SUNDANCE

ALSO BY DAVID FULLER

Sweetsmoke

SUNDANCE

DAVID FULLER

RIVERHEAD BOOKS

a member of Penguin Group (USA)

New York

2014

Riverhead Books
Published by the Penguin Group
Penguin Group (USA) LLC
375 Hudson Street
New York, New York 10014

USA · Canada · UK · Ireland · Australia
New Zealand · India · South Africa · China

penguin.com
A Penguin Random House Company

Library of Congress Cataloging-in-Publication

Fuller, David, date.
Sundance : a novel / David Fuller.
p.   cm.
ISBN 978-1-59463-245-7
1. Sundance Kid—Fiction.   2. Ex-convicts—Fiction.
3. Adjustment (Psychology)—Fiction.   4. New York (N.Y.)—Fiction.   I. Title.
PS3606.U53S86   2014   2013046245
813'.6—dc23

Printed in the United States of America
1   3   5   7   9   10   8   6   4   2

BOOK DESIGN BY AMANDA DEWEY

TO TOM

and

TO MARK

and to their grandparents,

JOYCE AND JACK, RUTH AND SIMON

SUNDANCE

This is a work of fiction, a flight of the imagination.

We all know Robert Parker and Harry Longabaugh were shot and killed in 1908 in Bolivia.

However, their bodies were not found during a 1991 expedition to San Vicente, Bolivia. A German named Gustav Zimmer was found in the grave thought to be theirs.

at first he failed to understand it. His eye sought invisible horses that might be pulling it. After a moment he realized it had to be a motorcar. It came toward him making a metallic sound, and the trailing cloud was unlike the dust off the back of a wagon. He had heard of motorcars while inside, but seeing one in person made him keenly aware of the things he had missed. He was entering the world anew. He thought he heard the jingle of harness and clop of horseshoes as the motorcar passed, clearly his imagination, then was surprised when a horse and wagon came around from behind him. Surprised, but also relieved. The old world was not quite banished, but it had certainly eroded. In that moment he thought he understood why his saddle hadn't been stolen. In this world, there seemed to be less need for a horse.

He reached Front Street. Every sprouting town alongside the Union Pacific railroad line had a Front Street that faced the tracks, with saloons, hotels, and brothels, shoulder to shoulder to shoulder. Because of the tracks, these towns grew more rapidly, and were more modern than the rest of the West. He passed a number of busy saloons until he chose one at the far end that was clean and empty. He walked into its cool, dark interior. He set saddle and gun belt on the rough wood floor and straightened to face a bar shining with varnish. He watched the saloonkeeper feign diligence, running a white cloth over an area already spotless. The saloon was unnaturally quiet, which put him on alert. Something was wrong, something not immediately evident. He listened, but rather than find something present, he discovered an absence. He concentrated on the distant whine in his ears and after a moment knew it was in his head and he was listening to silence. This was something new, as it meant the complete lack of hiss. He had lived with hiss for the last twelve years. He sniffed and there was no smell of gas. The room held still without the sporadic judder of gaslight. He looked at glass bulbs aglow with steady electricity.

He tucked the olive bandanna deeper under his shirt collar.

The saloonkeeper watched him out of the tail of his eye as if in recognition. Harry Longbaugh tightened, then shrugged it away. The saloonkeeper had almost certainly served any number of recently released convicts, probably every one of them geared up in Longbaugh's haunted pallor and guarded eyes.

"Before you say a word," the saloonkeeper stashed his rag behind the bar, "I seen plenty of you boys come on down here from the pen, and it's always the same, 'Years since my last drink,' like it's my job to stake you. Well, you got yourself put there and my liquor ain't free, better to know that while you're sober."

Longbaugh dug out the coins the guards had returned when they brought his saddle, holster, clothes, hat, and boots. He set them on the polished bar. The saloonkeeper nodded, moved a glass under his nose, and poured. Longbaugh marveled at it—not the liquor but the glass. A real glass. Not a tomato can. A real glass in his hand.

"Guess you ain't had it in a while. Word to the wise, maybe you ought to go easy." The saloonkeeper put the bottle back up on the shelf as if that would keep it out of reach.

"One day someone will listen to that good advice," said Longbaugh.

He heard laughter from a table in back. "But not today!" said an older man's voice through a cackle. Longbaugh had not noticed anyone else there, and wondered not for the first time if he had lost his touch.

"Got a name?" said the saloonkeeper.

Without thinking, Longbaugh spoke the name he had been using for the last twelve years: "Alonzo. Harry Alonzo."

The older man snorted "Alonzo" as if in recognition, and Longbaugh knew he should be going. He drank his drink.

But he did not leave. He turned to consider the man he had failed to notice. The man's eyes were off, and he realized the old man had a lazy eye that drifted aside to admire the electric lights. Three shot glasses were lined up in front of him, each one full, each one untouched. The old man kept them out of reach on the far edge of the table, where he considered them disdainfully.

"You know me?" said Longbaugh.

"I know what makes men crazy," said the old man.

"Don't mind Orley," said the saloonkeeper. "He's harmless. *Most* days he sits and keeps his thoughts to himself." He meant to warn old man Orley by his emphasis.

"Most days nobody comes in. Not the smart ones, anyway," said Orley.

"They all come in, Mr. Orley," said Longbaugh, "smart, dim, ignorant."

"That so?" said Orley, confused but curious.

"And they insult you."

Orley sat straighter and smiled. "That they do, yessir, that they do."

"Shut your mouth, old man." The saloonkeeper wanted to keep his paying customer happy. "Really, mister. You don't have to humor him, he's a little light upstairs."

"Wouldn't be a bit surprised," said Orley happily.

Longbaugh stared at the old man, then at the three full shot glasses. "You see drink for what it is," said Longbaugh.

Orley nodded. "The Devil's brew is what it is. Turns men evil."

Longbaugh smiled and looked down at the bar. "Not much of an excuse."

Orley's wandering eye moved to Longbaugh so that he now saw him with both eyes. He grinned as if he had been waiting for a kindred soul. He came halfway out of his chair, leaned forward to take the middle shot glass, brought the glass to his lips, and drank the whiskey down. The saloonkeeper watched with openmouthed surprise.

"We had a drink together once, Old Scratch and I," said Orley, setting the empty shot glass down in front of him as he sat back down.

"Good company, was he?"

"Best you could know."

"Charming?"

"Polite. Good for a laugh."

"Why not. He gets what he wants."

"All he has to do is wait. We all get to him in time."

"Some sooner than others."

The saloonkeeper looked back and forth, from Longbaugh to Orley. "Orley? I never saw you drink before."

Orley appeared calm now. "Waiting for someone to drink with."

Longbaugh kept his eyes on the bar and spoke softly. "How long since she's been gone?"

Orley answered without pause. "My wife has been dead ten years. Give or take a decade."

"How?"

"Cholera, they said. Went fast. Not pretty."

Longbaugh spoke almost to himself. "That *is* hell." If Etta was dead, that could well be him in ten years.

Someone opened the door and Longbaugh saw a narrow silhouette cut the sunlight in two, gun belt strapped to his waist, holster hanging low by his hand. He could not make out his age. Longbaugh watched him duck his head to come in and the electric light revealed an awkward boy around seventeen. His hips were lean and struggled to hold up his jeans and gun belt, his shirt bloused around his reedy torso, while his neck stretched tall to reach his smooth chin and small head.

"Heard you was gettin' out today, mister." The very young man had a high voice, as if it had to rise to climb that neck. Dark fuzz was evident on his upper lip. Longbaugh saw something dried white along the edge of the boy's mustache hair and thought it was milk.

"You the welcoming party?"

"I have a personal acquaintance with sheriff's deputies, mister, and sheriff's deputies have a personal acquaintance with prison guards at the Rawlins Penitentiary. They tell me everything they'd'a told my daddy." The gun belt was a good one, well worn and comfortable, and obviously had originally belonged to an older man.

Longbaugh realized the young man had followed him from the penitentiary. He wasn't fooled by the narrow frame and high voice. The truly dangerous were the young. They believed their dreams to be real and that they would live forever. A tongue of fear licked the nape of his neck, and it was not fear of the boy. A situation like this had come on him early in prison. When it was over, no one tested him a second time. He was not proud of what he had done.

Longbaugh turned his back on the very young man and leaned over the varnished bar. He looked at the reflection of his motionless fingers in the high polish. He was unnaturally still, as if blood no longer pulsed through his body, and that absolute lack of motion commanded the attention of the others.

The young man spoke louder to his back. "You're why my father died."

"I never killed another man."

"You made his reputation, and you took it away."

"I did not know your daddy."

"The hell you say, mister, Bill Lorigan was his name, Sheriff William Lorigan, you remember him now? You do, you *know* that name, he arrested you and was bringing you in when you escaped and turned him into a joke."

Orley chuckled. "Sheriff died of a punch line, one picked lock away from immortal fame." Longbaugh grimaced, thinking, *Please don't help me.* Orley aimed a finger at Longbaugh. "Now I got your name: Houdini."

The saloonkeeper snapped, "Quiet, you," then turned to the young man. "Leave my customer alone, Billy, he ain't bothering you. Have a heart, boy."

"Already got one. Once it stops, I don't."

Longbaugh didn't care for the way the young man strove to sound dangerous. Then he wondered about this Houdini. The name sounded as if it had been made up. He watched the young man peripherally, aware of the itch in the boy's smooth fingers that hovered near the heel of his revolver.

"My sheriff . . . my *daddy*, Sheriff Lorigan, he said the Kid was the fastest."

At the sound of that nickname, Longbaugh turned to stone.

"This is Mr. Alonzo, and as long as you're in my place, you would be well advised to leave him be."

Longbaugh felt it coming.

"*You're* the Kid," said the young man.

And there it was.

"Don't be a jackass, the Kid died in Bolivia," said the saloonkeeper.

"That's the story," said the young man, "but I know better."

"This is Mr. Alonzo."

"My daddy told me more things about you."

"Daddy was wrong," said Longbaugh.

"Said you was most affable, and that made you dangerous, and my daddy warn't never wrong."

Longbaugh was not amused. "Maybe not so affable," thinking, Butch was the affable one.

"Asking you to leave, Billy," said the saloonkeeper.

"You ain't gonna trick me like you tricked him," said the young man.

"No one could trick your daddy." Longbaugh's words were free of mockery.

"Asking you to leave. Nicely."

"Let him say he's the Kid."

"Kid died in Argentina," said the saloonkeeper.

"Bolivia," said the young man. "And that had to be somebody else, 'cause I heard it from the deputies, who heard it from the guards that he was in jail the whole time."

Longbaugh kept his eyes from looking at him. He hoped to wait him out, exhaust his patience, and get him to give it all up. Either that or just wait till the boy shot him then and there in the back and put all this to rest.

"You don't got to say who you are, mister. I already know. I'll meet you outside when you're ready."

The young man backed up, never taking his eyes from Longbaugh as he left the saloon.

Orley got up from his table and limped to the window. "He's waiting, all right."

"Time for another drink, then," said Longbaugh.

The saloonkeeper was gravely serious. "Story he told you was true, his daddy was humiliated after the Kid got away, and, well, it sounds funny but it was like he died of a broken heart."

"I'm paying for it," said Longbaugh. After a moment he indicated that he meant the liquor for his empty glass. The saloonkeeper was solemn and troubled and still did not pour Longbaugh a second drink.

Longbaugh stopped waiting and bent over to lift the gun belt off the saddle horn. He pulled the piece from the holster and inspected it for the first time. An old revolver, single action, someone's cheap imitation of the Colt Peacemaker. He'd used one like it when he himself had been a very young man and could afford nothing better. It was a standard tool, just as it had been back then, a standard dull tool.

Orley could not resist elbowing his thoughts into the room. "Heard about this incarcerated fella. Told 'em a fake name when they booked him so they didn't know he was famous, and if they ever found out, they never got around to changin' it. Too much bureaucracy or maybe just laziness. But everyone inside figured out who he was.

"Then in '08 someone killed that famous fella down in South America, or so the papers said. Happened so far away, it were tough to prove one way or t'other, but that's what came out and folks believed it. Got me thinkin' about what it was like bein' that famous fella, stuck in the pen, hearin' everybody say he were dead. You figure maybe he wanted to let folks know? Wave his arms and say, 'Hey, I ain't dead, I'm right here, look over this way.' Or you think he decided it were better if he just stayed dead?"

Longbaugh saw the saloonkeeper staring at him with a significant look of pain. Longbaugh pointed to his empty glass.

"That young fellow's out there," said the saloonkeeper. "I don't know in all good conscience if I can serve you. One whiskey calms the nerves, mister, but a second might slow you down."

"Just might," said Longbaugh. "If there's a God."

Orley wasn't finished. "Couple years back, I heard somethin' else. Heard that after he died in Bolivia, this famous fella hurt some other prisoner when the prisoner said somethin' bad to him. Nobody seems to know what, though."

Longbaugh scowled. "Sounds like Tuesday morning in the pen."

"No, sir, our boy, he were a model inmate, nobody got his goat. Whatever that prisoner said was particular." Orley then leaned forward as if he could affect intimacy from across the room. "Maybe you tell me what it was made you hurt him. I promise, cross my heart, to carry it to my grave."

Longbaugh let silence carry the moment. He looked directly at the saloonkeeper, who finally gave in and poured. Longbaugh let the full glass sit before him, reflected warmly in the bar's shine. He leaned forward and plucked a rag from behind the counter, leaving the olive bandanna untouched under his shirt. He took apart the cheap revolver and laid it out. He took each piece in hand and cleaned it. No one spoke a word while he worked. He put it back together piece by piece. He tested the action. He scowled as he sighted down the barrel. He tested its weight in his hand. He stared into space for a moment. Then he loaded the gun and slid it back in the holster, finally bringing it out a fraction to test where it had to be so that the chamber could turn while still in the leather.

He lifted the glass to his lips and drank as if he'd never get another.

"There another way out?" said Longbaugh.

"Never took you to be a coward," said Orley.

Longbaugh's jaw clenched, but he waited on the saloonkeeper.

The saloonkeeper angled his head to indicate a back door.

Longbaugh stood, hoisted his saddle with the gun belt again hanging off the pommel, and went out that way.

He stepped into a quiet alley. An old dog with a skin condition lifted his head and stared at him through cataracts. When Longbaugh didn't move, the dog put his head back down. Longbaugh thought he had won this round, thought he was clear. He was relieved and his mind instantly moved back to Etta, as he began to recalculate how he would go about finding her. She had a special music inside that he longed to hear again.

Then he heard the high voice from around the corner, and the young man stepped into his view.

"My daddy said you was affable, but he also said you was slippery."

Longbaugh stood on packed soil in the back alley between buildings where the morning sun had been and was now gone. He kept the saddle resting on his hip. He had not had a chance to have his boots shined, to enjoy a shave, or soak in a hot bath. He had had two whiskeys. He had eaten nothing since breakfast. He grieved in that moment for the other things he would not get to do. Then he turned to face the very young man.

"My daddy said you was fast."

"One last time. I did not know your daddy."

"You still fast? Don't matter. My daddy taught me afore he died. What'd your friend say in there? He died a punch line. Well, no, sir. Nobody's gonna laugh when I make him a somebody, 'cause I got his name, and once they know mine, they'll know his."

"Heard a man say that the first one to draw always seems to lose," said Longbaugh philosophically.

Young Billy Lorigan was confused by the man's extraordinary calm. It made him uneasy.

"Got me to thinking," said Longbaugh. "Does he draw first because he needs an edge? Or is it the second man's reaction? One man draws, he acts. You draw second and you're quicker."

"How fast are you?"

Longbaugh stared at him. That was an unfortunate question, and he felt the old itch to show him. It appeared, however, that the young man was not going to give Longbaugh a chance to cinch on his gun belt. He shifted the saddle off his hip closer to his belt buckle so the holster was angled just so and in sudden reach.

"Maybe you'll show me if I draw first," said the young man.

"Haven't fired a gun in years." That was so, but he had stayed quick. A small voice reminded him that he was older now, and this wasn't his gun.

"Not my problem, exactly. Unless you think I should let you warm up?"

"I'd rather be on my way."

"My daddy told me what to expect."

"If I were who you say, you'd have already drawn your last breath, and I still hear you talking."

"You're him."

"No one here to help you."

Insulted. "Don't need no goddamn help."

The way the gun hung there, the leather sides of the holster would not hinder the revolution of the chamber, not for one shot.

He watched young Billy Lorigan's twitchy fingers.

The cheap gun was in easy reach. He didn't trust it, but this was the hand dealt, and if he had to he'd play it. He looked at the dried milk on the young man's upper lip.

"I'm going to try once more. Walk away. Remember your daddy for the good man he was, and forget what anyone else says. Let your mama watch you grow up. No shame in not drawing down on a man you don't know."

The young man remained still, and Longbaugh saw the words had not moved him. He wondered if Billy Lorigan truly intended to draw on an unarmed man.

Longbaugh knew what it was like to run, and he told him. "Your life will change. They'll come after you, you'll have to hide in the hills, you'll be hungry and cold. Your daddy ever teach you to find water? He teach you to hunt the badlands? It's lonely, you can't come back to visit your mama, and they'll come after you hard, so you better be smart and you better be cagey."

Confusion dimmed the young man's eyes. But his confusion changed to a surprising resolve, and Longbaugh realized the boy had taken the wrong lesson from his words. The boy had heard a concession, that Longbaugh was trying to dissuade him because Longbaugh believed he couldn't win. Longbaugh opened his mouth to warn him, then shut it because it was a waste of breath.

The young man smiled just before he moved. Longbaugh watched, and as quick as the young man was, and he was very quick, through Longbaugh's eyes he moved at a measured pace that stretched the seconds, fingers digging through dry air to grab the handle, thumb webbing hitting the back of the hammer, hand direction changing to bring the piece up, lifting metal against gravity, clearing the leather, other hand sailing across to get above it, barrel swinging up, but the barrel never came level.

Longbaugh reacted, hand to gun, wrist-angle, trigger squeeze, mid-air smoke-splash, ear-slap bang, and the boy dropped, clothes off a clothesline, scarecrow off his cross, exhaling into a silent ground.

Longbaugh set the saddle down, dull pistol smoking in the holster still hanging off the pommel. He moved to stand over the boy's body, feeling as if a frozen corkscrew had speared the top of his head and twisted down through his skull into his neck, back, and legs. *Your daddy was slow, too,* Longbaugh thought from within his cold, pitiless heart. *Taught you all he knew. And now look.* Longbaugh was disgusted, furious at the boy for putting him in an alley full of the smoke of death. Furious at his thin-skinned daddy who fumed at the mockery and trained his boy to be his avenger.

Once again the old dog set his head back down on the ground.

They would come for him now. He had to run, and he wondered if he would bother. But a return to the Rawlins Pen was not an option. He was done with steel bars and seething men and entitled guards. Cold spread out from his spine to his fingers and toes. He was surprised to see the saloonkeeper standing at the head of the alley, then surprised again when Orley peered out from behind him.

"I saw it. You gave him every chance," said the saloonkeeper.

"You saw it," said Longbaugh skeptically.

"Saw the whole thing."

"You saw it."

"All right, I didn't exactly see it."

"No."

"But I know what happened."

"Did you see it happen?"

"Well, no . . ."

"No, you didn't. And with my reputation, the truth will never hold its shape."

Heads were poking out of back doors after the sound of the gunshot.

"Take the boy's horse," said the saloonkeeper. "He don't need it now."

The saloonkeeper led him around to the front of the saloon, away from the peeking heads, to where the young man's horse stood. Longbaugh tasted sour in the back of his throat, and tried to swallow it back down. His legs were shaking, not from fear but from the cold running under his skin.

Longbaugh set his concentration on the horse. He might once have been a decent animal but he had been mistreated. Longbaugh made a slow, wide approach to the horse's side, watching out of the edge of his eye as it shifted, shying, assessing, blowing. Its large eye followed him, liquid and afraid. Longbaugh set a gentle hand on the horse's neck. He felt the creature shiver, then after a long moment with his hand flat along the neck, the horse eased and settled down.

He removed the young man's saddle from the horse's back.

"Get this to his mother."

The saloonkeeper took the saddle and held it awkwardly. Longbaugh scowled and rearranged it against the man's hip.

"You know his name?"

"Billy Lorigan?"

"The horse. Do you know his name?"

"Heard him call it Felon one time . . ."

"Figures."

". . . but he could have just been insulting it, like calling it son of a bitch."

"Felon it is."

"Look, mister, now I look at him, he's got a mean streak like his owner," said the saloonkeeper. "Livery's next door. We can trade this one, get you a new mount . . ."

Longbaugh did not move from aside the horse. There wasn't time to make a good connection, so he had to make do. He pressed his open left hand against the horse's broad cheek, slipped a rope around his neck, then removed the bit, a "spade," from the horse's mouth. He looked at the "spade," an ugly thing, engineered for cruelty. He looked at the horse's inner cheek and tongue where the bit had ripped flesh. The young man had ridden the horse hard on its mouth, and Longbaugh knew he would have to find time to let it heal. He experienced a furious dislike for the young man for mistreating his animal, then, with astonishing regret, he remembered he had just killed the boy and the two emotions wove into a taut mental braid that sizzled and sparked where they entwined. The horse sensed his tension, and Longbaugh moved his trembling palm away to regain control of himself. He blinked and stared into the street, seeking that inner sleeve where he could sheathe his emotions and safely reconnect with the beast.

Once calm, he walked the horse to the livery. The stable man pointed out a new bit, and Longbaugh threw away the spade. The horse came warily back to neutral, but he had expected no less. He had always been good with horses. The horse accepted the new bit. Longbaugh put his dusty saddle on the horse's back and cinched the girth. He finally wiped down the saddle, revealing an old friend in good condition.

The saloonkeeper took a position at the corner of the livery where he could see up the alley to the spot where Billy Lorigan had fallen. The saloonkeeper shifted from foot to nervous foot on his heels. He watched townspeople gather, speaking loudly as if to reassure the dead body that they were doing all they could to avenge him. The saloonkeeper looked at Longbaugh and opened his mouth to speak, then closed it again. The townspeople united in their outrage and raced to the lip of collective frenzy. Longbaugh saw the saloonkeeper lift his hands to urge him to move a little faster, an implicit *please* in his gesture.

"They're talking posse," said the saloonkeeper, balling up his apron in his hands.

"Talking about bringing rope." The saloonkeeper released his apron, then balled it up again.

"Men going for their sidearms," said the saloonkeeper, watching one of the men coming this way down the alley.

"Count twelve, no, fifteen of them." The saloonkeeper backed up a step and the man ran past.

"You got to go *now*, Kid!"

Longbaugh glanced up as the nickname hovered in air.

"Ride out the south side of town, stay left through the stand of piñon, they won't see you going into the dry creek."

Finally Longbaugh placed his boot in the stirrup and came up without swinging his leg over. He stayed there, standing on the single stirrup and patting the horse's side until he felt the horse accept him. He swung his leg over and sat. He was quiet for a moment, years since he rode, and knew he would have blisters as the calluses of the past were but a memory. He heard the familiar creak of leather under his buttocks and thighs, and continued to measure the state of mind of the horse. He was curious as to why the saloonkeeper and Orley had taken his side. The horse took a step and Longbaugh brought him back, steadied him, and when he felt the horse fully alert to him, directed him with a nudge of his knee.

He looked at Orley.

"You going to tell them?"

"You know I wouldn't."

Longbaugh knew that he would. The old man would not be able to stop himself, he had finally made a connection and it had brought him to life. They might not believe the old man, but they would come hard after him on the off chance that Orley was telling the truth about Longbaugh's identity.

He nodded to the saloonkeeper and Orley, and he and the horse named Felon rode out of town.

heads, where, arms fully extended, they stalled. A moment later, they heaved in unison and for an instant the automobile touched four wheels, but the momentum sent it leaning the other way, onto the far wheels, where it wobbled, almost going over onto the passenger's door. There it paused, groaned, then slowly came back to four wheels and rested.

The men whooped and shook hands. Two returned to the second vehicle, while the other driver went and helped the limper back to his position on the front of the lead vehicle. That confirmed what Longbaugh had come to believe, that the man had been perched on the motorcar's hood, attempting to track him, his face near the ground to follow Longbaugh's trail. Sobering to see them track from an automobile. He missed the old days, when his pursuers were knuckleheads on horseback. With the knuckleheads riding Fords, there was always a chance they could get lucky.

They came on again, more slowly. They had proved themselves amateurs, and at that moment it hit him, a delayed reaction to his release from prison. He was free. The air was warm on his skin and clean in his nose. He was free and he felt good, he felt . . . better than good. He was on a horse, watching profoundly stupid men attempting to track him, and they had no chance whatsoever. He abandoned all caution, remembering the feeling as similar to the first time he took a bank. He decided to have a little fun. He headed in their direction until he intersected with their future path, then took the horse through a series of maneuvers. He made his trail so obvious that even they could follow his curlicued flight.

He stayed out of their sight, keeping half a mile's distance between them, judging their location by the sound of their engines. He noticed a thicket of nettles with a space in between, judged the opening wide enough for the horse but not the vehicles, and saw a way to torment them. After carefully negotiating the horse safely between the bushes, he guided it to shelter in the rocks ahead so he could watch. The vehicles came up the trail following his tracks and drove directly through the space between the nettles, scraping any arms and legs that happened to hang outside the car's profile. The men yowled in pain, and Longbaugh knew if they did not soon apply creek mud, they were in for a miserable night when the rashes blistered.

They quit the chase early as the afternoon aged. Any decent tracker could have guessed where he was, but none of these men were that tracker. They switched off their engines and waited for night, lighting their kerosene lamps, and making a small fire. Longbaugh moved in on foot and listened to their conversation, but he went away bored as they discussed not their strategy as a posse but the stinging itch of the nettles. He paused by one vehicle, on the side away from the campfire, saw a holstered gun hanging there, but finally did not trade his sad revolver for the better piece.

He left them behind in the setting sun. He rode across rocks and hard ground where, even if they bothered to follow, they would struggle to track him. Eventually there would be others on his trail, real men with knowledge and wisdom to supplement their modern tools, and he would need to be clever.

He had hoped to find tepees in the next valley, and was not disappointed. Another part of the old life that remained unchanged; when the natives traveled between reservations, they still made camp here. He rode in slowly, with his hands visible on the horn of his saddle, a caution left over from earlier days. He dismounted and approached an older man, recognizing the series of small circular tattoos on his neck as Arapaho. He was an elder, a medicine man, once a proud killer of whites. The Arapaho pretended to know him and offered a warm greeting. The man and his family had come north by way of Arizona. Longbaugh was surprised to hear Arizona had been made a state the year before. The Arapaho spoke of the changes to the land over the past decade, and Longbaugh revised his plan of escape based on the Arapaho's particular account. Longbaugh was anxious to move on, but the man's woman invited him to join their family for a meal, and he ate rabbit meat with corn tortillas. He luxuriated in the pleasure of decent food well prepared, and thought of how Etta was a terrible cook, and how badly he missed her burned casseroles. Whenever possible, he had tried to get to the kitchen ahead of her to start a meal. He smiled to himself as he ate the Arapaho woman's food, thinking that if Etta knew he thought he was saving them from her cooking, she never let on. It was, of course, possible that she considered *him* the poor cook and had been humoring him. After the meal was over, Longbaugh refused the offer of white man's whiskey, as he had many things on his mind and he didn't want an intoxicant to distract him.

He stayed long enough to be polite, and saw they were glad when he was ready to leave. He mounted his horse and rode away from the tepees. The three-quarter waxing moon lit the hillside that carried him out of the valley. He traveled a long time until he was far from other human beings, in a barren place where the moonlight made few shadows. He consulted the angle of the Big and Little Dippers and judged the time to be near midnight. He was close to the canyon walls of an old hideout. The land was stark and silver with moon. It fit his state of mind. He hobbled the horse and left it behind, furthering his isolation. The ground was hard, cracked into puzzle shapes that curled up at the edges and crunched to powder under his boots. He found a tree standing alone, its trunk thick and gnarled, its arms weblike and almost without leaves.

He sat under it. Lightning flashed on the far side of a distant range and exposed its shape against the sky. He waited for the next flash. He was glad to sit alone and think, and he knew exhaustion in his bones. The past simmered and he allowed his mind to wander.

He thought of his time in prison. He had given himself up to protect her and was awarded more years than he had anticipated. Two different times in prison he had been involved in violent incidents. The first came early on and was unavoidable, but it had served to inoculate him for the rest of his stay. The second had happened recently and had surprised him. He had not expected it, a spasm of brutality from deep in his gorge. Old man Orley had pegged it. There was a story there, and in retrospect, it brought him grave discomfort. He had always defined himself a certain way, and now he struggled with his recognition of another side, no matter how he hoped to disguise it.

He was confused as to his true nature. How different was he from the man the world had defined? He was an ex-con as well as the man who had died a myth in South America, perceived as affable by the dead son of a dead sheriff, among others. In the first instance, he had been arrested and served time. Yes, he was changed, but in what way? The authorities used prison as a cudgel to punish a man's outlaw acts. Had he been punished enough? Or did he still owe? Perhaps twelve years was too long a sentence, perhaps he had been overpunished and was due a peccadillo or two. *Interesting thought*, he mused. So who was he now? Despite the opinion of the state of Wyoming, he did not believe himself to be immoral. His code was strong, severe in many ways. He had paid a price that the rest of the gang had not. Were they better men for not getting caught? Or did they owe on their debt?

He flashed on the dead young man. Could the moment have been avoided, or did he secretly welcome the violence? He had killed in self-defense, but that did not help him. He grieved for that arrogant boy.

His mind drifted again. Silent lightning struck miles away revealing a foam of clouds on the far side of the mountains, followed in time by a curl of thunder no louder than the growl of his belly. She had stopped writing to him two years ago. The real hard time of his incarceration had begun with her sudden, unexplained silence, impossible to believe from the woman he loved. Sitting under the tree in the moonlight, he heard metal gates clang, clang open, open to corridors of cells on a steep grade, sucking him back inside, and his brain warned that he was somewhere between awake and sleep, where he could not know reality from illusion. Gaslight flickered between bars, with unseen men taunting him from the far side of a cigar-smoke cloud. He knew he would be tested and a man burst through the smoke, Longbaugh ducking, a fist glancing off his ear, and he grabbed the man's throat, crushing it to papery flakes, as if it was insect-infested pine under his fingers. He fought to extract himself from the dream, but his arms and legs were leaden, immobile, and yet somehow he was walking, walking a path, a path that brought him to a narrow boy standing in a field of poison purple larkspur, pleasant enough until he saw it was a boy with milk on his mustache raising Longbaugh's good revolver and firing at his face, bullet spinning through a spew of yellow flame. A dream for sure, as he had time to duck from its path, and in that turn of his head he was facing the other direction and there she was at the chapel with the music in her heart and her infectious smile, slim in her wedding dress—do you take?—yes of course—say I do—all right, I will—laughing over it later in their honeymoon bed, between sheets, a lingering kiss, her smooth thighs cool against him.

She had helped him survive prison, the way she knew and understood him, the way she believed in him, allowing him to keep a grip on his identity. She did it with her words. With her letters. He fought to wake up, as he knew his dream was about to go sour, and he wanted to avoid the darkness of isolation and loneliness, but his exhaustion held him under and drowned him in imagery, and he remembered, remembered a train, train rushing, rushing below in the dark, and they leapt together, he and affable, round-faced Parker, known to the world as Butch, landing in unison on a passenger car, laughing in each other's faces, Parker, who had escaped that day.

Butch. Longbaugh had been disoriented in prison after reports of his own death in another land, reported in '09, a year after it was supposed to have happened, and he wondered, was he alive or had he died along with his name? It meant that Butch was gone, and the loss of his friend had carved out a hole in his marrow. But at least back then her letters still came from New York, for another two years they came, and, even more than before, they were his lifeline. If the unreality of his own death cloaked him in heavy moods, her letters were the link to stable truth, even if they were addressed to Alonzo rather than his real name. Her letters had come weekly, reliably, creating a need he did not know he craved, until there was nothing. A silence that had lasted the past two years. He took a step, expecting solid ground, and his foot fell through black space, dropping headlong into the empty abyss of her silence. He had blamed the guards, their one sure method of punishment, but the guards swore they withheld nothing. He continued to send his own letters to her until a visit from the warden, holding those very letters, all returned from New York City, someone else's scrawl refusing them. From the bottom of the abyss he knew the truth and he believed it, there would be no more correspondence, and in the blackness came a stunning ache.

Bringing on the second incident. The big man had snickered, the big man who thought he was important enough to tease the legend, making his insinuation about Etta public. Longbaugh did not remember reacting, he only remembered his eyes unclouding to find the big man on his knees, bloody and cowering. This shocked him, first that he was capable of it, then that he had lost control. There were no repercussions—the big man did nothing after it happened, the big man's friends did nothing, and no punishment came from the prison staff—as if no one believed Longbaugh capable of such fury.

The nightmare now let go and he drifted into an easy dream, the boy Harry growing up in Philadelphia, traveling west as a young man, breaking horses, living on ranches, the mind-numbingly dull winters, the first time he and the boys drank themselves stupid and robbed a bank, his favorite gun in his hand, a gun so polite that no one wanted to blame him.

His sleep went deep then, his dreams lost to him, and he rested.

HE RODE WEST for another two days and turned south near the Green River, heading for the Colorado/Utah border and the Outlaw Trail. He saw no one after him in that time and felt safe riding into Browns Park. He was on his way to an old hideout where he hoped to find certain things that he had hidden.

The way into the canyon was tricky and well disguised. Longbaugh maneuvered it effortlessly and saw no indication of recent visitors. The sun overhead pressed dense, compact shadows from every rock, tree, and bush, as well as one that traveled under his horse. The canyon was eerily empty, not that he wanted company, but he hadn't remembered the air being quite so dead between the canyon walls. Perhaps because he had so often ridden in with loquacious Parker. In the pressing heat, he felt a cold trickle between his shoulder blades. He had remembered a breeze. Only the air above him moved, bending limbs that were out of reach. He rode with his head on a swivel, ears stretching out, over-reacting to the sounds of nature. The noise of his horse's hooves seemed to come from behind him, the creak of the leather saddle following a second too late. The horse sensed his tension and thought to rebel, but Longbaugh urged him on. Longbaugh thought that even the horse believed they were riding into a trap.

The passage opened and the inner canyon lay before him. He rode directly to the post office tree, where members of the gang left messages. He found a rolled-up scrap of paper, brittle now and brown-yellow, with a faded message in pencil that had endured any number of downpours to reach this state of illegibility. If it contained a warning, the danger was many years old. He had an ominous sense that he was being watched. He looked up the face of the canyon and was not reassured. He dismounted under the shade of the tree and pondered the surroundings. His eyes ran up the ridge to where the cabin sat. He could not see it, but he knew it was there.

Not a thing felt right to him. The sun was high, the sky a special shade of blue, the smell of sagebrush strong, and all of that made the sensation odder. What could be off on such a fine, clear day?

He remounted the horse and rode slowly for the trail that would eventually lead him up the canyon wall and carry him to the hideout.

He spent more than an hour when the ride would normally take half that, rounded the bend and came in sight of the structure. It appeared unchanged. The immediate area had not been cleared that season or possibly even the year before. That brought him hope. The cabin had been built with a unique floor plan, four rooms, each with its own entrance, and none of the rooms connected inside. He approached the door to the front room and stepped into quiet. Human life had not moved here for months, maybe years. His boots made tracks in the dust on the planks. Stove, kettle, pans hanging on the wall, a couple of chairs, a cot, cobwebs, little else. He took the lantern and a box of matches, and returned to the outside, chased by a shiver.

He left the horse and walked the slim trail that took him up to the caves. He passed a series of cave mouths until he came to one in particular. He lit the lantern while standing in the sun, and was unsure in the brightness whether the wick burned. He held his palm over the chimney and felt the sharp heat. He climbed the boulder that partly blocked the cave entrance and took hold of the base of a small scrub oak bush that was thicker now and grew in a place that worked as a handle so he could lower his weight inside. Once in the dark, he held the lantern up as his eyes adjusted. When he was satisfied he was alone, he stooped and moved deeper.

He remembered the way, and after twenty yards was able to stand, taking a left, a left, and a right, until he approached the hiding spot. It was clean and dry, a thin layer of dirt underfoot that showed no footprints, and wherever possible he walked on smooth rock to keep it that way. He found the place and set down the lantern and reached within a crevice between large rocks, and for a terrible moment thought that either someone had found it or he was in the wrong place. But he reached deeper, his shoulder pressed hard against the cold rock, patting the ground until his fingers touched fabric and he was relieved to pull out the package. He unwrapped his old oiled canvas duster to reveal the Civil War haversack given to him as a gift by Etta's uncle. He took a moment to appreciate it. Her uncle had been a high-ranking Union officer, so it was a fine one. The haversack itself was crafted of good leather, and its single shoulder strap was of the same leather. The flap was buckled with a belt-style closure, and he fed the tongue up through the frame of the buckle, pulled the prong from the punch hole, then lifted the flap to reveal the contents. It was all still there, the bills and coins. Fourteen years, undisturbed. The bulk of his share of the Wilcox train job in 1899, hidden in a rare moment of foresight when he had also thought to sew coins into his saddle. He knew Butch would never have touched it, no matter how quickly Butch went through his own share, but the others were less righteous. He thought again of Butch, buried somewhere in the ground of South America, and, being in a place where they had often been together, his heart was hollow with grief. While these moments now came rarely, when they did come they brought on a swift, chest-clenching sadness, and he paused until the ache began to ease. After a time, he went back to his work.

Under the haversack, wrapped in a smaller piece of oilcloth, was one of his guns, a classic Colt Peacemaker. This was the brother to the one stolen from him at Rawlins. He spent some minutes wiping it, admiring it, reassembling it, and loading it. He unloaded the cheap revolver and was about to break it down when he heard a sound and knew he wasn't alone.

He spun on instinct and underhanded the old gun at the face of the man standing there, calling loudly "Catch!" The man dropped his own weapon and his lantern, and before the gun hit him in the nose, caught it with both hands. The man's lantern broke and the flame went out, so that only Longbaugh's lantern gave light.

"Hell and tarnation!" said the man.

Longbaugh strode past him, picked the man's gun off the ground, and saw that the weapon was unloaded and a piece of junk. He handed it back so that the man now held two useless shooters. He brought his own lantern close to the man's cleanly shaved face and recognized him.

"You were the cook," said Longbaugh.

"And you—hey, holy—it can't be, but—it's *you*, ain't it!?" The cook's expression was incredulous. He shivered as if he was talking to a ghost.

"I need to go someplace people don't recognize me," Longbaugh said to himself.

"Ain't this the damnedest thing, I mean, ain't it? You're really standing here, breathin' and all, you ain't a spirit or nothin'." He reached out to poke Longbaugh as if to prove he was made of flesh, then thought better of it. "Guess you're a might older, and I reckon you shaved your mustache. Damn, I thought, I mean we all thought, I mean, everybody, damn, Kid, you're supposed to be dead!"

Longbaugh moved back to his gear, relieved to see the haversack flap in place, the contents hidden from the cook's prying eyes. He did not remember the cook's name. Howard. His name was Howard. No, not Howard.

"What are you doing here?"

"Well, I reckon I followed you. Got a little lost in the tunnels back there before I saw your light."

He made his question clearer. "What are you doing at the hideout?"

"I guess I live here. How'd you survive Argentina?"

"Bolivia."

Longbaugh inspected the man's clothes. Cowboy clothes, but cheap, not made to last. A costume.

"Didn't see tracks," said Longbaugh. "No one's been in that cabin."

"Not in the front part."

"No," said Longbaugh, realizing his mistake. "But no tracks up here either."

"Got to taking the other way, in case."

"There's another way?" Harvey, not Howard. Or Pete.

"Well, I reckon we blazed it some eight years back. Damn, it's really you. You really are alive!"

Longbaugh put his weapon in his belt and walked past the cook and through the tunnel, carrying his lantern and his haversack.

He grabbed the scrub oak's trunk to pull himself out, and from this angle, looking for it, he saw the second path. It would have been near impossible to see when approaching from the other direction. The cook came out behind him.

"You said 'we.'"

"Yeah, that's, well, you don't know him. He's new. Havin' you here changes everything." Longbaugh's presence made the man disagreeably cheerful.

"He got a name?"

"John?"

"Is that a question?"

"No . . . I mean, his name is John."

"What do you go by?"

"Well, they call me, uh . . ."

"Take your time."

"You see, sir, we got this plan."

"You and John."

"Well, yeah." He puffed his chest and looked important. "And we promised each other we'd use our new names until we did it. Pulled it off, I mean. And, well, it's something you know about. We got designs on a train."

Longbaugh said nothing. The cook's smile faded until he looked a little ill. The longer Longbaugh was silent, the more uncomfortable the cook became.

"Look, it ain't nothin', I mean, you can have your name back. Both names. We didn't hurt 'em, much."

"Which one of you is Butch?"

The cook stood a little straighter. "Oh, I am."

Longbaugh reconsidered him. He was dressed similarly to the way Parker had dressed. At least the way Parker had dressed when everyone called him "Butch."

"So, John is . . . ?"

"Well, John grew a mustache and there's, you know, a resemblance. Sort of. Or there was."

The cook uncertainly pointed at Longbaugh's clean upper lip with a timid finger. Then a strange expression crowded his face and he looked down at his own clothes. "About Butch. Is he, well, is *he* alive?"

"No idea. They got it wrong once, maybe they missed him, too."

"So wait—so if you ain't dead, who was there?"

"How would I know?"

"Maybe some guy dressed up like you." The cook looked down at his own clothes, as if he was considering the irony. "Say, I reckon you could teach us. You could show us. No, wait just a minute, I know! You could come along! We could make a new gang."

Longbaugh said nothing.

"I'll pick a different name, of course."

"Keep the goddamned name."

They descended to the hideout and on the way down the cook mused aloud about "wasn't it something" and "he's alive" and "this changes everything," but as they drew closer to the cabin, the cook went quiet with something new on his mind. Just before reaching the cabin door, the cook said, "He's not a bad fellow, sir. And he likes being . . . well, he likes being you. That's a compliment, right?"

The cook opened one of the back doors of the hideout. Longbaugh held back, looking in. He did not like the cramped mess he saw. Clothes piled and dishes stacked, furniture buried under trash. He did not enter.

"Where the fuck you been, Sandy?" said John, then saw Sandy was not alone. John jumped to his feet.

Sandy, thought Longbaugh. *Yes. That was his name.*

"This here's . . . well, this here is . . ." Sandy turned and saw that Longbaugh had stayed outside. Sandy came back to the door. John followed. Better this way. Too many places in the room where a gun could be hidden, just out of sight under trash or heaps of clothing.

"Holy Christ!" said John, then looked at Sandy. "I thought you said he was dead!"

John was not quite drunk, but he was a few yards down the path. Longbaugh looked him over. He didn't mind that Sandy did not resemble Parker, but *this?* John was also cowboyed up, every piece of gear one step too obvious, lacking taste and class. Longbaugh was disappointed. Some legacy. Whatever legend he had created now crashed against the image of John in his cheap costume. A pip-squeak imposter with a pathetic mustache.

"Harry Longbaugh," said Longbaugh coolly, by way of introduction. He did not reach to shake John's hand.

"Why didn't you say he was still alive?" John spoke as if Longbaugh wasn't there.

"Hell, I didn't know."

"Ain't this somethin'."

John sized up Longbaugh's stance and demeanor, trying to mimic him, standing straighter, lifting his chin, sucking in his belly, tugging at a too-short shirtsleeve while sucking at the long strands of his scrawny mustache as if to bite them off his upper lip.

Longbaugh watched and waited.

"I was telling the Kid here that we got us some plans."

"Well, what did he say? He like 'em?"

"Liked 'em fine."

John tried to whisper to Sandy without moving his lips, as if Longbaugh wouldn't hear him, saying, *What about the split?* and Sandy kept his back to Longbaugh, saying, *With him along, I reckon we're bound to get two, three times more,* and John saying, *They bring extra just 'cause he's there?* and Sandy saying, *Glad you didn't call me Butch back there.*

Sandy wasn't his real name, thought Longbaugh. They called him Sandy because his food always tasted like it had something small and foreign in it.

Sandy turned to Longbaugh as if he had been reading his mind. "You hungry? You want something? Why'n't you c'mon inside."

A memory taste of dry grit caught in his back teeth. "No, thanks."

He thought he had better take this man John more seriously, and he gave him a full look. He couldn't help but see him as one more jackass looking to make a name the easy way. John believed that if he could think of something, it ought to belong to him even if he wasn't willing to do what it took to earn it. Unlike the young kid in the bar, this one did not have the excuse of a simmering grudge. He was simply built from greed and John was bound to decide at some point that he wouldn't want to share the name he had appropriated. Near as he could tell, John was unarmed, but if there was to be trouble, Longbaugh wanted it on his terms in a place of his choosing. He was glad these boys did not know what was in his haversack.

"We got big fuckin' plans," said John.

"No. You don't."

"We do. And we're willing to share, tell you all about 'em."

"You don't want to rob a train."

"We don't? The hell you say, I think we do."

"You do not."

"Well, then, you say it, what *do* we want to do?"

Longbaugh said nothing.

"We goin' to get ourselves in some trouble, is what we gonna do," said John, both prideful and belligerent. Sandy the cook looked a little sick to his stomach, watching John preen.

"You do not have the makeup for train robbery," said Longbaugh.

"We got to do *some*thing; we got to make up a plan and get out there and fuckin' get into all of it, otherwise we wasted all this time. We got to *do* something."

"Maybe you'll think of it." Longbaugh stepped backward into the sun and turned without another word and walked quickly to the front. They stood dumbfounded and unarmed, and he figured it would be a few seconds before they caught on that he was leaving, a few seconds more to run inside and grab their weapons, and he was counting on their horses being unsaddled. It would give him a small head start, and he wanted all he could get.

He put his foot in the stirrup and swung himself up and turned the horse and headed down the trail. He stowed the haversack in his saddlebag as he rode. Their voices started up behind him. A few minutes later, he glanced up and saw they were following. He kept a deliberate pace, knowing it was unwise to push his horse.

He reached the bottom of the face of the canyon where the land went flat. He figured them eight minutes back. They could catch him if they sprinted, but then their horses would be tired and he'd have the advantage. By now they were thinking, and even imposters would know to follow at a safe distance. He was, after all, notorious. They would be forming some off-the-cuff plan, and as they were less than professional, their plan would be unpredictable. By now, John would understand that Longbaugh had insulted him, and he would be looking to prove his manhood, and maybe lay sole claim to the name in the process.

Longbaugh rode through the passage, leaving the inner canyon behind, then rode out in the open flat of the valley, eventually fording the Green River as he made for a trailhead that would take him up into the Uinta Mountains. He saw them ford the river in a shallower spot downstream. They knew the land and had made up time.

He rode into the mountains and they followed. He listened for them, and every time he thought they had given up, he heard them again. He knew the way, but it had been years, and he encountered natural changes in the landscape that forced him to make quick decisions and, in one instance, to backtrack. Clearly, the cook Sandy was more familiar with this terrain. He stayed on the trail that ran between steep sandstone cliffs, and then he was at the top and began his way down the far side. He eventually came to a road he had remembered as nothing more than a trail, and he turned to follow it, still working his way down. Not long after, he encountered a small camp just off the road, a woman with her daughter of around twelve. He thought they were Cheyenne, although they wore the clothes of white women. A few niceties kept them comfortable, a picnic basket, a blanket to sit on, a white sheet draped between branches to protect them from the sun.

He slowed, wondering about this pleasant scene in the midst of such unwelcome country. The young girl of twelve smiled but her mother stepped in front of her with a protective frown.

"Two men coming," said Longbaugh. "They're not exactly friendly. I'd stay out of sight."

The older woman put her arm around the girl's shoulder but did not answer.

"Are you alone out here? Is someone taking care of you?"

The older woman turned her daughter away and the daughter now looked at him with alarm, as if realizing she had just tempted a feral beast with a taste for sunny young females.

He watched them pull down the white sheet and stow it behind the tree, and while he still wondered how they had come to be there, he was satisfied they would stay out of sight. He continued on.

He stopped after a short ride, thinking about why the old trail had come to be expanded. While there was no one else on the road, clearly it was in frequent use. He listened for his pursuers and did not hear them. Previously he might have welcomed that fact, but now he thought of the Cheyenne mother and her daughter. He stared back over the road he had just traveled, watching for any sign of the cook and the man named John. He turned the horse to retrace his steps but heard the sound of what was now unmistakable even to him, an automobile engine coming up the rise, from the direction he had been headed. His first thought was that it was the posse, but he set that aside as unlikely.

He waited in the road and a motorcar with shovels, rakes, and brushes, as well as suitcases, lumbered around the bend.

A gentleman in shirtsleeves and wearing a waistcoat was alone at the wheel and pulled alongside Longbaugh and stopped. He had a friendly face, but Longbaugh sensed a cool tension that ran below the surface.

"You pass a woman and girl?" said the gentleman.

"Just did."

"My wife and daughter. Figured it couldn't be much farther."

Longbaugh understood. A white man with a Cheyenne wife and half-breed child could not let down his guard.

"On our way to the dig," said the gentleman.

"Dig?"

"The excavation. Dinosaur bones. My daughter wanted to see the land where they come from. Figured we'd camp overnight." He waved his hand at the suitcases with an embarrassed smile. "My wife decided to bring everything we owned."

"You do the digging yourself?"

"Well, some, but mostly my workers. I'm a paleontologist."

Longbaugh did not know what that was, but the word was long enough to impress him.

"Daughter was a little motorcar sick, so we stopped. Then I realized, after making sure I'd loaded all the suitcases, I'd forgotten my tools. Thought it better if they waited out here rather than endure the back-and-forth."

Longbaugh guessed they had driven up from Jensen. "Motorcar sick. New industry, new ailment."

"Yes." The gentleman smiled. "I suppose that's right."

"This road. I remember when it was a trail."

"Lot of people working in there now."

Longbaugh nodded. He kept thinking about the two imposters. He should have heard them by now. But with the gentleman on his way back, he thought the women would be all right.

"Better get along, then," said the gentleman.

Longbaugh tipped his hat.

But he stayed in the road, sitting in the saddle, listening as the sound of the motor was lost in the wind. He waited another minute or more, then rode after the motorcar.

Before he reached the camp he heard a shotgun blast, then a second one. He spurred the horse and rode fast around the elbow in the road and saw it, the result of everything that had happened during the previous ten minutes.

The Cheyenne woman had a swollen eye and a cut lip. She sat on the ground, holding a blanket closed at her daughter's neck to cover the girl's body. The twelve-year-old fought to control her weeping, but every other courageous breath was followed by a cascade of sobs. Scraps of torn blue clothing were lying on the ground, and he remembered blue as the color of her dress. The girl shifted when she saw him, and the blanket briefly bowed open and he glimpsed blood on her inner thigh.

He took in what was left of John, facedown, the back of his head blown off by a shotgun blast that exposed his useless brain. John was naked from the waist down. His pants might have been anywhere, tossed aside in his grimy lust. He was unlikely to cause Longbaugh any more trouble. He stared at him, pressed flat against the sandstone that, below him, held millions of years of dinosaur bones, and he thought of how puny and insignificant John was lying there. Except to that girl.

The gentleman was tying off the end of a rope on the rear bumper of the motorcar loaded with tools and suitcases. The rope looped over a stout branch that had earlier held the white sheet, some eight or ten feet off the ground. The rope came down the other side of the branch, where it was noosed around Sandy the cook's neck. Sandy the cook's hands were tied behind him. Sandy was gut shot, his long underwear mottled and bloody with dark chunks of something stuck to the fabric. His eyes blinked to a beat, and Longbaugh heard his gasping intake of breath.

How had it come to this? Neither he nor Butch would ever have considered behaving this way, and would never have tolerated it from their gang. He was disgusted, appalled that these two men thought this was the way to emulate their role models.

Sandy the cook saw Longbaugh and knew he was saved. He relaxed and waited for Longbaugh to charge in and cut him loose. The gentleman rolled his eyes over and blinked red at Longbaugh, and he saw the stamp of horror, the ugly thing the man had witnessed that was now branded onto his everyday future. The gentleman snarled at him with boarlike ferocity, but when Longbaugh made no move, the gentleman went on with his nasty business. Sandy smiled, waiting. The gentleman finished and climbed into the front seat and started the motorcar and the vehicle jerked forward. Sandy the cook's eyes bulged, his intake of breath was cut off, and his feet left the ground quite suddenly, his forehead thumping the branch. The gentleman turned in the driver's seat to watch him wrench and shudder and kick and slam his forehead again and again against the branch, tongue swelling out of his mouth. His movements slowed, his body sagged, and his sphincter and bladder released.

Longbaugh did not look away as the man died. The gentleman turned to him, as if he might be next. Longbaugh met his gaze and saw something die in there.

The woman lurched to her feet, leaving her daughter sitting on the ground wrapped in the blanket. She moved to where their picnic basket had been overturned, picked a red apple off the ground, stood straight, then hurled it as hard as she could directly at Longbaugh. The apple fell short of where he sat on his horse. She continued to glower at him, breathing heavily, hands at her sides, her eyes full of a deep, coarse hatred.

He turned his horse and rode away from all that.

3

———⊷•⊶———

ilhelmina Matthews commanded her front porch like a ship's captain on a quarterdeck, keeping Joe LeFors standing on the dirt, looking up, two members of his posse posing behind him with rifles. One of his boys rested his foot on a rock so he could lean the buttstock of his rifle on his knee and aim the barrel at heaven. The other held his across the crook of his arms with fingers folded over the magazine.

"We have no idea, ma'am," said LeFors, "if it's your brother-in-law or not. But you're his nearest relative in these parts."

"You brought all these men because you think it's not him?" said Mina.

"Only got eighteen, ma'am."

"Twenty," said the man on his right.

"Twenty, well," said Mina, "then it's a fair fight."

LeFors and his boys looked at one another, not sure if it had been a joke.

Mina, her little sister's name for her, struggled with her emotions, as she was a naturally obedient woman who trusted authority, yet she found these men and their mission distasteful.

LeFors had the cocksure look of a man with a grand idea, waiting for it to pay dividends. "I could take him alone, ma'am. But I hid all those men in the trees to make sure nobody gets hurt."

"How very equitable of you," said Mina coldly. She tapped her foot in annoyance, caught it, and forced herself to stop. She was unaware that her fingers continued the tapping on her upper arm to the same beat.

"When does your husband return?"

"My husband is deceased, Mr. LeFors."

"I am grieved to hear it." He was not. "I wonder if living on a ranch this far outside Denver is safe for a woman on her own." He leaned in so that she would not miss his meaning.

She glared at him and he backed up in surprise. She turned away, at which LeFors waved his men back to the trees.

Mina came in off the porch and shut the front door. Thinking she was alone, she let her body deflate, falling back against the door, hands shaking. She brought them to her face. After a moment, she lowered them, then jumped with a small shriek when she saw him leaning against the wall, in shadow between two windows, out of sight of the outdoor posse.

"Lord have *mercy!*" said Mina.

Longbaugh sensed that something other than LeFors's presence was upsetting her, but he did not know how to ask her what it was. "Eighteen's not enough, but twenty makes a fair fight," he said with a half smile, trying to get on her good side.

"How did you get in here?" she hissed, as if the posse might be listening.

"I thought your husband was alive."

"He is. In Indiana with his new . . . family." She struggled for composure. "Care to tell me how you got past all those men?"

Longbaugh shrugged. "LeFors never was too bright."

"He's a lawman, perhaps you should show him respect."

"Something's wrong, Mina. What is it?"

"*You!* You scared me half to death!"

He knew better than to press her. He was silent a moment, then said, "Where is she?"

"You are some kind of brazen, sneaking in here like this. But you always did sneak around." There she was, the old Mina he had expected, the haughty sister-in-law who looked down on him.

"So you're back to being Wilhelmina Matthews. No more Mrs. Fallows."

She glared at him and he was sorry to have retaliated.

"Will you at least tell me if she's all right?" he said.

"I'd say it's fortunate that Mr. LeFors told me you might be alive. I would have had you for a ghost. I should call him back in right now."

"Why don't you?"

"That man is a nincompoop, he doesn't deserve to catch you. But I'd do it, Harry, I'd do it. Only she wouldn't like it."

"Where is she?"

"New York! Where *you* sent her!"

"She's still there?"

She crossed her arms. "I do not know." He thought her anger was forced. She may have disliked him, but once again he guessed she was covering something. He looked around to give her a moment to collect herself. He had always liked this room, large and masculine, heavy wooden furniture, a fireplace made of large stones and walls stained dark brown, although now that her husband was gone, so were the old hunting trophies. The room had been softened by flower and landscape paintings, with doilies under lamps. The foreman would have stayed to handle the ranch for her. He was a good man, and would not have left a woman to try to run it by herself. He didn't remember the foreman's name, and he flashed on the moment in Browns Park when he hadn't remembered the cook's name, then realized all that had happened only three days before.

"You were a fool to come here, Harry."

"I'll be gone soon enough. When did you last hear from her?"

"A year, I suppose. Or two—it's not safe here."

His pulse quickened. "A year or two?"

"Does that surprise you?" Mina smiled coldly.

Longbaugh said nothing. She would be pleased to think that her baby sister was out of touch with the man Mina disliked.

"Fine. Stay and risk yourself. I'd feel sorry for you, except for what they told me."

"What did LeFors say?"

"He said that you killed a boy."

"I see."

"That's it, that's all? No explanation? No justification?"

Longbaugh said nothing.

Her voice softened, impressed that he made no excuses. "I've never thought of you as a killer, Harry."

"I want to find her. If she's done with me, she needs to say so."

Mina watched him in the shadow. "Apparently the newspapers were mistaken about South America."

Again he said nothing. Etta had told her early on that he was in prison, but Mina's response had been so full of I-told-you-sos that Etta had told her nothing more. Mina must have assumed he'd been released. When the newspapers said he was dead, she had no reason not to believe it.

Mina stared at him a long moment. Then, without warning, she walked into the next room. Through the open door, he watched her search for something. She opened a drawer, and he realized the drawer was full of her sister's things. He saw Mina pull out and set aside a collection of papers she had saved, work done by Etta's former pupils. While he was curious as to why Mina had kept them, seeing them again carried him back to an earlier time.

When he first met Etta, she had been a schoolteacher. He had been impressed by her intelligence, knowing how limited opportunities were for smart women, particularly in the West. He thought back to the day they met. Etta had been astonished by him, this interesting, handsome cowboy who also happened to rob banks and trains. Longbaugh wasn't astonished in the least. He had known her immediately, believing that he had met the right one. He wondered why she didn't know it, too. At the time, she had been engaged in a flirtation with a clever young fellow who was a teacher in a nearby town. Longbaugh thought the flirtation irrelevant, as chemistry was chemistry. But he did wonder why, for her, it came down to a choice between men rather than the thunderbolt it had been for him. That lack of perception on her part was the first warning sign, and he took a mental step back.

The other man appeared to be the very model of civility and stability, too good to be true, and then he was indeed too good to be true, as she discovered he was married. Even so, young Etta had managed to convince herself that, to be modern, perhaps a married man was what she was supposed to want. Longbaugh considered that a second warning sign, and took another mental step back.

By now, Longbaugh knew she was too young for him. Chemistry was not enough for him to lose his heart, and the thunderbolt did not saddle him with an emotional obligation. Surveying her with a cool head, he acknowledged issues of timing and age compatibility. He rationalized now, thinking it was a great deal to ask, even of a mature woman, that a female member of polite society might commit to a man whose very name was associated with a life on the outside of that society.

It was time to get on his horse and ride away fast. He was more than ready to do just that. He knew it was the wise move. And yet, he did not. Something about her potential kept him there.

But potential could only be fulfilled by time and patience, and that was not in the cards for a man in his occupation. So he pressed the matter and put her to the test, fully expecting her to fail. Recklessly, he took her to visit a bank in a neighboring town, not to rob it, but to show her how he might go about robbing it. He wanted to know her reaction.

He parked their carriage off the main street. She was appropriately curious and excited as they approached the bank, and seemed to be taking in all the details, as if this was a onetime event and she wanted to be sure to remember it all for her diary. Once inside, bad luck struck immediately, as he was recognized. He showed no panic. But Etta was anxious for him and wanted to get him away. Enjoying her display of nerves, he lingered to watch the whispered news of his identity pass from teller to teller. He was flattered to be recognized, and further flattered to see her impressed by his fame. Finally, he led her to a side door to the hallway that would take them out through the back. But once away from bank employees and customers, she took his hand and pulled him toward the stairs. She wanted to go *up*. It seemed a questionable move, but he saw something in her eyes. He took a chance and, again recklessly, went along. Armed lawmen burst into the bank through the front, met a roomful of excited wagging fingers pointing out the outlaw's escape route, rushed out the side door into the hallway, past the stairs, to the rear door, where they came face-to-face with more lawmen.

Now on the roof, Etta led Longbaugh to the ledge, where it was but a small jump to the roof of the next building. As they leapt together, she jubilantly tossed her hat high in the air. It fell in the exact wrong place, dropping between the buildings all the way to the alley below.

She looked at her hat two stories down in the dirt, and he heard for the first time that special laugh that he would later learn was just for him. She smoothed her hair, gathered in her mirth, took his arm, and soberly led him down the stairs into the general store. They went out the front door while the owner and his customers were glued to the big window, seeking a glimpse of the famous outlaw who had been recognized in the bank next door. She pulled against his arm to go back for her hat, but people were coming out now and he met her eye with an almost imperceptible shake of his head. She immediately understood and went with him the opposite direction, across the street and around the corner to their carriage. No one noticed them ride away.

Etta was hooked. But so was he. Before they had entered the bank, when he thought she was simply trying to memorize the moment, she was appraising the landscape. She had seen that the roof of the general store was the same height as the bank and the buildings had been built close together. She had formulated an escape plan when he hadn't imagined they would need one. She was thinking more like the Kid than the Kid. From that moment on, they were together.

Mina had found the old letters under the student papers in the drawer, and she came back to him with one of the letters in hand. He understood something then. Etta had, rather casually, left those old school papers with her sister years ago. It was Mina who had decided they were precious. They were not precious to Etta, but as a part of her baby sister's past, Mina cherished them. His heart ached for Mina's love. He recognized the envelope Mina carried, but was surprised to see it torn open and smudged with fingerprints. He saw the handwriting and recognized that as well.

Mina looked sadly at the envelope. "This was her last letter. It came two years ago."

So Etta had stopped writing Mina as well. It gave him a moment of comfort, until he realized it suggested another possibility.

"You think Etta's dead," said Longbaugh.

"*No* one thinks she's dead, and her name is *Ethel*!" Her rage was quick and inappropriate, and he knew it had nothing to do with her sister's nickname. "Despite the Pinkertons writing her name wrong, which you and she thought was *so funny*!"

"Tell me now. What's wrong, Mina?"

Mina was ashamed of her outburst, ashamed that there was something else, and ashamed that he had seen through her to know it. She shook her head back and forth.

"Men came. Two years ago. They had this letter."

"What men? Who were they?"

"I don't know."

"What were they like?"

"They were like big monkeys in suits," she said belligerently.

"Were they local, had you seen them before?"

"No." She sagged. "From back East, maybe. They had accents of some sort. They frightened me, Harry. They frightened me and I never heard from Ethel again."

Longbaugh looked at the letter in her hands. "Is there anything in there that tells you what it was about?"

"Do you truly imagine I did not read it carefully? It's one more in her series of newsy letters."

"Did you write her back, did you ask?"

"All my letters were returned."

"All right. All right."

They were quiet then, across the room from each other, Longbaugh still in shadow.

"Are you hungry?" she said, as if remembering her manners.

"Kind of you."

"I'd fix a plate for the Kaiser himself if he was cold and lonely and happened to knock on my door."

"I didn't knock and it's quite pleasant out there."

"You're here because you're family."

"Thank you." After her small kindness, he thought to return it. "I don't know who they were, Mina, but I'll find out."

Mina perused the letter. "She was associated with do-gooders, Henry Street something, it's somewhere in here, Settlement, Henry Street Settlement. A woman created it, apparently some kind of nurse."

"Lillian Wald, and she started it to help immigrants."

"Oh. So Ethel wrote you about that as well."

He saw the return address on the envelope. There she had written "Etta Place." Place was Longbaugh's mother's maiden name, an alias that provided protection from the authorities. Longbaugh realized Etta had been cruel to use that name on letters to her sister, which meant she was still angry that Mina didn't approve of him. Etta could hold a grudge.

"Most of her letters were about the Settlement. I can't imagine why it meant so much to her. After all, it is in a tenement." Mina shuddered. "But she did like to shock me. Don't argue, Harry, it's not my imagination, she avoided personal feelings when she wrote to me. I suspect she thought I would judge her. But now she may be in trouble."

Longbaugh was sorry for Mina's pain.

"She loves you," he said. "You're her big sister. She doesn't mean to hurt your feelings."

"You always had her heart, Harry. I tried to protect her from the bad things she loved, but you had her heart."

"I'm sorry—"

"It doesn't matter now." Mina turned away.

Longbaugh knew that it did matter.

"I'm afraid for her," said Mina. "Maybe this time it's good that you are who you are, maybe you can do something. I know I can't."

Mina turned back and offered him the letter. Her lower eyelids held back her tears, just the way her sister's did when she was about to cry, but he had no empathy, as he was greedy to hold Etta's words in his hands.

Seeing the smudged, torn envelope up close made something rise in his blood. He knew Mina had not defaced the letter. Someone else had treated it shabbily, and probably not the two men who had come to threaten her. It was as if Etta herself had been violated. He feared for Etta and what the last two years had brought. He turned his attention to the letter itself.

It was written just after her last letter to him. He brought the pages to his nose and breathed her scent, stronger here than in the letters she had sent him, but he had left those envelopes open too many times. The special hold she had on him returned in a rush of thrill and melancholy, and his cheeks burned. He had a terrible premonition that she was dead, and that if he didn't preserve her smell in this letter, she would be lost to him forever.

"Where will you go?" said Mina.

"You know the answer to that."

"Will you find her?"

He said nothing.

"Did you actually kill that boy?"

Again he said nothing.

She stared at him, somehow knowing there was more to the story than what LeFors had told her.

"If you didn't go to South America, why do they say you're dead?"

"I used a different name in prison. And I'm guessing Parker went down there with some of the other boys, so they thought it was me."

"Parker?"

"Cassidy. Butch. His real name was Robert Parker."

Night had swept in around them. It was time to go.

"This is the part you'll like. Go tell them I'm here."

"You want me to tell them? Won't they catch you?"

"No, they won't. I'll find her, Mina. I don't think you'll be bothered again. Go on now, tell the posse."

She snorted, amused.

"I can see why she loved you. I suppose I always could. But you're a bad man, Harry Longbaugh. You don't mean to be, but you're a bad man. Maybe for the first time I'm actually glad of that. Whatever she's gotten herself into, I'd wager that that's what she needs right now."

She opened the front door to the fresh night breeze, stood on her porch, and called out to LeFors's men and told them her brother-in-law was there. Every one of the posse members did the opposite of what he had been told and came bumbling out of the bushes and trees and scrambled to get close to the house to be the one to grab him in case he really was the notorious outlaw he was rumored to be. In the commotion, Longbaugh slipped out the same window he had used to get in and was past them, walking into the stand of trees along the edge of the property and out to where he had tied his horse, by their parked vehicles.

He stopped to listen to the disturbance back at the house, then turned, and was face-to-face with the lawman Joe LeFors.

LeFors stared at him but did not draw his gun.

Longbaugh realized LeFors did not recognize him. He had only ever seen Longbaugh from a distance, and in between Longbaugh had aged and shaved his mustache. He was also making no effort to run.

LeFors prided himself on his looks and on his clothing, a fussy little dandy, tailoring his wardrobe to simulate the brilliant lawman he thought he was. But LeFors's reputation, like his wardrobe, was self-promotion. If he knew the other lawmen did not respect him, he did not show it. LeFors had chased Cassidy's gang after they had engaged in a bit of cattle rustling, and had bragged to anyone who would listen that he had put a stop to it. In reality all he had done was ride around in circles while Butch laughed at him.

"They got him surrounded at the house."

"So where *you* going?" said LeFors.

"I was coming for you, Joe. Didn't think you'd care to miss it. Heard you'd gone to town."

LeFors nodded and looked over his shoulder at the sound of the commotion. "So they got him. So now he's mine. Siringo thinks he's the one, but when I bring him in, they'll know it was me all along."

At the sound of Siringo's name, Longbaugh went cold. He knew Charlie Siringo, had even, at one time, considered him a friend. Unlike LeFors, Siringo was a damn good lawman and a dangerous adversary. Siringo had been a Pinkerton, but unlike most Pinkertons, he worked alone and on his own timetable. He loved the chase and had been known to spend months on individual fugitives. Someone must have forced Siringo to include LeFors and his posse, which was a lucky break for Longbaugh—if Siringo had been at the house instead of LeFors, Longbaugh could never have slipped through so easily.

"Where is Siringo?"

"He's the one went to town." LeFors laughed, merrily, complacently, arrogantly, exultantly. "He misjudged our boy. Said he wouldn't show up here for another day or two. And now *I've* got him!"

"I'll ride in and find him. By the time he gets here, you'll have your prisoner."

He looked at Longbaugh, and for a moment he thought it was all over, that LeFors had identified him. Longbaugh's hand moved closer to his holster.

"Did you see him?" said LeFors. "Is it really him?"

"Probably not."

"No. You're right, probably not. Guess I got excited. I didn't really believe he was still alive. Couldn't be that lucky. By the way, what's your name?"

Longbaugh simply could not help himself. He had so little respect for LeFors that he said, "Alonzo," and smiled.

"Much obliged, Mr. Alonzo."

. . .

AT THE LIVERY by the train depot, he watched a stableman from a distance to see how he was with the horses. When it became clear that the horses trusted him, Longbaugh approached him. He offered the stableman the horse named Felon as long as he agreed to not use a spade bit, in fact to use no bit on him at all for at least a week so the horse's mouth could heal. He left his saddle behind as well, now empty of coins with the seam restitched.

He knew that after LeFors told Siringo about the man named Alonzo that LeFors would again be exposed for exactly what he was. He did not expect it to make Siringo mad. He thought he was leaving all of that behind when he went to catch a train going east.

4

———⊰•⊱———

The train traveled out of the light into a blackness that seemed endless. Longbaugh suspected they were not just in a tunnel but burrowing underground. The other passengers, however, were passive to the point of cataleptic. He asked a conductor, who then bragged on his own personal connection to the modern marvels of the industrial world, explaining they were in a tunnel that had been dug directly beneath the Hudson River. Longbaugh glanced up at the ceiling of the passenger car and pictured water over his head.

As there was nothing to see out the windows, his thoughts turned to the journey she had taken to get here, years ahead of him. She had traveled by train as well.

Etta had lived in Rawlins and taught in the school so she could visit him in prison regularly. But he knew she could not keep her life in stasis to wait for him.

Their conversations would follow a pattern. She would sit opposite him on visiting day, and inside he would rejoice. But he would try to appear solemn.

"You have to stop coming," he would say.

"I will," she would say.

"You're staying in Wyoming just to see me once a week."

"I suppose I am."

"You mustn't."

"Next week I'll stop."

"I can stay in my cell. I can refuse to see you."

"Then that's what you should do."

Then they would talk about anything and everything, but he would become solemn again when it was time for her to leave.

"Don't come back next week."

"All right," she would say with a smile. "I won't."

And the next week she'd be there to meet him.

He'd be solemn again, disguising his absolute delight.

"You have to stop coming here."

"I know, you're right, and I will," she'd say.

"You can't keep doing this. Get away from Wyoming. Live for both of us."

"I'm already making plans," she'd say.

Then they'd start talking. Every week she tried to wear something new or do something different with her hair. He'd always see it and compliment her, and it always pleased her that he was paying attention.

This went on for years. But over time he knew that as important as it was for him, it was no good for her.

One day she visited and he wasn't there to see her. He asked a guard to hand her a letter he had written.

It was a good letter. He had spent the entire week writing it and at the last second had almost not had the will to send it with the guard. But somehow, during what would have been their hour together, he had sat, very still, on the cot in his cell, imagining her reading it, then imagining what their conversation would have been if he'd been there with her when she read it.

She would have said, "This is a good letter."

"Then you'll leave? You'll go to New York?"

"Yes. I'll go tomorrow."

"You'll really go?"

"Of course I will."

And then she would have come back to the prison the next week.

At the end of visiting hours, the guard came to Longbaugh's cell with a response from Etta. Longbaugh read the single sentence over and over: "This time I believe you."

It was terrible not seeing her, but the following week a letter came from her, postmarked New York City. She wrote about her train journey across the country, but she hadn't mentioned riding under the Hudson River. Perhaps she had crossed by bridge or ferry boat.

The train slowed and entered a station. The passengers found their feet and collected their baggage and belongings. He took his own and stepped out onto a platform. The underground station was large, very large, but he managed to control his reaction. He followed his fellow travelers as they funneled to a staircase. He walked up with the others, each step bringing him closer to a light above his head until at the top of the stairs he was in an enormous room. He blinked to prove he was awake. His mind did not know how to absorb the size of this modern shrine of steel and glass. He leaned on a balustrade, craning his neck. It wasn't that he didn't know large spaces. In the West, he rode under expansive skies where he occasionally watched massive weather systems slam together. The desert spread endlessly, ashimmer with heat and mirage, where men and horses were baked into hard leather. Sleepy mountain ranges disguised their vastness and treachery, taking days, sometimes weeks, to cover, their endless beauty driving men to despair. But this space was indoors, man-made, littered with hundreds of tiny walking humans, and he was amazed. He tried to collapse it down into smaller bits, to understand the individual parts so that it might eventually make sense. Dozens of pillars were built on square bases made of a black metal grille with a repeating X pattern that carried up, way up, higher still, until branching out in four directions to flower into metal arches that crisscrossed under a roof that was yet higher with yet another giant series of arches. But then he saw a bird flying up there, which brought his perception back to the whole space. He did not understand how it had been conceived, how it had been designed, how it had been built, but somehow a bird lived in the space and called it home.

"What the hell is this?"

He was surprised when a passerby answered, "Appears to be a train station, if you haven't noticed." The man slowed after a glance, then came back grinning to look Longbaugh up and down, cowboy hat to boots. "You're in Pennsylvania Station, pardner. The main concourse. Nothing like the lone prairie, uh?"

"No." Longbaugh endured the man's superior air.

"You lost? Get turned around?"

"Not that I know of."

"Well, you're going the wrong way." He paused for effect. "Haven't you heard 'Go west, young man'?"

"We've got a western Greeley says, 'Gettin' too crowded, go east.'"

The man nodded at the cowboy's comeback, but his attitude lingered. "First time in New York?"

"You worked that out."

"You win, pal." The man smiled genuinely, his tone flirting with respect. "It opened some three years ago. Everybody came then, big crowds." He looked up at the ceiling as if noticing it for the first time. "Now they've seen it, especially with the new one opening, Grand Central." He again looked Longbaugh up and down and shook his head as he was on his way. "Jesus. Good luck to you, pardner."

Longbaugh walked a long way to be out of the grand inverted canyon of glass and steel, found exit doors and escaped to what he hoped would be the safe outdoors.

He stepped onto a sidewalk in the middle of the island of Manhattan, a man of the West, standing in his boots on the racing, bustling heart of the great eastern city. He stared at the fevered nightmare madhouse around him. Pennsylvania Station was a side attraction in comparison. He was unprepared, despite, or maybe because of, his boyhood in Philadelphia, as he had thought he knew what this would be. Sound. Size. Smell. Everything larger, oversized, swollen, gorged.

Modest buildings here dwarfed even the grandest structures of the West. He faltered in the maw of excess. How would he find her here? How was it possible to navigate this place, among so many people? How to start, how to become even functionally adequate in appreciating its nuances so that he could track her journey? In his awe he realized he was searching the face of every woman who walked past, looking for her.

Many women passed, even in that short breath of desperation. People and vehicles and buildings laid out as far as he could see, block upon block in every direction, until he forced himself to stop and seek perspective. He brought his mind back to the things that he knew. He compelled himself to remember that nothing had changed, even in a city so ominous and imposing. It did not matter that the city overwhelmed, it did not matter that men had looked for her and had threatened her sister. Her trail was still cold by two years. Searching faces on a city street by a train station was idiocy. He had arrived with a plan, trusted it enough to get him here, and with that thought he replaced his anxiety with manufactured calm. The plan began with her old boardinghouse, where he hoped to connect with those who had known her. Small steps would lead to more small steps, all of which would add up, but it wouldn't happen quickly. The trail was cold. If the man who sent the thugs to frighten Mina had found her, then it was too late anyway and it didn't matter.

He gauged the sun and engaged his inner compass. Her last-known location on the return address of her letters was for a boardinghouse that she had described as being on the lower part of the island. He had to go south. He walked to the corner, and the street signs read 31st Street and 7th Avenue. He felt more confident with a purpose and destination and he stepped off the curb directly in the path of a team of horses pulling a dray. He jumped back, the flanks of a horse brushing his shirt, horse wind touching his nose. An automobile came close on behind, steering aggressively to pass the dray. Adrenaline surged, but he sized up the competition and timed his cross. From the middle of the street, he noted the extended wall of tall buildings, a line of them all standing six stories or more, sidewalks bristling with people, streets clogged with streetcars and vehicles. A block away, a locomotive went by in midair, and after a moment he realized it was on an elevated track.

He was surrounded by words, everywhere words, by way of announcements, advertisements, store names, promises, and reassurances, permanent plaques and temporary proclamations. The city's walls were covered with words. How could there be so much to say, so much to sell? The germ of an idea began to take shape in his head, something about all the names, all the hucksterism, all the billboards grabbing for attention. There was so much of it, and it was seemingly impenetrable. The words were large and within their assault he was small.

He looked again at the horses.

The street endured the creatures, many of them sick or ill used. He watched as a teamster unhitched a horse from his team after the old boy had gone to his knees. Without the support of the others and the traces, he rolled to his side. The teamster led the other horses away to keep his schedule. This one settled in the gutter, chest rising, dropping. Hooves of an oncoming team rained down near his head, very close. A second team came closer still and hooves stomped meat. The old horse whinnied and brought up his nose, but the strength wasn't there and he fell back to cobblestones. Another hoof landed, and he jolted but made not a sound. Longbaugh looked away, squinting. He understood then that horses were finished here, dismissed as obsolete. Motorcars and cruelty crowded them out.

He watched locals in their stop-start dance crossing streets, never following a straight line, never getting too far without a compensating step back. The streets had rhyme and meter.

He was surrounded by true skyscrapers, sharp-edged monsters jutting through the ground to thrust into sky, and he cricked his neck in appreciation. Over time he would learn their names, Flatiron, Metropolitan Life, Park Row, Singer, and the fact of their being named spoke of their peculiar hold on men's imaginations. Yet it was a building in the distance, glimpsed while crossing a street, that grabbed his own attention. It was unfinished. He was drawn to the visible guts of the skyscraper. The base was finished, a stone façade ran up dozens of stories to a rectangular extension, maybe half the size of the bottom, partially covered with the same façade. Above that was an unfinished skeleton of naked steel beams. Yet another, smaller rectangular skeleton crowned that, the penultimate step to the sky before reaching a framework spire.

The bones of the beast beckoned and he went, knowing it was a long walk, but at least it was in the same southerly direction as her boardinghouse.

As he walked, he learned to mimic the city's beat. He saw men dressed in coats and waistcoats, in top hats or bowlers or skimmers. He saw other men, young, proud, and muscular, in overalls and black slouch hats. He saw women in the sort of clothing that was more revealing than he expected and knew he had been away a long time.

Reaching the building's base, he encountered a sign that named it Woolworth. A foreman waved him off. "Back away, buddy, men working here."

Longbaugh looked at him and didn't move.

The foreman gave it right back. "Nice hat, 'dude.'" Longbaugh didn't react to the insult but he felt the challenge. The foreman turned away.

He angled his head to see the top. Something caught his eye that he initially identified as a swooping bird, but it was falling in too straight a line, coming directly down, and he watched it drop all the way to the sidewalk. It landed a few feet from him, a newsboy cap. He stepped over to it, and looked up to the top of the building, from where it had come. He thought of Etta's jubilant hat dropping. He picked up the cap, turned it over in his hands and felt himself smiling. He looked at the foreman, who was checking a ledger, then he looked to the outside wall where a freight elevator waited for a final stone slab to be secured. Men smoked there, sitting or leaning on the stone pile in the elevator, waiting to ride. He went behind a stack of concrete sacks by the wall and stowed his cowboy hat and gear there. He tugged the newsboy cap onto his head, lifted a sack of concrete to his shoulder to block the foreman's view of his face, and followed another worker in his own newsboy cap onto the elevator.

He was lifted off the ground, knees bending at the force, watching the foreman's outraged face vanish below, whisked up into unfenced air, a short step off the edge into nothing. He was high quickly, dizzy with the rise, now above the shorter buildings, now passing the taller. He looked across a full city that carpeted an island and spilled out over land that stretched beyond the rivers. A rush of wind snatched his breath and his chest went hollow so that he inhaled hard and filled up suddenly, and the massive city itself came into his lungs. In a matter of hours his idea of what was real and possible had changed. He now understood what the city could do for him. He looked at the bay, then at the rivers that girded the island. He saw the bridges men had made to conquer them. Dozens of ships lay in the miles of docks that fringed the shore and many more ships traveled the rivers, giant ocean liners with multiple smokestacks, old wooden ships with sails and rigging, ferries, containerships, steamships, and uncountable smaller craft that slashed white between them. Farther out in the harbor was the statue. In letters, Etta had described her as something truly fine, and Longbaugh was glad she had not been disappointed. As a girl, Etta had collected pictures of the statue, published when it had been unpacked and constructed in the harbor in the 1880s. Her sister, Mina, after a visit East, had brought her a toy memento that Etta had graciously accepted, then placed high on a bookshelf, where only Liberty's arm and the torch could be seen. She had found the toy ugly, the head too large, the face too square and masculine, a poor representation that did not come close to the magazine drawings of the real thing. But she had kept it and, as far as he knew, still had it as an adult. Mina wasn't the only nostalgic one honoring a sister's affection.

The freight elevator stopped at the top of the main body of the building and men came aboard to unload it. One of them stared at his boots.

He stepped off the elevator. He was higher off the ground than he had ever been. He took it all in, and his eye fell on a hatless welder. The imp rose inside him. He took off the cap and approached the man.

"I think you lost this."

The welder looked at it. "Yeah, that's mine—hey, how in the world—?"

"I caught it for you."

The welder's mouth fell open as he looked over the edge, where he had last seen his hat in free fall. He looked at the hat, then at Longbaugh, trying to picture him jumping after it and catching it in mid-drop. The welder suffered an inadvertent shudder.

Longbaugh walked away, leaving the welder to contemplate the mystery.

He climbed into the steel skeleton of construction. The sun made one side of the steel hot, while the back side stayed cool. He was aware of the height of his boot heels, and minded his step. He climbed and hung on to a vertical beam, and leaned out to look down. Far down. Thousands of buildings were lined along complex street patterns that uptown broke out into a grid. He was small, innocuous, anonymous. He found that fact both unnerving and comforting.

Longbaugh spoke to a nearby worker.

"How far up are we?"

The worker squinted. "You joking, pal? Fifty-seven stories."

"How high is that?"

"How high does it look? The tallest thing in the world, taller'n the Eiffel Tower. Who're you again?"

"No one in particular."

" 'Cause I know everyone here and you ain't no sky boy."

"Would you believe if I said the new man?"

"New man with the plumb gang?"

"Sure."

"Nope. Not for a second."

Longbaugh was full of cheer. "Me neither."

The man glowered, picked up a basket of bolts, and walked away.

Longbaugh watched a low cloud cover come directly at him, then surround him in a soup of gray. Everything above and below vanished. He floated on a steel beam that disappeared a few feet away, encircled by foggy nothing. He was alone. In the midst of more people than he could have imagined, he was unseen and anonymous. The city could not only hide him, but here he could slay his nickname and bury it. That idea had germinated when he saw the signs shouting for attention. He was in the right place. He could search for her and cause less than a ripple. He could even reclaim his real name.

The cloud moved on, laying out the city below him as if a map unrolled, revealing the Statue of Liberty, the rest of the bay, the lower point of the island, buildings and streets, until he was looking straight down at tiny people and motorcars beneath his feet. He turned with the back of the cloud rushing away and watched the northern part of the island gradually revealed. Construction workers strolled on steel girders as sure as cats. They were intimate with the air and shared a fellowship in their work, knowing that they saw what ordinary men did not. For a moment, Longbaugh was one of them.

THE ADDRESS of Etta's boardinghouse proved to be a run-down old mansion, but it still had some pride, as the windows were free of the ubiquitous clotheslines bearing sheets and trousers that downgraded the other buildings in the area. He had expected New York to be younger, and while there was extensive construction up north, down here he had a sense of a place already passed by. A young woman in the midst of chores stepped out the front door. She might have been pretty but a vertical line between her eyebrows was as deep as her look of exhaustion. She held her lips taut, her eyes were strained and wary, and strands of hair clung to her forehead and cheeks.

"Looking for a room if you have one."

The furrow between her eyebrows ran deeper. "There's a room, but it's one of the bigger ones. Probably won't want to afford it."

"Let me decide."

"Suit yourself." She looked at his boots and cowboy hat, then at the gear over his shoulder. She walked inside and he was meant to follow.

She led him through a vestibule that had once been quite the thing. The dark wainscoting was as high as his shoulders. The rug might have been the original, and while clean, it was just about done, faded and in some areas thinned to the floorboards. A few small paintings decorated the walls, but if there had been pieces with style, wit, or talent they had taken flight. The staircase was grand but wanted paint, and the banister waited on a carpenter. He followed her up to the second floor to a heavy door that she opened with a key. The room was simply furnished, clean like the rest of the house, and when she spread the curtains, a good amount of light came in.

"This will do."

She looked surprised. "It's nothing special. Was nice once, but the owner didn't believe in upkeep."

"Good enough."

"Well." She was unsure how to continue with her new tenant. "I am . . . you may as well call me Abigail."

She told him the rate and he paid her without haggling. He set down his things. He asked where to buy clothes and she mentioned a local men's clothing store.

"You might find something there, but I wouldn't be surprised if it's too fancy."

"You're very young to be so disappointed."

She pinned him with a malignant eye, as if he had just tapped her on the head with a whale bone from a corset. Then she showed him her profile, chin raised. He thought that he would be wise to keep his thoughts to himself. He waited, and when she had collected herself, she led him down the hall. They came to the door of a privy indoors. He smiled at this place, New York City. A facility on his floor with running water. Luxury.

"Wash up here, I suspect you're tired." After a moment, she said,

"You won't be disappointed, this here's the most opulent jakes in all the five boroughs."

"As well as every state west of the Mississippi."

She almost smiled. He was anything but disappointed. He certainly stank after days of travel and was ready to be clean. She demonstrated the hand pump, and water came through a faucet and into a basin. She put a hand on a towel he could use, then stepped outside and closed the door. On the far side, she did not move away. He waited and a few moments later heard her tiptoe down the hall. He turned to consider the room.

His eye was drawn to the color of a small olive ribbon about six inches long that appeared to have been forgotten, stuck between a drinking glass and an old tin of Toilet and Baby Powder. He was reminded of Etta, as the ribbon was the color of his bandanna, and then thought that if her room had been on this floor, she would have spent time in this privy. He pictured her standing at the mirror, curling a strand of hair around a finger, turning her head to one side, then the other, as she imagined a different shape to her nose, holding her finger along the profile trying to see her sideways reflection. Years before, he had caught her doing just that, with total sincerity. Later she did it to tease, reminding him of his previous objection. He was fond of the shape of her nose.

After washing up, he returned to his room and unpacked. In the process of placing his few belongings in drawers, he found items left behind by previous boarders. In a drawer a single man's black silk stocking, in the wardrobe a lady's hat, under the bed a book, *The Poetical Writings of Fitz-Greene Halleck*. He flipped it open and found the man in thrall to exclamation points. He went downstairs and did not see Abigail. He went into the street and followed her directions to the haberdashery.

The sun was long off the streets, a victim of the heights of buildings. Electricity winked on, flooding the pavement with a light he had never before experienced, and there was such an abundance of lights that the sidewalks appeared to glow from within. This was inconceivable, all this illumination at night. He was used to the moon, which, once out of its sliver, reflected enough light to ride. Of course, cities he passed through on the train going east had lights as well, but not on this scale. He appreciated it with childlike glee.

A young boy on a bicycle rolled down the sidewalk and swerved into an old woman and knocked her flat on her back. Longbaugh watched, surprised, as the boy, instead of apologizing, loudly berated her as if it had been entirely her doing. Other pedestrians paused to observe the drama, and had he been more alert, he might have made something of the fact that a handful of children slipped into the belly of the growing crowd. Bicycle Boy explored his vocal range with the bravura of a heldentenor, and Longbaugh wondered what made him so angry. He did not exactly feel the hand that moved to take his wallet, but some inner instinct alerted him and he grabbed a narrow wrist, bringing around a boy in his middle teens who faced him with a feral snarl. The boy yowled, and Bicycle Boy quit bellowing, grabbed up his bicycle and, looking over his shoulder, pedaled away. Longbaugh held up the thief's hand and pointedly took back his wallet. The boy's false yowl grew louder. Longbaugh looked around. The team of nimble-fingered youngsters side-glanced their targets to read their reactions.

Longbaugh used the captured hand of his pickpocket to point out first one, then another of the boy's cronies until the pedestrians understood they were being robbed. They turned on the boys, women battering children with umbrellas, men shaking them as if their stolen money would somehow pour out of them like granulated salt.

Longbaugh twisted the boy's arm behind his back, and the fake yowling stopped, replaced by a sincere "Ow!" Longbaugh held him that way long enough so the boy pickpocket got the point. Then he set him free. The boy stepped a few feet away, shaking his arm, and looked back at Longbaugh with baffled surprise. Longbaugh remembered he was wearing boots and a western hat, so he said, "Git, ya little varmint." The varmint hightailed it.

The victims all came over to shake his hand, one woman bemoaning that she had not been quick enough and her things were lost. Longbaugh nodded noncommittally, as he was not yet finished.

He scanned the edge of the crowd and located the "drop bag." If the drop bag was there, then at least one pickpocket was still at work. He picked him out in a moment. Longbaugh strolled to the corner and grabbed the shoulder of the boy holding the burlap sack. The boy wriggled silently, but Longbaugh's grip was sure. He now caught the eye of the last pickpocket, the oldest of the boys, most likely their leader. The pickpocket froze to assess Longbaugh's state of mind. The pickpocket indicated the pocket watch in his fingers, then nodded to the Drop Bag Boy, offering an exchange. Longbaugh nodded his agreement. The pickpocket slipped the watch back into the waistcoat of the man in the straw hat who never knew it had been taken. Longbaugh took the sack from the Drop Bag Boy and gave him a small push toward the pickpocket. The pickpocket offered a respectful grin. The Drop Bag Boy considered Longbaugh with the look of one who had never before known charity. "Professional courtesy," explained Longbaugh. The boy ran to the pickpocket, who cuffed him alongside his head, then pushed him ahead as they both ran away on cobblestones. Longbaugh looked at the stolen purses and wallets in the sack. A professional operation. When leaving the crime scene, drop the goods in the sack so that if caught, the evidence was off your person.

"Ma'am," he said to the sniveling, not-quick-enough woman, "would this be yours?"

She blessed him and he handed her the sack to allow her the pleasure of returning the rest of the possessions to the others. In the fresh commotion he slipped away. One person watched him go, a small Chinese boy. At first Longbaugh imagined him to be another pickpocket, but all the thieves had been white, and if New York was anything like the West, they would have more readily trusted a freckle-faced girl than a Chink.

He arrived at the haberdashery. He looked in the window where a robust, headless dressmaker's dummy was wrapped in a boldly striped suit with a loud waistcoat, stiff collar, and a colorful cravat. The dummy's torso was on a post, so the trouser legs narrowed to a point at the bottom. He could not imagine himself in those clothes and turned away, but he turned back as the benign shoes at the foot of the dummy caught his eye. They were simple, straightforward, and a reasonable alternative to his boots. He went inside. General stores in the West were jammed with merchandise, filling every spare inch in every corner, and not just with clothing, but with items for the kitchen, bedroom, and garden; children's toys, bolts of cloth, nails, tools, just about anything you could imagine. This place was only a clothing store for men. What an odd concept. How could there be so many things for a man to wear? Shirt, trousers, shoes, hat. What else did a man need other than a gun? And there was room here to consider each piece of clothing individually without having your eye pulled to something else. Yet there were still too many choices a city man could make to decorate his body. He saw shirts, he saw soft collars and stiff collars, he saw studs, cravats, bow ties, and four-in-hands, he saw pocket squares, ascot pins, underwear, socks, spats, shoes, waistcoats, which the salesman insisted on calling vests, overcoats, top hats, bowler hats, slouch hats, newsboy caps, skimmers, as well as a collection of "off the rack" suits. The salesman was an enthusiastic sort, proud of the public service he performed by offering quality goods for sale.

"I take it, sir, you are here for a new look. Not that I object to the rustic. Your clothing almost appears as if you had actually come from out west."

Despite being daunted by the variety of choices, Longbaugh was entertained. "Yes. A new look. I am done playing cowboy."

"Excellent choice. I'll have you fixed up in no time. Let's start with a suit, shall we, and we can build the rest of your look off that."

"Something to blend in." Longbaugh felt lucky to have managed the courage to steer the conversation to his own preferences.

The salesman disguised his disappointment. "Of course, sir. Some prefer not to stand out, to make their statement more subtly."

"I like the dark one." Longbaugh pointed.

"Navy blue, a classic, excellent choice, you have a wonderful eye, sir."

Longbaugh knew what the salesman was doing, but he was flattered all the same.

He tried on the suit's jacket, and the salesman assessed him. "You're the sort of man who can handle color. You must see this vest." He moved toward something splashy, one eye on Longbaugh's reaction. Longbaugh gave him a quiet look of dismissal and the salesman immediately veered to a different, less obvious vest. At that, Longbaugh thought he might have a chance to walk out wearing something he liked.

He lifted the jacket off Longbaugh's shoulders and draped it over the back of a chair, then fit him with a soft collar and shirt. He stood back and assessed his work, "Yes, we're coming along fine now," stepped in close and reached for his bandanna, "Maybe try it without this," Longbaugh's hand caught his wrist and the salesman's head bowed, "but why would you? olive is your color, in fact I have a neck cloth to complement it, olive and lavender are a very common combination." Longbaugh adjusted the bandanna to rest flat under his new shirt. It had grown so thin with age that it was almost as if it wasn't there. Nevertheless, he would have felt undressed if it was gone.

He chose the shoes he had seen in the window and learned they had rubber soles. They were too low to the ground for his taste, but any shoe would be that way after his boots. They were remarkably quiet when walking. The salesman made a comment about factory bosses loving those heels as they were able to sneak up on workers, a comment Longbaugh did not fully understand.

He topped off his outfit with a bowler hat, but angled it rakishly.

The salesman wrapped his old clothes, hat, and boots in brown paper. Longbaugh tucked them under his arm and returned to the street. His step was awkward as he adjusted to the low rubber heels and saw that the same Chinese boy, leaning on a railing partway down the block, resisted laughing at him.

He made eye contact, but the boy did not come closer. He also did not turn away.

"Hey?" said Longbaugh.

The boy looked at him skeptically.

"You ever hear of an Eiffel Tower?"

The boy gave him a short nod.

"Okay, just making sure he didn't make it up."

Longbaugh started to walk away and heard the boy say, "Paris."

Longbaugh turned back.

"The Eiffel Tower. It's in Paris."

Longbaugh hadn't been sure if the boy even spoke English. The boy had no accent, which surprised him.

"Okay."

"In France."

"That part I got."

Longbaugh saluted him off the narrow brim of his new bowler, then continued on his way.

Longbaugh returned to the pickpocket corner. A few of the victims were still clustered, discussing their adventure. He stepped closer so that they might see him in his new clothes. He overheard them discuss the cowboy who had saved them from being robbed, one fellow looking around for him, his eyes rolling to Longbaugh, then rolling on. The tale of the savior-westerner grew legs until it dwarfed lampposts, straddled fences, and hurdled skyscrapers. He walked directly to the woman whose purse he had rescued and said, "Evenin'." Her eyes touched him and she smiled unevenly. He should have been relieved, but was instead disappointed, as he had liked being recognized for his goodness and valor. He had always been the outlaw, and here, with a good deed in his pocket, he was forced to disguise his better angels.

He steered for his new home. He knew he was being followed. He paused at a street vendor and bought two wrapped candies. He dropped them in his pocket and returned to the boardinghouse. Once there, he set one of the hard candies on top of an outdoor banister and went inside. Through lace curtains he watched the Chinese boy glide up, snatch the candy, and put it in his pocket. Longbaugh unwrapped the other one and put it in his mouth.

. . .

LONGBAUGH wandered through the downstairs. He stood in the breezeway to the dining room and watched Abigail two rooms away, through the open door into the kitchen.

She moved with an effortless grace that had been missing in his presence, exhibiting an innocent, careless charm now that she thought she was alone. He liked seeing she was not worn down by life, that a young vibrant girl still burbled within, and he was startled to realize how aggressively he was drawn to her. She turned sideways and he froze in place so that she wouldn't pick up his movement peripherally. She had changed her look. Her hair was pinned and neat, her face scrubbed, her cheeks wore a high blush, and her eyes had been accented to appear larger. He realized unhappily that all this had been done for him. While keenly attracted to her, he was not pleased to know she might want something from him. Nevertheless, he did not turn away.

She reached for a serving dish that held three heads of garlic, but her hands inexplicably stopped, hovering there without motion. After a long moment, he saw her move in a way that didn't fit her mission. A tiny musical wave rolled through her fingers, from pinky to ring to middle to index finger and back, gentle waves that rode up the sand, then rolled away. After a moment the wave washed up her wrists, then through her arms to crest in her shoulders. Her torso and hips joined the flow and her whole body was in heat. It was a moment before he realized she wasn't wearing a corset, and something shifted inside him. The beat began to move him, but he fought it, anchoring his foot to the floor. He felt the unheard music in her head, but tamped down the bump of his heart. He stood there watching her sway in her romantic trance and was suddenly overwhelmed by a surge of acute melancholy. He had been alone, a long time alone, and here, presented with something warm and young and pretty that he might take and have and hold in his arms, he realized he was more lonely than at any time he could remember. His heart dropped into a deep, soundless hollow. He wanted to touch and taste her to fill his emptiness, all the while knowing the only person who could sate him had gone silent. He lost his balance and put his hand out to touch the doorframe.

He watched her now as if from a great distance. She took up a garlic bulb, but the head was soft in her fingers. Her sway faded and she sniffed it, tossed it aside, and reached for the second bulb. She tested it and it was firm and she nodded, but her nod became a gentle head bob that then pendulumed to a fresh rhythm through her belly and hips. She crossed the room with the light step of a dancer, approaching a basket of tomatoes. She leaned in close to the basket and her head snapped back, the dancer frozen, the music silenced, nostrils flaring as she dipped her hands in the basket as if into ice water and came out cupping two oozing tomatoes frosted on the bottom with blue fuzz. She hurried them dripping to the trash. She wiped her palms with a dishrag and turned in a circle, lip curled, contemplating an alternate plan, and then she saw him. To her credit, she did not flinch.

He ventured through the dining room to the kitchen doorway.

"I thought you were a stranger. Good . . . good suit." She put the dishrag aside and smelled her fingers. Her taut expression returned as she slipped into her thoughts, and he imagined she was reviewing in her head the past few minutes of her performance. Or perhaps she saw something in his face that told her whatever fancy she'd created about him was not available to her.

"Appreciate the recommendation."

"You can get lucky there sometimes. Although I miss the boots."

"I saved them. Been here long?"

"I'm a little behind with supper. Nothing special, but it won't disappoint unless you're addicted to Maison Dorée or Louis Sherry."

"I meant living here."

"Oh. A few years. We were boarders and the owner asked me to take on the day-to-day."

"We?"

"My, uh, my husband and I."

"Then you know Etta. Ethel."

She became suspicious. "What's your name again?"

"Longbaugh."

"Right, Longbaugh. Etta's an unusual name. I think I would have remembered."

"She lived here up to two years ago. Maybe you moved in after."

"No," she said obstinately, "been here five years. You've got the wrong address."

He did not reach for the letter in his pocket. He well remembered the address.

"Maybe you made a mistake coming here, Mr. Longbaugh. Maybe this isn't the right place for you. I'll give you back your money, you'll find another place."

The dreamy young woman was gone, and he was sorry. He said nothing.

"So, just be on your way."

He thought he understood. "I'm not a stranger."

Abigail paused. "Men say those things when they want something."

"Although I suppose some men are always strangers to their wives."

Abigail cocked her head. "No. I don't believe you. She was married but her husband had a different name."

"Alonzo."

"Is that a guess?"

"Harry Alonzo Longbaugh."

She was slow to answer. "You could have heard that somewhere."

"So she did live here."

Abigail ran her hands down her dress trying to devise a proof. "Where were you? Where were you living?"

"Out west."

"No, sorry, her husband was in prison."

"She would not have told you that."

"When her husband's letters came, I sent them back." She looked smug, as if she had outplayed him at his own game. She leaned her low back against the counter and crossed her arms.

"Why?"

"Because she asked me to."

"Why?"

"Maybe she didn't want to hear from you . . . from her husband . . . again."

"That's possible." Without thinking, he pulled her last letter out of his jacket and absently tapped it on the table without looking at it.

Abigail watched the tap-tap-tap, and her arms dropped to her sides.

"That's one of her letters," said Abigail.

He looked at her, then at the letter.

"I recognize it," said Abigail. "You have one of her letters."

"Yes."

"Meaning you're her husband."

"Unless I stole this, too, along with his name."

"No. Stop that, don't tease me. You're Harry Alonzo."

"Is everyone in New York so suspicious?"

"I'm so sorry. I didn't know." She was flustered and she rushed to make up for her lack of trust. "She left suddenly. Like you said, about two years ago. I thought maybe she got sick of us, but I couldn't say why, I mean, we were friends, or I thought we were. She actually did say if letters came from you, I had to send them back unopened."

"Why?"

"I don't know."

"Do you know where she is?"

"No."

"And she didn't say why to send my letters back?"

"She left so suddenly, I never got to ask. I returned your letters and her sister's."

"Her sister's letters?"

She nodded. "Wilhelmina's. I wish I could tell you why she left. Maybe it had something to do with those people, but they only came after she was gone."

"Men came here?"

"Well, one was a man."

"Tell me what happened."

"A woman came the day after she left, one of 'those' women, you know who I mean, although maybe that wasn't so odd, since she tried to help different . . . different sorts of people." Abigail flushed. "Anyway, you know the kind I mean. That was her, the way she lived, helping people. But you knew her, you knew what she was like."

He thought he did not know her. Her actions were inexplicable, inexcusable, opaque. Somewhere in the choices she made was the woman he loved. But her choices were unrecognizable.

"Who came after that?"

"A day or two later a man came. He had a bandage on his cheek. He was handsome, dark hair, olive skin, what do you call that? Swarthy. He was polite, but I could tell it wasn't sincere. He scared me."

Clearly not one of the two monkeys who had visited Mina. He had thought that those men were hired to intimidate her and were therefore unimportant. Now he was convinced.

"Remember his name?"

She shook her head. "No."

"Ever see him before?"

She shrugged. "It was two years ago."

"Had she spoken about him?"

"When she wasn't talking about you, she talked about Lillian."

"Lillian Wald."

She nodded. "The founder of that Settlement place. I saw her give a speech once. Oh dear. Don't tell my husband. It was about suffrage and temperance."

"She wrote me about her."

"She liked it there. She'd come home and stop by the mirror and say, 'Etta, that was a pretty good day.'"

"She said 'Etta'?"

"Wasn't that her name?"

"Yes." He knew a strange relief. An encounter with the familiar, something that told him they were speaking of the same person. It was natural to call herself Etta with him, and even use it to annoy Mina, but that she had adopted it in New York meant something more.

"She'd take your letters and rush upstairs. Not exactly ladylike. She was less lonely when they came. After she read them, she was sadder."

Longbaugh pictured her on the stairs, holding up her skirt to run.

"I thought of us as friends, but she didn't always notice me. She had her own life. I liked her and wanted her to like me, but . . ." She shrugged. "Sometimes when she talked to me, it was like, I don't know, she had a sort of glow that I could almost, this sounds silly, but that I could feel. And I felt . . . I guess I felt respected."

Longbaugh understood. He had seen how idly Etta treated certain people. He had also seen her turn on that light and how people were drawn to it. She had been like that with him every day they were together.

"Abigail, I appreciate all this."

"Oh goodness, call me Abby," she said, then was flustered and turned to the side, running her fingers across her forehead to push away habitually loose hairs that today were not loose but carefully pinned.

"What did she look like?" He meant it as a neutral question. "What did she wear?"

"That's very sweet," said Abigail sentimentally.

Longbaugh cringed and said nothing.

"I suppose she looked like a New York City girl. Kept her hair up, wore shirtwaists, long skirts, like most of us." She looked down at her dress. "When we're out in the street."

"Anything more about this man, the one with the bandage?"

Abigail shook her head no. "You came a long way to find her."

He needed to steer her away from her maudlin appreciation of his marriage. "Thank you again, Abby." He looked over and saw a muscular young man in the doorway, dressed in overalls with a black slouch hat in his hands, like the young men he had seen on the streets. He would learn later that he was dressing like a Wobbly, a western miner, part of the Industrial Workers of the World. Tough men emulated by the young boys of the East.

Abigail looked as well. "Oh. Robert. You're home early."

She pushed up from where she leaned on the counter, but did not move toward him. Longbaugh thought her tone defensive, caught talking with a man in her kitchen, with her hair pinned and makeup on her face.

Robert Levi looked younger than he must have been. His shoulders were broad, his chest and hips narrow. His hair was short and his nose was a little off center, as if it had been broken. He crossed to her, but they did not touch. He took an extra step to command the space between his wife and this intruder, and Longbaugh knew he had an enemy.

"This is Mr. Alonzo," said Abigail.

"Longbaugh," said Longbaugh.

"Yeah," said Levi, narrowing his eyes. "Robert Levi, with an *I*." He waited to see what move Longbaugh would make. Longbaugh was patient. Levi gave him the same malignant eye Longbaugh had previously earned from Abigail, and he wondered who had picked it up from whom.

"I'm a sandhog," said Levi, as if that should mean something.

"It's not like that, Robert," said Abigail. "And you're not a sandhog anymore, you're a manager."

"Once a sandhog, always a sandhog."

"You don't need to be that way, he's our new boarder."

"You accepted a male boarder without checking with me?"

"What's a sandhog?" said Longbaugh.

"Who *is* this genius?" said Levi derisively. "'What's a *sand* hog?'"

"I'll explain later," said Abigail to Levi, wanting to cut him off.

"I was in prison, so I don't know from sandhogs."

"You said this man could live here? He was in *prison*!"

"You don't understand," said Abigail.

"Give him back his money, he's leaving."

"You don't understand, and he stays."

"I'm Etta's husband, so what's a sandhog?"

Levi stopped. "Etta?"

"Sandhogs dig subway tunnels," said Abigail.

"I worked under the river," said Levi, but still a step behind and less certain now.

"Takes courage," said Longbaugh. "And rising to manager makes you a man of ambition."

Levi stared at him, his mouth opening and closing, as if all former sandhogs had gills.

"I imagine you two have things to discuss." Longbaugh moved to the door, then looked at Abigail. "Which was Etta's room?"

"On your floor, two doors toward the back."

He left them to their spat.

HE KNOCKED ON THE DOOR that had once been Etta's and heard nothing. He knew locks, and it was a simple matter to spring this one. He stepped inside and silently closed the door behind him.

The rooms came furnished, so he concentrated on personal items. A man's things hung in a wooden wardrobe. Personal toiletry items were on the table by the window, a few papers by a small bed table. The boarder likely spent little time here. Longbaugh looked for any remnant of Etta, knowing it was futile. He searched behind and beneath things. He held out hope that she might have left him a message. The dreariness of that tragic romantic notion annoyed him, but with no other options, he persisted. He slid under the bed and felt between slats and mattress. He reached behind the wardrobe. He looked behind framed drawings on the wall. He tested floorboards and molding. He looked behind curtains.

He sat in the chair. He appraised the room. Etta's room. Even if a message had once existed, any number of things could have come between her leaving it and its being inadvertently moved or removed. He had the sense, and not for the first time, that he was chasing a phantom. If she had imagined him coming back for her, any message would have been covert, placed so only Longbaugh could find or understand it. *If* she had bothered to leave a message. His imagination wanted a message, so he wasted his pathetic time hunting for it. He disliked this need, thought it a weakness, but he knew that wouldn't stop him from looking next in the hallway. He hesitated to leave her room. He was one step closer to her in time. His eyes scoured the floor, the tables, the curtains. They moved up and measured the ceiling, and when he saw it he was amazed that he had missed it, as it was so obvious. Liberty's arm holding the torch, right there, on top of the wardrobe. He pulled the chair over and stood on it and brought the cheap memento down, and was further amazed to find a piece of olive ribbon tied around Liberty's middle like a sash. His mind went to the ribbon he had seen on the shelf in the indoor privy, and he understood. The two ribbons weren't placed randomly, they were a color match with his bandanna, and she had placed them deliberately. She had left a trail, and he was the only one who would know to follow it.

He sat on her bed, holding the toy, then lay on his side and curled around it. He pulled off the satin ribbon. About six inches long. Both ends of the ribbon were ragged, as if torn from a larger piece. He tried to picture the original, longer stretch of ribbon, to envision from where it had come. He didn't think it had come from a spool, as she had apparently left the boardinghouse in a hurry so she would have been improvising and wouldn't have had time to go to a store. It had to have been something she already owned. The trim from a hat's brim? Ornamentation on a dress? But there were no sewing stitches along the side of the ribbon, as there would have been had it been dress trim. Part of a decorative bow? But there were no fold creases other than where it had been loosely tied to make Liberty's sash. He turned to the Liberty toy. He looked for something there, maybe a scratched message on the statue's base. He turned it over, and the hollow bottom was empty. He sat it on the blanket and stared at it, all the while rubbing the satin ribbon between his fingers and thumb. He breathed fully. There was no message beyond the presence of the statue and the ribbons. She may not have known where she was going. This was her way to connect, to tell him there was a trail out there for him to follow, so that he knew what to look for.

. . .

HE OPENED THE DOOR and was face-to-face with an angry Robert Levi. He stepped out into the hall and closed the door behind him.

"What were you doing in there?"

Longbaugh shook his head. No answer would appease.

"You take chances, mister," said Levi.

Longbaugh spoke glibly. "No, just Liberty."

"What is that, a riddle? You don't take chances, you take liberties? Making fun of me?"

Longbaugh saw Levi tensing, about to come at him. So he moved first, stepped in close, bringing the statue's flame up near Levi's eye. The young man backed up, chin jerking close to his neck.

"*This* Liberty. Robert, listen to me carefully, I came all the way to New York to disappear. I served my time, and I'm not looking for trouble."

Robert Levi looked at the toy, still on his heels but rallying. Longbaugh was impressed that he so quickly recovered his belligerence. "What did you do?"

"Took this from the room. I don't know whose room it is, but this was there before your current occupant moved in." He lowered the toy and placed it firmly in Levi's hand. But he palmed the olive ribbon.

Levi considered the toy. "Why were you in prison?"

"I got caught." He secretly slid the ribbon into his pocket.

Irritated: "How'd they *catch* you?"

"Robbing a train."

Levi wasn't having any of it. "Sure, train robbery, because it sounds so romantic to the ladies."

"Feel free to try it if it makes your sun shine."

"You dangerous?"

"Not to the ladies."

"What are your intentions toward my wife?"

"Pay the rent on time. Compliment her cooking."

Levi growled. Longbaugh wondered what had gone wrong in their marriage.

Levi seemed to be chasing away a thought that would not let go. Finally it flew from his lips. "She *likes* you." His snarl was both threat and self-flagellation.

"She likes that I love my woman."

"Dammit, you *do* talk in riddles."

"Women like men who like their women. They like to imagine they're loved in the same way."

Longbaugh had confused him enough to momentarily geld him. Levi uncertainly handed back the Liberty toy.

"I love my woman."

"Glad to hear it."

"Aw, what the hell do you know?"

"Not a lot, since I haven't seen mine in years. But maybe there's hope for you."

Levi reached for a snappy reply that wasn't there. Longbaugh figured he'd think of one later and kick himself. "I'd love to get you down in the dig, show you how a sandhog lives, how a *real* man lives."

"All right."

Levi was confounded. "What do you mean, 'all right'?"

"Let's go. Show me how tough you are."

For that he had a comeback. "Sorry, nothing to steal down there."

"You're onto me. My plan is to rob a freshly dug tunnel."

"Mister, you wouldn't last five minutes there. Ever hear of a compression chamber?" Levi leaned in ominously. "Because you gotta go through one to work down there. The air pressure in there's so intense, the tunnel actually thinks it's just more bedrock."

When he didn't get the reaction he wanted, Levi pressed harder. "Know what a blowout is? It's when you hit a weak spot in the wall and the pressure pushes you through it, right through the dirt and rock till you hit the bottom of the river, then it blows your sorry ass up through the water till you're thirty feet in the air! Happened to a guy I know, and he lived. You think you're tough robbing trains, well you don't know tough."

Longbaugh looked at the rage in Levi's face and shook his head. "Maybe you should build a bridge."

"You son of a bitch."

"Okay, then. Show me."

"Who *are* you, mister? What is it with you?"

"You that desperate for my respect? I'm ready to be impressed."

"You think I want your respect? Jesus, I'm not taking you down there!"

"You just read me the book of Job trying to scare me."

"You're a damn civilian, Jesus Christ! What are you thinking?"

Longbaugh looked at him coolly and tried not to smile. There was more than one way to call a man's bluff.

Levi turned away, muttering to himself, "Keep your hands off my wife."

Longbaugh watched him until he had reached the stairs and gone down, out of sight.

He blinked as he stood there. He wanted nothing to do with their marriage.

He went to the indoor privy and took the piece of olive ribbon Etta had left there.

He returned to his room. He set the toy high on his own wardrobe, so that only the arm and the flame were visible. He brought out the two olive ribbons from his pocket and rubbed them together idly as he planned the next day.

5

He woke at sunrise. It was too early to leave, but he was restless and refused to stay in his room. He dressed and moved through the silent hallway and down empty stairs. He went outside, choosing to walk instead of just waiting. The sky was ominous and gray and pressed down on the city. The smell of rain rode the wind, but he walked on, heading north on Fifth Avenue. He was still dry when he decided to stop at the Hotel Brevoort at Eighth Street. He chose a small table in the main café, thinking the weather too uncertain to sit in the Parisian sidewalk café. He ordered strong coffee and looked at newspapers that were available for customers. He read without absorbing, his mind distracted. He thought about money and how to stretch it, as only that one time, after the Wilcox robbery, had he been wise enough to hide it away. Luckily, he still had most of that left. But if he was to fit into the city, he wondered if he should be like the rest of New York and find a job. He opened a newspaper and turned to the help wanted advertisements. He encountered a need for workers to fill jobs he did not know existed, and in some cases he did not know what sort of work they entailed. He envisioned entering the mind-numbing pattern of daily employment. During his early days out west, that pattern had bored him silly and driven him to crime. But his youth was past. Perhaps now he could better handle a tame existence. He reviewed ads that promised humdrum jobs inappropriate to his talents. The city was an immense industrial machine, and he lacked the skills that would make him employable. From what he was reading, he was perfectly qualified to start at the bottom rung of the ladder for slave wages.

He abandoned the newspapers in the café and went outdoors. A rainsquall had passed through while he was inside and had left the streets wet, but for now it had stopped. It was still early. He chanced the weather and walked again toward his destination. The air was clear and the city's edges were sharp, specific. He had given little thought to organizing his future, as organization had been imposed upon him for the past twelve years. He thought about his age and realized he was in his mid-forties. He wondered if he was slowing down.

He stopped on the sidewalk in the middle of a block, and took stock of his skills. He was a good horseman and an expert ranch hand with talents that had kept him in demand. He could handle a gun. He had a talent for escape, be it handcuffs or small-town jails. The penitentiary had been a different matter: there had been no way to escape from that establishment. He had made brooms there. He didn't want to make brooms anymore. But mostly, he knew how to rob banks and trains. These were western skills. He smiled ruefully as he thought of applying his skills to the new city. He opened and closed his fist, wondering how rusty he would be with a gun.

His vision cleared and he saw why he had ventured along that mental path, as the entrance to a bank was being unlocked in front of him, opening for business. He looked around to see if he had aroused anyone's suspicions. But everyone seemed preoccupied with the sky, expecting a resurgence of rain. The sun chose that moment to emerge briefly, a crease between clouds that illuminated bank and outlaw. A lesser man might have taken that as an omen. He checked his glowing reflection in the window, then squinted to see if those inside were in any way concerned about the man staring at them. When no one showed any interest, he experienced a sense of comfort and well-being. With a bank before him, he was curiously at home. He knew banks. He understood them. He was good at banks. They were obvious and consistent, as well as a source of income and self-esteem. A New York bank was likely to have better safeguards than a bank in Utah or Wyoming. Bank vaults would be stronger, more difficult to open, but his approach had never been to use force. He trusted human nature, gaining access through the incompetence of a manager, or the vain self-assurance of a vice president. The human animal was ever the same, it mattered little how technology matured. He looked up and down the block and mentally mapped escape routes. He saw two or three good flights off the street, alleys there and over there, cross streets, crowded sidewalks and busy intersections. He formulated one escape by foot, another by horse, then formulated a third option in case of emergency that utilized hacks and trolleys. He would require information about police schedules, patterns, the location of their precinct, and the number of officers on the beat. Not too difficult. It felt good to heat up the old muscles. He turned his attention to the bank itself.

He stepped inside. The atmosphere was cozy, especially welcoming after the wet streets and hostile skies. The light was warm and inviting. The employees smiled. He scouted the layout, noted the security guards on tall stools, the lineup of tellers, the desks and seating area at the far end of the room. His inner clock timed the walk from the front door to the tellers, the tellers to the safe behind them, the security guards to the security door. He went to the island and scribbled on a deposit slip, then patted his pockets as if he had forgotten his billfold. There were any number of ways to get information on the safe's lock, but then he identified the branch manager and his assistant and knew he could talk his way into the back. Yes, he could do it, he could take this place. A bank was a bank, whether in Colorado or New York City. He mentally assembled his team and scheduled more visits, at different times of the day, to know the civilian ebb and flow. It was doable.

He stepped back out into the gray day, feeling refreshed. He remembered without anxiety that it had been just such an act, albeit with a train, that had taken him away from Etta in the first place. He had no intention of robbing this bank. But the mental exercise made him feel like a kid again.

He arrived at the brick four-story building on Henry Street. He hadn't realized how far in the other direction he had walked, so he hailed a cab. The driver dropped him off a few blocks away, near the Williamsburg Bridge, not caring to brave the neighborhood. He smelled the East River mingling with the strong smells of cooking, cleaning, and garbage that came from the tenements. He approached the front door and knocked, and when a young woman answered, he asked for Etta. That caught her attention, and he was invited inside and told to wait in a parlor. The Settlement had been successful and had expanded to four other buildings on the same block of Henry Street, one of them a gymnasium, and he had gone to the wrong one initially before being sent here. After a short time he was led upstairs, taken to the back, and pointed to a rear porch that overlooked an inner courtyard dominated by a children's playground. Here, deep in the Lower East Side, was a welcoming, homey environment. Had he been Lillian Wald, he too would have spent his time here. Street noise was muted, she had a bird's-eye view of a tiny garden, and the empty playground, alert with optimism, was littered with the toys of a recent occupation. He waited for her to turn, and took advantage of the moment to observe her. She sat in a low chair, staring off while wrapped in her thoughts, a blanket around her shoulders, a sheaf of papers gripped hard enough in her hand that they curled into a cone. He realized she was probably his age, but she looked older, and had a presence about her that demanded respect.

She looked up to his face and was surprised. "You are not the one I expected."

"My apologies."

"Cynthia said a man asked for Etta. I expected another."

Lillian Wald rose out of her chair, leaving the blanket behind. She moved close to him and inspected his face impolitely. He did not move, but squirmed inside. Rarely had he been so thoroughly scrutinized. She allowed time to pass before she lifted an eyebrow and half smiled. "You are her Harry."

He stood taller and introduced himself with his real name.

"Have you news of her, Mr. Longbaugh?" She watched his expression, then answered for him. "No. But you're looking."

She went from direct eye contact to seemingly gazing just over his shoulder, and he realized she was thinking. She then looked at the papers in her hand. "This can wait," and set them on the blanket in the chair. Her voice was authoritative, and with her precise diction, he knew she was comfortable controlling a room. "Political gobbledygook, another useless report on our Federal Children's Bureau. To be expected with the Bull Moose gone." She shook her head. "Are you an optimistic sort, Mr. Longbaugh? I'm afraid I believed Theodore when he said we'd continue to enjoy the full support of government. . . . These days our representatives spend more time investigating the boll weevil than looking out for our young people. Apparently I'll have to go after them the way I did with the New York Factory Law."

He wanted to prove he could stand tall in the face of her power, but could only manage, "Factory Law . . . ?"

"Never mind, just politics, I'm talking to myself."

"No, I—"

"Prohibits employment of girls under sixteen for more than ten hours a day or fifty-four hours a week." Her words came like a fast river off her lips, as if spoken a thousand times a day. She smiled warmly. "You'll know better than to ask next time. Did they offer you tea?"

"No, ma'am, but that's not necess—"

"My people are wonderful, but busy, so it's not technically bad manners. *Cynthia!* She'll be along."

"You said you expected someone else."

"Yes, he came to see me once before."

But before he could ask about the one who had come, she changed the subject as she perused the low clouds overhead. "I forget to look around. We built the playground to keep the children from playing in the streets, but you know that. The neighborhood is changing, which is good, but change breeds anxiety. Just Monday, Mrs. O'Brien came to me in tears. Irish Roman Catholic, our Mrs. O'Brien, dismayed by the dwindling of the congregation." Then Lillian leaned in to whisper Mrs. O'Brien's secret: "All the new Italians." She shrugged at the frailty of the human condition. "Mrs. O'Brien is mortified that her children do not share her respect for religion."

Lillian Wald set her hands on the banister and gazed down at the children's playground. He chose to wait and was rewarded when he saw her transformed. Her shoulders opened, spread, and shifted the world's weight from off her back and onto the chair behind her. "Ach, the old woman grows long-winded. I am become strident, Mr. Longbaugh. I do it on purpose, mind you, it's difficult to get men in power to do the right thing. I trained myself to sound pompous and arrogant so that I impress those I must impress, and now it's habit." She turned and looked closely at him. "She was in love with you."

"Am I that obvious?"

"You mean did I think you needed to hear that, Mr. Longbaugh? Yes."

"You have a keen eye."

"I play politics with presidents and captains of industry, I had better have that and more."

She laughed and he smiled at the sound. She was quite full of herself, but she had a way about her that made it charming.

"Come, walk with me, did you see my little garden? It was put in for me, to help me relax, but when do I have time?"

At the bottom of the stairs they came out on a garden set off in a corner of the playground. They stepped over small puddles from the earlier rain. The garden was overgrown here, underwatered there. She pinched off a hard brown leaf from a parched plant and shook off water drops. "This one wants more than just a morning shower. I wonder what sort of plant it was," she said. She let it drop and a breeze scraped it along the ground.

"Etta was a wonderful teacher, but much of what we teach here is prosaic, cooking, cleaning, how to carry yourself, how to find work. Etta wanted to do more than prepare them for the grind of life, she wanted to educate them. She was a natural with the children. She took a liking to one difficult girl, and when she found out about the girl's troubled home life, she got overly involved. She learned the girl had an older sister."

"The girl, is she still here?"

"In fact she is. Many of them stay." She turned to gauge his mood, then took both of his hands in hers and was surprisingly serious. "Etta was courageous. You must prepare yourself for that."

With her direct and sober tone and the way she gripped his hands, he was aware of his heart beating.

She anticipated his next question. "And, no, Mr. Longbaugh, what we do here is no more dangerous than what people on the streets face every day."

He took his hands back and said something safe. "This is a . . . a good place."

"I saw a need."

"How did you get started?"

"Rather by accident. I was a wide-eyed nurse, and a desperate boy saw me on the street in my new outfit with my new medical bag and begged for help. I often say it was my first day, as I've learned to start an audience off with a good story, but in truth," she shrugged, "I no longer remember. He dragged me by the hand to his sick mother in her bed. I realized that the tenement was where I was needed. So I moved into the neighborhood."

"As simple as that."

"Well, I insisted on a decent toilet facility. But yes. As simple as that."

"I was good with horses," he said with humility, unable to compete.

"And Etta was good with the girls." She had missed his stab at humor. "We encourage young women to stay in school, further their education before job hunting, and," she gestured to the playground, "to experience play."

"What is it you need to tell me." It was not a question.

"Etta met the older sister."

"And that's why she disappeared."

"I imagine it had something to do with her leaving. In my experience, there is a thin line between helping others and getting too involved. I'm not sure even I understand where it needs to be drawn. You cannot save everyone." She shrugged. "This from the woman who every day tries to save the world." She sighed. "We all have our blind spots, Mr. Longbaugh, and we get caught up in things we would be wise to let alone."

He again heard the warning in her words.

"Did this older sister have a name?"

She hesitated and he saw a twinkle creep into her eyes. "Queenie Collette."

Longbaugh smiled.

"Yes, that's what I thought, too. I don't know her real name, but she was the girlfriend of an Italian gentleman, the one I expected to see when I heard a man was here asking for Etta."

He remembered an earlier conversation with Abigail. "Italian."

"It is said he is Black Hand."

He shook his head, not comprehending.

"Black Hand, *il Mano Nera*. Italian gangsters, although some newspapers say it's not officially a gang. They draw a small black hand in the corner of blackmail letters, then bomb homes or businesses if they don't get what they want. They prey on other Italians, doctors, bakers, the honest men."

"Is he around?"

"Joe? Yes, I see him occasionally."

"Joe what?"

"Isn't it odd. In politics, I remember everyone's name, and his I've forgotten. It starts with an *M*, I believe. Miss Collette is also still out on the streets, despite Etta's efforts to salvage her. She no longer commands the interest she once did, either on the street or in the heart of her Joe. Our poor deposed Queenie. She is now something of an old worn glove, despite being shy of the age of thirty."

QUEENIE COLLETTE's younger sister, Mary Smithson, a mature-looking fifteen-year-old, came from her classroom into the hallway. Lillian Wald held the door and watched Mary walk with an erect posture that was a shade too perfect. He found it impressive, but thought it might have been learned in a classroom. He glanced at Lillian and believed Mary's walk was meant to please the great lady. He knew then that with Lillian present he would never hear the truth from Mary. These girls loved their situation and they loved Lillian Wald and would not want to disappoint her.

He needed to speak with Mary alone, and that would never happen. A grown man was not to have a private conversation with a young woman learning to be proper, not without damage to her reputation.

He asked questions to which he knew the answers. He asked about Joe, but Mary knew little about him. He glanced at Lillian. She understood that her presence was deterring Mary, but she did not excuse herself. The safety of the children was paramount. He asked a few more questions, then thanked Mary when he heard the others coming out of the classrooms.

He and Lillian shared a few more pleasantries, and he said goodbye. She invited him back anytime, and while he appreciated her sincerity, he knew she had given all she could and would not return to the situation unless new information surfaced. Life had taught her not to put her energy into a lost cause.

He stopped on the sidewalk of Henry Street. He looked up and down as if he was looking for Queenie Collette and the mysterious Joe. But he knew they would not be so easily found, and the city remained as locked to him as the gates of the penitentiary. To blunder through neighborhoods while learning the rules was a fool's game. He needed a guide.

The sun came out then and made the street bright, and he squinted. A girl who was perhaps eight years old walked directly toward him and looked him impolitely in the face.

"Come with me," she said. She turned and, without looking back, led him across the street to the alley in the middle of the block. One of those odd life coincidences. Just as he had thought of needing a guide, this child had appeared. He missed his gun at that moment, but despite her authority, he reminded himself he was following a curly-headed eight-year-old girl.

Mary Smithson waited in the alley, deliberately out of sight of the main door of the Settlement. The eight-year-old bounded back across the street and took a position on the far side, to serve as Mary's lookout. He had a fleeting memory of his days on the outlaw trail.

"Don't got a lotta time," said Mary, showing nerves.

"Thank you for talking to me."

Her words came in a rush and were nothing like her proper indoor speech. "Could be my sister knows where Etta is, but Q takes off, sometimes for days, ya know? Got troubles, booze, and . . . whatever else she finds makes her feel good."

"Your sister. Queenie."

Mary nodded. "Q to me, though I gave her the name, my big sister the queen."

"You sound different than inside."

Her chin dropped to her chest. She looked up, a little ashamed. Some of the indoor polish returned to her words. "They taught me how to speak, but it sounds funny outside. I love it in there, I do. They're all so kind. But the girls are reading *Pollyanna*, and, nothing against it, but some of them want to start a Glad Club."

"And that's not for you."

"Nuh-uh."

"It's not real. You started on the streets."

"How'd you know?"

"Not so hard to read."

"The others girls come from bad lives, too, but, well, Glad Clubs?"

"I'm willing to bet it's too cheerful for Lillian, too."

"When I was growing up, girls with my look got started young and made good money. Men go for the sweet, pretty ones, and I thought I was the thing. But Q knew better. She protected me, ya know? She did. At the time I thought she was jealous, 'cause Joe, Giuseppe, talked so pretty to me, real romantic. I was sure he liked me better than her."

"Giuseppe . . . ?"

"Giuseppe Moretti. But she knew his pitch was hooey, he didn't want *me*, he wanted to sell me to other men. But the way he talked, so sincere, ya know? And he was handsome, and had nice clothes, and respect." She looked tensely around the corner to the Settlement front door. "Not sure why I'm saying all this."

Longbaugh knew why. In the Settlement, she was the clean and good Mary, and glad for it. But she never got the chance to tell her story.

"Q met Etta 'cause of me, so Q talked about her sometimes," said Mary.

Longbaugh's heart quickened to hear his wife's name brought into Queenie's streets. This time he glanced at the eight-year-old to know if someone was coming. The eight-year-old did not look his way.

"By the way, you should know, Etta's why I'm here. Someone I look up to." Mary took a step deeper into shadow and spoke both quietly and urgently. "Etta tried to help Q , got her to a place Joe couldn't find, which made Joe crazy nuts. Etta was smart, saw Q was good with fabric and knew to keep her busy, so she got her in the needle trade."

"Needle trade?"

"Garment factory job—this was early '11, right after New Year's. Etta took her over to one of those places, talked 'em into giving Q a job." Mary's expression changed then, as if a memory stepped in and she couldn't drag her inner eye away from it. "Etta thought having real work would keep Q away from Joe. It was a good idea, mister, really. Then Joe came after Etta. Called her names, wanted to know where Q was hiding. Etta stood up to him, I mean, she was something. After Joe went away, Etta figured Q was free of him, like for good. I mean, Q'd made her a promise. Seriously, mister, how was she to know what Q would do? Then, when it happened, well, everybody was pretty shocked. Joe was sort of the only person in the city who seemed glad about it, like he thought the whole thing happened just to give him this moral, I don't know, advantage or something."

Longbaugh was confused. "Moral advantage?"

Mary looked to the street and her expression changed. He turned and the eight-year-old was signaling.

"I got to go!"

"But—what happened?"

"The Triangle fire, mister," said Mary, and she ran.

LONGBAUGH walked away from Henry Street as if propelled by Mary's anxiety. He did not want to disappoint Lillian Wald by being caught talking to one of her charges. After a number of blocks he slowed. Every new thing he had learned about Etta's life unnerved him. He had missed it all, her growth of spirit and empathy, those early steps of change that gave her the courage to take risks on behalf of people Longbaugh would not have offered the time of day. A streetwalker. A gangster. Etta was intelligent and curious, but he hadn't really meant for her to go on living while he was away. He had expected to come out and find her the same, frozen in time until he could reappear to reclaim her. Instead, she not only had lived but embarked on a dangerous journey. But the part that wounded him was that so much of it had gone unmentioned in her letters. She had done all these things and had kept the bulk of them from him. He walked the streets, crossing easily, already unconsciously in step with the rhythm of traffic and city life. He struggled to reconcile the woman he had married with this courageous, obstinate person who had risked herself for a wasted soul. He was now that much more anxious to find her, to protect her and learn who she had become. Mary's words boiled in his mind. He had not gotten the whole story, but that did not slow him from trying to piece it together from the scraps provided.

He walked quickly, unaware of his surroundings, so deep in his thoughts that he turned a corner to find himself in the midst of a parade of women, accidentally in step with their tramping feet, beside him, ahead of him, close behind him, scores of protesters marching in militaristic unison. Silent, determined, some carrying placards, all of them walking with fevered purpose. Their collective silence was as much a surprise as the fact of being among them. The percussive tramping spurred him forward and he fell into formation. Learning about Etta had made him uneasy, restless, incautious, and he was glad to be propelled into this sudden adventure, although as with Etta's journey, he had no sense of its purpose. He saw intensity in the eyes of the women around him, a severe set to their mouths, the dedicated way they leaned forward, as if mentally armored against anything that might dive in at them. The one to his left smiled, the one to his right nodded, and he was welcomed as a brother. He sensed their fear, but other than the sound of their feet, it was their ominous quiet that roused him.

Half a block ahead, the marchers in front rounded a corner, entering a world of noise just out of sight. Those around him did not falter at the sound but drove up the pace, rushing to the clash, chins forward as the corner beckoned, each step nearer, tramp tramp tramp, placards angled into the wind, tramp tramp tramp tramp, those just ahead turning, and then he too was around the corner, caught in the noise and confusion as the silent protesters now opened their mouths and roared. Words collided, placards thrust skyward—"strike," "unfair," "working conditions," "white-goods workers"—as if passion and emphasis could change minds and hearts. From somewhere came the word "triangle," and his head turned, slowing, surprised when others pressed him from behind, elbows in his back, signboards banging his jaw, toes flattening the backs of his shoes. He was caught in the crush and he was exhilarated.

He cocked his head to try to see the objective between the thicket of fists and signs, and gradually he was shoved close enough to the targeted building where police in high helmets stood around the steps, although they didn't appear eager to defend the entry. The woman beside him yelled, "Triangle!" and another yelled, "They didn't die in vain!" Whatever "triangle" meant, these women were somehow a part of it. Their zeal was in contrast to the inactive police. The idea of police as bystanders perplexed him. But he gradually realized that others were doing their work for them. Prostitutes in garish outfits confronted gray marchers, yelling tooth to tooth, jaw to ear, with painted lips and heavy furs, their faces twisted in outrage, red mouths in wide screech as if to devour protesters' heads. The prostitutes were backed by grinning gangsters in overcoats, soft hats, and thick shoes, and he understood: The white-goods company had hired the gangsters to bring their hookers to do the dirty work. A prostitute rained fists on a protester while the police did nothing. In the absence of repercussion, the gangsters and hookers were bold, shoving into the crowd, cutting them into small groups and attacking. The marchers backed up and regrouped, then pressed forward again. Hookers swung purses at signs and faces, irritated that the marchers didn't stay beaten. He caught movement over his head, looked to an upper floor as a window was pushed closed, cold white faces looking down, framed behind glass.

And there she was in the crowd, thirty feet away, her profile visible for an instant, a glimpse that made his heart leap.

He moved toward her, blocked by shoving bodies, running bodies, fighting bodies, every few seconds seeing the back of her head, calling her name into the noise, leaning to his right and seeing her again, moving for her, pushing aside a hooker who had lifted her skirt to offend a striker. He followed and she turned and it was not her, someone else and not Etta, disappointed now, but the idea was planted. He couldn't stop looking, scanning every face until the faces merged and he no longer was sure what she looked like.

A protester near him went to a knee. He reached for her hand and was shoved from behind. He kept his balance, broadened his shoulders to create space and got her to her feet. Two smirking prostitutes smelled vulnerability and charged, then saw him and switched to another target. Their smirks had changed too quickly to fury, confirming the sham performance. This was paid street theater. He wanted to gather the protesters, tell them to hire their own goons and hookers. He felt the fury of the cause viscerally without having enough knowledge to understand it.

One prostitute grabbed a protester from behind and pinned her arms to her side as a second prostitute slapped her across the face. The lady protester boiled, jerked loose, and went at the slapper. The slapper pushed her to the ground. A policeman rushed in. Marchers backed up, inadvertently clearing space for the cop, and Longbaugh was left alone in the open, as he did not know how to back down. The cop came like an avalanche, nightstick cresting behind his ear, hungry to crunch the bone and meat of the protester's head. Longbaugh timed it, a step and he was in the policeman's path, his right hand rising to catch the cop's forearm in midswing and holding it there. They froze, his eyes drilling into the cop's rage, and he said simply, "Now you have a choice." The cop's anger wilted to confusion and he twisted to break free. The protester crab-walked backward on her palms and heels, belly and thighs splayed to the sky. The nightstick dropped from the cop's grip and Longbaugh caught it with his other hand. He set the cop free and watched him back up and run. He handed the nightstick to a protester who looked at it as if she'd been given a magic wand. Longbaugh sidled back into the crush to become no one again.

But the woman he had protected did not take her eyes off him. She found her feet and followed, grabbing for his sleeve. "Thank you, sir, a thousand times thank you."

Longbaugh backed away. "Forget it."

She came on. "Who are you? Tell me your name."

"I . . . better go."

"I thought he would kill me."

Nodding his head toward the cop. "Better stay out of his way."

She turned to where he had nodded, her cop gathering more cops, pointing toward Longbaugh. Police interaction was a bad idea, considering his history. If arrested, they might find out who he was. He seized the moment to slip away. Blocked by others, he saw her turn to find him gone. She grabbed at the closest protesters, asking if they'd seen him.

He moved out of the crowd and hid in a brownstone doorway. The pattern replayed itself, gangsters pointing prostitutes at protesters, prostitutes charging in, protesters fighting back, cops moving in to arrest only the protesters, dragging them bleeding into the backs of wagons on a side street.

He left the demonstration behind, the sound of the clash losing strength as the distance increased, echoing faintly through alleys and gradually growing so faint that the hum of battle meshed into the sounds of the city and was gone.

6

———◦━◦━◦———

alk to me about 'Triangle.'"

He had caught her off guard, coming in from out back, where she had stowed broom and dustpan. The sun caught her hair from behind and he was blinded by the halo, her face in shadow, eyes unreadable.

Her body tensed. "Triangle?"

"What does it mean?"

"Shirtwai—" The words caught in her throat and she swallowed. "Shirtwaist, Triangle Shirtwaist." Even with her eyes in shadow, he was aware of a liquid glint.

"Someone said it was a fire."

Abigail leaned backward as if she could put distance between her spoken words and her physical self. "March twenty-fifth, two years ago, 1911. Late Saturday, Saturday afternoon, at, um, four-thirty. Etta . . . Etta was there that day. I know you weren't here, you couldn't know, but everyone, everyone remembers where they were when it happened."

Her voice cracked and she pushed by him and inside. She smelled of soap and work sweat, the aroma of everyday oblivion, and it struck him that the word "triangle" snapped her out of unconscious daily existence into a fraught world he had yet to understand. She went to the door of the room she shared with her husband and closed herself in, and he heard the lock turn. He stood in the silence of the hallway. With bright sunlight falling through the door at his back, the light graded to black along the walls and he was unable to make out the staircase beyond. He knew better than to wait for her.

She did not serve supper to the boarders that evening, so they followed Levi's lead and served themselves. She did not join them at the table, and he did not see her at all that night. He grew weary of pretending to ignore Robert Levi's glower. Levi peppered his meal with occasional gibes. "Better food than in prison." Longbaugh concentrated on his plate. When Levi said, "We come by our supper honestly," Longbaugh excused himself and went outdoors.

He wandered the neighborhood, the island a meadow of lights, abristle with electricity. Heat came off the sidewalks despite the long-absent sun. She had planted the Liberty toy and the olive ribbons two years before. Things may have changed since then. Perhaps she didn't wish to be found. He chose to quash that frustrating inner voice. He had an obligation to know the truth. As he took the next of his small steps, he would seek out Queenie, then work his way to Giuseppe.

He stopped at a newspaper kiosk and bought a dime novel about the Cassidy gang, along with two pieces of hard candy. Wandering home, he left one of the candies on the post outside the boardinghouse, although that night he had not seen the Chinese boy.

He stayed up late, engrossed in the dime novel, sitting up in bed by a side table lamp, chuckling at the adventures attributed to him. He was entertained to know he had been heroic and dastardly, trigger-happy and dreamy, sentimental and cold-blooded. Perhaps the Kid in the book was, as Mina seemed to think, the ideal Black Hand adversary. He thought he would have been less amused had he read it when he was younger, before his visit to Rawlins.

He heard a noise on the other side of his door. His eyes twitched to the wardrobe where his holster and sidearm hung. A second sound and his body coiled. He watched the doorknob for movement, listening with his skin. Then the unexpected, a newspaper sliding under the closed door. He watched it inch in, then stop with three-quarters of it showing. Soft footsteps padded away in the hallway. He swung his legs and his feet hit the floor, he bent and took up the paper, a copy of the *New York Times*. It had yellowed. He read horrifying words, then ran his eyes to the nameplate for the date: March 26, 1911. A newspaper more than two years old. The day after the Triangle Shirtwaist fire.

The headline was stacked three lines high in the center of the page:

141 MEN AND GIRLS DIE IN WAIST FACTORY FIRE;
TRAPPED HIGH UP IN WASHINGTON PLACE BUILDING;
STREET STREWN WITH BODIES; PILES OF DEAD INSIDE.

A photo beneath the headline had a caption: "The Burning Building at 23 Washington Place." The photo was poor, framing only the upper floors, making it impossible to understand the building's height. A ladder rose from the middle of the photograph, but its reach was shy of the roof by three floors. In a small box in the photograph's corner: "Windows marked X from which fifty girls jumped—south side of building." A column of smaller headlines ran down the middle of the page beside the photo: "The Flames Spread with Deadly Rapidity Through Flimsy Material Used in the Factory. 600 GIRLS ARE HEMMED IN. When Elevators Stop Many Jump to Certain Death and Others Perish in Fire-Filled Lofts." The headlines went on, but his eyes blurred as Mary's words came back, followed by Abigail's words. Etta had been there.

He returned to the newspaper and read through the entire piece. Certain paragraphs gripped him and rang in his head, and he went back and read them a second time. The horror did not lessen with subsequent readings.

"Nothing like it has been seen in New York since the burning of the *General Slocum*. The fire was practically all over in half an hour. It was confined to three floors—the eighth, ninth, and tenth of the building. But it was the most murderous fire that New York has seen in many years."

"The girls rushed to the windows and looked down at Greene Street 100 feet below them. Then one poor, little creature jumped. There was a plate glass protection over part of the sidewalk, but she crashed through it, wrecking it and breaking her body into a thousand pieces."

"One girl, who waved a handkerchief at the crowd, leaped from a window adjoining the New York University Building on the westward. Her dress caught on a wire, and the crowd watched her hang there till her dress burned free and she came toppling down."

He read and reread deep into the night and did not look up until sharp dawn light flared in the window.

IN THE MORNING Longbaugh avoided his fellow boarders, leaving early through the back door. He made the long walk to the Hotel Brevoort. He was tired and sick at heart, and he carried the two-year-old newspaper folded in his suit's side pocket. He claimed a small table in the café. He left the old paper where it was and perused that day's newspapers one after another for references to the more than two-year-old Triangle Shirtwaist fire. He found none.

He was not clear in his mind as he read of the tragedies and triumphs of the previous day. The fire fell to the back of his thoughts until some offhand reference, often to strikes or working conditions, reignited his indignation. He nodded off at one point, awoke with a jolt, and did not know how long he had dozed.

He set down the newspaper. He closed his eyes and they burned. Images of fire curled in and scorched his mind's eye, and he could not escape the image of the girl with the handkerchief, caught on the wire, and then his brain could handle no more and he let go of her so she could fall.

He was surprised to learn that life could go on. He heard conversations around him. They washed by, frivolous, yet charged with a kind of importance for their simple confirmation of everyday existence.

To his left he heard someone mention the Castles in *The Sunshine Girl*, and a minute later heard, on the other side of the room, something about Irene and Vernon in that Sunshine play. This coincidence of timing triggered his imagination and he began to listen. It was barely mid-morning. Men were drinking their breakfasts, talking business, talking politics, bragging about their aspirations, underreporting their failures. Lubricated with drink, their voices waxed bold and supercilious. He overheard "Kaiser Bill," and the name sparked a debate by the front door, glowed and flamed near the windows, then spread unevenly across the room, where here he was a tyrant, there war was unlikely, behind him the war would stay on the Continent, and back at the front door Wilson would keep us out. This was a new phenomenon to him, a conversational virus infecting a big room, running here and there until the fever crested and played out. When German politics faded, there was a run on the new renaissance. A smaller trend burbled about how senators being elected directly threatened the survival of the timber industry, the steel business, and the whiskey trust. Then a wave on modern technology, it had peaked and everything was already invented, so don't invest in research, until at another table, invention was in its infancy, so invest all you've got.

Across the room he overheard the words ". . . not staging another Wild West Show." Longbaugh leaned forward to locate the source. He narrowed it to the two men aiming spears of tobacco juice at a spittoon. Etta had written him about seeing a Wild West Show. It had made her laugh.

He realized he wanted this diversion. Triangle burned too brightly in his mind, he feared for her safety on that day, despite the fact that it was well in the past. He found the Wild West Show idea interesting, his world brought east and dramatized.

Longbaugh approached the spitting men. "Did I hear you say something about a show?"

The fatter one folded tiny pink hands over a warm belly and eyed him suspiciously. "Something." He scrutinized Longbaugh through one open eye.

"Never seen one," said Longbaugh with open hands, apologizing for his naïveté.

"I gather you are unfamiliar with the West, sir," said the fatter one.

"Unfamiliar?"

"Everyone in New York first encounters the West in Buffalo Bill's show."

"I see," said Longbaugh, not surprised, considering all he had encountered about the East Coast's fascination with the West. "And where will it take place?"

"You're asking a man fresh out of that business."

"So you don't know, or there's no show?"

"Hasn't been a West show in New York since . . ." He nodded as if counting the years in his mind. "Well, a few years now. Whenever the Bills were in Madison Square Garden last. That's also when the Millers took their show to Europe."

"Bills?"

"Buffalo and Pawnee, the Bills, surely you've heard of Buffalo Bill Cody?"

Longbaugh snorted inside. "Surely."

"The Millers got their horses and stagecoaches confiscated by the British, someone over there thinks there'll be war. I was this close to investing in that one."

"You can invest in a show?"

"You can, and I did. 'Twas my business. But my new passion is song and dance, pretty girls showing a bit of ankle. Pretty girls don't need stables or shovelers."

"Although . . ." said his friend wittily, and they laughed together.

"Not *all* pretty girls drop their flops onstage," said the fatter one.

"Just their frocks," said his witty friend.

"From your lips." The fatter one returned to Longbaugh. "That's the future, my friend, that's where the money is."

Longbaugh dropped coins beside their glasses. "This round's on me." He picked a red apple from the bowl on their table, polished it on the side of his trousers, and headed outdoors.

He stopped on the sidewalk, about to bite the apple when he saw the hotel doorman shooing a small boy. The boy simply moved to another location whenever the doorman had to go back to hold the door open for an incoming gentleman. After which the doorman's artificial smile vanished and he charged the boy again, who simply ducked and moved. Longbaugh saw it was the Chinese boy.

Longbaugh tapped the doorman on the shoulder. The doorman turned and was abruptly professional. "Yes, sir?"

"That's okay, he's mine." The doorman looked at him as if he were out of his mind, but Longbaugh tipped him, and the man knew better than to argue with a customer. He returned to his post.

Longbaugh approached the Chinese boy. "You waiting for me?"

The Chinese boy nodded. "She's going over the line, cowboy," he said with a seriousness reserved for dire news.

"Who's going over the line?"

"Lady at your house."

Despite his confusion, Longbaugh held his tongue.

"Going to meet someone."

"A man, you mean," said Longbaugh.

"Yes."

"Abigail is going to meet a man who is not her husband."

"Yes."

Longbaugh nodded. He rolled the apple in his palm. "And you know this how?"

"I know the man."

"Friend of yours?"

The Chinese boy spat.

"I see."

"Hates Chinks. Hates immigrants, but he's got it special for me. Got a bar on the Bowery. Was a ward boss, but even Tammany's sick of him. Small brain, big mouth."

"Let me guess. You were following him, keeping an eye on him."

"Saw him talking to her. Outside a lecture hall. She was afraid to go in, and he got friendly. Made a time to meet her."

He looked at the boy, thinking him wise beyond his years. Then thought he was probably early teens, making him short for his years. Longbaugh waited, but the Chinese boy seemed to be finished. He continued to roll the apple in his palm.

"You want me to do something?"

"She seems nice. *He's* not."

"So I should stop it?"

"You like her. So help her."

"Help her, or mess with him?" said Longbaugh.

The Chinese boy shrugged. Either way.

Longbaugh scrunched his nose. This was not his business. This was not the Chinese boy's business. This was nobody's business but Abigail's. And her baffled and jealous husband's.

"Why don't you just tell the guy's wife?"

Han Fei looked at Longbaugh as if he was a fool. Longbaugh understood. No one would listen to him. A Chinese boy had no power in the white city.

"When is this supposed to happen?"

"Half hour."

That brought him awake. "Half hour from *now*?"

"Restaurant near here."

Longbaugh looked away, shaking his head. "Cutting it a little close."

He pictured how it had happened. The Chinese boy had followed the man to the lecture hall the night before and had been surprised to see Abigail there. He had watched the man make his move, and was determined to do something about it. So that morning he had followed Longbaugh to the Brevoort, but couldn't get past the doorman. Had Longbaugh dawdled in the café, Abigail would have been at the man's mercy. Longbaugh didn't want any part of this. Then he remembered her reaction to the Triangle fire and the way she had slipped the newspaper under his door. She had a good heart, despite being confused about her marriage, despite being a jangle of raw nerves on the verge of making a bad decision she was sure to regret for a long time.

Longbaugh looked the boy up and down. "The conscience of the neighborhood."

"Wouldn't know, cowboy."

Longbaugh wondered what the man had done or said to the Chinese boy to bring out such an intense desire for punishment. "You eat breakfast?"

"No."

He handed him the red apple. The boy considered it, nodded, wiped it on his shirt, and took a bite as he started walking. Longbaugh closed his eyes a moment, then followed. A few blocks later they were outside the restaurant. They lounged across the street, and after a few minutes, the Chinese boy pointed out two men coming from the other direction.

"There."

"The short one or the tall one?"

"Tall."

Longbaugh scrutinized the tall man. Not much to look at, but he knew downright ugly men who could charm the leather off a saddle.

"She's lonely," said the Chinese boy.

Longbaugh was impressed by the Chinese boy's empathy. "Why didn't she go into the lecture?"

"Too shy. It was called The Ideal of Free Love."

Longbaugh smiled sadly. Now he better understood the tall man as well. In the West, he'd seen predators just like him make their play. Apparently predators were no different here. The city just offered more and better opportunities. Like lectures for women about love and ideals. From what he knew about Abigail, she would have been curious, vulnerable, waiting across the street from the lecture hall, summoning her courage, wanting to know more about herself and her body. Her whole life she would have been told what *not* to do, and therefore she didn't know what she *could* do. She would have gone there to learn. The tall man knew women would come, and then be too shy to go inside. Longbaugh saw the moment in his head: When it was time to go in to hear the speaker, Abigail had faltered, ticket in hand. The vulture then swooped in with his sympathetic smile and sensitive eyes, and she was comforted, relieved to be understood. The tall man would have known what to say to make her feel desired and safe.

Longbaugh watched the tall man stop in front of the restaurant, showing off for his friend, conniving and smug, and he felt his stomach lurch.

He said nothing more to the Chinese boy, left him behind as he crossed the street, walking near the front door, then kneeling to tie a shoelace that wasn't loose. He eavesdropped on their conversation.

"—what happens after is I go home and maybe feel a little sorry, so, hey, I'm nice to the wife. Thing is, she's so happy for the attention that I get it twice in one day. It's like I did her a favor by screwing this girl."

His short friend laughed. "You're something else."

"Next time, come with. You check their left hands and pick the married ones, so, hey, what are they gonna do? Make a scene?"

"I'll stick with my wife. But I wanna hear all the details."

Their laughter propelled Longbaugh into the restaurant. Once inside, he looked around. Abigail had yet to arrive. If he knew anything about her, she would be unsure, she would hesitate, she would be late, and then in a frantic hurry because she was late. It was a long way from the boardinghouse, but he also knew she would come.

A moment later the tall man came in alone. The manager knew him and led him to a corner table in back. It had a curtain he could pull for privacy once she arrived. A dark corner for a dark rendezvous. Longbaugh waited for him to settle in his seat, then crossed the restaurant, passing the manager coming back. He grabbed the curtain and pulled it around the table so no one could see what he was about to do.

"Hey, this table's taken," said the tall man, reaching for the curtain to get the manager's attention. The tall man's voice was deep and melodious, perfect for charming innocent women.

Longbaugh took the seat beside him and kicked the man's foot forward so that he sat back down hard in his chair.

"What's the idea!" said the tall man.

Longbaugh looked him dead in the eye. The tall man was unsure as to his next move. He waited for an explanation and was greeted with silence. The tall man sized up Longbaugh. He was bigger than Longbaugh, younger, possibly stronger, but Longbaugh's eyes bored in on him and gave him pause. He decided to be forcefully polite.

"I got this table reserved, 'sir,' and I'm expecting my companion any moment."

Longbaugh maintained his silence, and the man's eyes shifted nervously, hoping a waiter or anyone would come by, trying to figure a way to get rid of this annoying fellow.

"I'm not sure where they seated you, 'sir,' but you can't stay here, I have an important meeting, and—"

"I know why you're here." Longbaugh spoke slowly and quietly.

"So, hey, that's it, I'm getting someone to throw you out." The tall man put his palm flat on the table to push himself up, and Longbaugh grabbed his wrist and held it down in a tight grip. The man froze, looked down at Longbaugh's eyes, and was frightened. He took a moment to decide what to do next, then slowly, slowly, sat back down.

"There's no need for that, mister, really. Look, I don't know who you are, but I'm sure there's been some kind of mistake."

Longbaugh said nothing but kept a firm grip on the tall man's wrist. The tall man suddenly tried to wrench and twist his hand away. He was unsuccessful, and as quickly as he started, he stopped. A new understanding of his situation came to him.

"Oh God, you're the husband. Hey, listen, mister, there's been a mistake here, I wasn't going to do anything, I swear."

The tall man's eyes trembled with panic. He tried to look at Longbaugh's belt, to know if he was armed.

"It wasn't me, I swear, it was all her, she came to *me*, she even suggested this place."

Longbaugh did not move, did not take his hand away, did not stop looking directly into the man's eyes.

Finally the tall man quit fidgeting and sat quietly, awaiting his punishment.

With his free hand, Longbaugh dipped the small spoon into the salt dish and carried a heaping mound directly over the back of the tall man's hand. He angled his head slightly without losing contact with the man's eyes. Then slowly his hand turned the spoon and salt fell out of it, bouncing, then piling up on the man's skin. The tall man stared at his hand as if he was being burned by lye.

"Oh God, I swear, it was a joke, I would never touch her. I'm a married man, I would never do that kind of thing. I'm a good family man, I swear." The tall man spoke quickly, desperately, in a full-out panic.

Longbaugh said nothing. He put the small spoon back in the salt dish.

"So, hey, listen, let me go, and I swear, I'll never do anything like this again. I won't even come back to this restaurant. I don't have time for stuff like this, please, mister."

Longbaugh reached down, took a pinch of salt off the back of the tall man's hand and flicked it at the tall man's eyes. An involuntary spasm shuddered in the tall man's cheek. "Stay away from her," said Longbaugh. "From her and the Chinese kid."

"No, I swear, I won't, I mean I will, oh God, please—"

"You know where the back door is." He let go of the wrist. The tall man lurched out of his seat, wiping the salt off his hand and scrambling away, out of the restaurant in a flash.

Longbaugh was glad to have terrified the tall man, but thought it would only stymie him for a week or so, and then he'd be back at it. He thought about Abigail, coming a long way to meet a man like that, although she was unaware that he *was* a man like that. Until he bedded her, the tall man would shower her with affection, as he had enough experience preying on vulnerable women to fake empathy. But something inside her wanted what the tall man had to offer. Longbaugh considered her marriage and wondered how she had ended up with Levi, then thought he was being too hard on the young man. Somewhere along the way, Levi had become uncertain. Perhaps it was Abigail's fault, perhaps his own, but Levi's uncertainty had led to jealousy, mistrust, and a drought of affection. It was possible her intent had been not to meet a man, but to attend the free love lecture as a way to help save her marriage. At the moment of truth, at her most defenseless, standing there on the sidewalk, the tall predator had swooped in, oozing charm and dripping with concern. Longbaugh ached for Levi then. He tried to picture Levi as a groom. Levi would have been a force of nature in the early days of their courtship, the risk-taking sandhog, teeming with power and life. He may even have looked like her best hope, a man who might have the inner confidence to allow his woman to bloom.

Longbaugh drew the curtain partway aside to watch the room. Abigail had yet to arrive. He hesitated to leave, as she was due any moment. He kept his eye on the front door, prepared to drop the curtain when he saw her. Customers came in, greeted warmly by the manager, menus in his hand. The restaurant was almost half full and the best tables were being taken quickly, the only ones still available in the middle of the room. More time passed as more diners were seated. He considered leaving through the back, but that way felt tainted by the tall man's escape, so he stayed where he was. A woman came in, leaning amorously on her gentleman escort, and for one unnerving moment he thought it was Etta with another man. He let the curtain drop, then drew it back again to prove it was not his wife. His heart beat quickly. A waiter drifted over, and he waved off the menu. It was time to give up the table.

He moved to the front door but skirted the center of the room so that Abigail would be less likely to see him. Then he realized that she was so late she almost certainly wasn't coming. His step changed and was lighter, and he was suddenly pleased, as if her rejection of the tall man was somehow related to any similar decision Etta might have made.

He reached for the front door at the same moment it was being opened from the outside, and he took a casual, polite step to the side. Two laughing men came in, and Longbaugh reached to catch the door as it closed behind them but stopped short when he saw Abigail across the street. He brought his arm back and allowed the door to slowly close so she would not see him.

He remained there in shadow, and a moment later, when the door was reopened by a party of three, Abigail had not moved. She stood very still in the same spot on the sidewalk. He then understood she had been standing there for quite some time.

She stared at the restaurant, her expression blank, trying to decide whether or not to go in. Her toes touched and she held her purse flat against her thighs with both hands. When the door closed, his view was blocked. But he stayed where he was.

Another hungry group pulled the door wide, and this time he noted that her hair was pinned, her dress lovely, but she wasn't as pretty as she had been that day in the kitchen, and then he was appalled at himself, as if he had some sort of proprietary claim on her because she had once shown an interest in him. As the front door closed on her again, he recognized the sadness at the core of her indecision, and it broke his heart.

Another couple came in, and he saw how the sunlight fell against her hair and shoulders, making a mournful shadow at her feet.

She had no way of knowing the tall man was not inside waiting for her.

The door closed and blocked his view.

The door opened. She was so very still.

The door closed and blocked his view.

The door opened and she was gone.

He waited, letting the door close and open again, then stepped outside and looked both ways. Abigail was nowhere in sight.

Once he was certain that she was gone, he made his own decision quickly, resolutely. He set out for 23 Washington Place. To know what had happened to his wife in the fire.

7

Charlie Siringo stepped off a train under the streets of Manhattan, climbed the exit stairs, and entered the main concourse of Pennsylvania Station. He was not much interested in the glory of the place and did not slow down. Siringo was there on a hunch.

Siringo was an unusual lawman. He was a loner as well as a dedicated bloodhound, known to spend months chasing one criminal. He'd worked as a cowhand for fifteen years, then was briefly a grocer, before spending twenty years as a Pinkerton. After he quit the Pinkertons, he clashed with them when they blocked publication of his memoirs. In a fit of pique, he wrote an exposé of their strikebreaking methods and rigging of elections. The Pinkertons bought up most of the copies of the books and confiscated the plates. Nevertheless, he was well known as a published author, and at fifty-eight years old, still a lawman, with the freedom to choose his quarry. Today he was after a murderer, a man who may have been one of his old friends.

Somewhere in the state of Utah he had lost the trail of the man who called himself Alonzo. He believed that this Alonzo, who had shot a seventeen-year-old son of a local sheriff, was now in the city of New York. Siringo had not been able to identify him with absolute certainty, but there was circumstantial evidence to convince him that the convict Harry Alonzo was in fact Harry Longbaugh, and not just any Harry Longbaugh, but the notorious former outlaw. Joe LeFors had seen him face-to-face and hadn't recognized him, but LeFors was an idiot. After that encounter, Alonzo/Longbaugh had vanished off the face of the West.

Siringo felt an affinity with the man. Longbaugh had often ridden with Cassidy, and Siringo had a history with both of them. In the late '90s, Siringo had infiltrated the gang as a fellow gunman, calling himself Charles Carter. He and Longbaugh had become friends, but when the gang's plans were regularly thwarted, Cassidy was told that Charles Carter was in fact Charlie Siringo and had been warning the railroad about every planned robbery. Cassidy had been furious and had gone after him. Butch cornered him in a canyon, and with no way out, Siringo expected to die. But Butch surprised him and backed off. Siringo knew no reason for it. Butch and his boys had simply turned and ridden away. To this day he wondered why, a mystery, and he disliked mysteries.

He went after the gang as a lawman, chased them across the West, and didn't quit until he was informed that they had fled the country. Some time after that, the newspapers reported they had died in a gunfight in South America. Siringo had recently been surprised to learn that Longbaugh may have been in prison during the time he was supposed to have been shot dead in Bolivia.

That started the fuss, making a simple killing of a sheriff's boy into a LeFors-led posse over a half dozen states. If this was a famous outlaw, as rumor had it, everyone wanted in. LeFors, however, was so inept that Siringo had been forced to take over. It was just bad luck that he hadn't been there on the night Alonzo/Longbaugh had visited his sister-in-law. He would have recognized him and arrested him or known it was someone else, either way making this journey unnecessary.

He had sent LeFors and his boys after Alonzo that night at Wilhelmina Matthews's home, knowing they would never catch him. Then, in the ensuing quiet, he had taken the opportunity to question Miss Matthews.

She had been gracious but not helpful. But when Wilhelmina was out of the room, he had managed to get a look at a letter from her sister and had memorized the return address in New York City.

LeFors, to cover his ineptitude, had told the world that he had seen the man in question and it was definitely not Harry Longbaugh. Because of that, the West quieted down, the posse went away, and no one was looking for this Alonzo character any longer. No one but Siringo.

Siringo spoke with the warden at Rawlins, and learned that while the prisoner appeared on the books as Alonzo, the warden believed it to be an alias. Under further questioning, Siringo learned that the warden believed it essentially because the prisoners and guards believed it. He had no proof. But Alonzo had been receiving letters from someone named Etta Place, who shared a name with Longbaugh the outlaw's wife.

If this was the same Harry Longbaugh, Siringo knew he would go to New York to be with her.

Siringo's first order of business was to locate a place to stay. He wasn't picky, and he didn't imagine he'd be here long. Longbaugh was the ideal prey, relaxed, unsuspecting, and confident that he had fallen off the map. The element of surprise belonged to Siringo. He would choose a hotel, freshen up, rest in the afternoon after his long train ride, then track down the address of Etta Matthews Place. He would move in slowly, ask around to see if anyone new had ventured into the neighborhood, and by nightfall he would position himself to watch the place and grab Longbaugh when he showed up.

LONGBAUGH worked his way back to Fifth Avenue, past the homes of the rich, through the Ladies' Mile, with the fancy shops and oversized department stores that sold, among everything else imaginable, the ladies' shirtwaists that had once upon a time been made at the Triangle factory. He passed motorcars waiting curbside for shoppers, the uniformed drivers standing around smoking. He slowed at Washington Square and gathered his courage to approach the Asch Building, where

Washington Place met Greene Street. While it was important to know her actions up to the time she vanished, he feared being there. Or, more to the point, he feared to learn more impossible things about her that he might not be able to reconcile. He tried to remember the timing—had he heard from her after the fire? He was sure that he had, but now, so close to where the fire had killed so many, his certainty fled. He worked backward to convince himself, of course she had survived the fire. He was sure of it. He almost remembered it clearly.

Washington Square was crowded. On that Saturday afternoon in late March of '11 it had apparently also been crowded. It had been a hard winter, but because of the unpleasant living conditions, people came out to the streets whenever possible, even when the weather was less than ideal. He walked up the block and came face-to-face with the building. He turned his head to the upper three floors. He was surprised to see no evidence of a fire. He had expected a scar.

He crossed the street onto Washington Place and walked along the exterior. The fact of normal everyday existence distressed him. Here was a case where history did not blurt its anguish, but whispered in his ear. There should have been a scar. But the building carried on, as if the past was the past.

At the corner of Greene Street, he came upon a small man setting fresh flowers on the sidewalk, holding in the crook of his elbow similar flowers that appeared almost as new as the ones he was putting in their place. This was where, according to the newspaper, so many of the girls had jumped. He counted the floors up to eight and nine. Then his gaze fell down the face of the building to the sidewalk. A long way down.

Longbaugh was quiet. The man with the flowers approached him.

"You I don't know," said the flower man.

"No."

"What I mean to say, I come here every day, and you I don't know. I know all the others, even the ones who did not have someone in the fire. Some come regular, some come just now and then, some don't come anymore at all. You I don't know."

"I was away."

"You knew someone, then?"

"Yes."

The man with the flowers pointed down Washington Place. The thicket of trees in Washington Square at the far end of the block seemed to billow from the ground, framed by the taut vertical buildings, like a low gathering of green clouds. "Death has a hold on this place. Down there is where they hung people."

"What do you mean, 'hung people'?"

"Before the Revolutionary War. And then later, in the Civil War with the riots. You spend enough time here, people come by and tell you stories." The flower man looked up at the ninth floor. "I try to imagine surprise death, how it feels. You walk down the street and people grab you and hang you and you're dead. Or a person goes to work filled with plans and hope, and decides in a minute that instead of burning to death, the only thing is to jump out a window to die faster."

Longbaugh pictured the girl with the handkerchief whose clothes had to burn off before she could fall. He was gripped by that image, seared as it was on his brain.

Longbaugh looked at the flower man looking up at the window. The flower man was a youth, barely a man at all, despite appearing older. The fire had made him an elderly young man.

"I went up there once, before it happened. All over were little bits of cloth, shirtwaists hanging, sewing machines pushed in close. Who's surprised that one dropped cigarette makes it go up? Those owners, they don't care, they locked the other door. The only other way out they locked, and why? To keep the girls from stealing. What is there so important to steal?" He forced himself to calm down. "But you've heard all this, everyone knows, everyone knows." He got a faraway look in his eyes. He rocked on his shoes. "You know the jury let those bastard owners off because they couldn't prove they knew it was locked that day? *Every day* they locked it. Blanck and Harris, the shirtwaist kings, took their insurance money and they walk around free right now."

Longbaugh was aware of fingers in his belly that closed into a grip on his insides.

"They had coats on," said the flower man. "Work was done, the girls waited for the signal to go home. The cigarette drops two minutes later, they live. Two minutes and she is standing here at my side, instead of you."

Longbaugh turned away from the flower man's calm face. He looked back up at the ninth-floor window, but his gaze caught on the wires. Strange that the man's words seemed unreal, while the newspaper's story of the girl with the handkerchief seemed not only real but made it seem as if he had known her personally. But then the girl with the handkerchief had his wife's face.

"I have this dream, every night the same," said the flower man. "The firemen let me on the sidewalk and I hold out my arms to catch her. My Rosa is standing on the window ledge, and points to where I should be. I go there and she jumps the other way. I run to catch her, but too late. She sends me to the wrong place so she won't crush me. I see her hit and burn on the sidewalk."

Longbaugh looked at the sidewalk.

The flower man looked as well. "You would think the fire would go out as she fell."

"Some got out." Longbaugh wanted to care about Rosa, but he only wondered if his wife had survived.

"Yes, some. On the tiny elevator, until it stopped. On the fire escape, until it pulled off the building. And the *owners* got out. They were on the top floor and went across the roof to the building there." The flower man pointed to the New York University building next to the Asch Building. "The tenth floor was above it and everyone up there lived. At least they should have the decency to die in their own goddamn fire."

"Easy, friend."

"I am easy." Yesterday's flowers were crushed under his arm. "This is me being easy."

"How did they identify the bodies?"

"Took them to the wharf, lined them up, and people came from all over the city and walked past them. Many were too badly burned to recognize."

Longbaugh watched her run, hair on fire, flames browning her cheeks, bubbling and splitting her skin. He watched her pounding on the locked door until smoke and flames won and she fell on top of the others who were dying to get out. He heard her voice, shrieking his name. These images were irrational, he knew intellectually she had not died in there, but he was not thinking rationally, so he watched her perish over and over in his mind.

Time passed and he eventually looked around, and the light was different. He didn't remember the flower man leaving, but he was alone.

He stayed until it was late. The city darkened with the setting sun, light rushing away above him, while the new incandescence slowly came up as if the city burned from within.

LONGBAUGH returned to the boardinghouse. He did not remember stopping, but as he approached the banister, he found one wrapped hard candy in his pocket. He didn't remember eating the other one. On this night he did not leave it on the banister, perhaps because he resented the Chinese boy dragging him into the middle of Abigail and Levi's marriage.

He stopped in the doorway outside the downstairs sitting room where Abigail and Robert Levi sat on opposite ends of a sofa. He entered with Triangle questions burning in his mind. He was so preoccupied that he did not notice the livid raspberry on the side of Levi's jaw. He did, however, notice that Abigail had changed out of the good dress she had worn while standing outside the restaurant. Only he knew about her earlier temptation. While Longbaugh had scared the vulture away, she did not know that the tall man had not been in there waiting for her, as it had been her decision not to go inside. He pulled the folded two-year-old *New York Times* out of the pocket of his suit coat and dropped it on the table in front of her.

"How did she survive?"

Levi glowered at his wife. "You saved this?"

Abigail looked at Longbaugh. "She?"

"You said Etta was there that day."

"I specifically said throw it away," said Levi.

"That day?" said Abigail, confused. "You mean—?"

"Triangle, the fire, did she make it out?"

"I know you lost a friend in there, but keeping this is morbid," said Levi.

"Yes, of course, Etta was fine," said Abigail to Longbaugh, talking over her husband.

"How did she get out?"

Levi gave him a hard look and reached for the old newspaper, but Longbaugh brought his fist down on the headlines.

"What happened?" In the wake of the falling fist, his voice was so quiet that Levi barely heard him.

"Etta didn't work there, she just went there that day. She was angry, she, she pulled some woman away from her sewing machine and forced her to go upstairs with her," said Abigail. "Something about the conditions."

"Upstairs?"

"She was on the top, the tenth floor," said Abigail. "With the owners."

Longbaugh stepped back. She had gotten out, yes, she had gotten out with Queenie and now he saw it—angry about the working conditions, she had marched Queenie upstairs to confront the owners, and when the fire broke out, she had followed the owners over the roof to safety. That was her instinct, to go up, just as she had in the bank on that day so long ago. Even if it had been the owners who knew where to lead her, she would have sensed it as the right move. The girl on the wire was suddenly anonymous, and he lost her face and his mind's eye turned away from her terror. He remained sad for the others, but his feelings shifted now that he knew she was not among them. In his selfish joy, the other women were dead and buried instead of kindred souls. He sat in a chair opposite husband and wife and was not proud of his lack of compassion, and while he tried to make excuses for his elation, he could not. He had to live with his happiness, that his search had found new life.

He registered Levi's jaw injury, then looked at Levi's telltale raw knuckles.

"What happened to you?"

"Nothing. Something at work."

"Something about work?" Longbaugh's tone was so skeptical that Levi came clean.

"No."

Abigail shifted uncomfortably on the sofa. Longbaugh found it difficult to make eye contact with her, even though he knew she hadn't seen him inside the front door of the restaurant.

"Let me guess," said Longbaugh. "There's another sandhog down there, knows you from the old days, so he figures he can say whatever he likes, and he made a comment about your wife."

Abigail looked away, blushing, biting her lip, her arms crossed. He had hit the mark. From Levi's expression, Longbaugh understood that Levi had defended her honor without believing in it. Men always fought hardest for the things they could not prove.

But as Levi and Abigail exchanged guilty looks, his mind returned to the Triangle fire. Etta may have gotten Queenie out, but for Moretti it was moral ammunition to use against her, as Etta had exposed Queenie to the worst fire in the city's history.

Longbaugh abruptly stood up and left the room. He needed time alone, to celebrate his relief in shameful silence, and to regain his empathy so that he was no longer pretending to care about the grieving families, the sad lovers, and here in Etta's former home, the brooding couple.

He took the stairs two at a time, but at the top he heard someone coming after him. He turned to see Levi at the bottom of the stairs. He heard a door slam downstairs and knew that it had been Abigail.

"Is it you?" said Levi.

Longbaugh was impatient and invincible and in no mood after the good news about Etta. He had already helped the sandhog once today. "It's not, but if you need to take it out on someone, then come on."

Levi appeared ready to accept his offer, but stopped three-quarters of the way up, and Longbaugh couldn't help noticing the frayed rug under his feet. Levi closed his eyes to tamp down his anger. Longbaugh watched as Levi talked to himself, and after a moment lifted his hands in a reluctant gesture of capitulation.

"Look, I—I think I . . . but . . . aw, hell, I don't know," Levi mumbled.

Longbaugh was disgusted.

"I know I shouldn't have." Levi came up abreast of him, chastising himself. "First the newspaper, then, well, all the other things."

"Was that you looking to apologize?"

"No. Okay, maybe."

"She told you to."

"Well, no."

"No?"

"I think I'm confused, I mean, if it *was* you—"

Longbaugh took hold of Levi's muscular upper arm and led him to the second-floor parlor, sat him down, and kicked the door closed behind him. "You are not good at this."

Levi hung his head. "She says I have too much imagination."

Longbaugh growled in the back of his throat because something had almost happened at the restaurant, meaning Levi's imagination was on target, but he fed him the lie. "Yeah, and you're thinking too much, you're *looking* for betrayal, and when you look that hard, you can bet you'll find it, because anything you look at that closely will suddenly look like proof. But just because you can see it that way does not make it so."

Levi looked up at him. "It's not that I don't *want* to trust her."

"Make up your mind, Levi, doubt or trust." Longbaugh shook his head, irritated, standing over him. He became quiet as he thought it through.

The pause grew so long, Levi shifted uncomfortably in his chair.

Longbaugh was conflicted. If he started this, it was sure to turn awkward in a hurry. He had to keep Abigail's secret while reassuring Levi and maybe give their marriage a fighting chance.

"You loved her once."

Levi decided he might be insulted. "Still do."

"And you won her."

Less certain this time. "Yes."

"So something was different then."

"What do you mean?"

"You're a long way from the heroic sandhog."

"So maybe I was more . . . easy, more like myself."

"You were cocksure, with a head full of hope, and now you're eating your own tongue."

Levi looked as if he'd gotten all of it embarrassingly right. "I thought once we were married and got, well, together, it would be okay."

Longbaugh squinted at him in irritation. "What about little things?"

"What is this? Who are you to—"

"Ah, so now you don't have *enough* imagination."

"Say!"

Longbaugh again turned it over in his mind, not caring that Levi went fidgety whenever a pause stepped into the conversation. He knew too much about where each of the partners stood. He did not want to give advice. He preferred to be the affable uncle who shared wicked truths, as opposed to the earnest, well-meaning father hoping to protect his children from repeating his own ancient mistakes. But after seeing her outside the restaurant, knowing that if things stayed the way they were, that something like it was bound to happen again, he was intent on making Levi understand. Part of it was Etta's escape from the fire. Part of it was the bruise on Levi's chin. Part of it was the predatory son of a bitch in the restaurant who didn't deserve her. But another part of it was the uncomfortable memory of how he had felt when he watched Abigail as she danced.

He spoke slowly, as if he did not trust his own words. "You see a bird with a broken wing."

Levi looked behind him as if someone else was in the room. "What?"

"And a cat lurking."

"What's this got to do with . . . ?"

"Do you step in or leave it to fate?"

"I have no idea what you're saying."

"Simple question, how do you see the world? Broken wing. Hungry cat. Take part or leave it to chance?"

"I don't—"

"Cat's closing in."

Levi sat up. "Where am I, the woods, the street?"

"Do nothing and that cat gets dinner. Step in and the bird has hope."

"Shoo the cat away?" said Levi uncertainly.

"He'll come right back when you leave."

"Suppose I could move it."

"Bird just saw the cat."

"Um, pick it up?"

"In your hands?"

"Yeah, okay, but this is strange."

Longbaugh opened his own hands, exposing his palms. "Show me."

Levi threw him a scowl, hesitated, then made a cup shape with his raw-knuckle hands, but he flew them apart as if the bird's fleas were crawling between his fingers. Longbaugh left his hands in place. Levi reinforced his scowl, but brought his hands back together. When Longbaugh didn't move, Levi took the next step and mimicked picking up a wounded bird from the floor.

"Careful, she's nervous," said Longbaugh. "If you're going to help her—"

"—you got to make her feel safe."

Longbaugh nodded almost imperceptibly so as not to spook the bird.

Levi sat with the wounded creature cupped on his lap. Then he realized he looked absurd and set it free with a violent shake. He jutted out his chin. "Abby's not wounded."

"No."

"That's not what this is about."

"No."

"Or is she?"

"Maybe not."

Levi nodded then, to himself. "Because I'm the one. Because it's me."

"You can change it."

"You think I haven't tried? But the way men look at her . . ." He swallowed his thought, exposed and ludicrous.

Longbaugh was still for a long time. Levi looked as if Longbaugh was the cat and he was the meal. Longbaugh thought long and hard and tried to choose his words carefully, as there would be other predators in other restaurants, and while only she could put a stop to that, she'd have to want to. Then, suddenly, he realized he was angry.

"Shut off your idiot brain, give her the benefit of the doubt, god-damnit. Do something, some little thing, just . . . hold her hand, touch her cheek, Christ, help yourself out."

Levi raised his hands helplessly.

"Rub sand in your suspicious eyes, *pretend* to trust her, maybe you'll start to do it. But don't, dammit, just don't push too hard."

"What if I've already tried?"

"You always give up so easily?"

"Aw, hell."

"Or just with her. Because you think she's looking around and you've got your pride."

"Okay, all right," said Levi from under a pile of self-disgust.

"You were a sandhog, for cryin' out loud. Toughest bastards in the state of New York. And she was the right one."

Levi thawed with the memory. "She was . . . something."

"Think there's a reason she wears your ring?"

"Sure," said Levi, attempting a joke. "I asked."

"And she said yes."

"Damn, no wonder Etta loved you."

Longbaugh looked aside. The sound of her name brought something else into the room. Longbaugh gazed at a spot as if he could see her there. He drew a long, slow breath. "A man asked me once about a thing that happened in prison. Said he'd heard about a fellow who wasn't violent, yet he'd beaten the hell out of a much bigger inmate. His knuckles looked like yours."

Levi looked at his own hands.

"He'd just had his letters returned, ones he wrote to his wife, all unopened. The big man was shooting his mouth, 'She's like all the rest.'" Longbaugh's eyes were dead cruel. "I remember how he looked afterward." He then looked directly at Levi, still cold, as the memory lingered. "Tell her . . ." He wondered how far he should go, and then he knew what to say and his voice changed and grew quieter. "Tell her you love her, tell her—you hear music inside her. Tell her that."

Levi stared at him as if he was afraid to move and uproot the fragile moment of revelation. He jerked to his feet. "I have to go, I have to see her."

Longbaugh laughed softly. "Slow down, sandhog, easy, it took time to get here, it won't clean up overnight."

"No. I understand. You're right. I know that."

Levi stood in place, looking this way and that, trying to physically slow himself down. His whole body shook with the effort. Then he didn't care.

"I have to see her."

Longbaugh shrugged. "Go."

Levi left the room in too big a hurry. Longbaugh watched him with envy. He wondered if he had been insane to try to help. He could be making things worse. In reality, he wasn't convinced Levi could ever again reach Abigail. She might already have given up. After a few minutes he was sorry he had not called Levi back to lower his expectations.

To his surprise, Levi came back to the doorway with a grave look in his eyes.

"Oh, no, what did you do?" Longbaugh regretted their conversation now, another mistake to add to the list. Levi had pushed her and taken it too far too fast, destroying all his evident goodwill.

Levi spoke in a whisper. "A kid downstairs, looking for you."

Longbaugh thought it must be a mistake. "A kid?"

"Some Chink, mentioned Paris."

Longbaugh moved out of the room and to the balustrade. He looked to be sure he could not be seen through any of the windows. Levi now grasped his urgency and turned off the hall light behind him, but Longbaugh said, "No. Leave it."

Levi turned the light back on. Longbaugh looked down to the first-floor hallway where Abigail blocked the Chinese boy.

"Cowboy," said the Chinese boy.

"What is it?" This could not be about Abigail again, not in front of her and not in front of Levi.

"Man outside, all afternoon, asking questions."

"Still the neighborhood conscience. What questions?"

"About any new people. In the neighborhood."

"New immigrants show up every day, you sure he means me?"

The Chinese boy made a face. "You're different. So is he."

"Okay. Where is he now?"

"In front. Watching for you. Very patient."

"Who'd he talk to?"

"Came in a circle. Started two blocks east, asked stuff." The Chinese boy pointed his finger in a new direction. "Then went south, same questions, then west and north. Then he came closer, one block in, east again. More questions but a smaller circle. Like he knew you were here."

"Clockwise. Who did he talk to?"

"Cart vendors. Deliverymen. Boys on steps."

"Squeeze till I'm in a pinch. What was he wearing?"

"Cowboy stuff. But no hat."

"No. That would be too obvious."

Longbaugh started toward his room, and Levi said, "Stay away from windows."

Abigail looked at Levi with surprise.

Someone came in the front door, and Longbaugh stepped back into the shadow of a doorframe and saw it was another boarder. He could see nothing outside through the briefly open door.

He went to his room and left the lights off. Without moving the curtains he looked out and took in as much street as possible. His limited view revealed nothing, and he could not confirm the identity of his stalker. But he knew. Siringo was the only one smart enough to follow him here. In retrospect, he saw how Siringo must have tracked him. He had gone to Rawlins after the boy was killed, spoken to the warden, learned about the letters. Somehow gotten the address, although he wasn't sure how. Longbaugh was lucky to have the Chinese boy. He left much of his gear in his room, but took his holster and his gun. He would need them now.

He went downstairs.

He stopped in front of Levi. "Doubt or trust." Then he pointed to the red, swollen jaw and said, "And ignore that loudmouth."

He looked at Abigail. "If you see her . . ."

"I'll tell her," said Abigail.

He glanced out the window, again without moving the curtains. The Chinese boy shook his head, clucking. "Not that way, cowboy."

"I know," said Longbaugh. Then to Abigail, "Is the light on by the back door?"

"Yes."

"Good."

Longbaugh saw the Chinese boy giving Abigail a long, disapproving look, as if he couldn't believe she had even considered sleeping with the odious tall man he so utterly despised, and Longbaugh moved to get the boy out of there before he gave it all away.

He led the Chinese boy past the back door to a window at the far end away from the light. He opened it quietly and put his head out to look both ways, then slipped out into the backyard. The Chinese boy followed.

They stopped in a shadow. They watched and listened. Neither moved, as if they both ran on the same inner clock. They made eye contact and went together across the street.

They found another shadow and stopped to listen. He saw movement a few doors down, then recognized a cat stretching.

"You see him?"

The boy shrugged. "Maybe still out front."

"What's your name?"

The boy was surprised to be asked. "Han Fei."

"Nice to know you, Han Fei. Harry." Longbaugh watched the shadows. "I'm starting to appreciate the neighborhood conscience. Good that you mentioned Paris instead of that other thing."

Han Fei gave him a look that said, *Do I look stupid?*

"How did you get onto him?"

"I watch things. What's he want?"

"He's a lawman and he thinks I'm a killer."

"Guy you killed deserved it."

"Just like that?"

"You saying he didn't?"

"You didn't know him, why take my side?"

"You helped the woman."

"Okay." He reached in his pocket for the piece of hard candy. The boy took it but put it in his pocket.

"Not hungry?"

"Don't like those. I give them to my mother."

"Which do you like?"

"Ginger."

"Next time."

"From a place near Five Points."

"I'll get more for Mama."

"Probably best, cowboy."

Longbaugh had been staring at one particular shadow, finally convinced it was empty. "I want to get close to him."

"Under-arrest close?"

"I need to be sure."

Han Fei led him two blocks away, where they looped, just as Siringo had done, but counterclockwise, and came back toward the front of the boardinghouse. A block out, they went in the back door of a tenement and up the stairs to the roof. Keeping their heads low, they moved to where Han Fei pointed at a fire escape, then realized it was empty. He was surprised, and looked back and forth. "He was there."

"I believe you."

"For a long time."

"I know. He's good."

Longbaugh looked behind him, then up and down the street. He looked across to other rooftops. "Let's go."

He and Han Fei went down the stairs and out the back door to the street and away from the boardinghouse through an alley. Longbaugh felt a presence in every window, every doorway, on every rooftop, in every shadow. Nevertheless, he was sorry to go. If she came back, she wouldn't find him.

HE STRETCHED OUT on a lumpy bed in a dark hotel room, light from streetlamps, advertising signs, and automobile headlights reflecting to the ceiling. He inspected the patterns in peeling paint, and saw mountains, valleys, rivers, as might be portrayed in a cartographer's drawing. After he'd looked at them longer, the shapes became faces that reacted to the moving light, and seemed to change expressions, grim to surprised, curious to pleased. Siringo's face was there, or how Longbaugh remembered it. He thought of Siringo alone in the confusing city, and wondered if he had friends or family here, if he had a place to stay. Then he wondered if Siringo had contacted the local police. But it was pointless to try to outthink him. Longbaugh's only move was to leave altogether, find another city. But that was not an option. Siringo would find him because he knew what Longbaugh was after. Longbaugh would have to quit his search if he was ever to lose him. As that would never happen, his next best hope was to stay a few steps ahead.

Longbaugh listened to the conversations around him, through the ceiling, from across the hall, then was surprised by a voice almost against his head, inches away, on the other side of the paper-thin wall. Siringo could be in the next room and he wouldn't know. As could Etta.

. . .

THE NEXT MORNING he started out in the area of the city that had been known as the Tenderloin, playing the ignorant bumpkin, an out-of-towner looking for a honey and a good time. He told everyone of the type of lady he liked, describing Queenie to the best of his ability, and let the word spread. Eventually he found a neighborhood where she had worked, and the people who knew her told him her name. I know what you want, mister, as if by some magic they had conjured up an exact match. But she had been missing for days. Not unusual, they said, she might be on a bender or just sleeping one off. She would eventually turn up, at which time he was welcome to her, and in the meantime offered him a consolation companion. He waved them off. He insisted on Queenie or no one until someone said if he was that determined, he ought to speak to a guy named Joe, and might find him at a certain bar.

He went to the Tall Boot Saloon in Little Italy that night.

8

His suit labeled him out of place; the clothes bought to help him blend in now betrayed him. He inched his bowler low to shield his eyes, and scanned his neighbors. Every joker in the place was gut-checking his resolve, as here was a prime pullet to be plucked. It would be tricky to get out, but that was for later.

The saloon called Tall Boot was a few steps down from the sidewalk. When a man was standing in the doorway, his eyes were level with pedestrians' knees. Indifferently secured planks were flooring, naked bulbs threw raw shadows, the walls were undecorated, and the bar ran long under a close ceiling, crowded with shoulder-to-shoulder drunks. Longbaugh smelled bathtub booze and smoke, puke and syrupy hair oil, and the rank, nervous sweat of heavy, unwashed men. It was familiar, homey, comfortable, and he liked it just fine. He'd known many similar bars, especially one particular hole in Boise. The bartender slid a glass of something in front of him. He bent to it, and the smell of ammonia snapped his head up. He heard laughter at his expense and realized how closely he was being watched. He pushed the glass an inch to the side with the back of his hand and the lug next to him snatched it, downed it, and slammed the empty back between Longbaugh's elbows inside a pair of blinks.

Longbaugh glanced at him sideways. "Easy, professor, you'll bruise the gin."

The fellow grunted and went away. The bartender poured him a second and hovered for his reaction, expecting payment for both.

Longbaugh reached for change in his pocket. "So where's Moretti tonight?"

The bartender collected Longbaugh's face along with his coins, offered a disinterested sniff, and walked away. Longbaugh watched him bypass customers brandishing empties to get to the far end of the bar, where he spoke into the ear of a slick, the only other patron wearing clothes as good as his own. The bartender never looked back, but the slick darted his eyes to Longbaugh, then ducked into the crowd.

Longbaugh waited, and the second drink waited on the bar with him. No one touched it, and he had elbow room, as if Moretti's name had suspended him in a bubble. Nearby conversation was uninformative, so he let it all fuzz into a hum. Someone would come, but it would not be Giuseppe Moretti.

A full ten minutes passed before he felt the fingers that pinched his wallet. This time he did not grab the hand that fleeced him. The lift was second rate, but as it was the opening move, he suffered it like a mark. He stared ahead and waited. It was a full two minutes before a space cleared beside him, and another minute after that before the ample lad with the demeanor of a festive bear crowded in beside him. The bear held out Longbaugh's property.

"These are the times that try men's souls," said the bear. "As well as their mistresses, livers, and wallets."

Longbaugh stared ahead. The bear was not drunk, but his words crowded his ears, as if they had volume and weight and a surface covering of fur.

"Ought to be more vigilant, tourist. Got your purse appropriated— but I gloved the fingers."

"Did you."

"No no, now don't hurry to thank me," said the bear with honeyed sarcasm.

Longbaugh moved his eyes without reaching for his property. "Looks familiar."

"Ought to, since it belongs to you."

"You sure?"

"Let's just say I watched the fingers swipe it."

"And where is the swiper?"

"Oh, way too slippery for an old bear. Be grateful for the important things in life, which include the return of your property."

"Open it," said Longbaugh.

"It's all there. Got him before he turned it inside out."

"Indulge me."

The bear scratched himself, then looked inside. The billfold was empty. No money, business cards, or club memberships. A lot of nothing.

The bear pawed through it. "Now wait just a damn minute."

"Is that *my* empty 'purse'?"

"Bastard Flexible was only supposed to—aha, yes, there it is, I see it now." The bear was instantly jolly, his embarrassment forgotten, a thing of the past. "You that much smarter'n you look, tourist, or just dumb lucky? Neat trick, emptying it up front. You don't look the clever type. But trust me, in this I am innocent as a puppy's nose. Got a name?"

Longbaugh said nothing.

"Well, you have earned mine. Agrius Hightower will now carry your skimmer . . . and buy you a drink."

"You must know a place that serves alcohol."

Agrius Hightower certainly was merry. "We'll manage all right." He nodded to the bartender, pushed Longbaugh's untouched second glass away, and two fresh glasses arrived with liquid that appeared respectably brown. Longbaugh watched Hightower lift his glass. Hightower saw him watching and paused with his lip on the rim. "Do what you like, tourist, but my policy's to drink the real juice when it's offered." He drank.

Longbaugh raised his glass to his nose. Creditable whiskey. He drank.

The slick was back at the far end of the bar, pretending not to notice Longbaugh and Hightower. Longbaugh understood then that the slick was Moretti's boy, but probably not muscle. Hightower was likely to handle that, although he was too smart to be just an enforcer. Perhaps he also did something else for Moretti. Longbaugh imagined the slick was Moretti's messenger. If so, Moretti was smarter than he expected, keeping layers between himself and the gang's operations.

"Didn't take long to find me."

Hightower was not insulted. "Was I looking? I happen to live here."

"No," said Longbaugh with abrupt, harsh certainty, "you don't."

Hightower shot him a wintry look, and met menace with menace. His words grew thicker still, more substantial. "I owe allegiance to nobody."

Longbaugh returned an innocent smile. "No doubt. But you moonlight for *il Mano Nera*."

Hightower looked him over as if he would not underestimate him again. "Mind you, I care not at all, but what would you do with Giuseppe Moretti if he were here?"

"Nothing to cause you any trouble."

"He do something to you?"

"He knows my wife."

Hightower's manner changed, as if his respect for Longbaugh vanished with those words. "Oh, tourist, I sincerely do hope not." He stood back from the bar. "There's my problem, I trust my instincts, got to learn to wait before I befriend a man." He hitched his trousers and stood taller, delivering boilerplate: "If your wife chooses life on the boulevard, that is her decision and we cannot be held responsible." Hightower stepped back to leave.

"You already know her name."

"I sincerely doubt it. Not her name, nor any other of her physical advantages or attributes."

"Etta Place."

Longbaugh watched his words' impact. Hightower came back to the bar.

"Interesting name."

"So it is."

"But she had no husband. We would have known."

"You'll take me to him."

Hightower nodded. "I will. And I hope that will make you as happy as it's going to make him." He knocked on the bar twice to get the bartender to refill his glass. The bartender turned his broad back to him. Hightower smiled and nodded his head without satisfaction, having come to the limit of his leash.

"Shall we?" he said.

Longbaugh followed Hightower away from the entrance and toward a rear door. He felt the collective disappointment of the other patrons that he was leaving under escort. He saw, blocking the door, a small Italian *paisan* in a loud checked jacket who presented a toothy, liquid smile that brought Longbaugh no warmth. Here, likely, were the fingers that had lifted his purse. The smiler turned and was out the door a few steps ahead of them. By the time they reached the alley, he was not to be seen.

"By the way." Longbaugh ducked under a fire escape a step behind Hightower. "I don't own a skimmer."

"And I would never carry one," said Hightower knowingly.

Longbaugh followed warily through the narrow, ill-lit alley. He wanted to slow down, observe and memorize, but Hightower was quick for a bear. He let Hightower get ahead, trying to memorize the route.

He knew he had misjudged the situation when he reached a fork in the alley and Hightower was nowhere to be seen. He walked a few steps to the left, then came back and tried the right. Hightower might have gone either direction. Now he listened for something else, because he had been played for a sucker and had walked right into it. He wasn't surprised, had in fact expected it, but he'd hoped his lesson would come after he'd gotten to talk to Moretti. Now it would be harder. He stayed by the corner, but left his gun hidden against his low back. Three hard boys stepped out. He had overheard talk in the bar that most of the men there were Sicilians, and these boys were dressed the same. He felt but did not see one more behind him. Four. No. There was a fifth, up ahead in the shadow, hovering behind the first three, the *paisan* with the teeth and the loud checked jacket. That the *paisan* kept a discreet distance suggested he had the wisdom of a coward and the wiliness of a bully. The *paisan* would be happy to kick him, but only when he was down.

"You got something belongs to us," said the hard one who was their leader.

"Wait, don't tell me," said Longbaugh. "My life or my money?"

He leaned sideways to contact the wall closest to him, a side glance at the boy behind. A young one, tall and lanky, with pimples.

"Take 'em both, if you don't mind," said the hard one.

"You may need to work a bit."

The corner gave him an advantage, and none of the boys were showing firepower. Why bother, when the odds were so in their favor. He waited for their move. The three in front spread out and closed in. The one in back would also be moving. Longbaugh watched for any flinch, twitch, or tremble.

Hightower came up behind the *paisan* and slapped him so loudly on the ear that the others all turned. The *paisan* said, "Ow," and grabbed the side of his head. "You never learn, do you, Flexible? This one's mine."

Longbaugh saw the silent message signaled from Hightower's eyes to each of the boys in turn. The main four went sullen, trudging now, slow as erosion, losing that catlike step that had impressed him. When they did not scatter quickly, Hightower signaled the leader with an abrupt jerk of his head. Once they were gone, his irritation turned on Longbaugh.

"Maybe you best stay close, tourist." He moved near enough to bring Longbaugh into the pull of his gravity. This time he walked ahead more slowly. "Thought I had you pegged in there. Now not so sure. You're a little green for being that Place woman's husband."

"You think I was in trouble?"

"If they'd wanted to hurt you, they'd have had guns."

"In their pockets?"

"You truly are a tourist. There's a city law against carrying. The Sullivan Law, automatic jail sentence if you get caught with a gun. Punks like that sew their pockets closed so cops can't plant one. They get their girlfriends to carry. If they're willing to risk that little cop trick, that's when they're serious."

Longbaugh smiled mirthlessly. Curious that Agrius Hightower had more respect for his woman than for him. He brought his hand out from under his jacket, leaving his pistol hidden. Hightower watched Longbaugh's hand, but Longbaugh knew Hightower had not seen the Peacemaker.

"What did you call him, Flexible?"

"His name's Felice," Hightower pronounced it in perfect Italian, feh-LEE-chay, "but I don't speak Wop, and he's a twisted little turd, smile at you one minute, kick your cheek in the next. That makes him flexible."

"Giuseppe live around here?"

"Signor Moretti moves around. If he stays in any one place more than a night, I'd be surprised," said Hightower over his shoulder. Then he stopped, turned, and came at Longbaugh to look him directly in the eye. "Moretti is a man so thin-skinned, he bleeds when he takes off his shirt." Longbaugh thought about the warning, knowing it had meaning without knowing why.

They entered a building and navigated tight hallways with scant light. Longbaugh smelled frying onions and garlic, heard a juicy cough through a wall and an aborted scream over his head. He had absorbed the lesson and stayed close to his guide. That way, if anyone took a shot, they risked hitting Hightower. Again to the outdoors, but before he found a street sign they went into another building, out the back, then through another alley. Longbaugh quit trying to memorize the way.

They could be anywhere, they could even have circled back to the same building that housed the Tall Boot. He followed until they were into another doorway, up stairs, down a second-story hall to an unmarked door, where Hightower knocked.

Time passed. No sounds came from within. Hightower waited without knocking a second time. Longbaugh heard nothing until a girl opened the door, a lean and pale creature, not unattractive, with hair unruly as if she'd been interrupted during strenuous exercise, breathing through her slack and puffy mouth. A thin robe hung to her knees, her nipples a distinct shape against the cotton, her bare, thin legs standing on large feet, making her seem young and coltlike. She resented the intrusion, but one look at Hightower and she nodded her head to come in, opening the door wider.

"He said it was you. Who else'd come unexpected?" she muttered. Her voice was lower, duskier, older than he would have imagined. She closed the door behind them. "Better be important."

Hightower nodded, and she looked at him with flat, sleepy eyes, not giving a damn about his problems, standing there in her white skin and blue veins, black hair and white robe.

She turned slowly, wandering away with one finger trailing along the wainscoting, as if she were numb or stunned and needed support to stay balanced. She was too young to be Queenie, but he had an unexpected memory of the half-Cheyenne girl on the road to the dinosaur excavation.

Longbaugh looked at the busy hallway, crowded with things, objects, stuff, as if the owner couldn't decide what he liked and simply bought everything, fitting each new piece into whatever space was available. Longbaugh's senses were bullied by decorations that may have been expensive but appeared garish, one piece clashing with the next, from the wallpaper to the lamps to the chairs to the rugs to the sculptures to the wall hangings to the paintings. His eyes rested on the girl's simple thin white robe, but then she stepped into a doorway and was gone. He turned to check the hallway in the other direction. A man in a good suit was half in, half out of a doorframe, and Longbaugh saw one leg, one ear, one eye, and his right hand holding a sandwich. The slick messenger bit into the sandwich and stepped back, out of sight.

He followed Hightower across the hall through a door into a parlor with yet more opulence, but the focus of this room at least had a theme, framed pornographic daguerreotypes that hung on the walls. The frames were wide, carved, and lavished with gold leaf, almost more eye-catching than the poorly printed nudes. Longbaugh wondered what this place was, thinking they had entered a whorehouse through the back way, but there was no madam, no other girls or musicians, and no offer of watered-down booze. It might have been an immigrant's idea of a private club. Or perhaps this was what all those Fifth Avenue private clubs were like.

Hightower indicated he should sit, then leaned against the wall behind him. Longbaugh turned in his chair to measure him, then turned back to face the empty room and the exposed women laughing in their gold frames.

Moretti came in immediately. He was clad much like the girl, but his robe was luxuriant with gold brocade. He had not bothered to belt it and his oily erection shone between the curtain of parted fabric. Its size was impressive, more so for its resilience in the company of men. Longbaugh was unprepared for Moretti's youth, as power rarely accrued in one so young. Moretti was handsome, with smooth olive skin and black tousled hair, dark eyes and long black lashes. His heavy beard must have been difficult to keep shaved so close. A horizontal scar across his left cheek kept him from appearing too pretty. It was recent, within a year or two, as it still reacted to his changes of mood. Here was the man whose cheek had been bandaged when he came to visit Abigail. Longbaugh noted the sneer on his heavy-lipped mouth, that cruel place women found irresistible, but also the place where his true feelings could not hide.

Moretti lashed out at Hightower. "If this concerns negotiations with our friend, I have had a conversation with that *ingannare* Wisher, and you will need to set him straight, and why is there a witness to my words, Agrius?"

"This is not about our friend."

"But have you spoken to him? I want an agreement, I want a partnership, use the information we have on him, I want—"

Hightower cut him off deliberately. "I will speak to him. This regards another matter."

"*What* other matter?!"

Longbaugh looked at Hightower, who nodded at him. "*You* say, tourist."

He had taken a chance, letting Hightower stand behind him, but while he imagined Hightower to be a treacherous animal, he didn't peg him to shoot a man in the back. He'd have someone else do that.

Longbaugh took his time before he spoke. "Etta Place."

Moretti's erection pulsed. "You know where that *puttana* is?"

Longbaugh stood and his feline quickness and brutal eyes disrupted Moretti's enthusiasm. He did not know the meaning of the word, but he understood it. Hightower came off the wall, but Longbaugh was ready for him if he made a move. Moretti's erection plunged.

"This would be her husband," said Hightower with musical delight in his voice. "I never did catch his name. Mr. Place, I suppose."

Longbaugh liked the sound of that. Mr. Place was his maternal grandfather's name.

A sneer hooked the corner of Moretti's lip, but was quickly replaced with unguent charm. He pulled the wings of his robe together to conceal his softening rod. "I did not know she was with spouse. How very interesting. I wish I had known, the things I could have done with that information. I have been looking for her for quite a little bit of time."

"I'm sorry you don't know where she is."

"Perhaps you will be the one to tell me."

Giuseppe Moretti sat down. He waved Longbaugh back to his seat.

"You are a supremely lucky man, Mr. Place, to have married such a woman. When first I met her, I am not ashamed to say I was enamored.

How she held herself, how she acted. Strong, that one. No fear. She was not so tall, but she appeared tall with confidence." He watched closely to see how his words affected Longbaugh. "Maybe you did not know her that way. Sometimes it's not easy for a husband. We out here get to know them better. I even told her she would make a wonderful companion on a cold night by a fireplace. Can you imagine such a thing?"

Longbaugh said nothing. One of his fingers dug into the fabric of the arm of the chair and pressed hard against the sharp point of an upholstery tack.

"She reacted, of course. A very quick reaction, I would say. And I will never forget what she said to me next: 'Some other time.' Your wife, she was clever with words."

He missed the controlled anger in Moretti's voice, as his own eyes blurred, trying to picture Moretti's story.

"But I am acting rude. I have not allowed you speak. You are here for . . . ?"

"For you." The room became very distinct with danger, the air sharp and dry, whistling through his nose.

Moretti leaned in closer. "She told you about me, then."

"Why would she bother to do that?"

"She didn't mention me, the last time you saw her? When was it, this morning?"

"No."

"You mean to bargain for her well-being, then? For her physical safety?"

"You're not the bargaining type."

"You are a visionary as well as a husband."

"I came with a question."

"And if there is no answer?"

"That's an answer."

"I will reply to any question, but first tell me—why look so hard for . . . a woman?" Moretti rubbed the scar on his cheek.

"Why do you?"

"Oh, your spouse and I have business of the unfinished variety. But to a man like you, she's little more than," he shrugged, "a wife. There are marvelous creatures out there to sample, such variety."

"Like Queenie?"

Moretti was startled, darting a glance at Hightower. "How does he know this?" The scar on his cheek reddened.

Hightower put his hands up in a defensive shrug. "First I heard of it."

Moretti was off balance, so Longbaugh pressed, hoping to surprise him, trick out the truth. "And your search for Etta, this unfinished business?"

"A matter of principle."

"Still mad about Queenie?"

Moretti stood up, glaring, and for a moment Longbaugh thought he had him. "Are you under the impression that Queenie is no longer in my power?" He swung at a lamp and sent it crashing to the floor. "Because she now begs to be in my presence. Begs! All is right with the world."

The moment was lost, Moretti had turned his anger to Queenie and not given himself away regarding Etta. Longbaugh changed tactics. "But you're good to them, your women, a generous employer, although strong when you need to be."

"Yes." Calming down.

"And you're consistent. They always know what to expect from you."

Moretti was back on earth. He sat down again, closer to Longbaugh. "How well you understand me, Mr. Place. Perhaps you are a better mate than I first suspected. I had to be strong with Queenie, of course, but that was a surprise to no one. Sadly, Queenie outlived her good looks. Happily, I took full advantage of her best years." He could not resist showing off. "There was a time, Mr. Place, when she had class. She also had a number of high-class clients, which she thought she could keep secret from me. But I always knew and I always collected from them. Of course, now she's free to go back to them, but who would want a worn-out sack of a whore?"

"Not you."

Moretti smiled grimly. "You have not asked your question, Mr. Place."

"Haven't I?" Longbaugh said nothing more and let the pause crowd the room until the others were uncomfortable.

"It's two years since she's been missing. Why do you come here now?" said Moretti.

"I've been busy."

Moretti watched his eyes, then sat forward. He meant to sound calm and reasonable, but Longbaugh knew it was the tone Moretti used to frighten women.

"I do not give advice, Mr. Place. I prefer action. I am not a man who feels the need to explain himself, or even offer warnings. Someone crosses me, he gets what he deserves, not an explanation. When he thinks back on it, he does not know why he is dead. With that in mind, I think you would be wise to watch yourself. Do not think of getting in the way of the business I have with your wife. You are not up to that. And anyway, that would go badly for you and do nothing to help her. You would not wish to force me to do things you would regret."

No one spoke to him that way. No one. But he controlled himself. He controlled himself. He saw himself giving Moretti precisely what he deserved, but he did not act. He controlled himself. If this man had known who he really was, he would not have dared speak to him that way.

Moretti smiled. "I hope we will meet again."

"Assuming I recognize you without your cock."

Moretti did not know what to make of that. He stood up, looking at him as if he'd misheard. "I thought you might be helpful to us. I see I was wrong."

"You don't know how to be wrong. That would require the ability to learn."

Moretti's eyes burned, but he did not explode. "I see I was wrong." He repeated the sentence stiffly and slowly, looking directly at Hightower, as if the words carried a deeper meaning. "You do not even know as much about her as I know." He left the room, the door closing quietly behind him.

Hightower whistled. "Oh, but you own a set of leather balls, tourist. You just ran a burr up that man's backside. I guess I better show you out before he thinks about it and asks me to do something."

Longbaugh, still flush with confrontation, let himself be led out of the room to the hallway and to the stairs.

On the way down, Longbaugh separated himself from his rage and found his voice. "What's your part in this, Hightower?"

"I promised Moretti I'd find her."

"Why does he care after all this time?"

"He said it himself, a matter of principle. And these Sicilian guys never forget and never let go. Ever."

"Still mad about the Triangle fire?"

Hightower stopped on the stairs and looked back up at him. "Too damn smart for your own good, tourist. But no."

He turned and headed down again, and Longbaugh followed him out into the alley.

Hightower took him in the other direction, and was quiet for the first block. Then he said, "Notice his scar?"

"I saw it."

"She gave it to him."

Longbaugh stopped. "She? *Etta?*"

"Your wife went to see him, to see if Queenie really had betrayed her trust and gone back to him. That time, *her* pride was injured. Queenie had promised she was through with him. But the fire scared the little whore and she ran back to his protection. He'd won and he knew it, and when Etta showed up, he laughed. She knew he was planning to send people to hurt her, but she showed up anyway. She had serious guts, your wife. Even he respected that. Once she was there, he sent his boys away and moved in to taunt her. Got a little too close. Said he'd let her live if she'd take Queenie's place. Then he asked her to join him at that fireplace. She pulled something out of her purse."

"Something?"

"Something sharp. Swung it at his face, cut him across the cheek. That's when she said it."

"'Some other time,'" said Longbaugh, fitting her words into the story.

"He was too stunned to act. Too much blood. She walked out of there with her head held high. By the time his boys came back in and saw him bleeding, she was gone. But she got his attention."

Longbaugh thought, *Oh yes she did. Two years' worth of his attention, and counting.* Moretti was waiting for that "other time." No wonder Hightower was more impressed with her than with her husband.

Hightower continued to lead him through a maze of buildings and alleys, and Longbaugh thought it was to keep him from memorizing the way back.

He knew what she had used to cut Moretti. She had bought the toy because she was planning to plant it for her husband. And Hightower was right, she knew Moretti's reputation, she knew even when Moretti had Queenie back, he would want his revenge. But she couldn't help herself, she had to go back, she had to know if Queenie's betrayal of Etta was Queenie's choice alone or if Moretti had forced it. So Etta had had it in her purse when Moretti made his proposition. Now he was sorry he had left the toy at the boardinghouse. He wanted to know if there was blood on the flame.

Hightower brought him out to the middle of an empty, dark street that dead-ended behind them.

"You'll find your way from here."

"How'd you get involved with him?"

"He pays."

"I hope he pays well."

"Better than Pinkerton. Good as Tammany, although Tammany was more regular."

"You were a Pinkerton?"

"Strike buster. But the country's changing, going progressive. Never liked being on the wrong side of history."

"*Mano Nera*'s the right side?"

"Crime has a future, tourist."

Longbaugh thought about his own criminal past. Then he thought about the dime novel version. Crime ran through the future's filter and came out as romance.

"Interesting run, Hightower. Pinkerton, Tammany, Black Hand."

"Tell me my next stop and you'll tell me my future."

"Appreciate your help."

"Didn't do it for you."

"No. You didn't."

"You got a funny way." Hightower scratched under his armpit. "First you're the concerned husband, then you're nothing like it. I'd like to split you open, tourist, see what's inside. Although I'm starting to think you're no tourist. Like the opposite. What do they call that?"

"Irony."

"I was thinking native. You've been somewhere that doesn't match those clothes and that hat."

"Just looking for my wife."

"Let me know if you find her."

"That'll be the day."

Hightower went through the doorway of a different building and was gone.

Longbaugh was alone. The street was dark without streetlamps, empty, quiet. He listened to the night. The city seemed far away until his ears were hit by the deep-throated blow of an ocean liner's horn, much closer than he might have expected. It moaned for an extended breath, cut off suddenly with an echo that boomed across New Jersey, and the rest of the world was hushed. His ears slowly retuned to the distant clopping of horseshoes and automobile engines and voices of people he could not see. The cross street ahead was well lit and busy, and he was about to walk to it, but his feet were reluctant, cemented to cobblestones.

When he didn't go, he wondered why. But he trusted the alarm inside his skull that told him he'd missed something. Moretti's arch words about being wrong may have been code, meaning Hightower may have delivered him here under orders. An elevated train clattered a few blocks over. Once he reached the busy street ahead, he would be fine. Getting there was the issue. Unless he was imagining things. Unless there was no problem.

Something moved behind him and he started, turning toward the flick of a long, narrow tail. He kicked and it leapt sideways and stood to chitter insolently. He shook his head to ward off the tension, maybe the rat was what he had been sensing. He started toward the big street.

Then he knew. He had been dumped in an industrial area. No lights. No witnesses. Even in dodgy neighborhoods, people jammed the streets day and night, as their apartments were small, cramped, over-crowded. Only in the limestone mansions on Fifth Avenue did people go into their homes and stay. He walked slowly, because he knew it would come, now it was just a matter of when.

They came out early, too far away, a mistake, in single file from a doorway near the lit-up street at the far end, lining up to face him. He was blocked in the dead-end street, but their impatience gave him the edge. Now he had room to maneuver. They were backlit from the thoroughfare, the same five boys from the alley, including the *paisan*, Felice. What was it Hightower had dubbed him? Flexible. They hadn't thought to position someone behind him this time. Their second mistake.

"No one here to save you this time. So we *will* take both," said the leader.

Maybe they thought he would try to run, or maybe they thought he would try to get out through the door Hightower had used, but Longbaugh wasn't interested in getting away. Only Flexible did not reach for his belt or shoulder bag. Each then brandished a pistol. Longbaugh remembered Hightower's explanation of the law. They had gone back for firepower, and were forced to carry their weapons somewhere other than their stitched-up pockets. But he did not recognize their guns, as they were flat, with a rectangular shape. The darkness hid details, but the gun silhouettes did not resemble a revolvers. There was no cylinder. He did not understand how they might work, but he also did not underestimate their power. Another invention of the modern world sent to teach him a lesson. Flexible kept his hands by his sides and backed up a step. No surprise there.

"You going to make this easy or hard?" said the leader.

Longbaugh reached under his collar and pulled his bandanna up over his nose. He liked the feel of it on his face when he went into a situation.

"Now you have a choice," he said.

He reached under his jacket and drew out his Peacemaker. He thumbed back the hammer to spin the cylinder with his opposite palm so they could hear it whir. He thought it only sporting to give them fair warning.

They opened fire immediately, all arms raised and blasting, and he marveled at their impatience, not to mention their rude lack of fair play. He did not move. The old sensation returned; when in battle or crisis, he was both exquisitely present while being a small step outside himself, watching. He had little fear, perhaps because he understood the moment. New weapon or not, these guns had no better range than his revolver, and right now they were too far away. He watched them leap and fire their pieces with manic incompetence, jerking off round after round, pointing without aiming, bullets zipping this way and that, ricocheting off buildings, breaking a window, one very lucky shot whining close to his ear. They moved toward him, but the shots were coming more slowly now, their fingers tiring from pinching off rounds. They were moving into his range while running out of ammunition. Flexible did not come, watching the other four pose and jump. They seemed unwilling to believe that their fancy new guns, facing the prehistoric revolver, had not decimated their target. The firing stopped and they stood stupidly, breathing hard, guns smoking, one of them still trying to fire, but some sort of odd sliding mechanism on top of each of the weapons had kicked back. The leader withdrew a flat, rectangular object that Longbaugh would later learn was a "magazine," or clip. The others simply gaped at Longbaugh. They could not believe he was still on his feet.

"And now it's my turn," said Longbaugh affably.

They looked at one another, confused. A sudden flurry of activity as each of them hurried to eject the used clip from the handle and reload. But now they were close enough. Longbaugh moved.

He dropped to a crouch, his weight on his bent right leg, stretching out his left to give himself a base. His pistol came up and he fired once, targeting the leader, because you always begin by cutting off the head. His heart was full with the noise and power of his weapon, his shot tearing through the leader's shoulder, the force of the projectile twisting him, and he went down in a clumsy pirouette. The leader howled in pain and his piece skittered across cobblestones behind him. Longbaugh's body was electric with thrill, the gunfighter unleashed, and all the old ecstasy rushed in with the muscle memory, his quickness, his accuracy, knowing in his fingers there was no one better. He fired his second shot, splitting the flesh of the next boy's side as that boy had turned to watch his leader go down. The second boy did a near somersault while his breath was knocked out of him, and for a moment he sat with his mouth open, gulping for air. Longbaugh savored the moment, no rush now. His third shot thumped smack into the exposed rump of the third boy, who was in reckless flight toward the big street. The bullet parted the lower muscles of his buttocks and drove that hip forward, while his other leg was still kicked up behind, and he did an awkward split that initially may have caused more pain than the bullet. The fourth boy, the pimpled one, was surprisingly courageous, still holding his ground, magazine in hand after fumbling to eject the empty clip. He was another tall, lanky creature, not unlike the sheriff's boy in Wyoming. Longbaugh admired his nerve to be standing there. His eyes were comically wide, staring at Longbaugh, then looking down, frantically trying to insert the clip, looking back, and Longbaugh grinned as he took careful aim. But he hesitated, again seeing the Wyoming boy, and instead sent one just over the pimpled one's hat. That was enough. The boy spun, heels rising, toes tapping in a dance of full retreat, running past the others, who were crawling, dragging, or limping away from the mad gunman.

Flexible did not run. Longbaugh rose to his full height and considered the runt, who with both hands took hold of the lapels of his jacket and pulled them away from his body and kept them open that way, exposing to Longbaugh his shirt and belt to prove he was unarmed. There was a moment when the *paisan* considered the bandanna over Longbaugh's nose and mouth and his smile wavered, but he still marched toward him, his innocent smile wide, coming on while holding that jacket open. Longbaugh let his weapon hand fall to his side, amazed by Flexible's gumption, somewhat hypnotized as Flexible walked toward him, close now, steps away, closer, always smiling, jacket flared, four steps, three, too close—and Longbaugh saw it late, the glint of steel in Flexible's right hand, kept hidden under the lapel of his jacket as he held it out there. Longbaugh twisted away to protect himself, a late dodge, but Flexible was on him, running the knife into Longbaugh's flesh.

Longbaugh barely reacted, although he knew the steel was deep in the meat of his side. Had he not dodged, it would have found his belly. He kept his expression flat, and doubt flashed in Flexible's eyes when he seemed not to be hurt. He swung his gun and the butt end cut across Flexible's face and broke his nose and wrecked his smile, taking teeth. Flexible dropped and Longbaugh pulled the knife from his side. Pain stabbed him and he knew it was bad, bleeding heavily under his jacket. Roaring with rage and frustration, he jammed the knife into a space between mortar and bricks, and snapped the handle off. Flexible was motionless on the ground, not conscious of Longbaugh's actions. Longbaugh didn't want the runt to know he was hurt, so he placed the bladeless handle in Flexible's palm. He yanked off his bandanna, wiped the blood off the ground, then held the bandanna tight against his side to keep from leaving a bloody trail and got away from there.

He wanted the moment back. It had been satisfying to open fire, to release his aggression on a gang of rude predators. He had lost himself in it, and the *paisan* runt had taken advantage of his joy, as if he had known that violence was his one true vulnerability. He had stood there like a flat-footed, punch-drunk, dull-witted mule and let it happen. Any self-respecting gunman would have pressed the barrel smartly against Flexible's temple and run a bullet into his brain.

He stopped under a streetlight and let go of his side and lifted his coat and shirt and examined the wound. Not good. He was hurt, and even if the blade had missed organs, the danger of infection was real. He could go back to his hotel, but as he looked at the fresh flow of blood, he knew he could not stitch it himself. He didn't know how much time he had before the adrenaline wore off, making him unable to maneuver.

He closed his jacket over the spot and saw he still held his revolver, his own blood dripping off the end of the barrel. He looked around, and two or three people stared. He tucked the revolver in his belt, noticed he was on his knees, came to his feet, and walked. He found street signs at a corner and considered where to go. Abigail came to mind, but Siringo was onto that location, and Levi was a wild card.

He walked the streets, legs shaky, and for entire blocks he did not know how he stayed upright. He eventually reached a street he knew and banged on a door. He fell then, with a vague recollection of the door opening to a familiar woman's face, but things were blurry and he could not stop the slide into a blissful sleep, where he started to dream.

9

He lay in a soft bed and did not care to move. He was warm but found the sensation of sweat drying on his forehead to be soothing. He had been in and out of sleep for days, or so he thought, and during that time, his side had tendered him significant pain. Today he had discovered a good position on his back with his palms facing up and his feet lightly tented by the sheet. It was all right, lying like this, and he stayed still, just quiet, unmoving, and still. He adjusted to the pain, and with that, the pain shifted, as if it took a small step outside of him. It did not quite leave, it remained within reach, but it did not grip him so tightly. The sensation of the absence of pain was tranquilizing, and he drifted in its spell, in a dream state where he floated over mattress and pillows, comforted in warm air, body weightless. He was immersed in a loud, pervasive hum he could not identify, something generated by a machine, likely from outdoors. He accepted the sound, gliding on its rumble. People were speaking, but the hum absorbed all deep bass notes, as if it were a heavy low fog and the tinny voices were ejected spouts of cloud through the fog's roof, quickly blown away.

Gradually words filtered in. He did not, however, open his eyes to identify speakers. Once he thought he heard Lillian Wald. She was explaining something about sacrifice, the words strange without context, until she said, "When everyone sacrifices, there's no incentive to fight," which sounded both odd and curiously reasonable. He slept again until his head lifted up to stretch against the thin veil of waking, taut against it but not breaking through, hearing Queenie's sister, Mary, in the room with him as she spoke to another girl. Her words took physical shape, so that the spoken name J. P. Morgan transformed into the young J. P. Morgan in person, standing beside Longbaugh's bed. This did not seem unusual to him, and he somehow understood it was fifty years earlier, part of the Civil War past, as Morgan was taking the first step in building his empire. Longbaugh watched the infamous moment where Morgan bought defective rifles from the government on the cheap, then sold them right back to the government on the following day, unaltered, for an obscene profit. The figure of Lillian Wald then appeared, pointing acidly at Morgan, cursing him for his deeds. They both faded back into the hum as Mary's words labeled Lillian a leader of the anti-preparedness movement. He did not know that word, and he pushed through the veil and opened his eyes. The room was different than what he had imagined, smaller and more blue, with sun on the street and reflected light streaming in the windows. Even when she looked at him, Mary did not notice him awake and went on whispering to her companion. He closed his eyes again and shifted in the bed, and pain came back into his side. He must have made a noise, because Mary stopped talking and came over to arrange a pillow. He did not speak to her but fell back again underneath the veil.

The next day or maybe an hour later, he woke to find Lillian Wald sitting in a chair, reading documents. She looked up when she saw his eyes were open. She said nothing, and after a few moments, he closed his eyes again. He imagined her there for the rest of the time he slept, reading her papers, occasionally looking over to see if he would ever open his eyes again.

He came fully awake some time after that and was alone in the room. The hum was gone. He saw his things in a corner. Someone had fetched them from his hotel. He did not know how that was possible, as he alone kept the secret of where he was living. He was thirsty. The room was small, the door was closed. It was uncluttered, with a nightstand and chair by the bed, curtains on the windows, and a framed child's painting on the wall. This did not seem to be prison, although he had no experience with how New Yorkers incarcerated their own. He tried to sit up in the bed but felt a pull in his side, and slowed way down. He cautiously brought himself to a near-seated position, managing the pain. The pain was less than it had been.

Mary came in, and her face lit up to see him awake and she told him the fever had broken and how worried they had been and how Miss Wald herself had gotten her old nurse's bag and cleaned his wound herself. Longbaugh was happy to hear all those things, but he wanted her to stop talking and bring him a glass of water, as he really was very thirsty.

"WHERE ARE WE?"

"Settlement house. Not the building you were in the first time, down the block."

"How long have I . . . ?"

"No one will find you here. You're in a back room on the third floor, where we house women," said Lillian Wald.

"How did I get here?" said Longbaugh. He was different somehow, as if he didn't quite know himself. Unsure.

"You knocked a couple of weeks ago," she said from her chair by his bed. "We let you in."

"Have I thanked you?"

"Many times, especially that night. You didn't want to be a bother."

"You haven't asked about it."

"I have an idea. Something to do with Joe, I suspect."

"I can't prove it was Joe. Giuseppe Moretti." Saying the man's name aloud made his heart race. That surprised him.

She nodded. "I'm not surprised you can't prove it, as I imagine he is Caesar's wife."

He raised his eyebrows.

"'Caesar's wife must be above suspicion.' Did you learn any more about Etta?" said Lillian.

"No."

"I understand. By now, you only know where she is not."

"How did my things get here?"

"Your Chinese friend."

"Han Fei? How did he know where—no, never mind, I can guess." Han Fei had been with him the night he left the boardinghouse, so he knew about the hotel. How he knew Longbaugh had come to the Settlement was a question for another day. A good friend to have. And Longbaugh did not have many friends. He looked at Lillian in the room and thought of Mary's attentive nursing. Perhaps more than he knew.

"Has he been by?"

"With clocklike regularity."

"I'd like to see him."

They were quiet together. He looked for something safe to discuss. He remembered the low hum.

"Was there some sort of noise?"

"You mean the irritating rumble under all our activities, yes, the trucks were parked along the sidewalk as they delivered extra lights and decorations for the pageant. I asked them to turn off their motors. I don't think they could hear me."

"People were whispering."

"People were trying to let you rest."

"Something about war and preparation. Did a war start while I was out?"

She shrugged. "The Balkans are on fire again, but no, technically we are not at war, not yet. And about the rest, you wouldn't be interested."

"I think I would."

"Mr. Longbaugh, I am the last human being on the face of the earth to shy from discussing politics, but you need to heal."

"And conversation delays healing."

She was less than amused. "Very well. They were discussing 'anti-preparedness.'"

"I see." He did not. He waited for her to explain, but she was more adept at waiting than he was.

"All right, what is anti-preparedness?" He wondered if he would have been the first to speak back in the old days. He caught himself—in the days before he had been knifed.

"I am among those who believe wars no longer need to be fought."

"Optimistic."

"So say our critics."

"So anti-preparedness is essentially what it sounds like, don't be ready."

"So say our critics. Now you must rest."

"What do *you* say?"

"Mr. Longbaugh, after an injury like yours, I've seen patients struggle with depression and anxiety."

"What do you say to your critics?"

She looked aside as if deciding whether or not to answer. She looked back. "That those who profit by manufacturing the tools of war incite both sides. A buildup has been in progress for some time. A certain gentleman, an armaments manufacturer, Mr. Spense of Great Britain, insists to my face that he would never ever do such a thing." She paused. "He would, of course, and does. Without it, perhaps war would be less . . . inevitable."

Longbaugh remembered the man in the hotel café who had said Miller's Wild West Show had had their horses and stagecoaches confiscated by the British.

"What does that have to do with sacrifice?"

She stared at him.

"I heard you say it to one of your people."

She graced him with a tart smile. "When you were with fever, no doubt. I will speak to the girls about all of us remaining more circumspect." She sighed as she looked about, choosing a way to make light of herself while bringing the discussion to a rapid close. "The idea, to be perfectly pedantic, is if we all step away from politics and sacrifice for a change, particularly if our men of business choose to *not* profit on war, then, to flog a dead horse, perhaps, *perhaps* it would be less inevitable."

"And your critics call that naïve?"

She smiled in spite of herself. "Very subtle, Mr. Longbaugh. But we won't know unless we try."

"And if they stockpile and we don't?"

"The providers of the raw materials of ordnance are often the same for both sides, like Mr. Spense. If he chose to join the sacrifice, then at least part of the buildup comes to a sudden and fortuitous end." She stood and made a small bow. "This discussion is now over, and you shall get some rest."

"I've been unappreciative."

She self-consciously forced herself to settle down. "And I'm a little touchy. I recently discovered that I dislike the humiliation, the presumption of naïveté, and the general laughter at my expense. Although I suspect I was no more fond of it when I was young."

"Will there be war?"

"Almost certainly."

His spirits sank a notch. He was glad the discussion was at an end. She, however, had something more.

"But if I am naïve, if there is no way to stop it, I will use all my political might to fight the J. P. Morgans and keep the Spenses from adding to their fortunes, for at the very least our boys should have weapons that perform. That is a business sacrifice of which I must insist."

"Very sensible," he said, his eyes starting to close.

HE WAS NOT a good patient and was up and walking around sooner than the nurses would have liked. But a nurse named Jennifer took pity on him and decided, if he was determined to walk around, let him walk around in his own clothes. She brought them to him, cleaned and folded. He noticed immediately that his bandanna wasn't there and began to go through his pockets. Jennifer watched him.

"Something missing?" she said.

"Bandanna."

"You had a bandanna?"

"It was green, olive."

"Oh. I'm afraid I thought it was a rag."

"It's not here."

She knew that her news wasn't good. "I tried to get the blood out of it, but it wouldn't come clean, so I scrubbed it and, well, it came apart in my hands."

"And you put what was left of it where?"

"I'm sorry, Mr. Longbaugh, but I'm afraid I threw it out. I never would have if I had known it had sentimental value."

Longbaugh sat on the side of the bed. She saw the expression on his face.

"I've done a terrible thing."

"No, Jennifer, it's fine, please, don't give it a second thought."

She sat on the chair opposite him. "I am truly sorry, Mr. Longbaugh. I did notice it, it was such an unusual color. But wait, I know I've seen bandannas at the department store, very nice red ones."

"You've done so much for me, I cannot thank you enough. It was just a rag."

Losing the bandanna caused Longbaugh to think about the ribbons Etta had left for him. The ones he had found along the way were still in the pocket of his trousers. He wondered if Etta might have left one here. But as he thought about it more, he realized she would not have. Between Abigail explaining that she had left in a hurry and Hightower's story about her confrontation with Moretti, he knew she wouldn't have taken the time to come back here. Just enough time to leave one in the boardinghouse privy and another in her rented room. Nonetheless, as the days passed and he grew stronger and expanded his walks through the Settlement, he caught himself looking for anything that shade of olive.

. . .

HAN FEI FIDGETED. He and Longbaugh sat on a back porch so that Longbaugh would not be seen from the street. Significant activity was taking place on the street, out of their sight, as the city brought in bleachers for the pageant. The heavy hum he had thought he imagined when he was with fever was back with the large delivery trucks.

They spent long, quiet stretches listening to the noise. Longbaugh wanted to let the young man know how much he appreciated his help, but it seemed as if Han Fei was uncomfortable being thanked.

"You ever been to a pageant?"

"Not with white people."

"Seems like they're going to a lot of trouble."

Han Fei nodded. "Seems."

"They say they could have ten thousand people."

Han Fei nodded. "Ten thousand."

"Where will they put them?"

Han Fei shrugged. "Not at my place."

"I know this is a silly question, but how did you know I was here?"

"Looked for you."

"And ended up here."

"You came here before. And they have nurses."

A few of the Settlement girls had heard rumors on the street that someone had been shot and stabbed by the Black Hand, but he must have been some kind of supernatural spirit because he hadn't died. Longbaugh figured Han Fei may have heard the same and somehow put it together. Longbaugh thought it was possible Siringo could make a similar leap. Siringo had been by to speak to Lillian Wald about Etta, but as far as he knew, he had not been back.

"The other one, the one like me. He still around?"

"Still around."

"At the boardinghouse?"

"Sometimes."

"You know when he's not there?"

"I can find him if I look."

"He's good."

"I can find him if I look, cowboy."

"It wasn't an insult."

"Okay."

Longbaugh tried to find a safe topic.

"How are they doing, the Levis?"

"She's happier."

"No more meetings with tall Chinese haters?"

"You said something to him."

"What would I say?"

"He doesn't curse me now. Just acts like I'm not there."

"Maybe he's reformed."

"No. You said something."

"How about Levi? How does he seem?"

"Saw him smile. Right after she smiled at him."

"She smiled at him?"

"He took her hand."

"And she smiled."

"She smiled."

"Well." Longbaugh was pleased.

The noise stopped. The lack of activity made them both turn their heads and wait. Then it started again.

Longbaugh nodded. "Pageant. Funny thing."

"Yeah."

"Songs and skits?"

"So they say."

"For the twentieth anniversary of the Settlement."

"Twenty years is forever," said Han Fei.

Longbaugh smiled and wondered how old he was. Another quiet moment, then something on the street, out of sight, crashed. Han Fei's eyes went wide. "*That* didn't sound good."

"If you go back and you're sure there's no Siringo, I left something."

"I brought everything."

"Statue of Liberty toy."

Han Fei wrinkled his nose in disbelief.

"They sell those off carts. I can lift one faster than blow my nose."

"This one's special."

"Those aren't special, cowboy. They're ugly as sin."

"You're right. It's not important."

An immigrant looked up from the courtyard below and spotted Han Fei. He elbowed the man nearest him and pointed.

Han Fei sat back, and Longbaugh stood up and stared at the man below, and the man looked surprised and turned away.

"What's that about?"

"The little Chink."

"Yeah, and everyone comes here, so why do they care?"

"Good question." Han Fei looked away, bitterly.

"She accepts anyone, I mean, she accepts former slaves, and you know how popular they are."

"Almost as popular as Chinks."

"So why don't they hate her, didn't she help start that negro association?"

"National Association for the Advancement of Colored People," said Han Fei. "You have faith in people, cowboy. But they don't care what she thinks. Just glad someone's lower on the totem pole."

Han Fei looked at the way he was standing. "You're doing better. Moving around."

Longbaugh realized it was true. The pain was such that, although still present, he had begun to ignore it.

THE NEXT NIGHT, on the night of the Henry Street pageant, Han Fei brought him the Statue of Liberty toy. He also brought Siringo.

The streets around Henry Street were so busy with the pageant that Han Fei had missed seeing Siringo follow him in the crowd.

Longbaugh wondered how Han Fei had managed to get in. "House chiefs," chosen from the students and staff, were at every door on the block, strictly monitoring the crowd and admitting a maximum of five people per window to watch the pageant down on the street. The whole building had been buzzing and busy for more than two hours. Longbaugh considered himself lucky that his room was on the other side, so he was undisturbed.

Han Fei came in with the toy, proud that he'd gotten through. Longbaugh took it and looked at the point of the flame, and thought there might be a fleck of dried blood in one of the folds. Longbaugh was trying to think of some way to show his gratitude when the nurse Jennifer opened his door, walked in, and began to pack his clothes.

"There's a man downstairs looking for you," she said.

He watched her pull his extra shirt from a drawer.

"You left your post, Jennifer. You're a house chief, and you left your post," said Longbaugh.

She added his shaving gear, closed up his bag, and held it out to him.

"I put one of the little ones in charge. You know how the little ones are, no one gets by. Hey," she looked closely at Han Fei for the first time, "how'd *you* get in?"

"What man, and why are you sure it's for me?"

"Because men like him don't come here for our services, and he's not interested in the pageant. Time for you to go."

"Oh, cowboy," said Han Fei miserably, knowing what must have happened.

Jennifer was in control. "I have him searching the ground floor. A lot of people here, Mr. Longbaugh. You've got time. At least thirty seconds."

"Thank you, Jennifer." She closed the door as she went back to her post.

"It's all right, Han Fei, not your fault." Longbaugh lifted his bag.

Han Fei's expression said he believed it was.

"I've been here too long already."

Han Fei was determined. "I'll get you out."

"Not this time."

"I can do it."

"Yes you can, but I need you to do something else."

. . .

CHARLIE SIRINGO moved from room to room, casing the second floor, having satisfied himself that Longbaugh was not on the ground floor. The rooms facing Henry Street were difficult, as he had to check every celebrating person watching the pageant while hanging out a window in a group of five.

He moved fast, but it was unlikely to be fast enough. If Longbaugh was there, someone was bound to warn him. He took the stairs two at a time and on the third floor he saw an open door at the far end. There he found a sickroom with someone under covers. He crossed to the bed and yanked back the sheet. The small Chinese boy he had followed rolled over to look up at him, fully clothed with his shoes on. The boy offered a false look of surprise, but Siringo was already moving back to the hallway. He considered throwing open every door, but knew it was already too late. His one chance was to go to work on the Chinese kid.

He returned to the boy on the bed, a Statue of Liberty toy in his hands.

"Where?"

Han Fei's eyes darted up over his head for a second, then glared at him with stubborn defiance. "Downstairs."

"The roof."

Han Fei looked stricken. "Yes, that's it," he said finally, as if Siringo might assume the opposite.

"Yes," Siringo said, smiling, "that's it."

Han Fei made a halfhearted effort to get around Siringo to block his path, but Siringo was quick, down the hall, taking the stairs up, two at a time. He found the door to the roof and hesitated, thinking a fore-warned Longbaugh might be armed. He drew his gun from his holster, and pushed through the door into the night air.

A crush of onlookers lined the Henry Street side of the roof, watching the pageant below. He walked behind them, occasionally tapping a man on the shoulder who would turn and prove to be someone other than Harry Longbaugh. He looked down and saw the street filled with people, thousands and thousands of them, surrounding a staging area in the middle of the street with a large fire built there. The history of lower Manhattan was being played out, Indian squaws meeting the incoming Dutch. The Dutch were portrayed in fanciful costumes that included windmills, wooden shoes, and tulips. The lighting was bright, as if the sun was setting between the buildings.

Siringo turned away, disappointed. He walked back to the door to the inside, then scanned the open space, his gaze falling on the roofs across the way that also flanked Henry Street. He stopped when he saw Longbaugh. He crossed to the back corner of the building and put a hand on top of the cornice. The street below was quieter than the one on the other side, where the pageant played out, but this street was also powerfully lit, jammed with actors in costume awaiting their cues to join the festivities, some quietly singing, some rehearsing their lines, some laughing in anticipation of their big moment. Siringo looked up at the moon, near full, two hands above the tenement roofs. He looked over to where Longbaugh grinned at him, and there wasn't a thing Siringo could do about it, as Longbaugh stood on another rooftop across the street.

"Hello, Harry."

"Hello, Charlie."

"So it is you."

"You came a long way to find out."

"Pretty long." Siringo couldn't help but smile. The hunt would go on.

"You want to shoot me, Charlie?"

"Wouldn't be very satisfying, that." Siringo saw he still had his gun in his hand and slid it back under his jacket.

"What you got planned?"

"Arrest you."

"Do it, then."

"You're under arrest."

"Feel better?"

"Nope."

"Any particular crime?"

"Boy in Wyoming. Billy . . . something. But you knew that."

"Funny how no one remembers his name."

"Unless you've done something lately."

"You mean like to freshen my offense? Naw. Just him." He didn't consider his encounter with the Black Hand boys to be pertinent.

"Well, that's why I'm here."

They shared a quiet moment looking down at the well-lit street.

Siringo pulled on the soft drop of his ear. "Something bothering me."

Longbaugh laughed in spite of himself. "Something I can help you with, Charlie?"

"It's just not like you. Shooting that boy."

"Maybe I've changed."

"Could be. Either way, I'm going to have to catch you."

"Expected nothing less."

"Of course, you were always faster than I was."

"Fast enough."

"On the other hand, we're both older. Never can tell who's deteriorated the most."

"Who told you I'd deteriorated?"

Siringo smiled. That sense of humor he had always enjoyed when he was Charles Carter and they were outlaws together. Then he was serious again. "There's something else."

"I've got time."

"Back in the nineties, when Butch found out about me—what happened there?"

"You got away."

"He had me cornered, had me dead to rights, and he was mad."

"Changed his mind."

Siringo watched him across the way. It was too far to read his eyes. He wondered why Longbaugh didn't know. Or if he did know, why he wasn't telling. But he clearly wasn't going to get an answer tonight. Still, he hated mysteries.

Siringo changed the subject. "What if I get *you* in a corner. You going to shoot it out?"

"There is that possibility."

"I don't believe it."

"Ask the sheriff's boy."

"Wish I could."

Longbaugh nodded thoughtfully. "So do I."

Siringo heard the tone of his voice and again fingered the soft part of his ear. "Like I said. Just not like you."

"It happened, Charlie, I can't change it."

"If I had to guess, I'd say you didn't mean it."

"He's dead, isn't he?"

"If it was self-defense, you can say so."

"Will you believe me, Charlie?"

"I might."

"Will you believe me and stand up for me and convince the judge and the jury?"

"I can try."

"Then I best keep running."

"Fair enough."

They stood under the big moon and stared at each other, trying to read the other's face in the light from below.

"I did what I had to," said Longbaugh. "And now you're doing the same. Don't lose sleep over it."

"I hope you find her before I find you."

"That would be all right."

Siringo watched Longbaugh step away from the edge of the roof and slip off into the shadows. He considered rushing down the stairs into the street, to see if he might make the hundred-to-one right guess as to his escape plan and then have the luck of Theoderic to catch him in the crowd.

He did not.

10

ongbaugh had a new appreciation for roofs. In the West he'd been
leery of them, even of the bank roof with Etta, as a roof was an elevated dead end offering limited escape, and in a chase could end only
in a shoot-out or step-off-the-edge-and-drop. Western buildings rarely
stood above two stories, so off-the-edge-and-drop was an acceptable
option, although with four outdoor walls, any smart posse should have
been able to surround him. But seeing Siringo confined to a neighbor
roof with no way to reach him had brought unexpected pleasure. And
here, in the tenement heat of summer, where whole families abandoned
their steaming rooms and carried sheets and pillows up to the roof to
sleep under stars, he had stayed long enough to become part of the
landscape and now blended in with the masonry.

He took his place, a corner he had made his own, and scanned the
street below. Streetlamps glowed and gradually took over from the setting sun. He had been watching the front entrance to the Tall Boot
Saloon. Every day he spent watching, he felt his side hurt a little less.

He had become more patient. The time spent recuperating had re-
trained him to accept the value of waiting. It helped that Lillian had
told him he likely had lost no time. "You were learning new informa-

tion," she had said, "so it seemed urgent, but it was fresh information only for you. Wherever she is, she's far enough ahead that Giuseppe and anyone else looking can't see her. She doesn't know you're trying to catch up, she's just moving and hiding."

Moving and hiding. Rather than reassuring him, it made him question how actively Moretti and his men were hunting. The presence of a newly discovered husband may have spurred them to intensify their search. At times he doubted his patience, fearing he was employing it as an excuse to be cautious. But, coming back around, he decided that caution was warranted, it would be devastating to blunder into a situation he had not anticipated and accidentally give her away.

And there was the problem. He was no longer certain of the edge delineating action from prudence. His hesitation unnerved him. He knew he was not the same since the stabbing. He pressed himself to heal mentally as well as physically. He caught himself reviewing his responses, comparing them to the past to see if his actions were consistent with those of the man he had been. His timing was off. He was thinking rather than reacting, and that was making him slow. While the one who draws second often wins, what if you fail to react? What if you fail to draw at all?

He thought about courage. It was a topic that had never before occurred to him, but then, he had never had cause to distrust it. With his courage in doubt, he began to question its source. These days courage seemed to come from a thing or a state of mind, a bottle or a full belly, for example, or maybe a good night's sleep when he didn't remember his dreams. He wondered if he could bank his courage for future access, to balance the grim moments when the pain in his side sucked it out, or when he doubted his judgment, his quickness, his aim. Was courage a pose? It never had been. Could he simulate courage and thereby bring it back? Did he dare test it now that it was no longer second nature?

He had neglected a chore, and that troubled him as well. He had planned to replace his bandanna, but so far he had not. He told himself it was due to time constraints, as he was busy hunting for Hightower. But he feared it was one more manifestation of his uncertainty. Without the bandanna, he might be less willing to go into action. He watched the street below. He was of two minds, and wondered which man he would be when the bear showed his face.

He did not know if Hightower frequented the Tall Boot, or if it merely served as the occasional meeting place. The bear might have been more likely to enter through the back, but there was no spot in the alley from where Longbaugh could watch without being seen. He was betting there was nothing to keep Hightower from using the front door if he happened to come from that direction. Longbaugh had been on the roof close to a week, convinced that sooner rather than later that day would come.

He did, on occasion, see Moretti's messenger, the slick in the good suit, but he was not interested in Moretti at this time.

Living on a tenement roof offered one other advantage in that it put time between Siringo and himself. Siringo was unlikely to give up, but he might be convinced, if his vanishing act carried on long enough, that Longbaugh had found his wife and left the city or had given up in order to evade arrest. Not likely, not even truly plausible, but maybe not impossible. He also appreciated the value of this location in that Han Fei had yet to find him.

Longbaugh had taken advantage of early mornings to scout the neighborhood. Gangsters were nowhere to be found at that hour, when the rising sun lit the faces of skyscrapers. Those boys were too busy dragging themselves home or sleeping it off. He learned the surrounding streets and alleys. He had tried to find the building where he had initially met Giuseppe Moretti, but so far had failed.

The day came when Hightower rambled down the sidewalk. No one could mistake that walk, those wide arm swings, and that deep, furry, uninhibited voice. Longbaugh smiled with his quarry in view, admiring the man's gregarious charm.

Longbaugh went down the narrow stairs and out onto the street. He watched passersby and looked for an appropriate candidate, one not yet inebriated, so that when Longbaugh threatened him, the threat would have the desired impact. He also wanted someone who was not a Tall

Boot regular, and therefore could not be a Hightower ally. Longbaugh cut his choice out of the herd, and bribed the man to go in and tell the bearlike creature at the bar that Mr. Place was outside. The candidate grinned, took the offered coin, and made a merry step toward the saloon where he would now drink for free. Longbaugh grabbed his shoulder in a calculated display of ferocity, drew him close, showed him the gun tucked in his belt and met his eye. The candidate returned his look with appropriate solemnity, and his sincere promise to fulfill his task convinced Longbaugh he would do that for which he had been paid.

AFTER HIGHTOWER verified that the man had said Mr. Place rather than Mrs. Place, he hurried out the back of the saloon into the alley, not bothering to look both ways as he hustled toward the side street where Longbaugh stepped out to block his path.

"You tip him?" said Longbaugh.

Hightower gurgled in fear, almost losing his balance.

"The man who told you I was waiting, did you tip him?"

Hightower shook his head no and collected himself enough to do a serviceable imitation of steadiness. He affected a blustery smile and shrugged. "These are the times that try men's souls."

Longbaugh resisted the urge to break his arm. There would be time for that later. He felt akin to his old self at that moment, but something held him back, and he hoped it was expedience rather than reticence. He hoped the bear would go for his gun or throw a punch or run, so he could test himself, so he could react. He reminded himself that this man had led him into a trap. He tried not to overthink it.

He took hold of Hightower's arm and led him to the street, down the block and around the corner, down another two blocks, and into a creditable saloon, one that Longbaugh had found during his early-morning scouts. He was not surprised that Hightower made no effort to get away. By now, he would be curious and working out his own plan. He guided Hightower to a small booth in back and used force to sit him down. He was immediately sorry, as his display of aggression had done nothing to frighten Hightower, while Longbaugh felt resurgent pain in his side. He frowned to cover his wince and sat opposite.

"Cozy," said Hightower, looking around. "I should get out more."

Longbaugh waited.

"Looks like you got a little stitch in your side."

Longbaugh stared and gave away nothing.

"So. Can I get a drink?"

Longbaugh glanced toward the bar and nodded. The bartender brought whiskeys. Hightower drank his and after it was gone, Longbaugh pushed over the one meant for him and Hightower drank that as well. Longbaugh imagined Hightower had his hand on a gun under the table.

Longbaugh continued to wait. He chose not to mention the night Hightower had set him up with Flexible and his friends. He was therefore surprised when Hightower brought it up himself. Of course, if pressed, he could deny it had been a trap. He could say those boys had it in for the tourist all along and had simply disobeyed him.

"There's a story making the rounds. Funny story, maybe you heard it. Got most of the boys on edge, so maybe not so funny to them. Of course, they're superstitious louts. You probably remember those punks, the ones jumped you in the alley?"

Longbaugh listened.

"The ones I pulled off you? You remember that, right? The way I saved your hide?"

Longbaugh listened.

"Well, something happened later that same night. With the timing, I thought maybe you would know something about it. But how could you? After all, here you are, flesh and blood."

Longbaugh listened.

"Can I get another drink?"

Longbaugh did not react.

Hightower shrugged and his thick-tongued words came out archly.

"If one isn't offered, I shall not pout." He took one of the empty glasses, drained the last drops into the other glass and angled that over his mouth for whatever dregs would fall.

"So those boys, Flexible and friends, said they'd had this encounter. Didn't name names, although they could have been embarrassed, considering how it turned out. They did say he wore some sort of mask. So they met this fellow in the street and made him an offer. But *this* fellow, well, he was different. He seemed somewhat put out and decided to resist. They did not find much to like in that. It's an intolerance they should probably be made aware of, one of their many faults. He drew a gun, this fellow, and before you say anything, let me point out it was their Christian duty to defend themselves. But here is where the story gets interesting. The boys said they shot him before he even fired. Not just shot him, but riddled him, dozens of hits, with their automatics, and you know those things don't miss much, but I tell you this and I am sincere, he just would—not—die. They did not believe their eyes. They had guns smoking in their hands, and there he stood on his own two feet. They were beginning to think there was something supernatural at play, and they were also beginning to feel a wee bit of the nerves."

Longbaugh listened.

"You could help here, a little grunt, a little nod, just to show you're paying attention."

Longbaugh offered neither.

"Well, there they were, practically unarmed as they had already emptied their guns into him, and he retaliated, he actually opened fire on them. How many spirits do you know carry a gun, much less know how to use it? It makes as much sense as, say, someone like you doing it. And this fellow, he was a deadeye, took them out one by one, a bullet apiece, and when he was done, they were in sore need of medical attention."

Longbaugh said nothing. At least one of them had been uninjured, but to correct him would be to give himself away. Maybe that's what Hightower had in mind.

"But that is not how the story ends. You remember Flexible? Well, he swears on a skyscraper built of Bibles that he got close enough to stab that fellow in the belly, and the fellow didn't flinch, didn't bleed, just lifted his finger and broke Flexible's nose and two front teeth. Flexible woke up to find his knife blade in the wall. Here he thought he'd stabbed a man in the flesh and he found out he'd stabbed a brick wall instead. Now they're all convinced he had to have been a ghost."

"A ghost," said Longbaugh.

"Otherwise they'd have made him one, if he'd ever been human in the first place."

"You know who they were after?"

Hightower was innocence incarnate. "Not a clue."

"A mystery," said Longbaugh.

"Better than a mystery, it's a damn spook story. He's a new legend, got the rest of the gang sleeping with their eyes open and cricks in their necks from looking over their shoulders, expecting the specter to come for them. Although with the ghost laying low the last few weeks, they're starting to get brave again."

Longbaugh considered him. Hightower knew. But he couldn't be sure, as the story made no sense, not if he'd survived bullets and stabbings. Until Hightower could make it make sense, he couldn't swear it had been Longbaugh.

Hightower also knew that Longbaugh knew Hightower had set him up.

"Why tell me?" said Longbaugh.

"No reason."

"Uh-huh."

Hightower chuckled. "I only know I'm not their ghost. Innocent as a puppy's nose."

That was the second time Hightower had used that expression, and Longbaugh could not decide if a puppy's nose was innocent by virtue of its curiosity, or, considering where it ventured and what it encountered, the least innocent thing on the planet.

He had yet to decide what to do about Hightower. He had knowledge Longbaugh did not, so for the time being he was prepared to pretend Hightower had not tried to send him to his death.

"So tell me: Why am I here, what can I do for you, Mr. Place?"

"Find my wife."

"Still looking for her?"

"What's your bargain with Moretti?"

"Like I told you, I promised, for a fee, to locate her, and as you can see, I'm not getting any richer."

"So we have the same goal."

Hightower scratched himself. "Although you're not likely to help me get Moretti his revenge."

Longbaugh said nothing.

"I do wonder why you're so intent on finding her," said Hightower.

"You and Moretti seem to share that question."

"Does she owe you money? Is her daddy rich? Do you need divorce papers signed because your mistress is with child?"

Longbaugh said nothing.

"Oh, now, wait just a pelican's breath, it can't be *that*, no, sir, not that easy. It isn't love, now, is it?"

Longbaugh said nothing.

"Jesus, Mary, and Joseph, it *is* love. It's love and it's been love the whole time. I tell you, it was right in front of my nose and I missed it. Serves me right for being a cynical bachelor. I'll be damned and go straight to Hell. Oh, don't worry, tourist, I am a sucker for love. And I'm going to help you, because, and I'll admit it without an ounce of shame, I'm a sentimental guy."

Longbaugh was skeptical. "You're going to help me."

"You found my weakness. *Amore.*"

"You'd give up a payday from Moretti?"

"A farthing, a pittance, barely worth a dice throw. I answer to a higher power."

In the end, Hightower's reason didn't matter. If he pointed Longbaugh in the right direction, whatever unpleasantness Hightower had in mind could be dealt with then.

Longbaugh thought to test Hightower's new sentimentality. "One thing. Were you the one after her when she ran off so suddenly?"

"Well, that was a while ago. It could have been anyone." Hightower began moving the empty glasses around in front of him. "Sure, Moretti wanted revenge because she'd been hiding Queenie, but he really lost his temper when she cut his cheek. Threatened to dynamite the boardinghouse she lived in. And Moretti has built his reputation by executing the extended families of his enemies. She was smart, she cut off contact with everyone she knew. It was like she put up a wall, I couldn't get a line on any of her people. I didn't even know about you."

Then Longbaugh understood. She no longer dared to write, and all letters from husband and sister were returned unopened so that Moretti would not know. It was either bad luck or poor timing that Etta's last letter to Mina had been intercepted. Etta had imagined Mina opening her door to some hired lug with a loaded shotgun. Mina had been lucky to get off with a warning. Etta had imagined Longbaugh stepping out of prison into the cross fire of Black Hand flunkies. She had been protecting him.

"Where does the trail begin?"

"Trail? What trail, there is no trail. She disappeared, she's gone. Like she never existed."

"Someone knows. There's a clue out there, somebody knows something."

"You tell me who and I'll talk to them." Longbaugh heard danger return to Hightower's voice for the first time that night.

"Queenie."

"Oh, tourist, you're barking up the wrong pussy. I talked to her, talked to her twice, and again on Sunday. She knows less than nothing, that pretty little head full of rags has been broom-swept of all intelligent matter."

"Then it's my turn."

"Think you can do better? Good luck, she's gone missing the last few weeks."

Longbaugh leaned in to flatter him. "*You* can find her."

Hightower was more than willing to be flattered. "Well, of course, I usually can, but I haven't bothered this time, not since Moretti lost interest."

"How do we start?"

"Now, tourist, let's not get overly excited . . ."

"Did you forget so soon? You're a sentimental guy, and this one's for love."

"Playing on my weakness. And I do love a happy ending. All right, tourist. We'll dig up Queenie. But lower your expectations, because she's not going to be able to help you."

11

Longbaugh continued to be conscious of his physical actions. He weighed his movements in advance, trying to leave nothing to chance, as he still did not trust that his muscles would respond the way they always had. He analyzed his walk and tried to affect the old stroll that would return him to fearlessness. He caught a glimpse of himself in a store window and his stride looked performed. He tried to walk without thinking, but when he did, his side ached and he started thinking again.

He forced himself to visit a department store on the Ladies' Mile and bought a new bandanna. It was too new, too stiff, and a color they called forest green, although it was the closest color to the original he could find. The color would age, but it would never approach the old one. It did not feel natural, but it was the one thing of his own he wore the first night of the Hightower pilgrimage.

Hightower had outfitted him in working man's clothes and said not to shave.

Longbaugh inspected the dirty shirt, the double-breasted reefer jacket and the shapeless slouch hat. "I wonder if Etta did this to escape Moretti."

"What, dress like a working stiff? Could explain how I lost her trail."

They met at the Hotel Algonquin, then started their search in the old Tenderloin area. He ordered nothing in the first bar. Hightower shook his head. "You order, you pay, you pretend to sip. Then put it down. Keep the bartender happy."

They continued throughout the night, visiting a series of bars. In one place, Hightower mentioned that they used to have a blind tiger. That night there was no tiger and no Queenie. Longbaugh's clothing, however, brought challenges from drunks in more than one bar. Hightower finally came clean, laughing while telling him that in the early nineties the righteous Reverend Parkhurst had hired a detective to take him on a sojourn to the seamier side of the city, and the detective had dressed the reverend in similar clothes. Parkhurst's ensuing sermons had famously exposed the city's underbelly. The following night, with Longbaugh back in his regular clothes, he and Hightower hit the dance halls, then visited bordellos in the days after that. He was relieved that the opportunistic Hightower did not take to calling him "reverend." Still no Queenie.

Longbaugh wondered aloud why they weren't looking at places on Fifth Avenue. Hightower laughed at him. "Fifth Avenue belongs to the rich," he said. "No Queenies there."

"How'd it get to be for the rich?"

"You mean, why aren't the rich living in their waterfront properties?"

"I don't remember any waterfront properties. Just docks."

"Exactly. Docks and warehouses. On both sides of the island. You know what Fifth Avenue is? The farthest you can get from the water."

They prowled streets and dark alleys, then ventured into deeply shadowed avenues under elevated train tracks. The shadows there bred fear and violence, a natural habitat for gangsters who lingered and attacked their prey without mercy. Hightower was on occasion recognized and sometimes welcomed, but usually merely tolerated. The one time Longbaugh was attacked, Hightower made quick work of the assailant. Hightower feigned nonchalance afterward, and Longbaugh wondered what it was Hightower needed from him, to have protected him that way.

Hightower did not mention Queenie by name as they questioned the locals. He played the part of an unlucky vendor attempting to rebuild his stable with "older" prostitutes. No one questioned his story, as there were plenty of bad ideas masquerading as wealth schemes, and there was no competition for the crone whore. The haunts of older prostitutes were uncovered, and Longbaugh and Hightower spent a series of nights in crawly rooms where half-naked women sprawled on dingy sheets, their backs and thighs dotted red with the bites of bedbugs.

The women, after donning exotic smiles, would grow churlish or tragic or both on discovering their visitors were not customers. After that, they did not mask the damage and desperation of their lives. Longbaugh wondered why these women did not merit the outrage of strikers who fought for better conditions. A naïve thought, perhaps, and while he knew the answer, the question lingered.

Queenie continued to be nowhere.

Longbaugh waited for Hightower to abandon the search out of weariness, but carried on as if he had weeks to burn. Longbaugh wondered if Moretti's desire to find Etta was so fierce that Hightower would continue this odd journey in the hope that Longbaugh's long shot was his best chance to find her. He studied the man, but Hightower's good humor never wavered. That was troubling.

A coincidence can on occasion appear supernatural, but Longbaugh understood that luck involved maximizing opportunities. It had worked in bank and train robberies, and it worked here. When a net is cast over a vast area, the chance of catching your prey increases. They met an aging prostitute old enough to be past pathetic and on the road back to respectable. When she learned of their quest, she reached for her long pipe and a small brown cube wrapped in waxed paper. She loaded the cube and smoked in front of them. She smoked quickly, and he knew her opium tolerance was high and she would need to smoke a good amount to arrive at the sought-after euphoria. Longbaugh asked if many of the girls smoked and the old woman chuckled at being labeled a girl. Even in her altered state, she maintained the dignity of a dowager. But Longbaugh and Hightower now had a new destination. They were going to Chinatown.

THEY CONVINCED the myriad owners of opium dens that they were not police. Each owner in turn had immediately offered them a bribe, and while Hightower would have been happy to accept, Longbaugh had waved them off.

They found Queenie on their third stop. The interior of the den was kept in deliberate gloom, with individual pallets for the good spenders and bunks for the rest. Longbaugh breathed in opium smoke, which had a sweetish smell, flowery, pungent, and amiable, and was not like tobacco. Hightower stayed back, hat pulled low so that Queenie would not recognize him. She sat on the side of a wood-framed lower bunk, vein-marbled feet flat on the floor. A quiet Chinese girl prepared a pipe. Longbaugh wondered about Queenie's tolerance and how long she could remain lucid. He made eye contact, but the quiet girl did not slow her preparations. An older woman snarled Mandarin at the girl, who then worked more quickly.

Longbaugh pushed in to press the situation, kneeling by the side of the bunk.

"Aw, honey," said Queenie when he invaded her space, "you come on back later, I'll take care of you then. But right now I got this other thing." She patted his knee.

He put his hand on her hand to keep it there. "Been looking just for you."

"Y'have? Now ain't you the sweetest." She slid her hand out from under his. She was conspiratorial. "This ain't the place. We'll go some-where later and I'll show you a good time. You want a pipe, honey? Make the time go faster."

"Not right now. How long you been here?"

"Oh, few days."

Longbaugh put his hand out to stop the quiet girl from giving Queenie the pipe. The girl's eyes flashed.

"That's mine!" said Queenie harshly.

The quiet girl looked triumphant.

"I just want a minute to talk."

"You give it here, that's *mine!*"

Longbaugh backed off. The quiet girl held out the pipe to Queenie with two hands. Queenie laid her head on the pallet and curled her feet under. The quiet girl set the pipe between Queenie's lips and danced a flame over the bowl and Queenie took a deep inhale. She leaned away, then came suddenly back to the stem and sucked in a second time to get every last essence, pressing the smoke down into her lungs. He waited until she exhaled.

"Talk to me."

"I'm a little busy, honey."

"Talk to me and I'll buy you a second bowl."

"What kind?"

"Just stay awake."

Queenie was lucid when she spoke to the quiet girl. "No *yen pock*, I want the *yen shee*."

"*Yen shee* is the box that holds the ashes," said the quiet girl condescendingly.

"You know what I mean. No rooster blend, I want the other, the good stuff."

"*Li yuen*," said the quiet girl.

"That!" said Queenie. She turned a belligerent eye on Longbaugh to see if he would agree. He nodded to the quiet girl.

"Sucker," said Hightower softly.

"Okay, honey." Queenie's manner changed so quickly that he knew her earlier act had been put on to be rid of him. "We talk now."

The quiet girl held up one finger and Longbaugh put a dollar for the *li yuen* in her hand. The quiet girl looked at it and went away.

"Key to happiness is good health and a bad memory," said Queenie. "This is how I get back my bad memory."

Longbaugh wanted her memory intact. "Can't you remember without feeling bad?"

"I used to try to forget so he wouldn't know. I knew he could read my mind, see? He sees everything, of course, but I had this idea, if I could fool *myself*, then he'd be fooled when he went in my head."

Hightower's eyebrows rose and he made a mock sign of the cross over his crotch. At first Longbaugh had thought she was talking about Moretti, but realized she must have been talking about her god.

"Some days it got so intense that I thought he wanted me to forget so it'd be easier for him to forgive. But nowadays I can't remember what I did. Strange, too, 'cause just when you think he wants you to be good, he gets imaginative."

Longbaugh reacted to her peculiar theology.

"He had real different ideas about what to do, like he knew the bad things I'd done and wanted to try 'em."

Longbaugh sat upright. This was not theology. If it was, then her notion of a higher being was unique. And deviant.

"I guess he got tired of me, although once I'd been his heart's desire. I let Joe get in the way. I always let Joe get in the way."

Nothing theological there. Longbaugh half smiled at his own misunderstanding.

"Tell me about him."

"Which one? My Englishman?"

"Start there."

"He was somethin'. Did you know he survived the *Titanic*? I coulda been in love with him, or at least I tried to be. I coulda been a countess or a duchess or somethin' English. *I* coulda survived the *Titanic*!" The opium was softening the edges of her words. "But let me tell ya somethin', honey, he wasn't like Joe."

"Giuseppe."

"Yeah, Joe-zeppi. He hated when I called him that. Fidgy was nice, but . . . That's my Englishman, Fidgy. Elegant. And too nice. Except when he was readin' my mind. I forgot who I was when I was with

Fidgy. He could make the past seem like it never happened. He said stuff like, 'When you don't live in the past, you travel beyond guilt and just live.' He talked like that. But with an accent."

Longbaugh wondered if her memories of Fidgy were an attempt to convince herself she had been important. He looked at her face, the harsh lines and hurt eyes, and remembered Lillian had told him she was not yet thirty years of age.

"Ah, here it comes." Her body relaxed. "I love to forget. Only thing I remember is how pretty I was."

Fishing for a compliment.

"You're still beautiful."

"Aw, honey, ain't you a charmer. I *was* pretty. Ain't no wonder Joe don't want me now. Joe don't want me, Fidgy don't want me."

"Where is Fidgy?"

"Back in England."

"Did Etta know him?"

Queenie flashed anger. "Fidgy was mine. Even Joe didn't know about him. He was my secret."

"But you trusted Etta. Maybe you mentioned it to her, some late night when you needed to share your memories so they wouldn't get lost."

"No. Never once." But inside of a breath, her adamance toppled. "Although I might have. He always had such beautiful guns, did I tell you about that? He was a collector. Kept them in wooden boxes, polished antiques, even the boxes were polished, beautiful guns."

"Why did Etta help you?"

"She saw Joe hit me once. Why do I always gotta fall in love with someone's not nice to me?"

"Etta, Queenie. Talk about Etta."

"At least *she* thought I was worth saving. Although she had dreams too, mostly about helpin' people. She got me that job, away from Joe."

"Needle trade?"

"Yeah, but then there was a fire."

"She saved your life."

"I couldn't be alone in my place after that, so she made sure I stayed hid from Joe."

"Where did she hide you?"

"Oh, on Henry Street. Joe came lookin', too. I was hidin' and heard him yellin' at her. Etta said she didn't know where I was. She lied pretty good for a nice girl. But in the end I only had one place to go. She sent Joe away, then went to find me, but I was already gone. I felt kinda bad about that." She yawned. "I think she got mad, since she went back to see Joe." Queenie nestled in and closed her eyes.

Longbaugh pressed. "She went to see Joe." He wanted her side of this story.

"To find me, yeah." Her eyes fluttered open, closed.

"So you went back to him."

"Had to, honey. Had to."

"Had to? But you told her you wanted to get away from him, you promised you'd stay away for your own good. She came back to face Joe to find out if you'd betrayed her trust."

"I couldn't help that, honey. It was Joe."

He watched her conveniently float away, as she didn't care to face this. "Don't you stop now, not if you want that second bowl."

She opened her eyes reluctantly, forcing herself up on one elbow. "Hey, listen, it's what she wanted to hear. But I loved Joe. How could I help myself, he came all the way to Henry Street to get me back. It was so sweet."

He came all the way to Henry Street so he could dump you in the ash can, thought Longbaugh.

"But when Etta went to see him at the end, lookin' for me, that proved to Joe she was the one, so he had to teach her."

"You disappointed her."

"Did the best I could. Didn't want to hurt her feelings."

"She saved you from the Triangle fire."

"Yeah, but Joe said she also got me in it. I wouldn'ta been there at all if it wasn't for her."

Longbaugh backed off. "Okay."

"Not like I didn't give it a chance. I worked there for months. I was real good with that new sewing machine, three thousand stitches a minute—old pedal ones only do thirty-four."

"Could have been your calling."

"Nah. Not after what I did. A couple years before me'n some of the girls got hired to beat on strikers. So now I'm workin' with this girl I'd smacked with an umbrella. She's right on my aisle. I always turned my head, even though I don't think she knew me."

"You might've fit in over time."

"First I hit her with an umbrella, then she dies in the fire."

That brought him up.

"They just wasn't my people. They called guys like Joe *shtarkers*—I had to ask what it means. Tough guys. Yeah. That's Joe, all right. A *shtarker*. And I was his whore."

He was losing her again, and maybe a little of himself in the opium smoke. She rolled away, but Longbaugh pushed one last time.

"You know where she is?"

"Don't bother me, honey. I'm restin'."

"Etta, where is she?"

"Well, if he ain't killed her, she's probably hidin'."

"So he still wants to kill her?" Longbaugh looked at Hightower when he said it. Hightower apparently had an itch on his backside and was digging under his trousers to reach it.

"She cut his face. Never saw no woman do that, not to a Sicilian. They don't forget that stuff."

There was no reason to continue to torment her. He had emptied her of information, and her current condition made her useless.

"Okay, we're done. You can sleep now, Q."

Queenie came around from the wall and sat upright. "You call me Q?"

"Did I?"

"You know my sister."

Longbaugh nodded, acknowledging the human connection. "I met her."

"Whatta you doin' to her, you bastard, you fuck my sister?" Longbaugh sat back. "You keep your filthy hands off her. I thought you was nice. You here to compare us? Well, stay away from her and go to Hell or, so help me God, I'll kill you."

Hightower pulled Longbaugh away.

"Come along, Romeo, you've done enough."

At the door, Longbaugh stopped to face the quiet Chinese girl. "You give her that second bowl, that *li yuen.*"

Hightower made a face. "What the hell for? She'll never know the difference."

"She did what I asked." He turned to the girl and said, "Make sure."

"You think that helps, feeding her addiction?" said Hightower.

"Not like she's one missed bowl from salvation."

Longbaugh pushed by him and out to the street.

The sun was strong, the day hot. Hightower laughed with self-congratulatory glee. "Probably shouldn't tell your wife what you were doing with Q's sister. By the way, where is this adolescent lovely? She look anything like the young Queenie?"

Longbaugh showed no emotion. "Find your own way to Hell, Hightower."

"Hah! You sound just like her."

Longbaugh blinked in the sun.

"You're feeling it, aren't you, tourist?"

"What?"

"You can't help but get that feeling in the den, all that smoke."

"I'm fine."

Longbaugh looked across the street and was surprised to see Han Fei leaning against a banister. For a moment he wondered if Han Fei was an opium-induced illusion. He let his eyes move past, pretending he hadn't seen him so that Hightower wouldn't be alerted.

"Okay, tourist, you're doing fine."

"Enough of this. I'll see you tomorrow."

"Yes, sir, good time to sleep it off. I, however, will corrupt myself with an imbibe-able."

"Don't be sore, even your friends need a little time away from you."

"Are you my friend, tourist?" Hightower displayed a sarcastic grin.

"Without a doubt."

Longbaugh walked away from Hightower, then glanced back to see that he was still going in the opposite direction. Longbaugh continued on, half a block, but Hightower seemed unconcerned with his actions, now disappearing around a corner. He took the chance and came back to Han Fei.

"I think I found her," said Han Fei.

"Thanks, but we were just talking to her."

"Your wife. I think maybe I found her."

12

———✦———

They were better than halfway across the Brooklyn Bridge before Han Fei turned to scan the expanse behind them. He stepped up on an empty bench to get a better look. A white woman tsked at the Chinese boy taking liberties on her bridge, but Longbaugh met her eye with a cold stare and, startled, she scurried along, whispering to her companion.

Longbaugh kept his eyes looking ahead, toward Brooklyn. "See him?"

"No."

"Hard to miss on foot."

"It's why we walk," said Han Fei with the certainty of a mother or a schoolmistress.

"Unless he saw us walking and took the train and he's riding with his feet up." Another train to Brooklyn ran by close, flapping the fabric of Longbaugh's trousers. He tried to see faces in the passing windows, but that was impossible from this angle. Longbaugh thought, *He's waiting on the other side.*

Longbaugh was worried. Despite Hightower's having said he was off to get a drink, Longbaugh knew he had to be somewhere nearby, he had to have come back to follow him, and Longbaugh didn't like that he still couldn't locate him. How could he know when to lose him if he couldn't find him in the first place?

He was in a hurry to get to her, but agreed when Han Fei advised caution. Any recklessness at this point could expose her. If she was there now, she'd be there in an hour, or a day, or a week. Now that he had a location, her safety was the priority.

He tried to distract his mind, looking at the bridge around him, a structure of mature beauty. Fencing in the center footpath and creating a kind of steel intimacy was a row of vertical cables running up to connect with the thick main cable that curved its way to the full height of the bridge's towers. The vertical cables kept pedestrians from walking into rushing trains as tracks ran close on both sides. On the outside of the tracks were cable cars, and beyond those, private vehicles.

They were closer to Brooklyn than Manhattan, and crossing the East River freed them of the smoke that grimed both banks. The briny air scrubbed any residual opium smoke trapped in his nose.

Han Fei broke in on his thoughts. "You talk to him like you trust him."

Longbaugh was sorry to hear his jealousy. "Han Fei, I wouldn't trust him to resist a bad oyster. But he knows things I need to know."

"Like?"

He decided it best not to answer.

The pleasure in his surroundings retreated with Han Fei's discomfort. His thoughts returned to her, the colors of the world receding, having been overly vivid with Han Fei's news and opium-fueled hope. Better to tamp down expectations, as he had been willfully ignoring the warning voices inside his head. Han Fei may have believed he had located her, but he had not seen her, and would not have known her if he had. Longbaugh also thought about the circumstance of her living as a recluse. That suggested something else might be wrong. Perhaps she was in a desperate emotional state and wanted no one to find her, not even her husband.

Han Fei had discovered her through a rumor about a woman who had shuttered herself in a rented room for months. Impoverished squatters dared not leave a condemned building even for water or food, as their spot would immediately be taken, but cloistered behavior was unheard of for immigrants. Immigrants struggled to improve their situations, and the moment they had saved enough to move to a better neighborhood, they were gone. Han Fei had investigated and found the rumor true, but went to find Longbaugh only after he learned she had communicated by a basket attached to a clothesline and signed her notes with the letter *E*.

Longbaugh was wise to himself; he knew he had every reason to want to believe it was his wife, but even with that prejudice in mind, when he put the pieces together, it all made independent sense. Etta was afraid of Moretti, so she had chosen a place to hide that was outside of Moretti's territory. In case the Black Hand somehow got lucky, she had stayed off the streets so as not to show her face. And then there was the use of the letter *E*. It was not only the first letter in her name. She knew Longbaugh would be tracking her, and she knew along the way that Longbaugh would have learned that Queenie's sister used the letter *Q* when referring to her. He would have put the two together. *Q* and *E*. Here was the sort of clue worthy of her—subtle yet specific.

He looked back again for Hightower, combing the bridge with his eyes. If Hightower were to learn of her location, he would go to Moretti, and Etta would find herself knee-deep in Black Hands. The bridge bristled with pedestrians, it would not take a Pinkerton to keep up with them. Nevertheless, the sizable Hightower would have stood out. Longbaugh later realized he had been so focused on the one man that he had neglected to look for anyone else.

"You were after that Queenie."

"That's so."

"Why not come to me?"

"Not sure where to find you."

"No, you were testing me. See if I could find *you*."

"Okay."

"Your friend's looking, too."

"Siringo? For Queenie?"

"No, cowboy, for you."

"Where is he?"

"Watching the boardinghouse. Asking about your wife."

They reached the Brooklyn terminal and split up to search for Hightower. They met back at the entrance and expanded to the street, scrutinizing carriages and motorcars, circling them, looking underneath, then peering in automobile windows. They split again, circled to probe shadows, side streets, doorways, alleys, then returned to reconnect. The more they looked and did not find him, the more Longbaugh's concentration faded. He was ready to see her.

"Take me there."

"Cowboy. A smart man could still be watching us. Maybe we missed him. Maybe we look again. And this *E*, maybe she's your wife. Or maybe not. Maybe you shouldn't be so sure."

"You're right. I completely understand your hesitation. Now take me there."

Han Fei gave in.

They hailed a cab and Han Fei directed the driver. Longbaugh was glad that the man drove as if he was insane, swerving, stop-starting, speeding up only to suddenly brake, playing chicken with pedestrians and trolleys. He decided that anyone who might be following them was likely to lose them.

Han Fei had the cab stop a few blocks from their destination, and they walked the rest of the way. Her street was delirious with traffic, as trolleys came from everywhere. Longbaugh and Han Fei stepped forward, sideways, adjusted, slowed, and rushed. Longbaugh looked at the crosshatched streetcar tracks embedded in the cobblestones and wondered how the trolleys avoided creating metal monuments at every intersection.

Longbaugh noted yet another in a series of advertisements.

"That's the twelfth sign I've seen for base ball."

"Brooklyn Robins." He shook his head. "Forget them. You want base ball? Come back to Manhattan. We'll go see my Highlanders . . . only . . ."

Longbaugh was amused. "Only?"

"Only they changed their name." He was very unhappy. "To the Yankees. What kind of name is *that*?"

Han Fei stopped in the middle of the sidewalk. "We're here." Longbaugh looked around. Han Fei pointed to a corner building that was very like every other building. "Up there. Second floor. See the corner? Count four windows in."

Dozens, no, scores, of clotheslines crisscrossed above the street, waving the neighborhood flags, drying laundry hanging in a random palette of colors, shapes, and sizes, creating a sky so full of flutter that it was difficult to pick out that particular window, and then to see that a clothesline ran from this side directly to the window and all the way inside. The curtains were drawn, so no one could see in.

"We going up?"

"Talk to the woman who helps her. Make friends."

Han Fei led him upstairs to the woman's door on the second floor across from E's place. Longbaugh knocked. No answer. They went back out to the sidewalk to wait.

They wandered among the dozens of carts, and Longbaugh was again impressed by what could be sold on the street, from vegetables to rugs to medicinal tonics to sheet music. Within half an hour, Han Fei elbowed Longbaugh to point out a woman in a yellow dress heading their way. The woman was round and soft, and slow and deliberate, carrying heavy shopping bags. The yellow dress made her look like a stuffed canary.

"Introduce me."

Han Fei shrugged. "I don't know her."

Longbaugh was surprised. "You don't know her? You put all this together from watching the street?"

"It's your wife, you talk to her."

Longbaugh was not prepared. He tried to think on his feet as she approached, but too much was at stake. His mind went blank. She waddled close to them and was about to pass by when Han Fei made a high-pitched noise of anxiety in the back of his throat. Longbaugh stepped forward.

"Ahh, excuse me, ma'am."

The woman stopped, turned. "Ma'am? Ain't heard *ma'am* in a coon's age."

"Didn't mean to be rude."

"Ma'am ain't rude." She set down her shopping bags and rubbed her forearms. "That ain't your Chink, is it?" she said accusingly.

"Not mine in the sense that he—"

"Don't know this *yutz*," said Han Fei, moving off theatrically. But he slipped back to stand behind her where she couldn't see him.

"Do something for you?" said the woman.

"The name's . . ." and he hesitated. Should he be Longbaugh, Alonzo, Place, or someone else? He often made that decision on the spot, when cornered by the law. But here something more was at stake. He had to anticipate the name Etta was using. If he got it wrong and later tried to explain that he was her husband, it would sound like a scam. "Name's Harry."

"Well, Mr. Harry, you can call me Phyllis. Or ma'am." She laughed at her own joke.

He decided to be direct. If she was protecting the second floor shut-in, he'd find another way.

"You're the neighborhood Samaritan."

"Well . . ."

"Yes you are, helping a woman in need." He pointed at the window across the street.

Han Fei angled his head skeptically. Maybe too direct? Longbaugh stared over his head to ignore him.

"I try to do what any decent God-fearing woman would do." She looked him up and down. "Now, I know you ain't the landlord. And you sure ain't no real estate tycoon."

"Lucky me."

"What kinda trouble she in?"

"No trouble. Don't even know her name."

"Then I would be confused."

"Looking for a missing woman. I heard your friend doesn't come out."

"Been a couple months now. No. More. And you still ain't said who you are."

"Harry."

She shook her head condescendingly and waited. Han Fei looked away, to avoid watching him topple in failure.

"I was asked to find a friend of the family," said Longbaugh. "She's lost, and when I heard about your shut-in, I thought it might be her."

"I don't think this one's lost. Could be a little haywire."

"Hiding?"

"Life gets mean for some folks. Different folks handle it different. Not for me to judge." Phyllis looked at the shopping bags at her feet, ready to move along. Han Fei made an urgent nod to get on with it.

"She have a name?"

"Signs her notes with the letter *E*."

"Have you seen her?"

Phyllis shrugged a noncommittal yes. "She looks like people."

"How old?"

"Thirties."

"You know what the *E* is for?"

"Ethel, I think. Unless it's Evelyn. Not Eleanor, she don't look like no Eleanor. Could be Elizabeth."

"Not Etta?"

"That's a funny name."

The name Etta would have been too specific, particularly if she was actively hiding. Phyllis had initially said Ethel, which was Etta's real name. He moved on. "How does it work?"

"When she needs something she sends a note in the basket, with money in the envelope. I ain't no charity, after all. Mostly she waits till the laundry's dry, but not always. Then I got to take it all down and send her things over." She was not happy about the extra work. "And if you ask me, she could use a new envelope, this one's thin as an old pillowcase." She shrugged. "I wish she didn't want cans, my arms get sore. I ain't so young as I used to be. Probably should charge for delivery." She frowned as she thought her words didn't sound quite right. "Don't get me wrong, Mr. Harry, I'm an honest woman, I don't take no advantage, although I could, Lord knows, she never offers for my trouble. But I say to myself, Phyllis, I say, it's hard enough already being her. There but for the grace of God."

"How do you get the cans to her?"

"In the basket, like I said."

"Not to her door?"

"Did once, but she got mad and wouldn't open it."

"So you've spoken to her."

"Sure, and she said use the basket."

"You have one of her notes?"

Phyllis patted a dress pocket. She drew out a flimsy envelope. Inside was a folded scrap of paper.

"From this morning."

The handwriting was raw, nervous, more scratch than penmanship. But a few cursive letters could have been made by Etta's hand. It was two years since her last letter, and any number of things may have affected it—injury, alcohol, madness. Or she might have disguised it intentionally.

He looked to see the things in the shopping bags on the sidewalk. "Any of this hers?"

"Most of it. Sending it over soon's I get upstairs."

"I'd like to add a note." Han Fei nodded, and Longbaugh was glad for his sanction.

"Can't see why I shouldn't let you, Mr. Harry. You seem a nice, po-lite fellow. Can't promise she'll respond."

"If she is who I think she is, she will."

"If it ain't, here's hoping you didn't come too far."

Phyllis loaned him a pencil and he turned over E's note to write on the blank side.

"Ask her if maybe she wants to start doing some of her own shopping," said Phyllis with a sniff.

Longbaugh considered the words he might use. His eyes ran to the second-floor window. Curtains shifted with the breeze and he thought he saw someone. He looked at the blank paper. It was important to get it right. Then he knew it wasn't. If Etta was there, any words would do.

He wrote:

E.

It's Harry. I'm here.

He folded it and offered it to Phyllis. She nodded for him to follow, looked directly at the shopping bags on the sidewalk, and left them there. Longbaugh stifled his amusement and carried the bags after her. He nodded at Han Fei to see if he would join them. Han Fei shook his head with an emphatic no. The bigoted Samaritan would never allow him to cross her threshold.

Longbaugh followed Phyllis up the stairs, rebalancing the shopping bags as she searched for her key at the door. He blinked at the time it took her to find the key, then get the key into the lock, then get the door open. He followed her into her kitchen. Phyllis took her own sweet time sorting fruit and vegetables from cans. He looked out Phyllis's window, hoping to see past the curtain into E's rooms. Laundry hung from her clothesline, and he had to keep moving his head, as the wind moved the drying clothes and blocked his view. This time he saw that, among other garments hanging over the street, there were shirtwaists drying on the lines. He looked back to watch Phyllis arrange the cans in the basket to balance the weight. He watched her rearrange the cans. He bit his tongue. Finally she was done and he added his note, then covered everything with a napkin and tucked it around the cans. Then it was time to pull in her laundry and take it off the line. There were only a few things, but he saw that some were large, intimate items. He did not offer to help. She leaned out the window and pulled off the wooden clothespins, and he was grateful that she piled her things without folding them. She tied the basket to the clothesline and he stepped up and pulled on the rope loop to send the basket over the busy street to her window.

Phyllis patted his arm. "Not so fast, you'll tip it."

She took over from him and the whole business slowed down. He watched the basket's rhythmic passage above the carts, the neighbors, the traffic, toward a place where the world had been kept out. He watched the basket grow smaller among the hanging clothing on other clotheslines, as it passed over her sidewalk and neared her building, watched it clear the windowsill and part the curtains. Phyllis stopped pulling when the basket was well inside and could no longer be seen.

The curtains settled. Now they moved only when nudged by a breeze. He waited. An automobile driver sounded his horn at a hound who had stretched out in the middle of the street. A deliveryman unloaded boxes in front of a pharmacy. A trolley clanged. Another man called his dog, who was finding the middle of the street somewhat noisy with that horn blowing in his ears.

As he waited, he decided he was being overcautious, he would stop all this nonsense, march across the street, up the stairs, and knock on her door. He would convince her of his identity and she would open up to him. It was what he should have done in the first place, this entire exercise was unnecessary. If Etta was there, then she wanted him to come for her. This adventure with Phyllis was just more overthinking.

Phyllis seemed to read his mind. "Give her time. She'll get around to sending thanks, but sometimes it's a while. I think she puts the cans up first. Generally, I brew a little tea, and by the time it's cool enough to drink, the basket's back. You want tea?"

"No, thanks." His eyes moved to Han Fei, down on the sidewalk. Han Fei was looking at the entryway to E's building across the street.

Longbaugh did not know what to do. Every passing minute caused him to doubt that Etta was there. He looked again at Han Fei, wondering if his young friend was right and this E might not be his wife. Han Fei continued to stare at the building's front door. Longbaugh caught something in Han Fei's intensity and looked there as well. He could not see what Han Fei saw, with the angle and shadow. Han Fei turned his head and their eyes met. Longbaugh was surprised by the boy's anxious expression. His focus now split between actively waiting for the basket and wondering what had unnerved Han Fei. His eyes went to the second-floor window. Nothing had changed. His eyes went to the entryway. This time he saw someone move in there. Not Hightower. But someone familiar.

Han Fei called up, a warning: "Cowboy—"

"Coming down," said Longbaugh.

"See him?"

"I see someone."

"Know him?"

"Couldn't say."

"Not the big one."

Longbaugh put his hand up to hold that thought and ran from Phyllis's kitchen and down the stairs. He came out onto the street and looked into the entry of E's building. Whoever it was remained in shadow. Then, for an instant, the shadow was backlit by the flicker of a match, and Longbaugh saw the young man's face illuminated as he used the match to light something. The young man looked up and threw the thing over his head, as if he stood at the foot of a staircase. The young man turned and came out quickly, looked around, and registered Longbaugh's direct gaze. The young man jolted. In that first moment, he thought the young man ran because he had been recognized. He knew him all right, Black Hand, the tall, lanky pimply one. Longbaugh had neglected to shoot him that night because he was reminded of Billy Lorigan. The bullet he had aimed over that pimpled head had sent him running away, in just the way he was running now. Longbaugh took a step after him and froze. Remembering Etta and the basket.

He looked at the second-story window. Curtains fluttered. It was not the breeze. Something was happening. The basket pushed through the curtains and out over the street, jerking along on the clothesline.

The instant before it happened, he knew, as the basket inched, he knew, as he looked at the young man running, he knew, he knew the flicker and he knew what had been thrown at the second-floor landing, but before he could turn and run, he was clapped to the ground as a huge invisible hand pressed his body against the sidewalk and held him flat. Smoke and flame shot out the windows, an obscene yellow-and-gray tongue, the closest laundry flying sideways. The end of Phyllis's clothes-line was blown free and momentarily arched high in the air like the curl of a whip, the basket shivering, suspended, then all of it dropped straight down, along with splinter-projectiles of brick and glass. Rolling to his belly to protect himself, Longbaugh twisted his chest toward the second floor, arm up against incoming shards, mouth open to warn her, too late now that the dynamite had hurled everything out onto the street. Any garments still pinched by clothespins now hung limply, helplessly burn-ing and waiting to fall.

The street froze, followed by pandemonium as vendors rushed their carts in all directions. A few people ran toward the blast, but most ran the other way. He charged the building's entry, where a cloud rose out of the doorframe like cigarette smoke from an open mouth. He dove into a dense wall of fume through which he could neither see nor breathe. After a few bullheaded steps into darkness, he fell to his knees, coughing, eyes streaming, lungs burning for air. He tried to turn back but he had lost his sense of direction. He crawled toward where the light was brightest. A hand grabbed him and pulled him in the other direc-tion, and he was back out the door, on the street, where life was visible. He did not know the man who had saved him, and although he looked around later, he did not see him again. He thought about the light he had crawled toward and realized it was something burning.

He saw the wide-open mouth of the crying baby before the sound punched its way through the oatmeal mush in his ears, saw the dog frantically barking before hearing its sharp yaps, saw the expression of terror on the face of a woman before he heard her screams. Small piles of laundry blackened and curled on the street as the flames gradually went out. It did not appear that great damage had been done down here, despite the litter of detritus, that the neighbors' responses were more about the shock of having their private lives butt up against impossible violence.

He looked up. Smoke was clearing around the building, revealing a hole in the sky of flags, and beyond that he saw blue with occasional clouds. He looked to the damage of the second-floor room, where no one could have survived. He himself was stunned, emotionally numb, as now he was convinced it had been Etta. He felt something on his cheek and touched it to find tears. His cool intellect determined that his eyes watered to clear smoke and debris, and as he thought it, he knew it to be only partly true, as an expanding hole of mourning spread beneath him and consumed his intellect and walled him in, rising so quickly over his head that he expected it to fold over and swallow him in darkness. He saw the basket on fire near the gutter. Any note she may have written in response was now ash, the last chance to know if it had been his wife. On the far sidewalk, Phyllis spoke to a policeman. She apparently had not seen him there in the gutter, even as she looked wide-eyed in his direction. Through the bloated deafness in his ears he thought he heard her say, "He was just there. I think he went inside." He may have been reading her lips.

Grief choked him, dragging a heavy cloak of apathy down on his limbs. Whatever interest Longbaugh had had in what might come next had been blown to shreds. Police rushed in from all directions, and his animal instinct for survival filled him as he looked for an escape. But just as quickly that instinct deserted him, and he fell back to apathy. The weight was too massive, he could not rouse his body to save himself because he had lost the desire to care. They could have him, the police, Siringo, anyone. If she was gone, then what difference did it make? He would remain there in his immobile gloom, and when they came to ask questions, he would tell them all of it, and they could have the rest of his wasted, lonely, useless life, because why the hell not? It had been just a matter of time, she had evaded the fire at Triangle, but not this one. He came alert for a heartbeat and realized he had been staring at something on the street beyond the basket. As he cocked his head and focused he saw it was a soft lump of clothing, not fallen laundry but human, with a shoe and legs and arms, and he recognized Han Fei, with his face down in the street. Anger rose in his gorge, the lethargy of surrender abandoning him. He refused to believe he could lose two of them in the same blast, refused. He lurched to his feet and was staggered by the resurgent pain in his side. He drew a full breath and strength gradually returned to his legs. He walked, a wooden man becoming flesh. He knelt down by the body. Han Fei's back and hair were white with ash and debris. Longbaugh brushed much of it away and rolled him over carefully, expecting the worst. Han Fei rested in peaceful silence, Longbaugh falling again under that dark cloak, heart sinking to the street, until Han Fei's body tensed, seized, his eyes jerked open, and he sneezed and coughed. Longbaugh laughed aloud.

He spoke and barely heard his own words through the thrum in his ears. "Can you move?"

Han Fei squinted at him, blinked a half dozen times, moved his tongue around the inside of his mouth, then spit out something black. He shrugged.

"Try your fingers."

Han Fei moved his fingers, then his hands and arms.

"Good, well done." Han Fei smiled as if the compliment was for a major accomplishment. "Now feet."

Han Fei wiggled his toes under shoe leather, then made circles with both his feet. He bent his left leg to bring up one knee.

Longbaugh looked up. Phyllis waved at him from across the street, "Mr. Harry, Mr. Harry!" He scooped Han Fei up and carried him away from Phyllis. He stopped to look down into the burning basket. If there had been a note, it existed no longer, as even the cans were scorched. Longbaugh turned in a circle looking for Hightower. He did not see him.

They sat side by side on a train crossing the Brooklyn Bridge back to Manhattan, Longbaugh propping up the boy in a seated position, leaning him against his side. His hearing was improving, particularly in his right ear. They exited the train but Han Fei faltered and Longbaugh picked him up and carried him to Doyers Street in Chinatown. Han Fei drifted in and out of consciousness, but came awake long enough to guide Longbaugh to a bright blue door. Longbaugh carried him up narrow stairs to his family's rooms. His mother bubbled and clucked, calling out in rapid Chinese through an open window to her sister, Han Fei's auntie, at another open window in a different apartment across the narrow air shaft. The room then swarmed with women, now giving orders, now carrying tubs of water and assorted ointments. Longbaugh stayed long enough to see that Han Fei was in good hands, and he slipped out. He reached the street but met Han Fei's auntie rushing toward him carrying bandages and towels. He nodded to her and tried to vacate the doorway to let her through, but she blocked his path.

"He'll be fine," said Longbaugh. "Nothing broken."

She took one of the towels and reached for his face. He flinched, his startled head jerking backward, but she persisted and he held his ground and let her come. The towel met his cheek and she wiped his face. He saw blood on the towel when she took it away.

"You're not cut," said Han Fei's auntie, inspecting his skin. "Someone else's blood."

"Ah," he said stupidly, and wondered whose. "You should probably take those inside." He again tried to leave.

"George speaks of you."

"George?"

"My nephew."

"His name is George?"

"George Washington Chen. My sister—his mother—wanted him to be as American as possible. Did he not tell you his name?"

"He said Han Fei."

"Han Feizi? He called himself Han Feizi, the philosopher?"

"Uh, no, just Han Fei."

"The *zi* is a title, it means 'master.'" She laughed to herself. "Very like George, he wouldn't presume to have earned that title. And so like contrary George to go the other way, all the way back to China."

"I don't understand."

"He was born here, so he is American. But he struggles in school. My guess is he wanted a name with strength."

"Wait, struggles? He's smart as an owl."

"The children tease him for being a Chinese named after the first president."

"And this Han Fei was strong? Sorry, Feizi."

"You would not understand. It is Chinese."

"Try."

"Legalism."

"You're right. I don't understand."

"Han Feizi believed people were bad, evil by nature, and you need harsh laws to control them. He was very harsh himself."

"George is a strange little guy."

"How did he get hurt?"

"Too close to a bomb."

"Your bomb?"

"No."

"Someone trying to kill you?"

"No."

"I see." She gave that some thought. "Why did you bring him back?"

"You mean why did a white man bring a Chinese boy all the way back to Chinatown?"

She held her ground and looked for the answer in his face.

"I like him," said Longbaugh.

Han Fei's auntie thought about that for a moment. "I will tell George. What you did."

"Tell him good-bye," said Longbaugh.

"But you said you like him."

"I can't have his help anymore."

"He will be disappointed."

"It's too dangerous."

"I thought you said the bomb wasn't for you."

"It was because of me."

She nodded. "I see."

"He needs to heal and go on to his own fights."

"I'll tell George, but I'll say it better, so that he can hear it," she said, and went inside with the bandages and towels.

He walked away from the bright blue door and left Chinatown behind.

His grief and gloom were replaced by anger. Hightower had had him followed, and a smarter move he had never made, removing himself from the situation. Longbaugh now wondered about his own intelligence, if he had ever been smart enough to take the fight to the city. He was steeped in doubt, his side burning, his left ear still logy from the blast.

Despite being dogged by his grief, he now began to convince himself she had not been in there. He had initially believed she was there because that was what he wanted. In the aftermath, by blaming himself for rushing to see her and thereby letting himself be followed, he believed he deserved to lose her, which helped convince him she was dead. The dynamite furthered his conviction, as if Moretti's unambiguous use of violence added to the proof. Why blow her up if it was someone else? But now, in reflection, it seemed possible E was not Etta. All his proof was emotional, based on his anguish and sense of responsibility. He knew he had to go back. He caught a passing glimpse of himself in reflection and returned to the store window. His clothes were dirty from the blast, but his face was clean, and he wondered why until he remembered Han Fei's auntie.

He hired a cab and asked for the Brooklyn morgue, and the driver looked at him as if he were simple and took him to Bellevue. Once there, he found a bureaucrat who seemed to be in charge. The man was disgusted by the lackadaisical way in which things were run and told Longbaugh that no one wanted to work there, so they had hired alcoholics to process and handle corpses. Longbaugh realized he wasn't joking. The man went through paperwork, but found nothing about a Brooklyn woman in an explosion. He told Longbaugh that, considering the way things were, it was likely the body had yet to be transported.

He returned to the bridge and boarded a train one more time, to the other side of the East River, then found his way to E's street, currently blocked to traffic. Children no longer cried, dogs no longer barked, and women no longer screamed. The police lingered but appeared to have completed their investigation. Firemen moved in and out of the damaged building, and the scorched facade dripped. Locals made clean spaces on the street with their small brooms and narrow dustpans, and he imagined, at that rate, it would be some time before the block was clear of debris. The hanging laundry was all new and clean, and any destroyed clotheslines were already being replaced. He did not see Phyllis. He walked among them as if he belonged. No one looked at him.

He entered the building's gutted entry and climbed the stairs, stepping carefully to find solid footing, avoiding rubble and mangled banisters. Halfway up, he looked back to the place where the pimpled boy had lit the dynamite to throw at her door on the second-floor landing. His eyes tracked its flight to where her front door had been. The walls were soaked, the ceiling dripped, the smell of acrid smoke and fire mingled with sodden wood and plaster. He stood beside where the dynamite had detonated. He made his way into the room. Police and firemen had been there but were now gone. He crossed through a smaller room into the main room where the windows to the street had been blown out. Just under the missing glass, a body was covered with a blanket. He approached it. He peeled back the blanket to see if there was anything to identify. Flies rose around his nose and eyes, and he blinked and waved at them until they dispersed.

Her eyes were half open, with one side of her face flattened and gelatinous, but intact enough to be identifiable. At the moment of the blast, she had been turned away, partly protected by an inner wall. The officials had laid her on a wood plank. He could see that her back had been scorched and pitted by explosive debris. A snug halo of crinkled, singed hair shaped her face, with a small smudge on her chin and another on her nose. He looked at her from every angle, as if the first glance had been an illusion, that somewhere in these unfamiliar features dwelled the face of his wife. But she was not to be found, as here was Eunice or Elizabeth or Edith or Eleanor, not Ethel Matthews Place.

He left the second floor without being stopped by police or firemen. He left the building and left the area through the roadblocks the way he had come, ignored as if he had belonged there in the first place, forgotten as if he had never been there at all.

He returned to Manhattan. He felt none of the elation he had experienced when he learned Etta had survived the Triangle fire. He did not know where to file his personal responsibility for E's death. He did not even know her name.

The lonely darkness remained with him, despite the fact that it had not been Etta.

He was not ready to confront Hightower. He didn't know if he could control himself. He walked, not aware of how far he had already walked that day, not noticing the ache in his side or the blisters on his feet. He did not know how long he walked before he came upon a bar with a name that caused him to stop. After he read and reread the sign to be sure he was not mistaken, he came very close to smiling. Here was an astounding coincidence. He entered the place as if it was a beacon from his past as well as an invitation to drown his immediate future. The name had meaning only to him, as it had likely been intended to celebrate the obscurity of the location. He was surprised to find it clean and modern. He sat alone at a table in the back, as far from the other patrons as possible. The first glass of liquor did not dull his brain as quickly as he hoped, and he ordered a second and waited for senselessness.

A man came in and sat at the next table in the chair directly behind Longbaugh. Longbaugh paid him no mind. He was in the grip of whiskey by then, and although the man had a familiar look, Longbaugh did not at that moment fully trust his instincts. He also did not trust his ears when the man said, "Hello, Harry."

The voice was familiar, too familiar to be real. He considered, ran it through his aural memory, and chose to ignore it.

"Harry," the man said again, and this time Longbaugh turned in his seat to look over his shoulder.

"Of course," said Longbaugh when he recognized him. He laughed softly, shaking his head in wonder. The darkness lifted.

"I thought you'd get around to coming here once you saw the name," said the man who had called him Harry.

"It was pure dumb luck that I found it. Wait, you didn't name it yourself, did you? Do you own this place, the new Hole in the Wall? Just like you to thumb it at them."

"I don't do that anymore. I dumb-lucked into it just like you. Started coming here the last few months. Had half an eye out for you. Thought you might wander in."

"Slow down, how'd you even know I'd come east?" Longbaugh turned his chair so they were sitting side by side, looking out at the room.

"Didn't. Not saying I expected you, I just imagined it so often that I started to believe it. Then I was on the street and overheard two geniuses trying to outscare each other about some ghost they'd seen, said he had a fast gun and deliberate manner—probably not their exact words—one body, one bullet, and cool as rain in the Rockies. I knew it could only be you. Not a more obvious signature if you'd autographed their ears."

"You being the one guy who knew I wasn't dead."

"The very one."

"So all this time I've wondered, who the hell did they shoot down there?"

"You mean if it wasn't us."

Longbaugh grinned. "Yeah, if it wasn't us."

"You didn't know 'em. Coupla prairie dogs in the wrong country in the wrong decade, wasn't worth the lead to bring 'em down. Although it worked out all right for you and me."

"Were they playacting, trying to be us?" Longbaugh was remembering Sandy the cook and his friend John.

"Nope. Just a couple of bank-robbing fools from Oklahoma. The locals heard we were in country, so if an American picked his nose, it had to be us. They're romantic that way."

Longbaugh shook his head, grinning idiotically at his friend. "Robert Leroy Parker."

Parker grinned back. "Harry Alonzo Longbaugh. When's the last time we saw each other?"

"Union Pacific to Salt Lake City. Sorry, on *top* of a Union Pacific Pullman parlor car on the way to Salt Lake City."

"It was after that."

"No, they had me after that."

"You gave yourself up, they didn't have you. And it was while you were being transferred to the courthouse."

"I didn't see you."

"There was a moment it was just you and a deputy. I had a mount ready. Why didn't you slip the cuffs?"

"Same reason I let them take me."

Parker waited.

"The whole thing was a crap run of luck," said Longbaugh. "I was coming back to Etta, turned the horse in at the livery, I didn't notice the blanket slide off the Union Pacific money bag, and these boys rode in and saw it. Turned out they were with the posse that had just given up on us. Suddenly there were a cool dozen of them looking at the bag and looking at me."

Parker shook his head. "Crap luck, all right."

"I could see Etta in the big window of the hotel, and she knew. Was about to make a fuss, so I gave myself up."

"They didn't recognize you? Just saw the bag?"

Longbaugh shrugged. "Gave them a false name."

"And you didn't mention me."

"Never came up."

"They *never* found out your real name?"

"Never bothered to check. And none of the old lawmen were there to tell them different. Booked me under Alonzo, tried me under Alonzo, and wrote it down in the ledger at Rawlins. Rawlins was brand new that year, they were busy getting the place up and running, and bringing all the prisoners over from Laramie. Nobody looked at me twice, I was caught in the shuffle. Bureaucracy can be your friend."

Parker was amazed. "You did it to protect her."

"Long as they didn't know me, they couldn't know about her."

"Newspapers kept reporting that we were still riding together. Couldn't figure out where they got that."

"They're romantic that way."

Parker thumped the table with his fist in amusement. He took a swallow from his glass.

Parker turned contemplative. "It changed after that. Got harder. Railroads got madder, went after the gang like they meant it. Got so frustrated, I came up with a crackpot theory about running to South America. Pretty soon it got so bad, it didn't seem so crackpot anymore."

"So you really went down there."

"And was living a perfectly respectable life."

"I am interested in your definition of 'respectable.'"

"I swear, Harry, I was on my best behavior. Then word came we were dead. Now that was interesting. I figured they might stop looking for us, long as I didn't happen to lift my skirt in front of them. Seemed like a pretty good time to leave South America."

"I love it when you lift your skirt."

"But before I left I went and visited the town where we died. Now, that's a thing to do. The whole time I felt like a wandering spirit. Seemed like my head was floating a couple feet over my body, like no one could see me. Hard to explain."

Not so hard, thought Longbaugh, remembering how it had been in prison when he had heard of his own death. And Parker's.

"You know they bury people on top of each other down there?" said Parker.

"Cozy."

"Left a clue or two to convince any official snoop that it really had been us. Then, good-bye, Bolivia."

"I still say you were the smart one, Parker."

"Smart like being back in the Hole in the Wall Saloon with you?"

"Point taken."

"We were lucky, of course."

"Were we? How so?"

"Dying in South America. That's a long way. No one to prove it wasn't so."

"Although there are those who know."

"A handful. And they're not sure."

"Oh, did I mention? Siringo's in town."

Parker's entire body tensed. "You did not. Does he know we're alive?"

"He knows I am."

"Why's he here?"

"Looking for me."

"A handful and one. Funny way to keep a low profile, Harry."

"Not for lack of trying. And you can relax, Bobby, he's not waiting outside."

Parker snorted, but he did slacken his shoulders. "Why's he want you? Didn't you do your time?"

"Twelve years. Got out and some kid was waiting."

"Oh. That."

"That."

"There are benefits to being dead. No one wants to prove anything over your corpse."

"Tell that to the kid."

A pause slipped into their conversation, although neither man showed any inclination to leave. They continued to sit side by side, but both of them angled their chairs so only the hind legs were on the floor and their backs were against the wall behind them.

"Sure are a lot of people inventing us since we died."

Parker nodded. "No shit."

"Ever find it hard to be someone else?"

"Nah. I like it, it's good for me." Parker drummed his fingers on the wall behind him. "The gang got to be too big a responsibility once the law got close. You?"

"Can't seem to get out of my own way."

Parker was matter-of-fact. "Because you got something special. That limits you."

"How you figure?"

"Fastest gun I ever saw. Like having a tail or wings, something you can't hide."

"I'm not that fast."

"Pretty fast."

"I keep telling you, it's about patience, nobody knows how to shoot."

Parker laughed. "You do keep telling me."

"And they come after *me*."

"You always say that, too. But you never back off or go halfway. Too much pride, Kid. It limits you. Oh, I don't blame you. If I was that good, I'd be the same way. And now you're the Ghost, got a whole new myth around your neck, like a nervous noose."

"You find that funny."

"I do, a little. But that's you, like it or not. People always tell you who they are, all you have to do is listen."

"What if I told you I want to be anonymous?"

"I'd say you can't help it. You may want to be anonymous but you're a legend all over again. Can't escape your nature, Kid. Now, me, I got nothing special. I wasn't fast or handsome. I'm getting good at being somebody else."

Parker stood up then and went to the bar, returning a minute later with a full bottle. This time he sat at Longbaugh's table across from him, filled their glasses, and set the bottle in front of his friend.

"Nice to talk," said Parker.

"Same."

Parker looked off, as if it had been awkward to make such a personal admission, and now he had to somehow pretend he hadn't done it.

"So how's Etta?"

"Haven't seen her."

"How's that?"

Longbaugh inspected the bottle. "Is this Kentucky or Tennessee?"

"You two split?"

"Not that I've heard."

Parker shook his head in amazement. "Well, if that isn't the most asinine thing. She was devoted to you, Harry. How do you not know where she is?"

"I didn't want her waiting around Wyoming."

"So, what, you sent her to New York?"

"Actually, yes."

"She get lost?"

"Stopped writing."

Parker was contemplative. "Something of a surprise."

"That she stopped writing? I'd say it was."

"Not that. You. Sending her away. Pretty damn gracious of you."

"What, I'm not gracious?"

"One of the most gracious sons of bitches I know, but this is about Etta."

"I'm not gracious about Etta?" He didn't know whether to be angry or amused.

"Took guts on your part. No offense, Harry, but I always thought you liked her being your little girl."

"Well, my little girl found a little mischief."

The light went on for Parker. "You're looking for her, which is why you're still in town, which is why you're not running from Siringo."

"I *am* running from Siringo. I just happen to be running right in front of him."

Longbaugh saw Parker was about to say more, then saw him swallow his words. Longbaugh couldn't face telling him the full story. It made him weak inside, having lost her, weaker still being unable to find her. And the story itself was complex and unfinished, so he had yet to discern its shape. But in life, stories are always defined after the fact. Longbaugh was unprepared to revisit the many roads he had taken, as he himself wasn't sure which of the offshoots could still prove important.

Parker's expression changed to one of curiosity. "You remember how you let Siringo go?"

"I didn't let him go, *you* let him go."

"That's a technicality. I had him boxed in. And I was mad enough to kill him."

"I remember."

"He wouldn't be here now if I had. You see where I'm going? It was because of you. Logan told me Charles Carter was Charlie Siringo, and you said no. You said you'd met Siringo years before and Carter wasn't him. So I let him go."

"That sounds about right."

"But it *was* Siringo. And I still don't see why you did it."

Longbaugh scratched his chin and shrugged. "Well, for one thing, I liked him. And second, you're not a murderer."

Parker was quiet for a while then, thinking all of it through. He pulled a gold coin out of his coat pocket and ran it back and forth along his fingers like a magician. Twice he almost spoke up, but each time he went back into his own head, running it around, remembering those days and what they meant to him now. Longbaugh noticed the coin was a boliviano, with a man's profile. He tried to think of the name of the hero of the country, then felt stupid as he remembered the country was called Bolivia, so the man was Simón Bolívar.

Longbaugh was thinking about things as well, and when he thought Parker had had enough time to forgive him and let go of his frustration, he looked at him ruefully. "My little girl. Funny way to put it. You really think that's how I saw her?"

Parker was tactful. "Maybe not."

Longbaugh poured again, overfilling the glasses, as if he didn't want to leave any behind, but there was still plenty left in the bottle.

Longbaugh shook his head grimly. "Once you've been with someone a while, you get an idea of how people see the two of you together."

"Go on, you two were close . . ."

"Funny to find out how people actually see you."

Parker waved that off. "Quit that."

"You're not so much a couple, really. Just two different humans sharing time together. When it comes to knowing what's in someone's heart, you're only guessing."

"Brother, we don't know what's in our *own* hearts."

"Makes you wonder what it is keeps folks together. Maybe our women stay with us because they're flattered by how we see them, as if it's how they like to see themselves. But I guess that's just another guess."

Parker kept trying to shift his friend's mood. "Or maybe they like us for reasons we can't understand. Lord forbid if I ever understood what any woman ever saw in me."

Longbaugh finally caught Parker's tone and forced himself to lighten up. "You're the original mystery, Butch."

Parker tried to end it, by being sincere and supportive. "Just because people change doesn't mean she's changed about you."

Longbaugh's face clouded over. "Hard to know anything when you're surrounded by silence."

Parker stayed quiet this time, recognizing his mistake. He absently toyed with the gold coin a while. When he spoke again, he had moved on. He talked about old friends, droning on in monologue. Parker knew who in the gang had lived, who was in jail, who had tried to go straight.

"Too bad we have to stay dead," said Parker. "The West has this city by the balls. We could make some serious money. Look what they've done with our stories. Would've taken an extra forty years to do all those things they said we did. They make us out to be heroes. It's like they need us to teach them how to be men."

"I thought the Wobblies were doing that."

"That's it, they are! You got it exactly. And that's the West. Big Bill Haywood's from Utah, you think that Stetson's a costume?"

"I read one of those dime novels about us."

"I bet you died in a foreign land."

"Heroically."

"Manly guns blazing."

"Truth is, I don't miss the West."

"Why would you, they threw you in the clink. But that wasn't really the fault of the West, was it? That was the big eastern railroads."

Longbaugh grinned. "You blame everything on the railroads."

"Bet your ass I do. They came after us, they hurt my feelings. But we got their attention. Made our own myth, robbed them blind, took back part of what they'd stolen from everyone else."

"Give up, Parker, we weren't Robin Hoods."

"Easterners don't know that. They'll believe anything you say happened on that side of the Mississippi. Riddle me this, who was the bigger thief, the railroads or us?"

"You could rationalize an earthquake."

"Which is a damn valuable skill to have. The railroads stole with both hands, and the government let 'em do it. Just as long as they connected the oceans."

"Didn't stop them from coming after us."

"Proving they're greedy bastards. Couldn't even share with a couple of nice fellows like us."

Longbaugh grinned. "You do go on."

Neither of them reached for the bottle again. Whiskey still beckoned from their glasses, but they were done. The bar was empty of other customers, and the bartender was asleep on a stool, leaning back against a shelf. The thin, gray dawn brought an even light to the front window, slowly seeming to dim the electric bulbs.

Parker stood up and hitched his trousers, slipping the gold coin in his pocket. "Glad to see you again, Kid."

Longbaugh nodded.

"Wish I could help you in this thing you have to do." Parker looked at him wistfully. "But you're no good for me. Whenever I'm around you, I get the urge to rob something."

"Was about to say the same about you."

"Those were good times, though, weren't they? I miss 'em, I do. But the two of us back together? I can't be famous again. I only just learned to be dull. It's not so bad."

"I would never ask."

"No. You were always good that way. Let a man choose his own path, even if you did lead him right to the trailhead."

They both laughed. Then Longbaugh looked at him with complete sincerity. "Bobby, you can't help me with this thing. I know you, you always want to help. But it's good this time to walk away."

Parker nodded. He reached out and Longbaugh shook his hand. Parker held on to it. He looked sorry. "I'm glad you're all right."

"It was good to know you, Parker."

"And you, Longbaugh."

Parker let go of his hand and left him there. After a moment, Longbaugh looked around, realizing Parker hadn't told him what name he was using. By then he was gone.

13

During the search for Queenie, Longbaugh and Hightower had often met at the Hotel Algonquin, as it bordered the Tenderloin. Longbaugh knew Hightower liked it there, so it was the first place he looked, in the busy, loud, huge restaurant in the hotel, and found him in a business meeting at his regular table, somewhere in the middle of the sea of diners. Longbaugh was determined to stay out of sight, but he was interested in Hightower's conversation. When a table came free not far from a waiter's screen at Hightower's back, he moved in to eavesdrop.

Hightower's adversary was an overdressed young sport in a colorful waistcoat, which may have been ostentation or perhaps a sly commentary on the sartorial choices of his business associates. On the other hand, as the rich did not need to shout, perhaps this young man was attempting to amuse his mentors with his frank, peacock-like display of appetite. Longbaugh leaned to see his shoes. Tired and worn. A few steps yet from his goal.

He listened.

Hightower's voice played in a different register, lower, slower, even more furry and deliberate than before. "It's time to reopen the discussion about my friend." Longbaugh gathered that Hightower's "friend" was Moretti.

"I will take back any message you care to send, but I can promise, with all candor, the answer will not change."

"My friend is looking to expand his business, and he thinks *your* friend is a good match."

The overdressed young sport was aloof. "Just so you understand, this is not personal, my friend is simply not interested in taking on partners."

"Your friend is in a dangerous business." Hightower was not happy. "Any man with extraordinary access to ordnance requires extraordinary protection."

"I repeat, it is nothing personal."

Hightower brooded. "My friend has a problem when people say no."

"Would he threaten us? The way he threatens his Italian kin, with a note and a child's drawing of a hand?"

"You know the information we have. It could make things uncomfortable for your friend, as he is too comfortable in the company of a certain type of lady."

"You overestimate your leverage. Do you truly imagine he fears for his reputation?"

"Perhaps he should."

"Perhaps you'd be better off threatening to use our own weapons against us."

Hightower showed his frustration. "You deliberately misunderstand, Mr. Wisher."

"I understand perfectly, Mr. Hightower, but blackmail works only when your quarry has a secret he needs to hide. My friend cannot be threatened and he does not want your friend's sort of muscle." The overdressed young sport named Wisher paused dramatically. "I, however, have his ear." Hightower perked up, leaning forward. Wisher smiled knowingly. "And I have never been averse to allowing a bit of grease to be applied to my own wheels."

Hightower was relieved. "Good boy, Wisher, I'm proud of you. That is a mature attitude. You're wasting your talent working for your friend. But much as I'd like to hire you away from him, you may not leave his employ before you make this marriage happen."

Their negotiation was at an end and Longbaugh slipped out of his chair. Wisher stood. Hightower stayed seated, his half-eaten breakfast before him. Longbaugh saw them shake hands. As he was interested to know more about Hightower's business, he moved out of the restaurant to wait outside.

The overdressed young sport named Wisher came out to the street. Longbaugh looked him over. He again thought that Wisher was replacing his wardrobe piece by piece as his finances improved. The grease for his wheels would likely slide him into a new pair of shoes. Wisher's eyes locked onto the bosom of an attractive woman as she passed. Appetite in other things as well. Longbaugh filed that away and stepped into Wisher's eye line.

"Pardon you," said Wisher unpleasantly.

"You have a match?"

"No."

"Say, I believe I know you."

"You do not."

"We haven't met?"

"Lord no."

"Not Mr. Wisher?"

Wisher did not bother to look closely at Longbaugh's face. "No."

Wisher moved around him and walked after the attractive woman.

Longbaugh went back inside, but stayed by the entrance. He caught the eye of Hightower's waiter, and tipped him to hand-carry a note to his customer, asking to meet outside.

Hightower took his time finishing his coffee, then paid his check. When he reached the street, he was wiping crumbs down his front. He was not unprepared, however, when Longbaugh grabbed his collar and pinned him against the wall, as Hightower brought a knife blade up against Longbaugh's throat.

"You called me out the last time, tourist. You're getting predictable."

Hightower heard a pistol cock and a cool metal muzzle blocked the sound in his left ear.

"Am I?" said Longbaugh.

Hightower drew a long breath. He lowered the knife. "You got a beef, Place?"

"You might say that."

"I'd like to know what I'm dying for."

"Why should you? No one warned *her* why she was dying."

"You're not talking sense."

"The Moretti way, remember? They don't know why they're dead, they just are."

"Queenie? Wasn't me, I swear."

"Of course not."

"Place, you've got a gun in my ear, I'll tell you anything you want to hear."

Longbaugh thumbed the hammer back gently against the cylinder. Hightower straightened himself and made his knife disappear under his coat.

"Oh hell. I think I understand. Not Queenie. Your wife." Hightower spoke softly as he began to piece things together. "And you think I did it."

"Dynamite."

"All right. I see why you're here. Moretti's signature, and I'm his employee." Hightower spoke with care, talking aloud as he worked through it. "You think I lit the fuse. Not an unreasonable assumption, I would think the same." His tone of voice was similar to the cautious way he had spoken to Wisher. "One thing you should know—even though Moretti is willing to let people die in ignorance, in this situation he would want to see her face. The ones who go anonymously are business associates. This thing with your wife is personal. He looks at her brand on his cheek every day of his life. My own theory is, if she was blown up, one of his people was taking initiative in an attempt to please him. Rest assured, Moretti will not be pleased, he dislikes initiative. Men with initiative always think they can do a better job than their boss.

Had it been me, I'd have had him there to watch. And make no mistake, if she's dead, that is not good news for your friend Agrius Hightower. If I've been kept in the dark, then Moretti's attitude toward me has changed. Now you have no reason to believe me, as you know me for a stout guttersnipe, but let me say this in all honesty, what you see before you is an innocent stout guttersnipe."

While Longbaugh thought Hightower was lying, he also thought he was lying very well—almost as well as Longbaugh was lying, leading Hightower to believe it had been Etta in the explosion. As his anger receded, he thought that if Hightower had been responsible, he was a coldly brazen bastard to so casually return to his table at the Algonquin and dip his buttered toast in his sugared coffee. Had it been a charade to appear innocent, then Hightower was more cynical than even Longbaugh's low opinion allowed. In the end, it did not matter. Just as long as he told Moretti that Etta was dead.

"Maybe what you say is true."

"Listen, Place, your wife just passed, I don't care how long it's been since you saw her, for all I know you could be relieved, but either way you have to be in shock. I'm buying you a drink."

Now that he no longer needed to sell her death to Hightower, Longbaugh began to deflate. The explosion had taken something out of him. Even with no connection between Etta and E's death, his sense of hope had been undermined by the blast. She seemed farther away and he despaired at the possibility of ever finding her.

They returned to the hotel restaurant. The lighting had not changed, but the room appeared darker, and Longbaugh realized that *he* was the darkness in the room. Hightower caught the waiter's eye and ordered.

"Where'd it happen?"

"Brooklyn."

"Brooklyn? Oh, nasty, dying in Brooklyn."

"Brilliant way to console a man."

"My apologies, that was clumsy."

The waiter returned with their drinks. Longbaugh did not want his, but he did not offer it to Hightower.

"What made you think it was me?"

"Other than the dynamite?"

"Never touch the stuff. Too unstable."

"I thought you were following me. Turned out to be one of Moretti's boys."

"Flexible?"

"Pimples."

"Silvio? You sure? You saw him?"

Longbaugh nodded.

"How'd he miss killing you?"

"I wasn't with her at the time."

"But you saw him tailing you?"

"No. I looked, but . . . I was watching for you." Longbaugh narrowed his eyes with profound self-loathing.

Hightower stared off, thinking. "When was this?"

"You playing Pinkerton?"

"Just conversation, tourist."

Longbaugh was quiet. He had no reason to share information. He didn't trust him, didn't want to know him, and didn't care to drink with him, but after running all that through his mind, he also sat in self-imposed darkness and realized he did not want to be alone, even if it meant spending time with a man such as this. He heard himself answer.

"After we left Queenie."

"Christ." Hightower rearranged the puzzle. "Silvio wasn't following you. Silvio was following *me*. Probably a team, one stayed on me when I went to the oyster bar and Silvio took you. Son of a teetotaler's bitch."

Hightower's face changed while appearing to remain still. A spark under his eyes sent a blaze of fury through his skull, flushing his cheeks and thinning his lips until he went cold, grim, and hollow. Longbaugh realized Hightower was not angry, he was humiliated. He had lost Moretti's trust.

"Would you have done it if Moretti had asked?"

"Before I met you, without hesitation."

"Now not so sure."

"Moretti must have suspected that."

Longbaugh said nothing. Again he thought the man a magnificent liar.

Hightower ordered a second drink.

Longbaugh had all he needed from Hightower. But he still did not leave. He fell into a brood, as if he were the grieving husband.

"Talk about her, Hightower."

"Don't be morbid."

"I wear morbid like a paper cut. Talk."

Hightower adjusted himself in his chair, widening his nostrils dyspeptically. His words came out archly, his voice a step too high. "She was a lovely woman, charming, really, quite pretty . . ."

"And that you can save for the eulogy."

Hightower's demeanor changed. "She's dead, Place, take your cherished memories and go back where you came from. Don't ask questions if you don't want answers."

"Talk."

"You don't want this from me."

Longbaugh stared at him and Hightower relented, narrowing his eyes and gathering his thoughts while deciding just how politic to be. He gave Longbaugh a full look.

"I did not like your wife. She was a thorny progressive nitwit who believed everyone deserved a chance, and all the rest of that Bull Moose rot. But then, she didn't much like me either. Thought I was a flunky pig for sale to the richest fat cat. The moose, the pig, and the cat, welcome to the zoo. While there may be truth in all that, she could at least have pretended to charm me. Look at me, am I so bad? I carry a certain rough appeal. She didn't need to judge me so quick. You're not so much better than I am."

He checked Longbaugh's reaction and saw he was not offended.

"Although I'll say one thing. She never showed interest in any man that I could see, so maybe it wasn't just me. How'd you get so lucky?"

Hightower stared off with a tiny shrug as if it was against his religion to share good news. Then he perked up with another thought.

"Oh, and one more thing, she was headstrong, the least appealing quality in a woman. She refused to compromise. She was rigid about everything. But then I am rigid about nothing whatsoever, a rabbit in springtime is rigid in comparison."

"Give you that."

"She'd get a look in her eyes, like she was thinking of something unexpected, off-key. A little smile, a glance to the side."

"I know that look."

"She thought she was outthinking everyone else in the room. That arrogant look of larceny."

"That's it, isn't it?" Longbaugh smiled with the memory.

"*You* get that look, Place."

"Do I?" He was caught off guard, then pleased to be tarred with the same brush.

"Oh yes. Makes me wonder who you really are. Combined with what it was that she saw in you, I am most curious."

Longbaugh turned his drink around and watched the liquid across the top send tiny circular waves toward the center. "You talk about her, and there she is out of the corner of my eye. People have been telling me things that she would never do, never. But she did them, I recognize her in the details. I've been looking for my wife and I found someone else." He stared straight ahead. "Like falling in love twice with the same woman."

Hightower raised his eyebrows. "Then you're a lucky man."

"Yeah, if she wasn't dead."

Hightower sneered as if that was just too much. Longbaugh thought that after seeing Parker, he had gotten used to talking and had carried this disagreeable habit into the daylight. Playing the widower had sent out imaginary tendrils of grief that had taken unexpected root. He looked at his untouched drink and did not want it. He looked at the room and wondered why he wasn't leaving. He looked at his hands on the table and saw a crumb next to his finger and brushed it aside. He tried to listen to conversations around him but quickly lost patience.

He tried to listen to the voices in his head, and had less patience. Time came and went. He looked at Hightower and wondered why *he* didn't leave.

"So what do you do now?" said Hightower.

"Do?"

"Now that your wife's dead."

He shook his head slowly. Hightower took chances. Unless he knew.

"Tourist, you need a distraction."

"I could change my mind about shooting you."

"Aw, you like me."

"I don't *dis*like you."

"Nah, you like me. And you need to make plans."

"Okay, now you can go away."

"You got money? A job? A skill?"

"I got a skill. I could shoot a part in your hair from fifty paces that wouldn't bleed. Unless I decided to miss and core your brain."

"No, something that interests you."

Longbaugh was indifferent to the question and the answer, but he heard himself say the first thing that came to mind: "The West."

"Ah, the frontier. Hopes and dreams for the drab city folk. What is it you know?"

"Wyatt Earp, Bat Masterson."

"No, no, something new, not all that heroic tripe they endlessly stuff down our throats."

"Heroic? They were outlaws. They didn't all of a sudden stop thieving when they became lawmen."

"Forget it, no one wants to hear that, even if it is true."

"I thought you said crime is the future."

"Only if you tell it right. No one wants to know their hero's a jackass. What else you got?"

Longbaugh sat back. "I could write a handbook on robbing trains."

"What are you, some Pennsylvania dilettante who once visited Promontory Summit?"

Longbaugh was surprised and insulted. It was surely coincidence that Hightower mentioned Pennsylvania, but the insult rankled and made him reckless. Yet the moment he said "Butch Cassidy," he regretted it.

"Dead five years, old news. How do you know about Cassidy?"

Longbaugh kicked himself and took the nearest exit. "I met his cook."

"Why hear it from you, why not talk to the cook?"

"Somebody hung him for being a jackass."

"Not enough of that going around."

Longbaugh cut off the conversation, reaching for his money to pay the bill. Hightower put his hand on Longbaugh's arm. "This is my party."

Longbaugh let him take it.

"You see, distraction is what you need. You're feeling better already."

And now you know more about me than I cared to tell, thought Longbaugh.

"Come work for me. You're good with a gun, from what you say. Although if you kill Moretti, you dry up a steady source of revenue."

Longbaugh thought to turn the tables, see if he could quid pro quo Hightower into spilling more than he wanted to tell. "Tell me what she did all these months."

"A little wallow, eh? I can respect that. Man's got to mourn."

"Where do you think she was hiding?"

"You're the one found her in Brooklyn."

"That was a new place. What about before?"

"How can it matter? She's dead, let her rest."

"Because I want to know." His voice came loud and harsh and heads turned.

"Easy now, tourist."

"I want to know who she was," said Longbaugh, more quietly but no less harshly.

Hightower shook his head in disgust. He tore the corner off a newspaper and took a pencil from an inside pocket, poised to write something on its blankness. "This is pointless, but I'm glad it's not my cross to bear. I tracked her to a place she was living, almost caught her, too."

He handed Longbaugh the newsprint scrap with an address.

"You helped me with Moretti today, tourist, telling me about Silvio, so consider this your reward. Now I get to mess up Silvio and get a little respect back. I imagine he's backtracking right about now, telling Joe it wasn't Mrs. Place after all. Little creep may never grow out of his pimples." He scratched himself as he stood up, leaving money on the table. "Oh, and the next time you see your wife, say hello for me."

Longbaugh was not surprised when he found the street with the address he'd gotten from Hightower. Another innocuous boardinghouse in an area full of boardinghouses, not too nice, not too shabby, a place for a person to blend in and vanish. He bribed the elderly landlady to let him in and went up the stairs to the room she indicated. Longbaugh entered Etta's old room to find it furnished. He pocketed the torn corner of the newspaper. The landlady had told him Etta had lived there as recently as three months before. This time he looked immediately at the wooden wardrobe in the corner. From the moment he saw it, he ignored everything else in the room. The wardrobe was fancier than the one in the Levis' boardinghouse, topped by a carved finial, a front piece that added five inches to its height. A line of books stood upright against it, their spines partially covered by the decorative wood. Behind the books he saw the very tip of the flame of a Statue of Liberty toy. He dragged a chair and stepped up to find it perched on a stack of letters held together with an olive ribbon. Her handwriting shaped his name on the top letter. He could smell her, a heart-surging whiff of perfume amid the dust. That letter also had a layer of dust, and he lifted the stack to find a clean, rectangular shape on the wardrobe's wooden top, where the envelopes had been placed. The top of the wardrobe had gone months without a cleaning. Etta had known no one would look there. Hightower had missed it, but he was only looking for her person.

He thumbed the edge of the thick batch of envelopes and realized she had continued to write to him every week. He was amazed. She had been speaking to him all along, all the while knowing he might never receive her words. He stepped off the chair and sat on it, filled with a kind of awe. The volume of her affection and the extent of her communication now rested in his hands. He undid the olive ribbon and fanned the envelopes out on his lap. She had sealed each one and acted as if she had sent them off irretrievably.

He chose the bottom letter, assuming it to be the oldest, the first that he had not received. It began as did all her letters, *My Dear.* He quickly went to the bottom of the second page, to see the closing sentiment, and he read, *Your Etta.* He sat in silence, so many of her words in his fingers, her gorgeous scent in his nose, and he closed his eyes, overwhelmed, and she was nearer to him than she had been in years.

He returned to the beginning of the letter and began to read. He had planned to skim it, as there were so many letters and so much to learn, but he was bewitched by the sound of her voice in his head and he inhaled her cadence.

My Dear,

I must not send you this letter, and for that you cannot imagine the pain I suffer. Signor Moretti's men captured a letter I had posted to Mina. I did not think it possible, but he showed it to me and said he knew someone in the post office. I know there is massive corruption in this city, but the Black Hand's reach surprises even me. He said he was going to send men to see her. He was warning me that he could find my family. I doubt if he bothered to follow through, I'm sure Mina only thinks I'm too lazy to write. Better she think that than know the truth. Nevertheless, I learned my lesson. As long as I don't send this to you, he can never find out you exist. It appears the Hand has many arms (laugh now, darling, at least I can still joke), and if he was to find this or any future letter, he would know where you are, and send someone to meet you on the day you are to be released from that dreadful place. You would never know someone was coming, as my letter would fail to arrive to warn you. I will not risk you, no matter how much pain my silence may cause. I know what it is doing to you, and I'd do anything in my power to keep you from hurting this way, but it's better you should suffer silence than be lost to me forever. I could not live knowing you were no longer in this world.

He stopped reading. He thought of his visit to Mina and the men sent to frighten her. Etta could not have known Moretti had followed through on his threat. Mina had been lucky. Perhaps Hightower had a heart after all, as it had surely been his men.

He returned to the letter.

The very act of writing draws you near, and I selfishly cannot bring myself to break the habit. I do now as I've always done, organize my thoughts days in advance of lifting a pen, as even thinking of writing to you makes me happy. As I plan what to say, that is an intimate time, and when I ink my thoughts into permanence, you are here in the room with me. When I picture you reading my words, I imagine that you can hear my voice, so I try to write as I speak, precisely and never falsely. Oh, my, I just reviewed those last words, can you imagine me saying "precisely and never falsely"? Maybe it's a good thing you'll never read this. But I know these words are for me alone. Again, how selfish of me to be speaking to you this way.

I am conflicted, my darling. I want you to come and find me when finally they let you out, but I also fear it because they will try to hurt you. If I'm lucky, my silence will keep you away and safe. But when you do come, because you will, you must be careful! Swallow your pride, stay safe. Beware of those men. And now listen to me, sounding like a nervous mother. Or maybe like a nagging wife. Why would you marry such a shrew?

I am safe and in hiding. My plan is to relocate frequently, so do not fear for me. I have no planned-out strategy, so they will not be able to detect a pattern. My hope is that they will tire of this game. If I read them correctly, they are childish and impatient. Eventually I will find a way to continue my work.

I met an anarchist named Mabel. You would dislike her. Oh, my, I laugh to think of you two in the same room. For all her haughty attitude, I would fear for her sharing the same room as you. Her philosophy may not be appealing, but the anarchists are a cautious, nervous, and furtive lot, all things I must learn to be. She thinks I am a fool, and perhaps I am, but to underestimate me proves she lacks imagination. No surprise there, after all, she's an anarchist. Or maybe she just lacks humor. What is it you always say? I can't abide a man without a sense of humor. Or in this case, a woman. I will let her believe what she will and hold my tongue (not so easy, thinks my husband), although I find her imperious and insufferable. Best not to underestimate her in turn. At one time when you and I were looking for hideouts (where were we? Colorado, I think), we would have laughed at the idea of accepting refuge from that sort of person. Now how funny it is to find it to be prudent.

I close now, as it is late and I must rest. I move again in the morning. I always think of what you would do to make sure I was well hidden, so now in your place I take extra care. You would be proud of my precautions, I think.

I love you in silence,
Your Etta

He did not know what to do. His heart was full, she was here, right here, in the room with him, her words lifting him, her humor, her wit, all there, her voice alive in his head, and yet she was gone, out there somewhere, in hiding, and he couldn't reach her. His mind churned in frustration.

It was time to leave the room. He had already fueled the landlady's curiosity, better not to fan it to flames. But wise as that notion may have been, he did not stand up. He looked at the many letters and tried to decide his next move. He reached too quickly for the last envelope to see if she had left a clue to her latest destination and accidentally knocked them all to the floor. They scattered, out of order. He went to his knees and collected them with care to identify the dustiest, the letter that had been on top, the most recently written. If worse came to worst, he would open each one, as she had dated them.

The olive ribbon had left a clean stripe in the dust on her final letter, making it easy to identify, but he also saw a clean square in the middle where dust had not fallen, and he did not at first understand until he remembered the Liberty toy had stood on it. He opened it to a date only twelve weeks before. Twelve weeks. A long time and yet no time at all, although had he missed her by twelve minutes, she would still be out of reach. He scanned it but her words gave no clue to her current location.

He rewrapped the letters in the ribbon and remembered the toy, on its side atop the wardrobe. He stood on the chair, took the toy, and vaguely noted that one of the books standing along the finial was upside down. He was in the hallway before that fact tripped him and sent him back to stand on the chair and bring down the book. A loose sheet of paper slipped from under the book's cover. He unfolded it, holding his breath. *My Dear.* He turned it over but there was no affectionate close. It was unfinished, words dangling mid-page, the last thought a fragment without a period. She had been writing and was halted mid-thought, the white expanse below a testament to imminent danger. She had had a mere moment, enough time to fold it and slip it in the book and turn the book upside down. He reread the fragment, her last words:

> *SFS has been traveling back and forth across the ocean and I'm starting*
> *to wonder if it has something to do with*

14

————◆◆◆————

Every spare moment was spent reliving the last two years through her letters as he read and reread them—at meals, before sleep, while traveling on trolleys and trains. He started at the beginning, first letters first, and read in order to own the context. He initially read through them quickly to make sure she was all right, then started again and read slowly for clues or codes. The second year of letters brought to his attention one particular man, an anarchist, and as he read, he thought there was a chance this man might know of her whereabouts. He was supposedly well hidden, yet ironically, from her description of his habits and manner, he might not be difficult to find.

Longbaugh rode out to Paterson, New Jersey, Silk City, to visit the hall where the Industrial Workers of the World, "the Wobblies," made their offices in support of the silk workers' strike. He carried the pertinent letters and reread them on the train. This particular man had come to Etta through the female anarchist, Mabel. Mabel the anarchist had looked down on Etta, and it amused her to put Etta together with one of her anarchist compatriots, identified in the letters only as Prophet. The origin of this moniker was unclear, and if Etta knew his name, she had neglected to mention it. He held out hope that the SFS in the dangling sentence of her final letter was him. Mabel the anarchist's idea of a joke was to play Cupid for Prophet. Mabel the anarchist believed in free love and sneered at "bourgeois" progressives like Etta. Mabel the anarchist seemed to have more patience for the posh class she so deeply opposed than for progressives who were closer to her political philosophy.

He jumped to a recent letter. Etta had written that Prophet was energized by the strike and had spent significant time in Silk City with the Wobblies. Prophet's early enthusiasm was akin to the ecstasy of a first love or a religious conversion. Longbaugh flipped to a letter dated three months later, where, as she had expected, she recounted Prophet's profound disappointment in the Wobblies and the strikers, his vitriol and disappointment as predictable as his initial infatuation. Prophet now saw the strikers as docile and ineffectual. But he still on occasion visited their offices. Apparently, he was lonely.

Longbaugh walked along the Passaic River through Paterson, passing a series of silent silk factories that lined the riverbank. He crossed the bridge over the Great Falls and found his way to the IWW hall on Main Street.

He entered the hall. A harried young woman crossed his path, with an armload of papers and no time for him. He stood in her way. She looked at him in the way that those who are chosen look at the ignorant and misinformed, over glasses perched precariously low on her nose, through hair strands falling in her face.

"Can you help me?" said Longbaugh.

"Apparently, I can't help anyone."

"Oh."

"No, I mean I can't help anyone, according to my boss."

"Is he some sort of idiot?"

She thawed slightly. "And you're not one of us."

"How can you tell?"

"No one calls him an idiot. Out loud."

"I'm looking for a man named Prophet?" It came out as a question, as he had never spoken the name aloud, and it sounded false and careless in his mouth.

"What could you possibly want from him?"

"Nothing good."

His answer bought him another moment of her time. "Well, you're not the law." That was not a question, merely the opening salvo of her critical assessment.

"No."

"And you're no Pinkerton. No rabid foam."

"I washed my chin just this morning."

"A reporter would ask leading questions."

"Do you think your strike is the only reason America is dying?"

She was enjoying this. She looked at his clothes. "Not an anarchist recruit. Can't see you joining Prophet's cause. You'd be better off with us."

"Not political."

"Right. But you've heard about us, the enemy of capitalism out to destroy life as you know it."

"That's what comes of better conditions and higher wages?"

"Apparently so. If we're not starving, we're not doing our part."

"A progressive with a sense of humor."

"One more thing I can't get right. Not serious enough."

"So which one is your boss?"

"See those men over there?" She indicated a line that had formed in front of a desk on the far side of the room. Each man in turn was handed an envelope. "He's the one giving out the money."

"Awfully young to be an idiot." She laughed out loud and he caught her glasses as they fell off her nose.

Longbaugh watched her boss and the line of men. "The union hiring picketers?"

"No, they're ours, broad-silk weavers. I visited the picket line and found out they're broke, although not quite starving. I thought maybe the union might help, from the fund."

"Your boss took credit for your idea."

"Girls don't have ideas. This strike is about boys, men, virility, and please don't mind me. At least our people aren't groveling and their children eat. Those men had been running two looms at a time until the company decided they should run four. For the same money."

"Making half of them out of work already."

"So you're not a cop, a Pinkerton, or a reporter."

"From out west."

"Riding horses, mending fences."

"Robbing railroads."

"No need for a union when you make your own hours." He nodded at her quick wit. "But wait, I see it now. You're a cattle baron. Should have known all along, the way you carry yourself."

He smiled a little. "Confidence?"

"Arrogance."

"I must be hiding my affable nature."

"You buy up land the railroad wants and sell it to them for a profit."

"And apparently I'm rather cynical."

"It's your lack of affection for the workers."

Longbaugh shrugged. "My wife supports you."

"Send her along, I'll give her a picket sign."

Before he spoke, Longbaugh hadn't given much thought to Etta's politics. But from everything he'd learned in her letters and from those who had interacted with her, he was confident that he knew exactly what she believed. His own convictions may have been unresolved, but hers were not.

"What does a cattle baron want with Prophet? Wait, don't tell me, secretly he's the son of a wealthy landowner and you need him to help you buy Indian land."

"Something like that."

"No, seriously."

"He's one of yours, why let him hang around?"

"He is definitely not one of ours. You can shoo a fly, but as long as you smell sweet, he keeps coming back. Big Bill got sick of his face and sent him packing day before yesterday."

"So maybe he's not coming back?"

"I'll believe that when I see it."

"Know where he lives?"

"Nobody knows. But if he's not here, he's probably spreading cheer in the big city. I'd check the newspapers and magazines."

"Anarchist press?"

"Heavens no, they washed their hands of him long ago. Try *The Masses*, they're the biggest socialist magazine. Socialists are more tolerant, and he's always looking for someone to convert."

"Thus the name Prophet."

"And the fact that so far I think he's been spectacularly unsuccessful."

"Thus the ironic name Prophet. You know his real name?"

"The odd thing is, I do. He took a liking to me, but I'm one of those females who happens to have arms, legs, feet, hands, and hair. He had a moment of weakness when he said he was Jonah Calvin."

"Jonah the Prophet."

"Oh. That's right. Missed that entirely. My boss also thinks I'm too dense. Could be right." She thought for a moment. "I was also a little dense, since I guess I found Prophet attractive for about a minute and a half."

"Not bad looking?"

"Actually, he looks like a squirrel, but looks don't matter if you have a brilliant mind. Or I thought he had a brilliant mind. He would say profound things that I'm ashamed to say I thought were original." She covered her face with her hand, still embarrassed at having been fooled. "Until one day he said something I recognized and realized he was passing off other people's ideas as his own."

Longbaugh was fascinated. "Like what, for instance?"

"Oh, let's see: 'Political Freedom without economic equality is a pretense, a fraud, a lie; and the workers want no lying.' I liked that, that was pretty good."

"But you caught him—"

"—when he said something I recognized, yes. 'Does it follow that I reject all authority? Perish the thought. In the matter of shoes'—

wait, no—'In the matter of boots, I defer to the authority of the boot maker.' I always liked that quote, we all have contradictions, even when we believe in something, and I just so happened to know it was Mikhail Bakunin, and not Jonah Calvin. I looked through my Bakunin and found out Prophet had shamelessly lifted every smart thing he said."

Longbaugh had never thought about men seducing women with ideas and words, particularly political words.

"So, who's Bakunin?"

"Once a cattle baron, always a cattle baron. Bakunin was one of the early anarchists."

Here was a world as different to him as the city had been on that first day when he had stepped off the train. "Well, miss, that's very enlightening, thank you. I must admit, I enjoyed talking to you."

"You never said why you wanted him."

"Indian land."

A commotion by the door caused him to turn, and a man came in who could only have been Big Bill Haywood, wearing his Big Bill Stetson and offering his Big Bill handshake to men who buzzed to him like bees to pollen, tripping over boxes and chairs to grasp that hand. Longbaugh backed up to look him over. *He is large and impressive*, thought Longbaugh, *very impressive, but I'm faster*, and then he thought, *Damn you, Butch! I do have pride.*

He sat back to consider the man. After a few minutes, he had a sense of him. Men and women were drawn to his bigger-than-life qualities, his size, his voice. Haywood knew that, and humbled himself, understanding that people could be overwhelmed. He was a born storyteller. His everyday conversation had a natural flow, a beginning, a middle, and an end, which drew people to him and made them want to listen. Longbaugh realized he was drawn to him as well, but reminded himself that he was not here for Big Bill Haywood, he was here to find a squirrelly anarchist that even his brethren disliked.

He may not have known how he felt about the silk workers' strike or the Wobblies, but he was beginning to know why so many workers bought into it.

On the way back into the city, he reread the letter where Mabel the anarchist had thought Prophet would make a darling companion for Etta. Mabel was amused that the self-professed extremist radical Prophet had lost his heart to a woman who was so conventional. Longbaugh was amused as well, to think of Etta as conventional. While Etta did not trust Mabel the anarchist, she knew Prophet offered an option if she got into trouble, as he inhabited sketchier neighborhoods, hiding out and moving often. She knew she could handle him, and if she needed to disappear in a hurry, here was a quick way out of Moretti's reach. Prophet's instability could work to Etta's advantage, as his movements appeared random, unpredictable.

A cab let Longbaugh off on Nassau Street, at the offices of the magazine *The Masses*. He was surprised to find himself standing in front of a closed and empty office. He stood at the window, trying to peer in, when a fellow pushing a knife-sharpening cart stopped.

"They moved a couple days ago," said the knife sharpener.

"What, the whole magazine?"

"Few blocks. Other side of Trinity Church, Greenwich Street. Ninety-one."

He walked.

While walking, he skimmed one of her letters, slowing on a paragraph about Hightower. She had met him through Moretti, and knew he had been searching for her. She disliked him and found that in his case, she was unable to disguise it. He remembered Hightower saying he wished she could at least have pretended to charm him. Something about seeing the same moment from both sides made Longbaugh smile. He put the letters in his pocket as he came to the address.

The new offices of *The Masses* were light and bright, full of energy and conviction, as well as the mess and general confusion caused by the move. Crates were stacked, waiting to be unpacked, but the staff worked around them, apparently determined to publish their magazine on time.

Longbaugh was able to stand in the midst of the disorganization without being questioned as to his intentions or identity. One floppy fellow, an editor of some sort with a rag doll mop of hair and one shirttail out, was attempting to exhort his troops. He was not doing well.

"People, there's an Isadora Duncan rumor that she's leaving France. Anyone?"

He was also not good at intimidation. Too likable.

"A rumor that she's moving back to the United States. Of America. Is someone on that story? I need someone to bring me that story."

In a moment of perception, Longbaugh was able to pick out the covert Pinkerton agent. As he watched him, he realized the agent was too obvious. Then he realized that everyone there already knew he was undercover and a Pinkerton. He wondered if that was to draw the attention away from the *real* undercover Pinkerton. He looked again. That might have been anyone.

He left the offices and located a bakery, purchasing a combination of pastries and doughnuts that they boxed for him. He returned to the offices and laid out the sweets. In short order, writers and editors came to him. *Flies to sweet,* he thought.

As a man with a handlebar mustache took a pastry, Longbaugh said, "Seen Prophet today?"

"Thank the Lord, no. He'll be along, though."

As a man with a limp chose a doughnut: "Someone said Prophet's coming by today."

"He thinks we'll take some piece he wrote."

"That bad?"

"Unreadable."

"What's he look like?"

"And you would be?"

"The one who paid for the doughnut you're eating."

The limper tossed the doughnut in the trash.

He leaned back to wait for someone more congenial to indulge his sweet tooth. He unfolded a letter.

Etta was forthright about her life and its dangers. She was writing the kinds of things he had never known her to share in the past, either in person or in the letters she had sent to him in prison. Perhaps now that she thought he would never get to see the letters, she was more comfortable expressing herself. Or she was changed by her journey and looked forward to sharing her new self. Or perhaps this was an act of valediction, a final accounting of the true nature of her flight. In the end, reading her honest words, he decided she was confiding in the man she hoped he would be.

The floppy literary editor with his hanging shirttail rambled over to gaze longingly at a pastry. He finally plucked it and became the first of the magazine's staff to acknowledge the benefactor and offer thanks. Longbaugh put Etta's letter aside and they slipped into conversation. Among other things, he learned that Prophet was small and had scary eyes. Longbaugh indicated the man across the room who had just come in. "Anything like him?"

The floppy literary editor turned. "Oh boy, just exactly like him." He shrank, biting furtively into his pastry with his head down, as if that would keep Prophet from noticing him.

Prophet was indeed small, and while the woman in Paterson had said squirrelly, looking at his ears, Longbaugh imagined another animal. His oversized coat, however, did look as if a squirrel was wearing a beaver's pelt. Longbaugh mused that he must be roasting on this warm day. His hair was light and sheared short, uneven enough to suggest he had cut it himself. Had he let it grow, his large ears sticking out from his head might not have seemed so pronounced. Then he saw Prophet's eyes. They were pressed down into hard, small, startlingly blue circles. Prophet put a soft white hand into a coarse pocket and brought forth a sheet of paper folded into eighths. He unfolded his work—Longbaugh saw cramped writing that covered the page like ants on a honey spill— and tried to give it to the man Longbaugh had earlier pegged as the editor in charge.

The editor, tall and handsome and possibly thirty, with wonderful hair and strong lips, brought his palms up by his shoulders. Longbaugh had seen train passengers do that, rather than raising them overhead.

Prophet attempted to push the paper into the editor's chest, as if it might be absorbed there to be accepted, appreciated, approved, and adored. The editor shook his head slowly, palms now flat against his chest, and Longbaugh saw Prophet frustrated.

Longbaugh was quick to dislike the anarchist. He knew he should stay neutral, and Etta had described him with empathy. But Longbaugh felt no need to extend her charity. On the other hand, it was bad policy to prejudge the man, as he needed information, and an adversarial attitude was not the way to get it. If he wasn't careful, he was likely to underestimate him and miss something.

Harsh sunlight reflected off a window across the street and silhouetted Prophet, turning his large ears translucent. The image was so comical that Longbaugh suddenly understood Prophet's entire life, the teasing, bullying, and humiliation, the forced isolation until he actively chose isolation, cropping his hair defiantly, and Longbaugh thought to himself, *He's an anarchist because of his ears.* Prophet peeled his paper off the editor's chest and refolded it with his white hands. He surveyed the room to see who had witnessed his disgrace. Everyone had looked away, not wanting to be the next target. Everyone but him. Prophet's eyes found Longbaugh, and read his disapproval. Prophet pushed his way past the editor in charge and was out the door so quickly that Longbaugh was momentarily frozen. He followed, onto the sidewalk, watching the fleeing coat flap like a cape. He ran after him. Prophet looked back, saw him coming, and ran faster.

Prophet ran past Trinity Church, heading east on Wall Street, then turned north on Nassau. Longbaugh stayed after him, and they both slowed to a trot, until Prophet reached the subway station at Fulton. He turned, gave Longbaugh a quick glance, and ran down the stairs. Longbaugh followed, slowing to pay his nickel. He wondered if the anarchist had paid or if subway fares conflicted with his principles. On the platform, a crowd waited for the train. Prophet's size and head start made it unlikely Longbaugh would luck on to him, but he continued to look. He heard a subway train approaching from inside the tunnel. He leaned and saw a light growing closer, brighter. A warm press of wind blew by as if a false train arrived ahead of the real one. The real one braked loudly to stop beside them, and every passenger watched the doors open. People came off. Then people got on. He craned his neck to see if Prophet was one of them, but he had already decided this was not the way to catch him.

He walked back to the offices of *The Masses*. He looked for the floppy editor and was told he had stepped out. The pastries had all been consumed while the thin box remained, a raft for crumbs.

Her writing confirmed things he had learned along the way. Some passages, however, were elusive, her words cautious, as if someone looked over her shoulder. He reread the letter where the initials SFS appeared for the first time, while thinking of her unfinished last letter, SFS traveling back and forth across the ocean. But he was unable to find anything to illuminate her later comment. In between, there were references to his journeys, as she concluded he was traveling exclusively on American ocean liners. Longbaugh did not understand what that meant.

He reread the section where she considered the benefits of hiding out with anarchists. This was written while she lived in the second boardinghouse, after having left Abigail's. He reread the paragraph where she wrote she would gladly enter the paranoid anarchist world if it would keep the Black Hand from finding her. Her only reservation was Prophet. He was in love with her.

The floppy editor returned, teeth sunk into an éclair, fingers covered in sweet.

Longbaugh smiled to see what he had started. "I should have brought more."

"I shouldn't be doing this. It'll spoil my wife's supper. But I'll eat all of that as well when she sets it in front of me. Sadly." He patted his proud belly sadly.

"May I ask you about Prophet? About Jonah Calvin?"

"Apparently you know more than I. For instance, his real name." Indicating the handsome editor who had rejected Prophet's piece. "Although surely Eastman knows it."

"Does he ever mention plans? Or where he lives?"

"Not where he lives. But he wants to be asked about his plans so he can pretend to be coy."

"Did you ask?"

"Never."

"So he didn't tell you."

"Oh no, he told me every chance he got."

"And?"

The literary editor looked at him suspiciously. "They tell me I'm a soft touch, but I'm fairly certain I should be more circumspect here."

"Do you get the best out of your people?"

"Actually, yes."

"Then whatever you're doing is working."

"You're not one of my people."

Longbaugh shrugged. "I bribed you with an éclair."

The editor nodded, acquiescing. "I suppose I can rationalize that. You want to know his plans. Not sure how to answer that. He's not your typical anarchist. He's like the cliché of an anarchist. He'd like to make a name for himself. But it was as if he was asking me for ideas on how to do it."

"I hear he likes to borrow other people's ideas."

"Oh yes. Quotation without attribution is larceny."

"You're doing that thing, taxation without representation is tyranny."

The editor cocked his smiling head, pleased.

"How would he make a name for himself?" said Longbaugh.

"Well, first I suppose he should blow something up. Preferably with people in the general vicinity."

"You suggested that to him?"

"Of course not. That's just how he would do it if he were the cliché."

"You think he has that in him?"

"It's plausible, to prove a point and make himself appear important. Unless he blows himself up first."

"So he doesn't inspire confidence."

"Not in me."

"And he'd use dynamite."

"That would be the cliché."

"Where does one get dynamite?"

"Well, 'one' gets dynamite either from one who provides dynamite, or one who needs dynamite and stores it for future use, like those in construction. When they built Central Park, they cleared out acres of bedrock."

"Central Park is complete."

"The subway is not."

Longbaugh smiled.

"Assuming," said the floppy literary editor, seeing his shirttail out and tucking it in, "you can picture him with the guts to steal for his 'cause.'"

LONGBAUGH risked a return to Abigail's boardinghouse. He approached as Siringo had originally, circling in from blocks away, lurking to know if Siringo lurked. As he was well acquainted with the neighborhood, he was able to see without being seen in order not to be recognized. He might have consulted with any number of local peddlers, urchins, or even a few unrespectable bartenders to know if Siringo was near, but he risked that they were in Siringo's pocket and the information would go the wrong direction. Han Fei's help would have been welcome. But Han Fei was recuperating, and Longbaugh had resolved to shield him from any more danger.

Once he satisfied himself that no one was staking out the boardinghouse, he moved in to begin his own surveillance. He had been there only about an hour when he got lucky. Abigail came out the front door with empty bags over her arm. Shopping day. He let her pass by him to see if she was being followed. He picked up nothing suspicious and eased into the flow of pedestrian traffic. He did not fear losing her, as he was familiar with her routine and would catch up to her at any number of her favored stores and carts. But Siringo might know her routine as well. Longbaugh stayed alert.

He shadowed her from across the street, then moved ahead of her. He entered the pharmacy, which was usually her last stop. Even on those weeks when she had no need for soaps or cleaning products or medicines, she would peruse them idly before indulging her weakness for chocolates, as if by her attention to serious things she had earned that small wrapped box, a thing to hide at the back of the pantry. He stayed near the picture window, feigning interest in a shaving brush as he scrutinized the waltz of the street. Difficult as it was to pick out an enemy, on two different occasions he targeted possible stalkers with eyes on Abigail. Each time it proved to be an admirer of her looks. She seemed not to notice, and he thought that perhaps things were better in the marriage. She lingered at a fruit cart and he continued to catalog those wandering by.

She crossed the street to enter the pharmacy. She did not see him. He paralleled her along the far aisle, moving toward the back of the store and the stack of wrapped boxes of chocolates. She concentrated on other goods. The nearest customer finished her shopping and returned to the front of the store. For the moment they were alone.

"Abby."

She turned, saw him, and froze. The furrow between her eyebrows deepened. "No, oh no, you can't be here."

"I need your help."

"You don't understand, you can't be here, men have been watching."

"Men? What men?"

"Bad men. They're watching us. They could be watching now."

"Did they hurt you?"

"No, they never, they didn't, they just lurk and watch where I can see them."

"Have you seen them this afternoon?"

"Well, no. But that's why I pick this time to shop."

Hightower had sent them. He pieced it together: Longbaugh knew that Hightower knew he had lied about Etta's death. Apparently he had decided it was because Longbaugh had found Etta, or was very close. Hightower would have told Moretti, and Moretti would have demanded action. Hightower had placed men where Longbaugh was likely to turn up.

"How does Robert feel about that?"

"About how you'd expect. He's hoping they make a move so he can . . . do something."

"I need to see him."

"Aren't you listening? You can't."

"It will make them go away."

"No, no, please, just go."

"When you get home, unlock the back door."

She shook her head, looking back and forth as if someone might notice them talking and get the wrong idea. "I won't, I can't."

"Abby."

She stopped then, looked at him, and thought hard. He knew that look, she was talking to herself, he could almost hear the words in her head, *Oh, Abigail, what a little fool you are. Why can't you just be strong, why do you always have to dither?*

"Come to the back in twenty minutes."

"Siringo. The lawman from out west, is he—?"

"He has a bowler hat."

ROBERT LEVI came home in the evening and Abigail met him at the door. She took his hand, surveyed the street, pulled him inside, and closed the door. She met his eyes as she led him to the ground-floor parlor.

"Abby, what is it, did something happen?"

Longbaugh stood as Levi came in.

"Robert, I need your help."

Levi's face hardened. It must not have been easy to see Longbaugh again. Longbaugh had helped him, true, but he had also brought new troubles to Levi's family. Nevertheless, Longbaugh liked seeing Levi's confidence and maturity. They were still together, there was a moment he saw them touch each other in a completely unconscious way, and he saw a strength in Levi's posture that had been missing the last time.

"Look, Mr. Longbaugh, I appreciate what you did for us, but do you have any idea the trouble you caused?"

Longbaugh knew. He waited, his eyes on Levi.

"Abby, leave us, please," said Levi.

"I'm staying," she said. "Whatever he says to you—"

"You can hear anything I have to say," said Longbaugh. "You're going to need to be a team in this."

"I want to know what this is about, Robert," said Abigail.

"You've put my wife in a bad spot, Mr. Longbaugh."

"I'm here to fix it, but what I'm asking could be dangerous."

"You know these men?"

"Black Hand."

"They're terrifying my wife! Whatever you did, you made them mad. I want them gone, Mr. Longbaugh."

"I lied to one of the men working with the Black Hand. He thinks I'm hiding something."

"Are you?"

"Yes. But they're after me, not you. I'm asking you for a favor. Get me into the subway. After that, they won't be interested in you, and they'll leave you alone."

Levi smiled grimly. "I gather you don't have the five-cent fare."

"If you don't know the tunnels, just say so and I'll go."

"You know I know the tunnels. How does that protect Abby?"

"Or where the dynamite is stored."

"Dynamite? No, Robert, absolutely not," said Abigail. Then, to Longbaugh: "He can't help you."

Levi looked at Abigail, then back at Longbaugh. Levi was a different man now, and it was clear he liked his new role. Longbaugh saw that it was new enough and precarious enough that Levi was not ready to let his wife make decisions for him, as if that might undermine his gains.

"Story going around about a Chinese kid and an explosion," said

Levi. "Haven't seen that little friend of yours lately. He used to come around, even after you left. Like he was watching after us. If I were the type to put two and two together, I'd wonder about that boy."

Longbaugh said nothing.

"I'd especially wonder, after that explosion, if I happened to hear that a friend of his had an interest in dynamite."

"If you were the type to put two and two together."

"And I'd wonder if it had something to do with revenge."

"I hate it when you talk like that," said Abigail. "It's not code, I understand you."

"I'm not interested in the dynamite for myself," said Longbaugh.

"I'm listening."

"Someone else wants it, someone I need to find. Before the Black Hand finds it. Or him."

Levi looked at Longbaugh's face and read his sincerity. Longbaugh thought that he would get the benefit of the doubt because of what he had done for them. He was not above using whatever he had to in order to get closer to finding Etta.

"Okay," said Levi. "All right. Maybe I can help."

"I don't know why I bother," said Abigail.

Longbaugh sat back and waited. Abigail was fuming, anxious eyes on her husband.

"When do you see these men?" said Longbaugh.

"A fellow comes around. He's not subtle. He wants us to see him."

"Yes, he does, he wants to remind you and scare you. Any particular time?"

"Sometimes during the day, but he's always there in the morning. Early, when I leave for work."

"With your permission, I'd like to stay the night."

Levi glanced at Abigail before he said, "All right."

"I apologize for this," said Longbaugh. "But it'll fix the problem, and it's with Abby's best interests at heart. Pack a few things, but it'll only be for a day or two. Pack light, Abby will need to carry everything alone."

"We going somewhere?" said Levi.

"The two of you are getting away from here."

"I'm not afraid of them," said Levi.

"This is how you protect your wife."

He knew this move would frustrate Hightower and annoy Moretti. But it was best to keep Abigail out of reach, in case Moretti wanted to make a statement.

"Robert, when you and I leave tomorrow, we'll pull the Black Hand shadow with us. He'll be glad to see me. Abby, you leave right after. Decide between yourselves where to meet, and tell no one. Not even me. You'll be safe after that. A few days and you can come home."

Abigail looked as if she wanted to disagree. But she looked at Levi and he nodded. She closed her eyes then, giving in, and she nodded.

HE SAT ON THE BED in the dark of his old room, alone and tired. Sleep would not come. They were out there, they could see him, but he could not see them. Siringo was close as well and had adapted to the terrain, hunting him in city camouflage. "He has a bowler hat" told him all he needed to know.

Longbaugh believed he was drawing nearer to Etta, but the closer he seemed to get, the more the circle tightened around him. Hightower had sent him to Etta's second boardinghouse on the chance he would find something Hightower had missed. They were giving him rope, as they knew he wouldn't stop until he found her, and his search made him both valuable and vulnerable. They could afford to wait, and they could afford to watch. He moved blindly forward, aware that he knew too little. Everyone else seemed to know so much more.

The night was thick and massive out there, and he picked out sounds from the street—any one of them could have come from one or more of his enemies. But he listened past all that, past the streets in the dark and out beyond the shadows, to the rivers on either side slipping along the island, shaping it, tracing it, building it up in places, carrying it away in others. The world was large and he was insignificant. She knew so much more of this world, and was at least fighting for something, whether he understood it or not, whether he agreed with it or not. He paused in his reflections as he realized Levi could save his own wife a great deal of trouble if he turned Longbaugh in to Siringo. Longbaugh thought he would not, although his imagined reasons did not fully convince him. He was relying on intuition. That made him unhappy. Experience taught him that intuition was a weak sense, a shallow sense. Intuition fooled men into thinking they had secret unconscious knowledge ready to tap when in fact it was no more than guesswork, and often poorly informed guesswork, based on past experiences that would never truly align with current conditions. Intuition was to be engaged for frivolous things, never for matters of life, love, or death. Intuition led men to quick judgments, and invited superstition. He was haunted by the men who waited in the street. His intuition told him they were close. He needed time, to think, to reason, and he did not have that time. That meant he was forced to trust his intuition, and the only edge that gave him was that it was the one thing he knew he shouldn't trust.

15

━━━━◆•◆━━━━

obert Levi walked to the end of the block pretending he was interested in buying a newspaper. He returned to where Longbaugh was waiting for him inside the open front door of the boardinghouse.

"He's alone," said Levi.

"All right. We go, and make sure he sees us."

"Just let me know when you want to lose him."

Longbaugh came out of the dark of the hallway and closed the door behind him. It was a risk, as there could be more than Black Hands waiting. He moved past the outdoor banister to the sidewalk, and was a few steps down the block when he realized what he had just seen.

"Wait," he said to Levi.

He went back. There, on the same banister where he had always left treats, was a wrapped candy. He picked it up and held it in his palm, grinning. He unwrapped it and put it in his mouth. Ginger. He no longer worried about Siringo, as his friend had just told him it was safe.

He rejoined Levi and they set out as the sun rose, Levi carrying a duffel to hold their gear. Longbaugh knew that within minutes Abigail would slip out the back with Levi's and her things. He was glad to know she would be safe.

Longbaugh wondered if Siringo knew about Moretti and the Hand. Siringo was smart, by now he probably knew all of it. He was probably a few steps ahead of Longbaugh. He might have already found Etta.

As they walked, Levi made small talk, and Longbaugh saw he was nervous. Levi explained what to him was obvious, that today was the best day to go to the Cortlandt dig, that a long-awaited shipment of dynamite had arrived in the night. No one had been able to get dynamite for weeks, so the shipment was widely anticipated as construction had been held up. War talk was everywhere, and Levi had heard rumors that earlier shipments had been diverted to the British, to be stockpiled against the Germans. Levi said that anyone looking to steal dynamite would be smart to come today, before the morning shift arrived and distributed it to the numerous dig sites. Longbaugh asked how anyone outside a small contingent of subway construction workers would know it was there. Levi then detailed the chain of access: Factory workers processed it, women workers packed it into wooden crates, then men loaded the crates onto trucks that were driven to a steamship. Every teamster knew what he was transporting, as nitroglycerin was risky and the trucks had to have padding and be outfitted with shock absorption. Stevedores moved the crates from trucks to ships. Every sailor knew when he was transporting hazardous cargo, as, again, safeguards were employed. After the trip down the Hudson, stevedores on this end unloaded it onto the dock, where subway crews carried it down into the Cortlandt Street dig, where it was at that moment. Subway workers, from foremen down to the man who lit the fuse, all knew it was coming. From factory to explosion, an extraordinary number of people had knowledge and access, most of them surviving on low wages and modest hopes, therefore vulnerable to bribery.

"Dynamite disappears all the time," said Levi.

"Very reassuring." He got a look at the Hand following them, but didn't recognize him. "Where's the most likely leak?"

"Depends. If it's graft, then it vanishes as a hidden delivery fee, taken by a middleman. If it's a disgruntled employee, or just someone needs money, it gets sold to criminals or gangsters. Some of it may walk off on its own. A slouch with a stick of dynamite hidden under his floorboards may feel like a big shot."

Longbaugh made eye contact with the gangster tailing them. The man ducked into a doorway. Another amateur.

"How do we get to it?"

"Pick a tunnel, any tunnel."

"Where?"

"Right here, if you want, under our feet," said Levi, "tunnels everywhere."

"How many can there be? There's only one subway line other than what they're digging, and then what, sewers?"

"You're walking on Swiss cheese, Mr. Longbaugh, tunnels of all shapes and sizes, including holes they dug, didn't use, and forgot about. Everybody and their pet reindeer's been digging down there. You got tunnels for the telegraph, the phone lines, old gas company lines and now new electrical wires, you got your aqueduct, and you got those old pneumatic tubes for mail delivery. A man could go from the bottom of the island right to the top without once coming up for fresh air."

Longbaugh smiled at Levi's confidence. They walked a ways and Longbaugh could tell that Levi was thinking.

"What you did for us back then, I just want to say—"

"Say nothing."

"No, it was important. She, the two of us, we—"

Longbaugh cut him off. "Things better?"

Levi looked at the sky and nodded. "They are."

Longbaugh glanced one more time at their shadow. Levi was aware of Longbaugh's itch. "You let me know when you want to lose him."

"I will."

They continued through morning-gray streets. Store owners unrolled awnings and flung soapy water from buckets against the sidewalks in front of their doors. Carts moved in to claim prime locations, hawkers yawned, scraping and rolling barrels into place, rearranging produce in wooden display bins, and counting coins for when they had to make change. A horse-drawn sprinkling wagon, carrying a large cylindrical tank, sent a heavy spray of water onto the street behind it. A one-horse street sweeper followed, dragging an angled brush roller that forced litter and filth to the gutter. A clean-up crew with shovels cleared the gutter a block behind.

"Lose him now."

"Good timing. We're right above a subway station."

"No, we're not, the subway's blocks from here."

"Trust me."

"I don't see an entrance."

"There isn't one."

They crossed the street to walk on the far side of the sprinkling wagon, keeping both sprinkler and sweeper between them and the gangster. They stayed out of the gangster's sight, and came to a grate that covered a ventilation shaft. Levi waited until the water spray had passed, then, with the sweeper coming, hurriedly lifted the dripping grate. He shouldered the duffel bag, made sure Longbaugh had a hold of the grate, then started down the shaft, using metal hand spikes that were hammered into the sides.

"Follow me, and let it close over you."

Levi dropped out of sight, displaying a comfort and aptitude that Longbaugh wasn't convinced he shared. With some difficulty, Longbaugh held the heavy grate up as he lowered himself into the shaft, then lowered it back in place over his head. The sweeper passed over and he covered his eyes to avoid the water that the brush roller splashed through the grate. He looked below and saw Levi had stopped halfway down, wedged there with his back against the shaft, his legs straight with his feet pressed against the opposite wall, as he opened his duffel to remove a carbide miner's light. He lit it, then continued to descend. Longbaugh followed, the light above growing dim while Levi's light slipped away below. He blindly found his way down, trying to keep pace. He descended out of clammy morning into dry cool, the smell of wet street gradually growing stagnant. He glanced up to see if the Hand was looking down the shaft. He saw only sky.

Levi waited at the bottom, illuminating the ground with his lamp. Longbaugh dropped to it, and Levi handed him a second lit carbide lamp, then led the way through the tunnel.

"What's this shaft for?"

"It's an air shaft, but they also used it to carry out the dirt."

"What dirt?"

"From digging the secret tunnel."

"What secret tunnel?"

"For the first subway. You'll see."

"First subway, when was this?" said Longbaugh, thinking there had been a false start a few years back.

"1870."

Levi set out ahead of him, as Longbaugh stood there, amazed, and counted out forty-three years in his head.

He had little idea of what surrounded him, his lamplight showing walls that were close. The dark made the tunnel snug, and the walls were rough to the touch. He shuddered at the unbidden fear of being buried alive. Levi dragged open a heavy door and the sound of the groan ran deeply out the tunnel behind him with the echo running back.

Levi led him into a large space. His light picked out a long steel shaft that ran overhead from an unseen room on the right to connect to a large gear on their left. For a moment his light stayed on that gear, which meshed into the teeth of a much larger gear mounted on the outside of an enormous steel machine. His light followed it up and then sideways to show it was more than twenty feet high and thirteen feet across. They climbed onto it and walked along the top, then worked their way down the other side, past a large opening, into a passage that served as an air flue. He was only seeing it in pieces via the carbide lamps, but he had a sense of its immense size.

"Okay, Levi, what is this thing?"

Levi looked back at the opening on the machine. "It's a blower."

"Not that compression chamber you talked about?"

"Naw, compression chamber's under the river. I forget what this thing's called, some kind of force blower."

Longbaugh's light found a sign on the machine's side. "Roots' Force Blast Rotary Blower?"

"Yeah, that's it." He looked at the sign Longbaugh was illuminating and laughed. "I was going to be impressed. There's this thing inside, like a fan, only a lot more powerful, strong enough to blow an entire subway car to the next station. And to bring it back, they'd reverse it and suck her home. Designed to be a giant pneumatic tunnel for delivering people. That other room back there had the boilers and the engine."

Levi's light guided them along the air flue to a door. They went through it, and by the sound of the echo, had entered yet another large space.

"Wait here." Levi's light moved away, circles of lamplight sticking to individual spots, flash clues to the room that were just as quickly inked back in by blackness. If his eyes didn't play tricks, they were surrounded by things that made no sense, windows, curtains, chandeliers, decorations. He heard the familiar hiss of gas being turned on. Levi struck a match, the flame twitched, and a gas wall fixture whumped alive, and light shaped the room. He had not hallucinated the splashes of decorations caught in Levi's light. They had entered an oversized parlor that would not have been out of place in an elegant home.

"The old waiting room." Levi's voice echoed.

It did not seem possible. "A force-blast blower and now this?"

"Subway station built right after the Civil War. First time I walked in here, it was like discovering Machu Picchu."

Longbaugh was never sure, because of his time in prison, if people were making things up to test him. "Machu Picchu," he said.

"You know, in Peru. Discovered a couple years ago, it was all over the newspapers."

The walls were painted a sterile white and were in decent shape, as it had been years since any crowds had contaminated it. Velvet curtains hung on the walls, and unless he was mistaken, covered windows. He reminded himself they were five stories underground, so windows to what? He walked to the closest velvet and pulled back a drape so old and flimsy that it seemed it would disintegrate in his hand. Behind it, a window frame had been painted on the wall, revealing a bucolic scene.

"Painted scenery," said Longbaugh.

"Yeah, Beach thought people would be less claustrophobic if there was a view."

"Beach?"

"Alfred Beach. Rich inventor, made his money publishing newspapers and magazines."

Longbaugh looked at a chandelier over his head, under one of a series of decorated arched ceilings. In the middle of the room was a sculpture that he identified as a dry fountain. A piano was against the far wall.

"There were paintings, but they're gone," said Levi.

Longbaugh saw a large rectangular object that was shaped like a crate, only with glass walls.

"And that?"

"A tank for fish."

Longbaugh walked to the edge of the platform. An unusual center track ran into a circular tunnel. The tunnel was nine feet in diameter and made of brick. Just inside the tunnel's mouth sat a subway passenger car. It was a cylinder and fit snugly within the tunnel. While it had surely been impressive in its day, it was now rotting.

"It's like a nightmare."

"Beach's daydream, actually. Traffic was so bad in 1870, he built his own subway to prove public transportation could work. Tweed and Tammany Hall were making money from the elevateds, so they were against it. Beach dug it out at night, in secret. It only goes a block, up Broadway. Old Beach sprung it on everyone, threw it open to the public, and the whole city came down for a ride. We should get moving."

"Why isn't it part of the IRT?"

"Money. Politics. Mostly money. And politics."

"How do *you* know about it?"

"We mapped it a few months ago. Stay here."

Levi went back and turned off the gas, bringing the dark back down on them, narrowing the room to the light from their lamps. He led Longbaugh through the subway car and out the far side into Beach's tunnel. They traveled the one full block to the end and climbed onto the opposite platform. On the far side of that waiting room, they went deeper into an adjoining tunnel and found metal handholds and climbed. Levi's light scanned the wall above them, located a small hole, and tapped just below it until he heard a hollow sound behind the bricks. He took a hammer from his duffel bag and expanded the hole until it was large enough for them to crawl through. They moved into a tunnel that appeared never to have been used. Time changed in the bowels of the dark, curving languidly into corners and decelerating in the blackness. They traveled on to a new juncture, then climbed an embankment that led to the sewer.

"Apologies to your nose." Levi covered his with a sleeve.

Longbaugh used his bandanna. Light from the street dropped through overhead grates at curbside, creating a series of glowing patches in the tunnel that grew smaller and smaller in the distance. The faraway street sounds rang against the concrete, the echo inseparable from the original noise, and he listened deeply to each sound as it lingered, its beginning and end infinite, indefinite. Close by was a steady, percussive gurgle of water.

Levi led him to a narrower, perpendicular tunnel, and they bent down to travel under gas pipes, moving away from both sewage and the reassuring fists of light. They moved in a crouch, and after a short time his back screamed. Levi showed no discomfort, so agile that quickly he had moved far ahead. Longbaugh pushed to catch up, knocking his head and shoulder against protruding pipe joints.

They reached the tunnel's end. The pipes kept going straight along the ceiling, as the ground dropped away, opening up on an excavation site.

"We're now under Cortlandt Street," said Levi.

The excavation was extensive. They appeared to be the only ones there, as it was early and work had yet to begin for the day. At the far end in the dark, an open tunnel connected to the larger passenger platform, but construction came to a stop at the wall beside them, awaiting dynamite that would blow open the next leg heading uptown. There was little light. The station was in the late stage of cut-and-cover tunneling, and wooden forms for concrete were in place overhead. Some of the concrete had already been poured, allowing street traffic to return to normal. Areas yet to be poured had been temporarily covered, and thin lines of white leaked between the wooden planks. Dozens of vertical beams held up the street, and mounds of dirt waited to be hauled away by parked motorized dump trucks with the name Galion Buggy Co. on their doors. All these obstructions would help keep them hidden. Levi put out his lamp. Longbaugh did the same.

As Longbaugh scanned the area, he leaned against a thick hunk of wood. At first he thought it part of another support column, but the wood under his fingers was uneven and had been damaged by fire. On closer examination, he was touching the rib of a very old ship, attached to the curved keel of a prow, with the planks, deck, and masts long gone. The keel looked to have sailed right out of the partially excavated dirt wall.

"What is this?"

"Oh yeah, we found a ship."

"A ship?!"

"Dutch sailing ship, it's pretty old."

"It's buried!"

"This used to be the edge of the Hudson River. She burned and sank maybe three hundred years ago."

"You care to tell me how you know this?"

"My foreman, Mr. Kelly, he's a big history guy. He even knows the name of it, something like Tiger, but in Dutch."

Longbaugh scratched his head. "First an air subway, and now there's a ship in the tunnel."

"Great city, huh?"

"And the rest of her?"

"Oh, she's in there."

"When do you dig her out?"

"Probably not in the budget, although Kelly's trying."

"Got to love progress."

"So what now?" said Levi.

"Now?"

"Up to you. We're here. There's your dynamite." Levi pointed at something down on the floor of the excavation near a motorized delivery truck.

It took Longbaugh a moment to see that he meant the pile of rectangular crates covered with a tarp. He climbed down to it. Levi followed.

Longbaugh pulled back the tarp. The crates were stamped with a logo, Spense Co. The top crate was open, and he moved it to see the orderly grouping of dynamite cartridges.

"This is when you get out of here," said Longbaugh.

"And if you need me to get *you* out?"

"No offense, but if that happens, no one can help me."

Longbaugh drew his weapon and checked it, spinning the chamber just to hear it whir. Levi watched his expert fingers in silence. Longbaugh replaced the piece in his belt.

"Thanks for getting me here," said Longbaugh. "Go meet your wife."

A loud scraping sound froze them.

Levi looked across and quietly explained the sound: "Temporary gate to the street."

Longbaugh pulled him down to a crouch and they backed away from the crates and took refuge behind a support pillar.

"Go *now*."

Levi leaned his head out to watch the silhouette of a man coming down the truck ramp.

"Security guard. I know him, Bill Marley."

Longbaugh jerked his head sideways to send him off. Levi gave him a look, but went. Longbaugh did not watch to see where. He watched Bill Marley.

Marley ambled down the truck ramp with the light from his lantern dancing at his feet. Longbaugh knew he would go directly to the dynamite crates.

Marley reacted before Longbaugh heard the sound. Marley baffled the light from his lantern. A sizzle of energy animated his body, as if he listened with his chest, his shoulders, his whole head.

In the far corner of the site, a wooden plank above them was wrenched out of place. Longbaugh looked from Marley to the intruder. Marley was moving in the direction of the dynamite crates. The intruder pushed his legs into the rectangle of light he had just created, then lowered his body down. He scraped the plank into place above him. In the gloom, Longbaugh watched the man slide down the dirt side of the excavation to the ground. He then rushed toward the dynamite crates in a motion not unlike a jackrabbit's.

Bill Marley waited quietly. Longbaugh heard the occasional curse as the intruder ran into unseen obstacles in the dark. He eventually slowed his pace. He had not bothered to listen for others, and appeared to have no idea he was not alone. Marley rose to intercept the intruder. The two shapes closed in on each other in the dark, a slow convergence, sailing ships on a collision course. Marley reached the crates and ducked down. The intruder arrived on the other side a few seconds later and put his hands on the tarp as if absorbing the magical emanations from a religious relic. Marley stood up across from him and shined his light in the intruder's face. "Stop right there."

Longbaugh was not surprised to see Prophet in the light, his eyes wide open, blue eyeballs surrounded by white, his hands on his goal, yet frozen, as if he dared not move.

"What do you think you're doing?" said Bill Marley.

Prophet moved his mouth, but nothing came out, as if tasting Marley's words to make sense of them.

This time, Longbaugh heard the others before Marley. Their dark shapes came from the mouth of the finished part of the tunnel, and Longbaugh tried to count them in the gloom. Four, five. Six. And one more over there, seven of them. No, six, hard to know for certain in this light. They were loud, and once Marley heard them, he dropped to a knee, turning his already baffled lamp completely off while gripping Prophet's shoulder to control him. Longbaugh wondered why Marley didn't hail them, as he assumed they were subway workers arriving for their shift.

The newcomers were out of the tunnel and crossing the long platform, approaching the dynamite. Longbaugh tried to figure some way to separate one nervous anarchist from six sandhogs and a subway guard. The newcomers' lamps illuminated the dust kicked up by their shoes, creating a low, glowing cloud below their waists.

He heard their voices now that they were closer. He recognized one of them and was surprised. The lisp further identified Flexible, as Longbaugh had been the cause of that lisp. Levi had been right. Too many people knew about the small window of opportunity.

"Don't come any closer!"

Bill Marley was standing. Longbaugh had expected Marley to be smart enough to stay out of the Black Hand's way. The man was taking his job too seriously. The six Hands spread out.

"Stop!" yelled Marley, standing up with spread fingers in the air.

Snatches of white animated the pistol blasts in the dark, giving away their positions, one coming from a close angle Longbaugh did not expect. Marley threw himself down, getting out of the way.

Longbaugh soured. He had little interest in protecting the anarchist who was in love with his wife. If he hadn't needed him, he would gladly have handed him over gift-wrapped to the Hand. They were closing in and would shoot Prophet in short order. While he imagined Moretti had sent his boys to steal explosives, it was possible—highly unlikely, but possible—that Moretti knew Prophet's connection to Etta, and his boys were there to grab him. Longbaugh considered his quickly diminishing options.

He counted the lanterns he could see in the dark: Four, two of them close together. He could at least put some doubt in their minds about going after Prophet, maybe scramble them, or chase a few, improve the odds. He drew his Peacemaker and came up, firing off four rounds in rapid succession, so quick that the blasts roared almost as one, and two of the lights vanished, while broken glass tinkled from a third. That one flickered, wavered, but did not die until the owner squelched it.

He had their attention. Nervous yelling amid a paroxysm of return fire, then their inept guns paused. One of them barked urgent orders, warning them not to hit the dynamite. Longbaugh broke open the Colt, dug out the spent casings, replaced them, slammed shut the cylinder and listened with a full load. He picked each of them out as they shifted, scrambled, reloaded, whispered.

Marley snaked his forearm around Prophet's neck and rose as he dragged him away from the crates. Longbaugh guessed that Marley thought Prophet was one of them, and was using him as a shield. Not the best idea, as he'd been protected by his proximity to the dynamite. When he was far enough away, a Hand risked a shot and Marley tumbled in a spasm of curses and pain. Prophet, now free of Marley's grasp, crawled back to the crates. Longbaugh rose and fired at the spot of the shooter and heard a harmonic curse to Marley's and knew the Peacemaker had done damage.

Longbaugh had forgotten about Levi until the sandhog decided to play hero. Down he came from safety to help the subway guard. Watching him run, Longbaugh understood that Marley was one of Levi's men.

The Hands saw him, and the gloom lit up like a meadow of percussive fireflies, their guns flaming in concert. Longbaugh saw Levi tumble, and he pictured Abigail's face when she learned his fate after finally getting him back, but then Levi was crawling, alive, rolling for cover behind the large tire of a Galion Buggy truck.

"Levi!"

"I'm okay. Damn! I'm okay," said Levi.

"Do what I say next time!"

"Right. Next time."

Longbaugh looked at Prophet by the dynamite crate. Damned fool, he thought. Not worth saving. Prophet leaned his back against the crate and reached up and over his head, grabbing dynamite cartridges as if they were forbidden candy, stuffing them in his coat pockets. Clearly he had given no thought to what a stray bullet would do to nitroglycerin.

Longbaugh focused on the Hands. He wanted better ground. He leaned and someone fired. He dropped and rolled, leveled his Colt, and fired on the position. A lamp flared bright white, capturing Silvio in his spin, mid-twist, hit twice, thigh and ass, filling the air with acid shrieks.

The shrieking gradually lost volume as Silvio dragged himself away with his face in the ground. "I'm hit, oh God, I'm hit, oh God, oh God, help me—"

The others marked Longbaugh's position and were coming, determined to run him and anyone else down. His position was not good. Levi was pinned behind him, Marley to his left vocally hosting a bullet, while his favorite anarchist was lining his pockets with explosives.

Longbaugh was amazed that Prophet did not run, continuing to greedily swipe cartridges as the Hand closed in. Prophet may have deserved his fate from Moretti's boys, but Longbaugh would not abandon him, not without getting the information he needed.

He braced himself for a suicide run, to get between Prophet and the Black Hand. He checked his gun, surveyed the terrain, then remembered Flexible. The grinning *paisan* was out there. And Silvio as well, so maybe a couple of others from that first night. Superstitious toughs who had imagined their own private ghost. Who was he to deny them their apparition? At that moment, they did not know who was shooting at them in the dark. Time to inform them. He pulled the bandanna up over his nose.

He called to Levi, "Lamp!"

Levi sent his lamp in a looping throw so that it landed in a soft mound of dirt near Longbaugh's shoulder. He set it alongside his own lamp.

Longbaugh looked for the best angle. He would use the lamps in tandem to make a stronger beam of light. He arranged them side by side, pointed at the nearby wall, then saw the bones of the ship and decided to aim them there instead. It was a big dumb risk, but less suicidal than his first plan. The moment he stood up in the light, he would be exposed to one or more of the Hands, but if he knew gangster mentality, when they saw what he was about to show them, the apparition just might hijack their attention. He was counting on them reacting without thinking.

They were shifting in the dark out there, coming closer and getting into position. No chance to test it. He made brief eye contact with Levi, who looked as if he understood what was about to happen.

Longbaugh lit both lamps.

The boys went quiet out there when the light hit the ship's ribs and threw curious shadows at the wall. He listened to their whispers, "What's happening?" "Where's that light from?" "What *is* that?" They were uncertain, but not yet aware that they were afraid. They still believed they had power in numbers.

With their attention diverted, Levi moved from his spot.

Longbaugh also moved, sliding along the ground just under the beams of light. To keep their interest on that wall, he had to make his entrance soon. He watched the wall as he crawled away from the lamps to make sure his shadow didn't show too early. He judged the distance, decided he was in the right place, and slowly began to stand. His shadow climbed the wall.

Longbaugh jolted when a sharp, penetrating whistle animated his climbing shadow, as if his shade was actually hissing within the ship's skeleton. For an impossible moment he thought his shadow was the source of the noise. Then he looked and saw Levi turning the handle of a steam valve. The blasting shriek grew. He realized in that instant *he* had been the credulous one. He nodded to Levi, who nodded back.

This was the moment. If Moretti's boys kept their eyes on the shadow, he had them. If they noticed him standing there in the open, he would be slaughtered in the crossfire. His shadow reached its full height, a frightening, damaged thing looming between the ribs of the ship. The loud steam began to lose intensity. But the effect had been better than he had hoped for, ominous and gruesome, and on that scale, if you were an ignorant and gullible sort, goddamn terrifying. The impossible unholy thing hovered over their heads and riveted them, chilling their hearts and inflaming their imaginations. As the steam fizzled out, he could better hear their squeals. He moved a step sideways and the horrible shadow twisted between the ship's ribs, and his heart was mean and glad as the superstitious boys cringed. The side of his body was fully lit by the carbide lamp, in plain sight of at least two of the Hands, but that massive shadow had them by the balls. They never once looked at him.

"*Gesù Cristo*, it's the Ghost!"

"*That's* the Ghost? *Egli è enorme!*"

"I *told* you he was real!"

"He's after us!"

"*Madre di Dio! Levati dai coglioni!*"

The Hands opened fire, but as Longbaugh had hoped, they fired at the shadow. Longbaugh saw bullets chunk the wood, pock the wall, dirt bursting into the air like water splashes, then a line of loose earth poured out of the holes like tiny waterfalls. The steam hiss was done, but it didn't matter. As more bullets hit ribs and shadow, he took a step closer to the lights and the ghost grew larger and more terrifying, as if he was moving closer to them. They yelled and fired as they backed away, fleeing, their aim ever more erratic. He raised his hand, as if reaching for them, and one of the Hands screamed and fell to the ground, trying to run on his knees.

Prophet looked directly at him. He had watched the whole thing. He pointed at Longbaugh, then at the shadow. He began to laugh. Longbaugh aimed a finger to keep him in place. Then Prophet yelled, "Save yourselves! Run, boys, save yourselves!" while laughing maniacally.

The gangsters ran, the gunfire silent but for the occasional shot over a shoulder. Levi closed the steam valve.

Prophet went on laughing, "Save yourselves, little grease boys!" Longbaugh grimaced at his unworthy arrogance, his casual racism, and he was tempted to call them all back and hand over the spineless coward.

He turned off the lamps. He listened to the pounding feet of distant runners, back near the tunnel, and once in there, the footsteps echoed louder. He looked at Levi, who stared at him with awe and respect. In the dark, to his right, already about halfway to the tunnel, Silvio continued dragging himself away, whining into dirt, calling out when he realized he had been left behind, "Come back, help me, don't leave me here with that thing—" But the others were too far away to hear him. He cared nothing for Silvio, not after Brooklyn, and his frightened whining did not move him.

Out of the dark came a tiny flash and a clap-sudden gunshot, and Silvio was silent. Longbaugh dropped to a knee, aimed where Silvio had been whimpering while squinting into the dark, looking for movement, anticipating an attack, already knowing what had happened and trying to pick out the shooter. For the flash to have been that small, the muzzle of the automatic must have been held directly against the target. After a moment he heard footsteps running in the other direction, leaving the silent Silvio and finding deeper darkness.

He was up and charging the spot, trying to see the escaping figure. The shooter was moving quickly for a big, bulky man. The small voice inside his head mocked him. There *had* been seven. The lamps were somewhere back there, and when he knew he wouldn't catch the shooter, he went back for one. He lit it and aimed the light at Silvio's drag marks, following blood until he reached shoes. He stopped, passed the light up Silvio's legs to the bullet wounds in his thigh and buttocks. But those wounds had not pinned the boy against the ground. The light tracked up the boy's shirt until he came to a small hole drilled into the back of his skull. He had died instantly and lost little blood. Longbaugh chose not to turn Silvio over to see the exit wound in the middle of his face.

He returned to Prophet, walking slowly.

"Run away, run away, little grease pigs!" Prophet's laughter was forced, as he tried to sustain his excitement.

"You can shut your mouth, they can't hear you."

"Little pigs," Prophet said more quietly, as if he had to gradually decelerate before he could stop.

Longbaugh wanted to rain the carnal fear of Hell down on the man, but he only said, "They'll be back. We're going."

"But you'll protect me." Prophet's knowing smile curdled the last morsel of his compassion. "They wouldn't *dare* mess with *you*."

Longbaugh walked rapidly to Prophet, grabbed him by the scruff of his coat, and brought him to his feet. Prophet continued his self-satisfied chortle and Longbaugh curled his fist and hit him just hard enough to amaze him, a quick thump to the chest. Prophet drew in a stunned inhale.

"What was *that* for?"

Longbaugh kept his eyes locked with Prophet's as he set his lips and reached down into the anarchist's pocket, unloading dynamite cartridges one by one by one, lining them back up in the crate. Prophet tried to object, but could only manage, "Those are mine—"

"One bullet, and you'll go up like some lunkhead carrying dynamite in his pocket."

He came to the last cartridge and his fingers found the folded paper Prophet had tried to give to the editor of *The Masses*. He put the last stick in the crate, and secretly slipped Prophet's article into his own pocket.

Prophet's expression changed, and Longbaugh read it as a revelation. "I *know* you."

Yes, thought Longbaugh, *you saw me at the magazine office.*

"From a dream, you were sent here."

Oh wonderful, thought Longbaugh.

"You're the emissary. You're the missionary, you're the tributary."

Please shut your mouth.

"You're the guardian angel. You're divine intervention, you saved me so I can make history."

The Prophet Jonah.

"You're the sign that I'm doing the right thing," said Prophet.

Longbaugh dragged him along to where Levi had finished binding a tourniquet around Bill Marley's upper thigh.

"He'll be all right once we get him to a doctor," said Levi.

"Can you get him out?"

"Crew'll be along, we'll take him in one of the trucks."

"Do what we talked about. Don't go home. Take care of your wife."

"And you?"

"You did well today, but for your sake I hope you never see me again."

16

Prophet made certain that he stayed close to Longbaugh once they reached the street above the cut-and-cover excavation. He was not aware that Longbaugh had scanned the area to see that they were alone. They traveled Cortlandt Street, away from the river, then turned north. The morning sun was low but bright, and Prophet blinked and squinted, as if his blue eyes couldn't handle the intensity.

"I got you this far, now you're on your own." Longbaugh's comment was disingenuous. He knew Prophet would never let him get away.

"No, what are you saying? We stick together, don't you know how this works? You're my spiritual guide. Why didn't you let me keep the dynamite?"

Longbaugh let silence answer that question. He walked as if unaware that Prophet followed.

"So what are you?" said Prophet. "Seraphim? Cherubim?"

"Something else."

"Right, good, an angel of death guarantees my plan's success."

Longbaugh promised himself he would be patient. He still had things to learn from this man.

"The first part of your plan better be to go home."

"Right this way." Prophet led him north. "My own private angel."

"You know how asinine that sounds?"

"I am prepared to convert to my angel's doctrine if it carries me to my goal."

PROPHET LED HIM through an alley to a room behind an oyster bar. Longbaugh was impressed by the well-disguised location. As the bar had its own rear exit, no one was likely to test this other door in the shadow. A door on the inside of Prophet's room would have led into the bar had it not been painted shut with the doorknob removed. No one on the other side would ever investigate.

Other than a small pallet on the floor, a chair and table were the room's furnishings. There was little space for much else, as the place housed dozens of piles of newspapers, each paper assigned its own stack, many of the stacks reaching chest or shoulder height, apparently arranged by their degree of irritation. The top newspaper on every pile had come under attack. Each individual story had been copyedited—underlined, circled, scratched out—with different-colored pencil or ink. He rolled back a few in the closest stack and saw that Prophet had attacked the earlier editions as well, and he noted editing marks at each fold all the way to the floor. His attacks had started some time ago, as the oldest editions at the bottom were yellowing. He scanned other piles. They were the same. It appeared as if almost every article in every newspaper had suffered his pique. What dedication! Here was a full-time job at an elevated level of outrage. And Prophet was nothing if not an egalitarian critic. *The Evening Call, The Evening Mail, The Times, Morning Telegraph, Evening Sun, Wall Street Journal, American Banker, New York American, The Press,* and these were just the papers close enough for Longbaugh to make out their names. There were more, many more. Not one was left unbloodied. In fact, the radical paper, *Free Society*, had been more savagely attacked than the others. Years of newspapers and magazines, each one read assiduously, each one disagreed with vehemently, edited with fury and discontent, the brilliant editor unmasking their idiocy, their infantile philosophy. Here was a rare and special madness that he very nearly admired.

"How do you like the place?" said Prophet.

"Astonishing," said Longbaugh.

"Thank you. It's one of my favorite spots."

"You've read all these?"

"How else can I expose their fallacies?"

"You should offer yourself as an editor."

"I do. Persistently."

"I am impressed."

"Thank you. Not many understand my dedication. I suppose that's why you were assigned to me."

Every time Longbaugh tried to give him the benefit of the doubt, Prophet said something annoying. "And give up the angel thing."

"Sorry."

Longbaugh looked past the newspapers and scanned the room for personal items, clothing, shoes, a suitcase perhaps. He saw nothing of the sort.

"What if someone finds out where you live?"

"I have other places."

He attempted wit. "Marble palaces, châteaus."

"We all sacrifice for our beliefs."

No humor allowed. Longbaugh decided to keep his questions neutral. "You pay rent?"

"Rent? Me?"

He could do this, he could ignore the undue arrogance. "I bet you come from money."

"You think I'm not serious."

I think you're harmless. Out of your ridiculous mind, but ultimately harmless. He tested the response in his head before he said, "I know how serious you are." Longbaugh turned to take in the room. "Although I guess you don't know many women." He was sorry the moment he said it. He had meant to be more subtle when turning the discussion to the women in Prophet's life.

"I know women."

"Ask one over sometime, maybe you'll be inspired to clean."

"I'll have you know I lived with a woman."

"Whenever people say 'I'll have you know,' it means they're lying." He couldn't seem to get off this tack, but Prophet kept serving it up.

"Right here in this very room."

"Your mother doesn't count."

Prophet grew more insistent. "She was beautiful."

Longbaugh looked behind a newspaper stack. "You smell something?"

"It was weeks and she was in love with me."

Longbaugh shook his head, because he just couldn't do it, so he quit all pretense. If he was lucky, Prophet would dub him an Old Testament angel filled with vengeance and hostility. He pulled out the paper he had taken from Prophet's pocket and proceeded to unfold it. Prophet recognized it immediately, and his hands dove into his overcoat to find his hard work missing.

"How did you get that?"

Longbaugh read the title aloud, "'The Great Leon Czolgosz.'"

"You have no right, give it back."

"Oh, did you write this?"

"Leon Czolgosz was a hero and a patriot, and I want it back."

"Since when do anarchists have heroes?"

"Give it to me."

He read on: "'Influenced by Gaetano Bresci.'"

"Bresci was an Italian, a great anarchist. He fought for the common man."

"Says here he killed King Umberto of Italy."

"Which inspired Leon Czolgosz."

"I bet you're mispronouncing that. And Leon—"

"Assassinated President McKinley."

"And you mean to tell me *The Masses* wouldn't print this?"

Prophet went pale. "How did you know that?"

Longbaugh sniffed, pretending to read silently.

Prophet collected his wits. "May I please have it back?"

Longbaugh heard the word *please* and put the paper on Prophet's table. "Leon used a gun. Why do you need dynamite?"

"Whatever suits the target."

"Must be some target if it's bigger than a president."

"I can't be tricked into giving away my plan."

"You've never used dynamite in your life."

"I have so."

"You mean, 'I'll have you know I have so.' Too bad you didn't get what you needed."

"I can still get it."

Longbaugh turned away dismissively. "Sure." It was foolish to torture the man. He looked for a way to take a step back. He was being impatient, but it was early and he hadn't had breakfast. He began to plan when in the conversation to mention Etta.

"You don't believe me," said Prophet.

"I don't see the same dedication as Leon."

"I, you, I'll have you know—" Prophet caught himself, scowled, cleared his throat. "I am a serious man, as serious as Leon. And I have a source for dynamite."

"Then why break into the subway? Why not go right to your source?"

Prophet looked at Longbaugh as if he were a newborn kitten he was intending to drown. "I don't like to pay for it. But I will if I have to. Fidgy will be back in a few days."

The name Fidgy rang a bell. "I knew you had to have friends."

"Friend? Fidgy? The *rosbif*?"

Longbaugh laughed in spite of himself. "The roast beef? Anarchy slang?"

"What the French call a Brit, 'the *rosbif* popped over from his castle in Twee-Sleeves.'"

"So he's a supporter of anarchy."

"Not our Fidge. He supports nothing. The *rosbif* was born without a conscience."

"No wonder you have to pay him. So how does it work, buying explosives?"

"I don't go to *him*, I do business with his man. That's the thing about the rich. They're so cheap that they force their people to be disloyal. Loney likes thinking he can step up to the good life."

"So 'Loney' sells it out the back door."

"He wants a little of his own."

"You know way too much about rich people to be an anarchist."

"You can't bait me."

"No. You're too true to the cause."

Prophet lifted his hand, as if toasting with a wineglass. "The cause."

"Taken to its logical conclusion, how can an anarchist pledge any cause? Don't you want to tear it all down to random noise?"

"As I always say, 'Anyone who makes plans for after the revolution is a reactionary.'"

Longbaugh immediately thought of the Paterson woman's story, realized what Prophet was saying, and went with his educated guess. "You're quoting Bakunin."

Prophet was stung. "Oh. Ah." And he began to cough.

Longbaugh chortled inside, bull's-eye, then nonchalantly plucked the closest newspaper from a pile and, with Prophet twitching, walked halfway across the room, set it on a different pile, and continued on until he was leaning against the far wall.

He hadn't seen it until that moment and was now glad he had decided to annoy the man, because otherwise he might not have noticed the olive ribbon hanging from between newspapers in one of the stacks. It was likely that Prophet was unaware of it. Longbaugh left it there, but it was good to find another crumb left on the trail.

"I don't much like you," said Prophet, very alert, staring at the out-of-place newspaper.

"I saved your life and didn't ask for thanks. Why wouldn't you like me?"

Prophet's eyes played tennis between the rogue newspaper and its home, one foot tapping as if needing to walk.

"How did you come to the cause?" said Longbaugh.

Prophet tapped himself up to standing. "It was revealed to me."

Prophet walked around the room, initially away from the misbehaving newspaper, a transparent tactic, until he stopped pretending and ran to it.

"Doesn't matter who you hurt," said Longbaugh. "As long as it's for the cause."

Prophet took up the newspaper. "How could it possibly matter? We live tiny, meaningless lives. We're nothing, we're insects."

"If we're insignificant, why not live and let live?"

Prophet carried it away. "If I can send the human race back to the Garden of Eden, I've done everyone a favor." He arrived at its original spot and laid it tenderly on top, aligning the edges with the newspapers below. "I'll be the serpent."

"I heard someone say the serpent offered knowledge." He was more convinced than ever that Prophet was a danger only to his own sanity.

"You'll thank me when it happens."

"I saw you with a woman," said Longbaugh.

"What woman? Eve? We still in the garden?"

"You know the one."

Prophet's lips drew together coyly, almost shaping a heart. "And what if I do?"

"Impressive."

"Smart women are drawn to powerful men."

Longbaugh looked to see if Prophet was making a joke. He was not. Prophet wanted to be known as a ladies' man.

"She lived here."

"Looks to be gone now."

"I wore her out."

Longbaugh kept a grip on his thinning patience. "Where could a woman go after experiencing this?"

"Not curious about my plan?"

"She wounded you."

"You got *that* backward."

"The pain must be unbearable."

"I barely knew her."

Prophet was getting tricky, changing his story. Time to bring him back. "Oh, I think you knew her very well."

"I knew she was naïve, but then, aren't all women? But this one was trainable. Most are so set in their beliefs, they can't see the truth when it's right in front of them. But there was hope for Ethel."

Longbaugh stopped his smile before it showed.

"Women fall in love with their teachers," said Prophet. "I couldn't stop her. What I could do was give her a path, change the way she looked at the world, change the way she dressed. This is the key to change, I'll have you know, alter the outward appearance of a person and you change the way they think."

"You'll have me know."

"Put a uniform on a soldier. Put the hat on a copper."

"Put rags on a bourgeois."

"Exactly."

If she wore rags, it was to blend in with the neighborhood. "So maybe you did know her."

"I said so, didn't I?"

"Where did she go next?"

"Don't you know?"

Longbaugh waited.

"To the *rosbif*," said Prophet.

"The rich one? The Brit? Fidgy?" The moment he spoke the name aloud, he remembered where he had heard it before.

Prophet nodded.

"I hear he's back in England," said Longbaugh. "She go with him?"

"No."

He fought to make his voice sound natural. "Then where?"

Prophet was suspicious. This angel had asked one too many questions about her. "Not sure. She hides."

He made a side step. "Will you see this Fidgy when he's back?"

"I'll see his man."

"When?"

"Fidgy's a collector. He'll be back in time for the show."

"What show?"

"Some bourgeois art thing."

"Fidgy. You don't even know his real name."

"Sydney. Sydney Fedgit-Spense."

There it was. Queenie's lover. Queenie had told Etta about her Englishman. But Etta wasn't interested in him because of Queenie, there was some other reason. He put it together as bits came from every direction. SFS, the dangling fragment. Spense Co. stamped on the dynamite crates. Lillian Wald knew an arms dealer, Mr. Spense. He had assumed Etta had gone into hiding with the anarchists because Hightower got too close, but maybe there was something else, maybe she had used Prophet to get to Fidgy. Prophet knew Fidgy, Prophet got his dynamite from Fidgy, or at least Fidgy's man.

Etta, what in the hell have you gotten yourself into?

"What?"

"I didn't say anything."

"Yes you did, you said, 'Etta, what the hell you got yourself into?'"

Longbaugh said nothing.

Now Prophet put things together. "You're talking about Ethel. You're the reason she's hiding."

Longbaugh bit his tongue.

"You're after her, you want to—no, wait, you're not Black Hand, you're another one of her conquests, you're in *love* with her. Christ, they're falling out of the sky. I can't believe she got to you, too, no, don't tell me, you can't be without her, you can't live until you win her back."

Prophet smiled from a place deep in the bosom of his victory. He had lucked onto Longbaugh's soft spot. Like all unloved, bullied men, he lived for the day when he could uncover someone else's weakness and become the bully himself.

"So you know, then, you know she was an untrustworthy cheat, only out for herself," said Prophet. "Her plans don't include folks like us. One look and she went to him, the big fish, not a second thought. Oh, he'll tire of her, all right, mark my words, and then where will she be? *Then* where will she be?" Prophet paused as if he was lucky to be rid of her, as if he had finally gotten even, as if he had put her far behind him, as if he was over her completely, but he couldn't keep it up, he couldn't make it so that he actually believed it, and out of nowhere he burst, he exploded, he shrieked as if every hurt he had ever suffered peaked in this one woman's betrayal:

"She made promises to me!"

His bellow was trapped and deadened between the piles of newspapers. He looked stung as he realized how completely he had exposed himself. He blinked and breathed through his mouth. But even then, to cover, he rushed to play the bully again.

"But it's worse for you. She left you to come to me."

Longbaugh forced a smile.

"Oh, now you have nothing to say. Now you've lost your voice." Prophet sneered. "Come on, broken heart, how does it feel, knowing what happened right here? Aren't you jealous of me?"

Longbaugh shook his head. "I can't abide a man without a sense of humor."

Longbaugh did not believe him, but even so, Prophet's words cut. Longbaugh was thinking, distracted.

Prophet picked up the folded article on Leon Czolgosz, and moved closer to the door. Then Prophet had his hand on the doorknob and was outside and running, and it was too late to stop him.

Longbaugh moved to the door and saw Prophet run out of sight around the corner. He had not learned anything about Prophet's plot. But that did not matter.

He went back in the room and took the olive ribbon from between the newspapers and put it in his pocket.

Sydney Fedgit-Spense.

17

─────◆─────

ydney Fedgit-Spense. The dangling initials in the fragment end of her last letter. He unfolded it while on the trolley, reviewing it for clues that might now make better sense, but despite Queenie's having mentioned her connection to the man, Etta had put very little about SFS in her letters. He guessed that, during that time, she had yet to understand his importance. Whatever had turned her energy to him may have occurred in the last three months.

He had slept poorly the previous night in his old room at Levi and Abigail's boardinghouse. The adrenaline from the violence in the subway was wearing off. A dull heat tested his eyes. He let them close for the smallest second, for some hope of relief.

His body was heavy, lulled by the creeping trolley rolling lurching rolling over cobblestones, cobblestones that came up, up to meet his forehead, and his subjacent mind took hold and whispered that something was wrong and he had misunderstood everything that had happened since he arrived. He was too late, to find her, to help her, to save her. She was gone, she had chosen to be gone, the trail of crumbs ran to the edge of the abyss and he was left behind, the trolley rolling, lurching. Images curled around him like curious smoke, images real and imagined, concrete and unreliable, untrue and completely, utterly believable. He was a Jonah swallowed by the city whale, aswim in gastric juice, wearing boots and Stetson, gasping for air in an empty fish tank five stories below the streets.

He clawed his way back to awake, hating the dream, touching his forehead, warm from the flat of the trolley window. Cobblestones hurried past and his mind was thick, rolling in fur.

The trolley turned at Greenwich Street, and he stepped off onto a sidewalk that rolled beneath his feet as if he was still moving. He smelled something on the wind, a change in the air. Flies were biting, rain coming. He watched the trolley roll and lurch away and something nagged, tugging his sleeve, but when he looked he saw only thread.

The darkness owned him, it spoiled the sun and held him motionless on the sidewalk. He was still there when the floppy literary editor came upon him on his way in to work. One look at Longbaugh's eyes and he took his arm and led him indoors.

The editor guided him to an out-of-the-way office and graced him with silence. Longbaugh combed his mind for small talk, a way in to a conversation he was not ready to have. "Did you find out about that person, that, what was her name, Duncan?"

"Isadora. Truth is, I made all that up about her coming back to America just to spur my lethargic reporters. Turned out to be true."

Longbaugh looked up. "So who's Isadora Duncan?"

"And that is the thing, who indeed? We go on about the private lives of public people when there is real work to be done."

Longbaugh had meant it as an actual question, as prison had left gaps in his knowledge, but, being mistaken for a wit, he let it pass.

"We make choices based on the limited knowledge we have. You never know where your choices will lead. Covering Isadora may draw certain readers but chase away others. Or perhaps we'll get lucky and all the old solemn readers will ignore our Duncan blasphemy and the new Isadora readers will stay and be converted."

"You believe that?"

The editor shrugged. "Precisely never."

"Would you print the Duncan story if you had it?"

"Probably not. Not important enough. Although I shouldn't judge. Things we believe in today may turn against us tomorrow and prove us completely wrong, all to our spectacular benefit."

"I imagine that happened to that fellow who shot McKinley. Except for the spectacular benefit."

"Leon Czolgosz. When our enemies are in their cups, and sometimes when they're not, progressives are tarred with his brush, the man who traded McKinley's tariffs for the Big Stick. How he would have hated TR, the direct result of his action. You're the second person in a week who's mentioned him."

Longbaugh knew who had been the first. The editor did not remember Longbaugh had been with him when Prophet was pitching his piece. He noticed his friend's shirttail hanging outside his trousers. Different shirt, same runaway tail. "I'm here about Sydney Fedgit-Spense."

The floppy editor was hilariously upbeat. "You mean that filth-spewing, pus-fingered brigand, that oily, diarrheic garden slug? The man's intestines should be unwound from his abdomen and threaded through his nostrils."

Longbaugh smiled. "That so?"

"I know, I go too far, after all, he's a thoroughly charming bloke, the old Brit. Why would you want to know the slightest thing about him?"

"To protect someone."

"Now *that* I buy. Old Fidgy-Spense is an ordnance broker who knows his consumer. He would start a war if he could increase his profit, playing one side against the other, and he sees nothing wrong in that. Lie to the Germans that the British are building up their armaments, and you sell them rifles and grenades. Warn the Brits that the Germans just bought rifles and grenades, and sell them howitzers. The cycle doesn't stop until they're so incensed by the other's stockpile that they have to use them. It's a little bit brilliant, actually."

"You don't think politics has something to do with it?"

"Politics has everything to do with it, my simplistic argument is an emotional screed, an unfair overreaction to a man I dislike, but then everyone's reacting emotionally—Austria-Hungary, France, Germany, England, Russia, the Balkans, Jesus, who am I leaving out, Japan, Belgium—anyway, nothing spices up a political disagreement like having a bomb or two in your pocket."

"So write about him, expose him."

"You mean if I happened to have access to a publication that would print the actual words I write? Problem is, we're already being sued this month. Can't advocate a new lost cause until September."

"Then why do what you do?"

"I defy augury." He watched Longbaugh's expression. "No? Shakespeare? I have to stop trying to impress people."

"I've been away."

"No no, it's me, just a tedious habit."

"As if your future had been foretold and you would prove it not so."

He smiled ruefully. "Doesn't seem nearly as clever when you put it like that." He thought for a moment. "I'd like to think we're building toward something. After Triangle, we seem to have the public on our side for the first time, starting to see workers as human beings. Even the politicians see it, with the hearings and new laws. I'd like to think that that tragedy will help make things better. People like Fidgy can never see it that way. He never looks back. I'm not sure he has a conscience."

"Funny. That's what Prophet said."

"Prophet is another one. Anarchy, well . . . men like Prophet, they misunderstand change. They want to tear things down and let the chips fall where they may. I'd like to think we all want things to be better. And despite my very real desire for change, it may be best if things move slowly. Go too fast, and you don't see the repercussions coming at you. Don't tell Eastman I said that. Hell, don't tell my readers."

"Where is Fidgy now?"

"Out on the ocean coming back from Merry Olde."

"I've heard him called a collector. What does that mean?"

"Art. Money. Homes. Women. It's said he had important paintings on the *Titanic* and they all went down without him."

"I grieve for his loss. I had heard he survived."

"What does that tell you?"

"He can swim?"

"You have a festive sense of humor, sir. The order was, women and children first. Yet he survived. What does that tell you?"

Longbaugh realized it had been a rhetorical question.

"One last thing," said Longbaugh. "I hear he's coming back for a show."

"The Armory Show. I have people covering it. It's an art exhibition of new European painters. Our readers and contributors are excited to read about it."

Longbaugh was grateful for the information, and said so. "I may need to meet him there."

The editor wrote down the address of the 69th Regiment Armory on Lexington, then grew serious. "You seemed quite beside yourself outside."

"Yes. It was a bad moment."

"I'm sorry."

"Don't be. It's better now."

"What changed?"

"I appreciate the way you look at the world."

LONGBAUGH thought that the most direct way to Fedgit-Spense was through Moretti. Hightower was a bad bet, he could not anticipate the man's agenda. But Moretti was more transparent, and there was a chance he would give himself away if pressed. And Longbaugh knew a way to get to him. Moretti may have kept himself at arm's length from the dirty work of his gang, but in order to maintain control, he still needed to give orders. He was too smart to write things down, as any written instruction would tend to incriminate. One person always had to have access to him. A trusted messenger to carry verbal instructions. And Longbaugh knew who that messenger had to be. He had seen him any number of times, the slick wearing a good suit.

Longbaugh went back to Little Italy and the Tall Boot Saloon. When he had watched for Hightower from the roof, he hadn't paid attention to the slick's comings and goings. Now he did. He watched from the same rooftop, tracking the slick when he came out of the bar, moving roof to roof until he ran out of roof. He went to street level and waited for him at the place where he had lost him from above. The messenger quit being cautious once he was that far from the bar. Longbaugh followed him out into the open, and the slick never once looked back, leading him directly to the building where he had first met Moretti.

Longbaugh waited in front until the messenger came back out. Then he entered and went upstairs.

He picked the lock and slipped inside Moretti's place. He closed the door behind him. He waited there, listening. A large clock tock-tocked. A door shut somewhere. Music played upstairs. A dog barked on the street. Somewhere else in the building someone blew his nose. The hall was dark, but light from individual rooms came through the open doors and fell geometrically across the floor.

He moved, grateful for the rubber-soled shoes that were quiet on both the wooden floors and on the rug that ran the length of the hall. He opened every closed door and peered into each room in turn and found them empty. He looked in the room where Moretti had come in that first night to meet him. Also empty.

He stopped outside one closed door and stood a moment, having heard a sound within. He leaned in close to listen, then put his hand on the knob and turned it as silently as he could manage. It was unlocked, and as it opened, it seemed to breathe inward.

The lean, pale girl, Moretti's girlfriend/whore, lounged on her bed, wearing the same thin robe she had worn the first night he'd seen her. She leaned on an elbow, narrow hip in the air, open magazine propped on a pillow. She appeared more attractive, but this time she wasn't being interrupted in the midst of fornicating with her boss. She looked up and was not surprised to see a man entering her room.

"And he said I was closed for the day."

"I'm not here for that."

"Doesn't matter, if he says so, it's so." Her low voice, aimed at him, was strangely inviting.

"What room is he in?"

"You just missed him." She lifted a pinky to the side of her pouty lips. "We have the place to ourselves."

"Where did he go?"

"He doesn't tell me things like that."

"Does he bring others here?"

"Only the very special ones. Like you."

"Uh-huh. Maybe a rich Englishman?"

"You can be anyone you want to be. An Englishman, an Egyptian, rich, poor. I'm awfully gullible."

"Uh-huh. Ever hear of a man named Fidgy?"

She let that pinky slide across her upper lip and blinked through cow eyes. "I'm not sure. Come over here and we'll discuss it."

She was so obvious that her act was subversively effective.

Longbaugh was not ready for this. Had he known what he was facing, he would have been better prepared. His wallet was where it could easily be lifted and he was wearing his gun against his back. Did she have information? Possibly. He took a step toward her, thinking anything that could get him closer to his wife was a positive step, but then he looked in her lifeless eyes and knew she was a dead end.

He stepped back closer to the door. "When is Giuseppe back?"

"Not for a while."

"I'll come back then."

"No. Stay. Come here to me."

"I am not ready for you."

"I'm ready for you."

The door behind him sighed open and he stepped sideways to look over his shoulder at Hightower coming in. "Now what would your wife say, tourist?"

Longbaugh's hand went for the Peacemaker, but stopped when he saw Hightower's gun already pointed at him.

The lean girl came upright, a growl of warning from her throat. "I got this one, Bear."

"You may not roll him, Edwina."

"You're no fun."

"Get out."

"I won't. It's my room, he said so. And anyway, I'm busy."

"Be busy elsewhere."

She stuck her tongue out at him. She sulked and got to her knees slowly, closing her magazine, plumping her pillows and tossing them to the head of the bed. He made a *tsk* sound to move her along. She put her feet on the floor, threw her head back to shake out her hair, then was up, moving slowly toward Longbaugh. Her eyes locked with his as she walked. Longbaugh backed up a step and she brushed past him, letting her robe catch on his arm so that Longbaugh got a full look at what he was missing. It was almost as interesting as she thought it was. Out of habit, he checked to make sure his wallet was still there.

"Figured I'd seen the last of you, tourist," said Hightower after the girl had gone.

"Where's Fidgy?"

"You here for Fidgy?"

"Figured Giuseppe would know where to find him."

"Well, he might. But so might a thousand others."

"Giuseppe has good reason to keep Fidgy in his sights," said Longbaugh. "And you never know what else he might say to me."

"What he might say to you, now that could be interesting."

"How long was Moretti collecting Queenie's fee?"

Hightower smiled at him as if he was an excellent student who had been listening in class. "From the start. Queenie thought she was clever with her secret lover, but it was Moretti's play from the beginning. He arranged the introduction and had money in hand before she ever heard of her Englishman."

"Fidgy had to go along with it."

"Why wouldn't he? He loves that sort of thing, it entertained him, but then, the man can tell a joke. It amused him that she thought she was giving it away for love."

Longbaugh thought Queenie would never have survived the *Titanic*. Fidgy would have flicked her overboard while commandeering a lifeboat for himself. Hightower had known all this when they interviewed Queenie in the opium den. Hightower was far too many steps ahead of him.

"Moretti is a real businessman," said Longbaugh.

"He's a whoremonger, but we all have to do something with our lives."

"He wanted Fidgy indebted to him. He wanted a business relationship."

"I'd have to say yes to that."

"Queenie wasn't the only girl Moretti sent to Fidgy."

"You're on a roll, tourist."

"He meant to blackmail Fidgy into making him a business partner."

"It wasn't the leverage he thought it was. Fidgy either didn't care that people knew he was a deviant with a taste for cheap whores, or thought people wouldn't believe it. What business do *you* have with him?"

"I'm interested in art."

"A clever lie, considering."

"You're right. I could never lie to you. Does he supply Moretti with dynamite?"

"He does, at times."

"I might like to get my hands on some."

"I thought you were looking for your wife."

"A pretense. Like he said, she's only a wife."

"Don't say things like that, tourist, I was invested in your love story. You surprise me. I never know what you're going to say next." Hightower scratched himself with his hand not holding the gun. "Oh, I thought I should tell you, I heard you come in."

"I hadn't meant to disturb you."

"So I made a telephone call."

Longbaugh didn't understand the ramifications of his statement. "I thought with a telephone you need someone to answer on the other end."

"That's so."

He couldn't wrap his head around it. None of Moretti's boys would have a telephone. "Who could you call? Not many telephones in the city, as I understand it. And Moretti already lives here. Although Fedgit-Spense might have one."

"He might at that."

"So you made a telephone call and someone is coming."

"Yes."

Hightower still knew more than he did, but how much more? He craved information, but feared that he gave away what he knew simply by his choice of questions.

Hightower began to put his gun away, then stopped and looked at Longbaugh. "I don't need this, do I?"

"You mean, would I leave if you weren't covering me? No."

"That's the way."

"You're good at pretending to be surprised by the things Moretti does."

"Am I?"

"He didn't put a tail on you."

"Oh, he did, and I wasn't pretending, I was actually surprised."

Longbaugh didn't believe him. "No, you're the one who takes care of his private needs."

"You flatter me."

"Like dealing Queenie to Fidgy."

"Can't say I'm above it, but Moretti handles the sex."

"You handle the muscle."

"When I have to."

"Intimidation."

"Only when it's necessary. I'm very genial at heart."

"Sending men out west to frighten women?"

"That you'll have to explain."

"You sent your boys to intimidate Etta's sister. I'm betting some old Pinkertons."

"I'm fascinated."

"You have a man in the post office who intercepted Etta's letters."

"I don't, but I know the man Moretti uses."

Longbaugh was skeptical. "So you're saying that was Moretti's trick and had nothing to do with you."

"If you say it happened."

Longbaugh ground his teeth. His gut, his *instinct*, told him Hightower's fingernails were dirty. Why employ an ex-Pinkerton if it wasn't to carry out your peculiar chores? He disliked being played for a fool, and he disliked the innocent look on Hightower's face. He wanted to flush Hightower out in the open.

"Don't treat me like I'm an idiot, Hightower, you've known Moretti's business the whole time. Moretti doesn't soil his hands, he sends others, and others means you. You handled that little piece of business with Mina."

"Mina? Would that be Etta's sister?"

The mock surprise on his face pushed him the final step.

"You tore open the letter and wiped your hands on it, then you gave it to those sons of bitches to scare her, and yes, that would be Etta's sister, you know Mina Matthews as well as I do."

Longbaugh had not expected Hightower's reaction. His face immediately changed, a moment of shock giving way to a wide, delighted smile, and Longbaugh knew he had made a mistake, but he did not know how or why.

"Mina Matthews." Hightower spoke the name as a revelation.

What had he said? Hightower already knew her name, what did it matter that he had said it aloud? Otherwise, how would Hightower have sent his people? But whatever he had done, he would make it right. Wherever Hightower went, Longbaugh would be there, if he had to ride under his lapel. He would keep him in his sight until he knew what was what.

"Moretti had lost faith in me lately, and I'd been looking for a way back into his good graces. Apparently I owe you one." Hightower's head cocked, hearing something Longbaugh did not. "I'm almost sorry for how I am about to repay you."

Longbaugh had not heard the footsteps coming down the hall before the knock on the skinny girl's door.

Hightower grinned. "Because that's for you."

"The telephone call?"

Hightower opened the door, and before Longbaugh could reach for his weapon, Charlie Siringo was in the room with his gun aimed at Longbaugh's heart. This gun he took seriously.

"Hello, Harry."

It was over that quickly, gone, all of it, Etta, his freedom, all of it, all of it, all of it. His eyes cased the room, watching his freedom slide like a whisper under the door and out the cracks between the sash frame and the window jamb. Too far from the window to crash through, too far from Siringo to charge, and Siringo was blocking the door. Lightning couldn't outdraw a pointed weapon. Whatever Hightower had learned from him, he would walk away with it and have no tourist's shadow to inconvenience him. His pride had done it. He had wanted to trip up Hightower and bring him down, and he'd fed him information instead.

"You are a patient man, Charlie."

"Worth the wait."

"By the way, tourist, if you were wondering, I had no idea where to find your wife. Until you told me."

Grasping at straws. "I don't know where she is, and now that you've turned me in to the law, you'll never know either."

"Fidgy's been dealing with a new art dealer these last few weeks, in anticipation of the show. A lady art dealer. Who knew the Brits were so progressive? He mentioned her name, he was quite impressed with her, but then, ladies are his weakness, they don't all have to be cheap. At the time, her name meant nothing to me. Matthews. Ethel Matthews. I never met her, and in what world would I? I don't give an elephant's fart about the fine arts, what use is that in the real world? I was trying to make an agreement between the Spense Company and Moretti, *that* was my job. Oh, and Moretti never trusted me for all those other things precisely *because* I had been a Pinkerton. He always thought my true allegiance was elsewhere. But isn't she clever, hiding out in the open, using what I assume is her real name."

Longbaugh was dead inside. They were both so used to using aliases, who would have imagined she'd come out as herself? But why not? He had come to New York wanting to use his own name. Why not Etta? He started very slowly to move into a position where he might access his gun, but Siringo saw it almost before he began, and angled his head. "Ah-ah." Longbaugh returned his hand to his innocent thigh.

Hightower moved to the door. "Now if you'll excuse me, gentlemen, I have just received an invitation to the opening of an art show. I hear it's a major event, they say everyone will be there. Maybe Fidgy and your Ethel can teach me something about culture. Naturally, I'll take Moretti as my guest. I'm guessing he's about to acquire a whole new appreciation for modern European painting."

Hightower put on his hat and smiled his way out the door, leaving Longbaugh to face Siringo's gun.

"Back up a step, please, Harry."

Longbaugh watched how Siringo held his gun. "How did he get you here?"

"Mr. Hightower has been in contact."

"He came to you?"

"Saw me watching the boardinghouse."

"One old Pinkerton to another. Professional courtesy."

"Was he really a Pinkerton? Seems a little overstuffed for that crowd."

"Did you notice he was someone you might not trust?"

"My interest was you."

"So you let him guide you."

"I wasn't interested in his character. You're the one's been taunting me."

"I saw him kill a man."

"File a complaint."

Longbaugh gave up. There was no justice to be had here. Hightower the immoral had played it brilliantly. "Does he know who I am?"

"He thinks you're an ex-convict named Alonzo, wanted by the law. I was surprised at how happy he was to hear that. You impressed him, but I know how immune you are to flattery."

"I don't always hate it. Just tonight."

"He was glad you weren't a civilian. Thought he was losing his touch."

"He reached you by telephone?"

"One at my hotel. I gave him the name when he offered to alert me if he saw you again."

"He didn't miss a trick."

"I wouldn't know."

"You would. You like to know everything. That's why you're listening to me now. I'm going to the Armory Show, Charlie."

"That could be a problem. I believe I already put you under arrest on somebody's rooftop. Seems to me where you're going is Wyoming."

Longbaugh walked directly at Siringo. "You're going to have to shoot me."

"That would be a shame."

Longbaugh watched Siringo thumb back the hammer. Siringo, of all people, would not be bluffed. It was a desperate move anyway, probably not worthy of him. If Siringo shot him, Etta would face Moretti alone. He stopped and took a step back.

"Let me go, Charlie." His voice was calm.

"Harry . . ."

"He'll kill her."

"Keep your hands where I can see them."

"You heard him, he's taking Moretti. Moretti thinks this is some private vendetta. He wants his revenge face-to-face."

"Everybody's got a story."

"She's using her real name, Charlie. That's so I could find her. It was a risk, but a risk she was willing to take. You think she should die for that? For using her real name?"

"You never know how these things will turn out. That's why they're called risks."

"You're going to let me go."

Siringo said nothing, but his gun did not waver.

"I know you don't want her to die."

Siringo said nothing.

"Make you a deal."

"Give it up, Harry, what've you got for barter?"

"My word of honor."

Siringo angled his head and narrowed his eyes.

"Let me go. Let me save her. Then, on my word of honor, I will turn myself in to you."

"You either think I'm awfully green or—"

"You know me better than that, Charlie."

"Do I?"

"I came here for her. Why do you think I didn't run when I found out you were after me?"

"You should have."

"You know why I didn't. Moretti is a vindictive bastard, and I don't have a lot of time if I'm going to stop him."

Siringo thought and then thought a little more, and Longbaugh waited for him in silence, because he had played his hand and he had nothing else.

Siringo rubbed the soft drop of his ear. "What happened with Butch, Harry?"

"What, you mean back in the nineties? That day at Hole in the Wall? He let you go." Longbaugh felt it coming then, the shift inside Siringo.

"Why?"

"You know why."

"Tell me anyway."

"If I have to tell you, you'll just think I'm desperate to get to the Armory Show, which I am."

"Humor me."

Longbaugh cleared all the emotion out of his voice and spoke plainly. "Because I told him to."

"Uh-huh."

"You were my friend, and I didn't want Butch to kill you. I thought you should be alive. Butch had never killed anyone before, and if he killed you, that would have made him into a different man. So I told him I knew Charlie Siringo from before and it wasn't you."

The gun wavered. Siringo showed the smallest hint of a smile, having the mystery solved about why he was still around to live his life.

A wash of relief raced through Longbaugh and he caught a full breath for the first time since Siringo walked into the room.

"I must be some giant chump, buying all this." Longbaugh saw that he had believed him, but let him enjoy his tirade. "I must be the biggest dupe saphead lawman on the whole goddamned turd-steaming, maggot-licking, pus-infested East Coast." Siringo kicked an overstuffed chair that landed on its side. "Goddamnit, Harry, you sorry-assed son of a bitch, I still have to take you in, but I know what it means when you give your word. I know you'll do what you say. Go on, get out of here, go save your wife, if you can, but I want you back and in custody by the end of the night. By the end of the night."

18

Great clouds rolled in off the ocean, their heads a high pile, their swollen bellies purple, chasing the setting sun into a clear sky to the west. A momentary brilliance at his back, gone before he turned his head. He waited for the drumbeat of thunder, which came more quickly than he had anticipated. His chance had come, risked on this one throw, and the small voice inside him wondered if it could be real, if he had any true hope of finding her on a night so forbidding.

He ran from Moretti's building down the long blocks and stopped when he reached the Bowery, fighting for breath with knees supporting hands, faced with a statue of traffic locked motionless in both directions. Any available trolley or cab had nowhere to go, and would be trapped in there for some time. He was a long way from the Armory.

He scanned the street and ran through his options. Speed had to be balanced with intelligent decisions, and he tried to force himself to think clearly. He wasn't sure where the Armory was on Lexington, which side of the street. He didn't know that area well, but he tried to picture the best route. North from here, certainly, and he remembered the Bowery running into Fourth Avenue, which would turn into Park. He thought then he'd be a block from Lexington. Still, a long way, and

Hightower had a head start. How best to get there, on foot or by vehicle? A long way on foot, and realistically, how long could he run and still have enough left to do what he had to do once he got there? He knew he needed to arrive not just on time but ahead of time to know the field.

The jammed motorcars and trolleys were of no help to him. He could start off on foot and hope the traffic would break up farther north, but as he looked in that direction, he saw no end to it. Then his eyes fell on an empty delivery wagon with two horses in harness. He moved for it along a crooked route between irritated, trembling automobiles.

The wagon's driver, a veteran of inert traffic, turned when he picked up unusual peripheral motion and saw a man running at him. The wagon driver's entire body shifted back in his seat as the running man looked directly at him and dug in his pocket for something.

Longbaugh made sure to approach at a wide angle so as not to spook the horses. As he reached the delivery wagon, he tried to press money in the driver's hand. "For your horse."

Hands in the air, avoiding the dollars. "I done nothing to you, mister."

"I'm serious here." He remembered how Prophet had tried to force his writing on *The Masses*' editor and how the editor's hands had gone up in just the same way.

"My horse, he not is for sale, and if you think you buy for *this*, you gone crazy."

"Not buying. Renting." He grabbed the driver's hand, brought it down and slapped the money into his palm.

"What, you are asking for the rig?"

"No, the horse. Him, that one there. I'm going to Twenty-fifth and Lexington."

"Armory Show, sure."

Apparently all of New York knew about the show. Except, of course, for him.

"Follow me once this breaks up and he'll be waiting. That's all you have to do. For that much money."

"Not one little chance in a million." The driver was, however, moved by the money already in his fist. He considered how to hold on to it. "But for this money, you can borrow the other."

"The mare? She's ready to drop." He looked at her uncertainly, a liver chestnut, the color of scalded coffee.

"Rig cannot get over there with her only as puller."

"Your rig is empty."

The driver shrugged, knowing he had the upper hand. "Wagon is heavy."

He looked at the massive snarl that stretched both directions and saw no other options. Meanwhile, time refused to pause. "Agreed."

The driver sat forward. Perhaps it had been too easy. "Just wait now, how I am knowing she will be where you say?"

"I am no horse thief, sir." His foot tapped the street, his fingers drummed the side of the wagon, and he waited aggressively, pretending not to show his frustration.

The driver studied his eyes. "No. No, I see that."

Now Longbaugh worked quickly, releasing her from the harness. He pulled her out, slightly swaybacked, wrapping the reins around his left hand.

He put a hand out slowly so as not to surprise her, and rubbed down her neck. She responded more quickly than he had expected. He kept peripheral contact to create a dominion with her. Her color was really more like a rich, dark brown. Perhaps he had underestimated her.

The driver watched, rapt. "What is this? She is old nag."

Longbaugh ignored him, speaking directly to her. "All right, here we go, here we are. What do you think? You have enough for this? You ready?"

Damned if the horse didn't lean into him.

He stepped on the side of the wagon and pressed his body against her flank, letting her grow accustomed to him, but time was precious and he couldn't afford an extended introduction. Before he thought she was ready, he hoisted his leg over her back and sat. He hadn't ridden bareback since probably some time in the '90s. But she was alert and patient. Crooked tines of lightning jabbed the sky, as if the rivers clenched to snap white rods up into clouds, making the whole island a silhouette. He feared her reaction to the sudden loud thunder, but she did not flinch.

"Got an apple or sugar cube?"

The driver made a face but took a carrot from somewhere inside his coat. It was firm, and Longbaugh put it in his pocket.

She responded under his knees as he turned her, and they slipped into a gap between vehicles and were off.

Drops touched his forehead and he cursed the coming rain, then mentally tried to negotiate with it to hold off so she could safely run the cobblestones. He thought he would beat Hightower to the Armory, but rain was not his ally. So far, the drops were isolated and the sky held its water. The Bowery continued in snarl for blocks as they rode north. He let the horse have her head and she responded eagerly, strutting high for a proud moment as if stretching her reality, then lowering her nose and going. He wondered if he had entered her dream, her last best chance to cut loose, remembering her filly days when running was her way. In that moment she knew speed and freedom, and to anyone who happened to be watching, she proved she had once been something special. His heart swelled alongside her pride, the wind strong in his face, and he bent down close to her neck, with her mane snapping against his cheek and forehead, and he roared inside for his own freedom. They rode north as one, weaving back and forth around stopped motorcars in the middle of the street, the white faces of awed drivers staring out their windows.

As he rode, some other part of him climbed back into his being, and he was the Kid again, riding full-out, his youth and determination revived. The early days were with him now, when he'd had no nickname and no plan, when he had robbed a bank before he knew any better and had run away with an idiot's desperation, the incredible exhilaration of a pocketful of stolen money once he knew he'd gotten away with it, and now his past continued to roll with him, the middle years riding alongside him, the confident days when he knew how to plan, and his plans worked to perfection with stopped trains and stowed horses and the faces of the posse as they realized they'd been outplayed, and finally the time with Butch was with him, too, the one man who truly understood what it was like, riding by Longbaugh's side on the outlaw trail, basking in the warmth of a true friend, and all of those memories buoyed him as he raced above the city streets on a game horse with rain threatening, the thrill quivering in his bones, the joy making thunder in his chest and lightning in his hips, and for that one small moment he believed, because he owned both the past and the future just as he owned this moment. If this was all, if this was his last ride—and he would keep his word to Siringo—then it was enough.

Maybe he would figure a way to go out in a fit of glory.

The rain continued to hold off, and they ran through a heavy cloud that misted his face. He watched her hooves land sturdily on the slick street. She would fly if he let her, and he gave her rein. Traffic broke as they thundered north, forcing them to slow to safely maneuver around motorcars that couldn't be trusted, swerving and braking. At Twenty-first Street he turned her right, toward the East River, for Lexington Avenue.

The block was dim after the bright Park Avenue, and an automobile sped directly at them, claiming the middle of the street, as if offended that some other species dared share the road. Longbaugh slowed the horse, and watched the headlights grow, lighting up the horse's chest, and he saw there was no mistake, the new Speedwell Roadster was coming directly at them, and he guided the horse to the sidewalk. He kicked out as the motorcar passed, a lucky heel wrecking the huge headlight bolted to the fancy fender. The driver braked to a squealing halt and rose over the steering wheel in a boil, brandishing his fist and cursing him. Longbaugh saluted him with two fingers off the brim of his hat, then urged the horse with his knees back out into the street to carry on. The Speedwell made a six-point turn behind him, its engine whining to catch up, but by the time the motorcar got close, Longbaugh had reached the end of the block and was turning the horse left up Lexington Avenue.

Lexington was another unexpected jam, this one caused by the exhibit. Traffic was drawn to the bright lights trained on the Armory a few blocks north on the left-hand side. Despite the frenzied flashing and the booming thunder, the rain still held off. The Speedwell revved hard and was unable or unwilling to brake in time, bashing the passenger side of a stopped vehicle and ramming it sideways into motorcars in the next lane. Now the furious driver had a new set of problems. Longbaugh left him and his rage behind.

The 69th Regiment Armory was ablaze with electric light, vehicles drawn like iron filings to the magnet entrance, where a man in a faux uniform yelled indecipherably through a megaphone in an attempt to enforce order. Patrons slid off backseats onto dry sidewalks, leaving the street mess to their servants, strutting under wide umbrellas that were thus far unnecessary, walking under the building's projecting gun bays, then climbing stairs beneath a great arched entrance under a rectangular sign, INTERNATIONAL EXHIBITION, MODERN ART. Longbaugh slid off the horse's back and guided her on the sidewalk to Twenty-fifth Street. Twenty-fifth was busy as well, with private automobiles lined up to wait. He knew time was critical, but he walked her to cool her down, praising her fine run. Chauffeurs stood in small groups, smoking as they gossiped, braving the threat of rain with collars turned high and hats pulled low. A few cleaned the insides of their vehicles, dropping trash in the gutter. One or two wiped down their windscreens and hoods while gazing at the flashing sky, knowing their time was wasted. As she cooled, he fed her the carrot.

While walking her, he saw Loney Wisher, Fidgy's man, come out of a side door of the Armory near Park Avenue. It started to rain hard just as Wisher slipped out the exit. Wisher wore not only a gaudy waistcoat—vest, Longbaugh corrected himself—but he was wearing new shoes. Wisher put up his collar and braved what was suddenly a downpour as he ran to a parked vehicle about three-quarters of the way back toward Lexington. He nodded to the chauffeur, who moved away. Wisher opened the back door of the vehicle himself and ducked inside, but he left the door wide.

Longbaugh led the horse alongside the building to a place where she would be dry and protected, and wrapped the reins around a pipe. He looked at the vehicle's open door and knew Wisher was waiting for someone.

It was a moment before he saw a man come out of the shadows in the hard rain, then he recognized the oversized coat. Prophet did not look around as he approached the open vehicle door. He also did not enter. He stood in the rain, although it appeared that Wisher was inviting him inside. Prophet passed an envelope to Wisher. After a moment, Wisher passed back a wrapped package that was the shape and size of a small batch of dynamite cartridges. Prophet slid the wrapped packet into his large side pocket, the one that had held his folded article on the killer of McKinley. Longbaugh guessed from the size and shape that he had purchased half a dozen cartridges. Ordinarily, the sale of dynamite to a civilian would have alarmed him, but the only person this man was likely to blow up was himself. Prophet turned and went back the way he had come, lost from sight in the dark, beyond a curtain of rain highlighted by a streetlamp. Wisher stayed inside the vehicle a moment longer, then was out, closing the back door, racing the long block back to the side exit, passing Longbaugh, standing out of the rain, and disappearing inside the Armory.

"You'll be all right here." He rubbed her cheek in appreciation. In the cooldown she had become an old horse again.

He moved after Wisher and checked the side exit door. Locked. Apparently during that time, Wisher had left it wedged open. Longbaugh turned to the front and, keeping close to the building to avoid the rain, hurried down the long block and around the corner onto Lexington, to join the other guests entering through the front.

The rain offered him cover as he moved from umbrella to umbrella, slipping between well-dressed invitees, pretending to be part of a large group as they flashed their invitations. He climbed stairs, shook rain from his coat and hat, and entered. A hallway led through this part of the building to the main exhibit, just ahead. He scanned faces, always looking for her, for Hightower, for Moretti, and now for Wisher.

He reached the exhibition hall and stopped just inside the entrance, with the entire show laid out before him. The Armory had a massive ground floor, and rose two stories to a high steel-and-glass arched ceiling that they had tried to disguise. He looked up and back at a great staircase that led to the second floor behind him.

He returned his attention to the main room. The designers of the exhibition had added decorations in an attempt to manage the size, so that the art would not be quite so overwhelmed by the setting. They had dressed the entrance with tall pines, and hung countless yellow streamers from the middle of the ceiling that fell in a soft curve out to the side walls to create a tentlike canopy. A military band played in the balcony, forcing the spectators to talk loudly.

He looked at the exhibit. The center of the first gallery, Gallery A, was dominated by a large white sculpture of a man with a knee down, the other knee angled, as if he was attempting to stand, holding up something that hung over his upper body. It might have been a sculpture of Atlas bearing up the world, except whatever he held was the wrong shape to be a globe. Longbaugh approached and circled it, and saw it was a depiction of a young man on a knee with an older man folded over him, embracing him, welcoming him, smothering him. He read the card, George Gray Barnard, *Prodigal Son.* Smaller marble sculptures surrounded it. A limited number of paintings were hung in this gallery on what were temporary walls covered in burlap that had been set up for the exhibit.

Beyond Gallery A, more temporary walls created a beehive of smaller galleries that organized the art and maximized wall space. Many spectators were gathered there, but not so many as to make it hard to move freely. The line of visitors coming in the entrance did not slow, and it would become significantly more crowded as the evening wore on. It would be difficult to find Etta, but no less difficult for Moretti.

A breezeway at the back of the first gallery on the right-hand side led him into not a rectangular gallery but one shaped like an octagon. He searched the faces of the spectators, and when he recognized no one, he took a moment to see what the excitement was about. The paintings leapt off the walls, jumped and grabbed him, shook and taunted and astounded him, the color, the design, the subject matter, the raw difference, the lack of indifference. The names of the artists were equally strange and he wondered how to pronounce Matisse, Gauguin, Manet, Picasso. He had little experience with art; any "important" paintings he had encountered generally portrayed some idealized realism, landscapes of the early West lit by orange-red sunsets with heroic clouds, implausible mountains, and unlikely cliffs. These were something else entirely, many of them almost childlike in their vision, yet they contained subject matter that was not for children. Confronted by colors and shapes that his own dreams could not have conjured, he was repelled and fascinated. New York had taught hard lessons of modernity and changed the impossible into the everyday; here the same thing was happening in the art, as if the act of looking scraped new passages in his brain. He backed out into the relatively placid Gallery A with the comparatively tame American sculpture. The father with his prodigal son was looking quite congenial. The explosive European paintings inhabited a hostile landscape where the natives spoke all at once, loudly, in rude tongues.

He felt for his gun and was reassured. He watched more spectators enter through the arch and in yet another vertigo-inducing surprise, he saw Theodore Roosevelt walking and talking, come to see the show, an actual former president recognized from photographs, now proven to be blood and bone. Longbaugh moved all the way back to the entrance and stood beside one of the decorative pines. He had to settle himself down, because Moretti and Hightower were coming, and soon, and if he was to do what needed to be done, he needed a clear head. He scanned the room through anxious eyes. He fought for control of his brain, needing to recognize Moretti and the bear the moment they arrived. But he was not focused, he was not ready.

He closed his eyes, pushed the noise and music off into a corner, then talked to himself until his thoughts returned to his task. His breathing lengthened, the moments stretched, and his thumping heart quieted. There. Yes. He opened his eyes and the room had slowed. When he was sure he was ready, he reentered the exhibit.

In that brief quiet he had observed more than he realized, develop-ing a feel for the exhibition and its hierarchy. He approached a woman who clearly held a position of power, as she was congratulated by arriv-ing guests. Guards sidled up from behind and spoke in her ear. She gave instructions without sacrificing her public concentration. He waited his turn, then stepped behind her, as if he was one of her people.

"Ethel Matthews here yet?"

The woman leaned back, still smiling at the crowd. "Later, with her client."

"Which client?"

"Fedgit-Spense, probably another half hour." A beat before she thought the question odd and made a full turn to know who was asking. "I beg your pardon, you are . . . ?"

"Harry." He put his hand out to shake. "Isn't this just marvelous what you've done."

"And you are with?"

"Don't tell anyone, but Fidgy thinks I should buy."

Someone distracted her other ear. She answered from the side of her mouth. "The price may be negotiable, but not tonight, next week if it's not sold." Coming back to Longbaugh. "His . . . man, his . . . *person*, that assistant, is in one of the back galleries, look in the Cubist Room, the farthest one on the left, in the corner. That's where they all start, what they're calling the Chamber of Horrors." She shook her head with great annoyance. "Where they go to laugh."

He thanked her and moved to the breezeway, this one on the left side, walked through two smaller galleries, more European paintings that he ignored, then entered the large back gallery under the giant clock. At the far end, he turned left into the Cubist Room, the most crowded of the spaces, with so many spectators gathered around one particular large painting that he was unable to get a good look at it. He did see the exit along the side wall, the door Wisher had used to reach the street and meet Prophet. He stopped next to a small sculpture of an oddly shaped mountain and scanned the space for Wisher. He looked at face after face, leaning and looking until he thought he had seen everyone there. He started watching the people as they came in, but something about the mountain sculpture by his elbow pulled at his attention and he looked down and saw it was not a mountain but a head created from rounded shapes and slices, as if the muscles and bones of the face had forcefully burst from the sculpture's core, like boulders shoving through the ground after an earthquake. After a moment of looking, the sculpture evolved into a woman's head, gazing down in what seemed a demure posture. He had been blind to it at first, had not even known to look for it. Now that he saw it, he could not unsee it, as it could be nothing else. The image was not generic but specific, and represented an actual person, so particular that, had she been there, he would have recognized her. He looked at the artist's name, Pablo Picasso, above the title, *Bust*.

He looked to the crowd as if to call out so that they might share this magical transformation. The crowd had shifted and he was brought back to his mission, as he now saw Loney Wisher among the spectators, although Longbaugh's view of the large painting was still blocked. Tonight Wisher was dressed less to impress than to express, working too hard even among this crowd of flashy fashion mongers. The spectators laughed at the large painting he could not see. Wisher chatted wickedly among them, his snickers mimicking theirs to curry favor, pawing the rich fabrics of their sleeves while secretly making notes. He seemed particularly drawn to one woman whose outfit was probably expensive.

Longbaugh made his way to Wisher's side. At a pause in the conversation, he stepped into it.

"I believe we've met."

Wisher turned and looked him up and down, in a way he had not bothered to do that day outside the Hotel Algonquin. "No. I would not have met you."

"Then there must be another Loney Wisher. No matter, I'll just talk to Fidgy."

At Fidgy's name, Wisher squared up. He moved Longbaugh away from the group, away from the painting.

"Silly of me, of course I remember. Buyer?"

"From what I'm seeing, yes, perhaps."

Calculation ran through Wisher's eyes. "Who's your representative?"

"I'm sorry, I—"

"Who explains things to you, who keeps you from being swindled, who have you hired to show you the ropes?"

Yes, thought Longbaugh. *Who will collect a percentage on your purchase?* "That would be Miss Matthews."

Wisher turned his note-taking pad and let it drift casually to his side so that Longbaugh could not read what he had written.

"*Mrs.* Matthews," Loney corrected him. "Remind me of your name."

"So you don't remember."

Wisher didn't miss a beat. "And she didn't remember to be here to take care of you."

"Yes, I wonder where she is."

"Wherever her whimsy carries her. That's the danger of putting your business in the hands of a woman. Known her long?"

"Practically forever. Weeks." He liked Wisher's competitive tone. It meant he would stick close.

"And yet you called her 'Miss.' You don't know her marital status. Do you even know her first name?"

"Ah . . ." Longbaugh thought he was about to be exposed, and tried to think of some plausible lie to get Wisher on his side.

"How rude of her." Wisher took his arm companionably. "You need someone who will be honest and direct with you. While Mrs. Matthews is good, the fact that she's not here is her loss, but if I daresay, your gain. My time, sir, is yours, as any friend of Sydney's, and all that. If you wish, she can always take over, assuming she arrives. Assuming she's not too busy with Sydney's business."

"I thought you handled Sydney's business."

"I handle many things at once. I promise you'll be satisfied."

Charm bled from Wisher's pores, and Longbaugh thought he had left an oily dark spot on his jacket where he touched his elbow.

"Fidgy thought I might like this man Picasso." He used the name because it was the last artist he had encountered and he thought he was pronouncing it properly.

"Picasso, oh no no no, next you'll be saying you want a Matisse, and that is nothing but filth, odious work, have you seen the one with the goldfish?" He pointed through to Gallery H. "It's obscene, show me an undraped woman who looks like that and I'll show you a walrus. Edward Hopper has an excellent sailboat over in Gallery M, or look at the other Americans from the Ashcan group."

Longbaugh considered the crowd around the large painting that so amused them all. "What about this one?"

Wisher snorted. "Well. Don't say I didn't warn you. I call it 'Explosion in a Shingle Factory.'"

A woman near him brayed, her jewelry tinkling. "Oh, that's *fresh*, Loney. 'Implosion in a Shingle Plant.' You don't think this Marcel fellow is *serious*, now, do you? I can't *wait* to see what the papers say in the morning."

Wisher touched elbows to separate the crowd and gave Longbaugh a full view of the painting in question.

Longbaugh looked with a cold eye. He thought he probably disliked it, although he didn't know for certain. Too many people had already had too much to say about it. He looked and looked. It certainly wasn't what he had expected, given the magnitude of the negative reaction. The paintings in the other gallery had desensitized his initial shock, but this was no less unusual to his eye. Much as he might have disliked it on his own, he disliked the idea of agreeing with Wisher even more. For that reason alone, he took more time. And looked. He glanced down and read the card. Marcel Duchamp. *Nude Descending a Staircase*. He looked back. The painting was rendered in warm ochres and rich browns, with some green as accent, close to Etta's olive. It was not as representational as its title. He saw what was meant to be a body in motion portrayed by what looked to be thin wood planks laid atop one another, some with curved edges, others more triangular. The body came forward from left to right, down an incline into brighter light.

The more he looked, the more he accepted the illusion of a body in motion, but he was damned if he could guarantee a woman in there. He looked for the staircase and identified only one sure stair, squared off with a right angle . . . but Loney Wisher was leaning in with his greasy smirk, so he stayed with it longer, until stairs began to emerge from multiple perspectives, as if every angle on a staircase had been considered simultaneously, despite the two-dimensional canvas. All at once, he recognized a sophisticated intellect behind the work. Interesting. Unusual, unexpected, and interesting.

Wisher waited for his laugh and studied Longbaugh's face. Longbaugh squinted and angled his head.

"You would take this much time with something so ludicrous? This 'thing' is a joke, a sham, not to be taken seriously by any cultured individual."

"Of course not," said Longbaugh. The more outrage he detected in Wisher's tone, the happier he was.

It seemed as if Wisher might take Longbaugh's cue and look at the painting again, but Longbaugh saw him talk himself out of that. Wisher tugged him away. "Time to visit the Ashcans."

"I wouldn't throw this out just yet."

"Oh no no no, the Ashcans are artists, Robert Henri, John Sloan. They paint the world as it really is."

"I couldn't say what the world really is."

"That's why we have artists, to tell you through their work."

This guy Duchamp is telling you, thought Longbaugh. *You're just not listening.* "I've been in prison."

"Uh? Oh yes, of course, very good, you're a wit, addressing our emerging sensibilities. A dangerous weapon, wit, I will remember your gibe."

"Steal it in good health."

Wisher checked the time. "Come with me. Sydney should be here any minute. Fresh off the boat, so to speak."

"Off the boat?"

"Just docked, saw it coming into the harbor on the way here. You didn't know?" Loney hesitated, as if a doubt was setting in. "He's coming directly from the wharf. Doesn't want to miss a minute of this."

"Why didn't you meet him there?"

"He needs me to catalog the art. He specifically wants to know which pieces people dislike the most. He can be very inscrutable. But I don't question, I just do my job." Longbaugh hadn't met Fedgit-Spense, but he thought he understood what he was doing and was surprised Wisher did not. Fedgit-Spense had little respect for the unsophisticated American taste and he was using that to help guide his purchases. Anything the Americans hated must be good, and Wisher was blind to the insult. Longbaugh was caught in the irony, as he had started to like the art only because Wisher did not. "It's my understanding your Mrs. Matthews is the one meeting him."

Longbaugh followed him through the galleries that banked Twenty-fifth Street until they had returned to the entrance. These smaller galleries held mostly American painters, and Wisher pointed out his favorite canvases from the Ashcan School as they went by.

They arrived at the arch by the entrance to wait. Wisher droned on, speaking of the American painters with affection. Longbaugh had liked their work, but was tired of Wisher's monologue, and he watched the crowd for Hightower, for Moretti. She was coming. She would come here, to this place. She was on her way.

Sydney Fedgit-Spense entered. Longbaugh knew because Wisher went for him without hesitation, leaving off in midsentence. Fedgit-Spense had a certain glow, unless it was caused by his habit of stepping into the cast of every strong overhead light. He was tall, thin, bony, with a schoolboy's straight blond hair flopping over an older man's face. His enormous nose led his skeletal frame wherever he went, and he looked as if he went wherever he pleased. After the things attributed to him, Longbaugh had expected someone more dangerous, or at least more handsome. Fedgit-Spense struggled to remove his heavy jacket, something more appropriate for a ship's deck than a rainy summer evening. Longbaugh watched Wisher flow to Fedgit-Spense, each step a metamorphosis, now the amanuensis, now the acolyte, now the apostle, until he was alongside his superior, "Welcome back, sir," lifting the shoulders of the jacket to allow Fedgit-Spense's arms to slip out. "Thank you, Loney, fine to be back." "I thought you might say 'home,' sir." "Not that good, Loney, despite your presence."

Longbaugh watched to see if Etta would come in with Fedgit-Spense, but Fidgy had entered alone. He looked and looked, and when the same people in the same plumage trading the same gossip and the same laughter continued to stream into the Armory, he began to think she was unreal, that everything he had heard about her had been manufactured to torment him.

Until he saw someone moving sideways against the current of the incoming crowd, back in the darkness under the arch, a woman slipping by in a blur of vermillion silk. He had a glint of recognition, the way she held her head, but . . . was he fooling himself, or had he truly recognized her? He'd been fooled before, especially when actively looking and hoping. The woman walked with her back to him, still going sideways through the crowd, different hairstyle, her dress of a color and profile he would not have expected. Had she always been so tall? He convinced himself it was not her as he started in her direction. She moved for a stairway that would take her to the floor below.

Wisher looked around for him. "Oh, by the way, Sydney, I met a friend of yours, now, where did he go?"

Longbaugh reached the top of the stairs as she reached the bottom. The lights were dim there, to dissuade the crowd from venturing down. He still had not gotten a look at her face, and he saw her turn to the left. He faltered, as if his legs were made of heavy liquid, but he forced himself to press on, holding the handrail for balance, going down as quickly as he could manage, watching his feet on the stairs, as he did not trust his step. He opened his mouth to call her name, but no sound came.

He reached the bottom of the stairs. The area was dark. There were apparently large rooms to the right as he saw arrows on the wall next to signs that read BOWLING ALLEYS and RIFLE RANGES. He concentrated on the hallway and saw her at the far end, in shadow, passing through a doorway, closing the door behind her.

He followed her down the hall. It wasn't her, he knew it wasn't her, this had to be another Ethel Matthews, it was a misunderstanding and he was chasing his imagination. He hesitated with his hand on the door handle. It clearly could not be her. He turned it, and the door opened quietly.

The room was dark. He heard her over there, shaking rain from her hair. She clicked on a lamp and a small cone of light illuminated a desk and her silhouette. Her back was to him as she opened a desk drawer and took out papers. He tried to speak but again he had no voice. He froze, sharing a room with her while she thought she was alone. All he could manage was to close the door behind him.

She turned at the sound. The light from the lamp lit a dark red sleeve, the curls of her hair, the underside of her chin, the lower part of her cheek.

They entered a microscopic slice of time that seemed to drag for an age, eyes connected.

He stood there, the ex-convict, the old lover chasing her through the new city, pathetic with hope, reckless with nostalgia and unrequited need.

A microscopic slice of time congested with thoughts.

Tell me. One way or the other, tell me, say it.

What is in your heart?

Not a full second had passed when she took that step toward him, leaving the light behind her, and there in the shadow she smiled.

"Hello, Sundance."

She came across the room as if the light propelled her forward, and he was lost to her, as that was all of it, he knew everything in that first honest step. She came to him and he caught her, wrapped her in his grateful arms, heart pounding against her scent, kissing her familiar lips, and feeling her excellent laugh bubble up in her breast.

They rushed to be together, making up for lost time, to prove that this moment was real and true, amazed to be holding each other, the years spent apart now slipping into an envelope that sealed behind them, as they touched that special one known from a thousand dreams and now made flesh, palms touching, fingers interlaced.

She grinned with the joy of discovery, her fingers inching back his bowler, fondling the fabric of his suit, the soft collar of his shirt.

His lips near her ear. "It's you."

Curling her arms back around him, she felt it against his low back and laughed aloud. "Sweetheart, you're packing."

"You've been associating with a bad lot. Thought I'd bring a friend."

"I'm well away from those people."

He leaned his head so she could see his eyes. "No. You're not. They're coming."

"But—"

"I wasn't quick enough. They're coming tonight. For you."

She took a full breath and held it a moment, her eyes looking over his shoulder. "I should never have used my name."

"I was too slow. I only found out after someone else put it together."

"But you found me, so it was worth it."

He touched her left hand, felt the wedding ring on her finger, and smiled. Mrs. Matthews. Then he affected a lopsided grin. "So. No corset."

"Nope."

"And that's a dress."

"That's red, Kid, and I knew you'd come."

"I wasn't sure you'd still want us."

"Yes you were."

His breath caught in his chest and he felt his smile tingle his fingertips and support his knees. The right answer. "Okay. Yes, okay."

She moved to adjust his collar, fingernail rubbing at her own lipstick, when she felt the bandanna.

"What's this?"

"The old one was lost at Henry Street."

"This is no good."

She loosened his four-in-hand, opened his collar, and pulled the too-green too-new bandanna away from his neck as if it must never be allowed to touch him again. He was surprised by the intensity of her dislike.

"Wrong color," she said.

She held it with two fingers over the wastebasket and let it drop.

She then gathered up the fabric of her dress to mid-thigh to reveal her petticoat. It was cream colored and constructed in two parts, the main section running from waist to just below the knee, and a bottom piece that fell almost to her ankle. Connecting the two parts was a series of evenly spaced fabric strips sewn to connect top and bottom with an open space in between. Weaving in and out of that open space was a decorative ribbon. An olive-colored ribbon. She took hold of one end and pulled the whole length of it out. His fingers went instinctively to his pocket where he kept the other pieces.

She let her dress drop back over the petticoat, brought the ribbon to his shoulders, and he felt her fingers slide the ribbon around his neck and feed the ends down inside his shirt to lie flat against his chest. The electric touch of her fingers stayed on the back of his neck, and the ribbon was alive against his skin. "That will have to do until we get a new one."

He drew the smaller ribbon pieces from his pocket. "Mystery solved."

"I needed something you'd recognize."

"I didn't, at first."

"Ran out of time that day. Just hoped you'd see them."

"You were so sure I'd know what they meant?"

"I bought this petticoat because of that ribbon. Only you would recognize the color."

He laughed. "We can discuss all this later, right now we have to go before they get here."

She looked at him seriously. "I can't leave the Armory."

"Don't worry, I'll get you out."

"No, I mean there's something I have to do here."

"Wait, no. Etta, your life is at stake."

"I know."

"And I just found you."

"I know."

He fought himself, trying not to say the things that came to his mind, trying not to be unhappy. He had found her and she was all he hoped she would be, except she was also intransigent, with an agenda that did not immediately include rekindling the marriage after the years they had been apart. He was here now, he had found her in time to get her out of danger, and she refused to go. He knew times were changing, it was everywhere and touched everything, but was it so absolute that a man was expected to let his woman willingly throw herself into the line of fire? He tried to hold his tongue but the words stumbled out. "I'm finally here after all this time, can't you let this go?"

"Are you asking me? Because this is something I have to do."

"Putting yourself in danger?"

She put her hands on his jaw, fingers on his cheeks. She touched the olive ribbon through the shirt fabric. She traced fingertips through his hair at the back of his neck. She looked him steadily in the eye, and he knew this was not up for discussion. "I have never wanted to run away more than I do right now. Be with you, run back to all that we are together. But there are things I learned once I got here. Maybe I didn't want to know them, but once you know, you can't just stop knowing because you wish you didn't."

He nodded. He wished he could disagree.

"I didn't know if I'd ever see you again," she said, "and until now I didn't realize how terribly I've missed you, and I was already missing you more than I could bear. But some things you have to see through."

She was certain, mature, and strong. That was no surprise, as he had been hearing about her from everyone he'd met along the way, but he hadn't expected it to be this way after he found her. He had thought she would see him and need him and go back to the good way it was. Good, except for maybe the railroads and the law on his tail. Good, except for maybe needing to use an alias and watching his back every day of his life. He was impressed by what she had become, without wanting to be impressed. Conversely, her strength made him want to protect her that much more.

He did the best he could. "I know you understand the danger, I've tracked you from Lillian to Queenie to Moretti, then Prophet to this Fidgy. You know how much Moretti wants a piece of you, and he's damn close. Whatever you're trying to do, you can't finish it if you're dead, and Moretti will not let go. *Come* with me."

"There's more going on than you know. More even than I know."

"I want you safe, if I'd been here earlier, maybe I could have protected you, or, I don't know, maybe I have it backward, but you have to understand, it's not like I'm trying to keep you my little girl—"

Her smile came up sideways. "Your little girl?"

"That was just, after talking to, never, never mind, forget all that."

She touched his cheek. "Sweetheart. I'm in this because of you."

"I don't understand."

"When you wouldn't see me that day at Rawlins, when you sent the guard with the letter, you hurt me. But then I understood. It was a gift. You sent me to New York, and I realized you did it because you trusted me. I could take risks, because you trusted me."

"Etta—"

"You didn't want me waiting. You gave me permission to live. I knew you'd catch up when you could."

"Damn it, Etta." He closed his eyes. "You could always charm me."

"I should certainly hope so."

He had yet to tell her about his promise to Siringo. He didn't trust himself to share that just yet, as if he hoped to find some way out of it. But now more than ever, he had to find a way to keep her safe. He could not face the prospect of returning to Wyoming in custody if she was still in danger. He was going back to face a murder charge. He would never be able to beat that. If he had to kill Moretti or Hightower to keep her safe, he would. A second murder charge would make no difference now.

"One thing. I think I have most of it. But there's a loose end. You learned about Moretti and Fedgit-Spense from Queenie."

"I thought I was helping her. Lord, I was naïve."

"But why use Prophet to get to Fidgy?"

She looked utterly confused until she put it together in her mind. "Oh. You've got it backward. I knew Jonah, Prophet, through that awful Mabel, and only hid out with him because Moretti's people were so close. Nobody disappears like an anarchist. I was after Fidgy before that. I thought I could get to him through his antique gun collection. Then I realized he'd never trust a woman about guns. Soon after that I heard about this exhibition. An attractive woman in the art world? That got his attention. Fidgy would never give Jonah the time of day. I didn't get to Fidgy through Jonah, I introduced Jonah to Wisher."

"But Jonah, Prophet, he was jealous of Fidgy."

"That was all his imagination, he assumed there had to be something between us. He wondered how I could even think of leaving him." She grew quiet, knowing how it sounded, and looked in his eyes. "My darling. You keep their attention when you give them nothing. Then you're mysterious. You give them any more, and you're used goods."

"Why Fidgy? I mean, I know what he does, but why go after him?"

"He stands between countries with more power than any individual should have. And I think he's trying to do something quite despicable. As it is, I'm not sure anyone else knows about it."

"Why do *you* have to be the one to know about it?"

"I was there, showing him a piece of art, and we were joined by a visiting member of Parliament. He had a very frank conversation with the man while I was standing there. I think he wanted to impress me. He did, just not in the way he hoped."

"Can this one man really be so important to world politics?"

"No. Not so important. He's one more small piece of what seems to be a universal march to war. But it's the only part I can affect."

"What makes you think you can expose him?"

"I have Lillian Wald. She has access to most everyone, including presidents of the United States. I haven't seen her in two years, but she'll be here tonight."

He was amazed. He had so many questions that he had essentially hit a dead end.

He shrugged and shifted the subject entirely. "So. Where are my letters? You've got more letters for me, and I want them."

"Back at my place."

"Good. You can read them aloud."

She fit her body up against his and moved in close, her warm, sweet breath filling his mouth and nose. "Pillow talk."

They held each other close again, remembering what they had missed and what was yet to come. This time it was different, quieter, as they were no longer in a hurry to confirm their connection. They eased up in their embrace, her nose nuzzled against his neck, as they took one last, quiet moment together.

He spoke seriously. "If we're going back up there, you need to stay close. He won't hesitate, he's coming, he's mad, and when he sees you, he won't give you a chance."

"Why do you think I married you. Nobody better than the Kid."

LILLIAN WALD was under the main arch as they came up the stairs hand in hand. She was delighted to see Etta, and Longbaugh saw the strong mutual affection they shared. Lillian took Longbaugh's hands in both of hers, knowing what it meant to him to be with Etta again.

Etta spoke quickly to Lillian, as a great deal had happened since they had last seen each other. Longbaugh listened with half an ear. He had been away from the exhibition for too long, Hightower and Moretti might already be in the crowd. It was difficult enough to find someone in a small room. The Armory was an enormous space, and it continued to fill up. But Moretti had an edge—he would have no trouble finding her once she met up with Fedgit-Spense. Longbaugh watched the entrance, trying at the same time to also scan the big gallery and beyond.

Etta mentioned anti-preparedness. Lillian nodded. Etta said Lillian had been right about Fedgit-Spense.

Between bodies in the crowd, there was a momentary space, and his eye caught someone familiar. Then the space closed and Longbaugh doubted his eyes. It seemed unlikely he would have come, but Longbaugh leaned, craning his head to see around fancy hats. No luck. Lost to him. Probably imagining things. He ran his eyes from entrance to gallery.

Etta speculated on why Fedgit-Spense so often traveled back and forth across the Atlantic. She had noticed an oddity, possibly coincidental, that he traveled only on American ocean liners. Lillian did not grasp the importance. Etta grew more passionate as she said he was transporting crates, as if moving oversized furniture. Lillian thought the information interesting but did not understand the connection. Etta pressed harder, determined to make Lillian follow.

"I think he's transporting the same crates back and forth without bothering to open them."

At that, Lillian straightened up. "It's not important what's inside. It's the fact that he's transporting his goods via an unexpected venue—he's using passenger ships for oversized cargo."

Etta nodded vigorously, pleased to be understood. "In time he'll stop traveling, but his 'luggage' will not."

Lillian cocked her head, looking off as she thought it through. "He wants someone *else* to know what he's doing."

"He wants the *Germans* to know what he's doing."

This time Lillian nodded. "So that the Germans will fire on American ships carrying American citizens, because they're also carrying enemy ordnance."

Etta's anger animated her words. "Which will infuriate America and bring another paying customer into the war. He's a dangerous war profiteer, Lillian, and I need your help to stop him."

Lillian patted Etta's hand and nodded. "Yes, we'll do it together."

Longbaugh saw him again through a hole in the crowd, and this time there was no doubt. Charlie Siringo. Son of a bitch couldn't wait. He turned his back as Siringo looked in his direction. This could further complicate matters that were already complicated enough.

"How close are you to proving this?"

"I overheard a conversation. I can't prove it. But this isn't just Fedgit-Spense. He's not doing this alone. This is bigger than that."

"Yes," said Lillian, "it is."

Longbaugh casually took both their elbows and escorted them through the galleries toward the back, away from Siringo.

Neither Etta nor Lillian seemed to mind. Etta leaned her head forward and addressed Lillian on the other side of Longbaugh. "I didn't say anything to him on the way over. I wanted to speak with you first."

Lillian craned her neck to answer. "Learn what you can, see if you can get him to brag to you."

As they reached the large gallery under the clock, Lillian nodded toward where Fedgit-Spense was standing in the breezeway between Gallery H and the Cubist Room, speaking to a man in a tuxedo.

"Straight off the ship and he's already working," said Lillian. "Chatting with Garrison."

"That's Lindley Garrison?" said Etta. "He's here?"

"Yes, my dear, the secretary of war is pretending to be interested in art. And if you're correct, Mr. Spense is no doubt urging him to prepare for the worst. Or, in his case, the best."

"You think Garrison knows what Sydney is up to?"

"Perish the thought. Mr. Spense would never let the Americans in on that sort of thing, and it's way too soon to show his cards. I imagine he's partnering with some sympathetic American entrepreneur. No, Mr. Spense is just watering the dirt to keep it moist for future seeding. We're Americans, after all, we don't acknowledge the threat of war. That's way over there with a great big ocean between us."

Roosevelt came in from another gallery. The moment he saw the secretary of war, a spring came into his step and he went right for him.

Lillian put her hand on Etta's arm to hold her back. "Wait, here comes Theodore. You won't get a word in edgewise. He wants a military commission so he can go fight the Hun."

Hightower emerged from the middle of the crowd that surrounded the Duchamp in the Cubist Room. The moment was so natural, and

Hightower so familiar that it was an instant before Longbaugh recognized the danger. Longbaugh now looked for Moretti, eyes scanning the room, trying to see through the patrons, ready to move Etta quickly in the opposite direction. But Moretti was nowhere to be seen. Hightower appeared to be alone. Longbaugh kept Etta beside him, still watching, not choosing an escape until he knew from where the Black Hand would come.

Fedgit-Spense graciously backed away from Roosevelt and the secretary of war to let the former president have his moment.

Etta saw Fedgit-Spense moving, momentarily alone. This was her chance. She started toward him, and Lillian's hand came off her arm and fell to her side.

Hightower crossed the room, working his way around the crowd, and went to the exit door, pushing it open. Moretti came in from the rain.

Longbaugh reached for her arm. "Etta, *now*." His hand found only air. He was startled, he looked, and she was halfway to Fedgit-Spense, moving in the direction of the Cubist Room, in the same direction as the leader of the Black Hand.

Longbaugh went after her.

Hightower stood beside Moretti and scanned the gallery as Moretti shook off the rain. Hightower was astonished at his luck, because right then his eyes met Longbaugh's. He smiled, shook his head, clearly wondering how Longbaugh had gotten away from Siringo.

Hightower yelled over the band. "Place!"

Etta's head came around at the sound of her name.

Hightower caught the motion of her head turning and he could not believe the magnitude of his luck. Longbaugh watched Hightower's surprised, and then exultant, eyes. Hightower was a prescient genius twice in a matter of seconds. He could not have planned it more perfectly. Longbaugh's hope of keeping her safe blew up around him. Hightower beamed.

Hightower's hand came up and his ecstatic finger pointed her out. Longbaugh reached Etta's side, arm around her waist, but when he looked back, he had lost Moretti in the crowd. He had to get her out, but which way? Moretti had been right there, how in the hell did he vanish? Which way had he gone? Longbaugh had no plan this time, he was on his own and the ground was crumbling beneath his feet. Standing by his side, although she hadn't seen Moretti, Etta understood the danger. But she knew her husband in these moments, knew how he was with danger near. She had seen Hightower pointing, so Moretti had to be there . . . and yet they still weren't moving. Something was wrong, but she knew to trust him. Her breath caught in her throat, she leaned in close, looked at him. His eyes scanned the crowd, but where was Moretti? Then Longbaugh realized he had been scanning the far edge of the crowd, where Hightower was standing—he'd been looking too far away. Had he focused in closer, he would have seen him, because Moretti had come around a cluster of people and was charging from his right, pushing through the crowd, rushing at them, automatic pistol rising in his fist, eyes full of fury and satisfaction, scar pulsing deep blood purple, a human arrow flying at Etta, close, way too close.

Longbaugh reacted, shielding her, turning his back to Moretti, making his body wide, driving her to the floor so that he could cover every inch of that red dress. He heard her breath go out of her as her back hit the floor. He went for his gun then, twisting to fire, hearing Etta's voice close in his ear, "Don't kill anyone."

A booming gunshot stunned the air, choked the voices, tripped the band, stopped the music. Spectators went down, dominoes flattening in every direction from the center point of the blast. The ensuing silence brought more fear than the original bang.

He looked at the gun in his hand and saw he had not fired. He felt nothing—if a bullet had hit him, he didn't know it, didn't feel it. He came up on an elbow, met Etta's gaze. She stared at him, clear-eyed and surprised. She said nothing. He thought she might have been in shock but he saw no pain, no blood, although her dress was that rich deep red. He ran his hands down her, feeling for wetness. Her palm came up to lean against his chest.

"You hit, you hurt?"

"No, I—don't think so."

Longbaugh turned, gun firm and steady, keeping his body between Etta and the shooter. He saw him then, Moretti on his knees not twenty feet away. Still dripping rain, a small puddle collecting on the floor. Standing directly behind him was Siringo, smoke leaking out the end of his gun barrel. Moretti was motionless, pistol aimed at Longbaugh, but soft in his fingers. His eyes were dull, fury greeting surprise. Longbaugh saw no blood on Moretti's shirt, but behind him the puddle pooled red between his legs. Moretti's arm dropped to his side and he went over onto his face. A bloodstain spread wide across his back already wet with rain.

The spectators stayed down in a mass cower. A few tentative heads peeked up from the floor. Others outside the room crowded in to get a look at what had happened. The secretary of war's arms were over his head, elbows protecting his nose. Sydney Fedgit-Spense's back held up a wall, his hands straight in front of him as if his palms could deflect bullets. The only man on his feet other than Siringo, the only one unmoved, standing there in the middle of the room, was Roosevelt. He rubbed the lens of his glasses and squinted at the scene.

Cowering, Wisher waved his arms at Siringo. "Whatever you do, don't shoot the art."

Roosevelt smiled and pointed at the Duchamp. "Actually, you can shoot *that* one." A couple of spectators on the floor laughed, and their relief and amusement spread as others heard the laughter and still others asked what he'd said, and the joke spread. Teddy's bravura gave them back their confidence, and they began to help one another to their feet.

Guards clawed into the room, trying to take over. Now the room was coming back, noise returning as guards tried to understand the moment and fifty people described it all at once. Lillian Wald was calm and poised among them, and the guards felt that and flowed to her out of respect. Her version became the official one, as she brought Siringo over. Siringo spoke to them, offering his gun. Lillian pointed to Moretti and the gun in his hand. The guards took Moretti's gun and allowed Siringo to keep his.

Etta looked over. "Hightower."

Longbaugh put a hand on her to stay where she was, slipped his gun back against his low back, then rapidly crossed the room through the confusion. Hightower was getting to his feet. He smiled and shrugged, and Longbaugh smiled back as he came on. But Hightower was wise to Longbaugh's smile and he straightened and tipped his hat, turned, and ran through the crowd as fast as he could, moving quickly for a big, bulky man. Longbaugh stopped and watched him go, and thought it was just as well. He wasn't sure what he would have done to him if he had caught him, and Etta had said not to kill anyone.

Wisher crawled to Fedgit-Spense's side in the confusion, guards running past, police now arriving to sort things out. "Come with me, quickly, before they start asking questions. Fenton's outside with the automobile."

Wisher hurried Fedgit-Spense through the Cubist Room, out the side exit door and into the rain.

Longbaugh went back to Etta, sitting on the floor. He reached down to help her up. Standing together, her arms snaked around his neck and brought him close. "You didn't go for your gun."

"Yes I did."

"You covered me."

"I just reacted, I had to be sure you were—"

"You love me."

"Well, yes."

She smiled.

"What's that got to do with when I pulled my gun?"

She grinned and kissed him. "Don't worry, I'll keep your secret." She indicated the exit door. "They went through there, come."

She took his hand and pulled him toward the side exit, past the small groups of people loudly reliving the incident. Longbaugh became aware of something in the side pocket of his coat. He felt it through the fabric, and had a memory of feeling the coins sewn in the underside of his old saddle. Etta turned, saw his expression, and stopped to wait. He dug into his pocket and took out a coin that hadn't been there earlier, gold, with the profile of Bolívar. Longbaugh looked up quickly and scanned the room, as the drop had happened inside of a moment. His eye caught a familiar shape walking away in the crowd, and he knew him, the same man who'd been waiting with a horse when Longbaugh was outside the courthouse, about to be sentenced. Longbaugh smiled and reflected that his friend had always been a quick and nimble pickpocket. Etta squeezed his hand, and now he went with her to the exit, looking one last time over his shoulder. Then they were out the side door and in the rain. Longbaugh would not see him again.

They stopped on the sidewalk. Longbaugh glanced and saw the liver chestnut was gone, reclaimed by her owner. Wisher stood just outside the exit, his arm extended, pointing out the automobile down the block near Lexington, guiding his boss to it from a distance as Fedgit-Spense ran, glancing over his shoulder at Wisher's pointing finger to make sure he was still going toward the right vehicle. Then his driver, Fenton, came out of the automobile and Fedgit-Spense saw him. Once Wisher knew Fedgit-Spense was taken care of, he turned to Etta and stepped in front of her to block her.

"I think he's had enough excitement for one night, Mrs. Matthews."

"I think he needs to talk to me."

"Have a heart, Mrs. Matthews, he disembarked an hour ago."

"Making the tales of his ocean voyage fresh on his mind."

Siringo came out the door and Longbaugh met his eyes. Then Longbaugh turned back to watch Fedgit-Spense at the end of the street as he reached his vehicle. The chauffeur, Fenton, opened the motorcar's back door for his boss. But Longbaugh saw they were not alone out there. A third person—not a chauffeur, as this man was hatless—lurked in the rain. Longbaugh saw his drenched shape on the far side of the motorcar. The man came around and approached Fedgit-Spense. He had been waiting all that time in the weather, allowing himself to be drenched, the fact of which alarmed Longbaugh. That meant that Prophet had had plenty of time to stew. Every moment that passed in the rain would have added to his resentment, as he was out to prove, in his strange, aberrant way, his resilience, his toughness, his willingness to absorb a physical beating from nature to prove his worth. He was demonstrating his will in order to fulfill his destiny. This, Longbaugh understood, was how Prophet perceived the world.

Longbaugh took a step for the motorcar, but it was so far down the block that he held back, watching, knowing he would never get there in time to stop what was about to happen.

Wisher saw Longbaugh start past him and turned to look.

Etta looked as well and immediately understood, as she knew Prophet better than any of them. "Oh, no."

Wisher saw Prophet with Fedgit-Spense and his hand went up as he screamed, "Oh no no *no!*"

Fenton the chauffeur also saw what was happening, but rather than help his boss, he backed away and ran the opposite direction. Longbaugh knew what Fenton had seen to make him run. Prophet held out his arms and used his soaked body to crowd Sydney Fedgit-Spense into the back of the automobile. He stayed outside, as if guarding the door. A small flame came to light, then went out in the rain. A second flame, protected somehow, stayed lit.

Seeing this, Longbaugh could not hold back, and he started to run to close the gap between himself and the vehicle, drawing his gun.

Etta called out to him, but he ignored her. He raised his weapon to fire, with Prophet's head in his sights, but realized he would be firing on dynamite and at the last moment he held his shot.

A fizzle of light. Prophet turned to face them all, with fury in his eyes. He had known they were there the entire time. His voice came from far away, yet cut the air through the heavy pounding of rain—

"ETH-ELLLLLL!"

—a wail of puerile, tragic want. Prophet dove into the open door of the motorcar on top of Sydney Fedgit-Spense. For a moment all was quiet except for the intense rain, then something flared yellow-red and very bright. In a shard of a second the frame of the windows and roof stood black, straight and precise, obliterated the next instant, the frame stretching, then gone, inside a yellow burst within a giant smoke ball, the first in a series of blasts that accelerated the flames spraying flat across the falling rain, while a simultaneous fireball shot up high to kiss the Armory roof.

Longbaugh was thrown back on the sidewalk from the pressure of the blast.

Etta watched, the light from the blast illuminating her face, her mouth set in a hard line, her eyes cold.

Guards burst out of the side exit and gaped in the rain. Police came down the street from Lexington.

Longbaugh came back to her side. "I'm sorry."

She moved into his arms, but her eyes remained grim. "We'll never know what he was doing. All we can do is say good-bye and be done with it."

"Etta?"

She turned her face up to his, and her eyes softened. Then her arms went around his waist and she held him tightly.

Longbaugh looked at the burning motorcar. "I feel sorry for Prophet."

"Poor ridiculous Jonah."

"He did it for you."

"He did it for someone he created in his mind. You did it for me. You're the one. You fought for me."

Longbaugh held her close. In time she would find a way to mourn them both, in her own way.

She came out of his embrace and her eyes darkened as she looked at Wisher. "But maybe the trail doesn't end with Fidgy."

Wisher was on his knees, blubbering, staring at the automobile burning in the rain, frying the last chunks of his employer. Etta showed him no mercy. "Tell me about his plans, Loney, tell me what he was doing. Do one decent thing in your life and tell me what he had planned, because I know you know."

Through stringing snot mixed with pelting rain, Wisher opened his mouth, ready to confess, wanting to come as clean as the rain, and then another small explosion rocked the burning vehicle and startled him, and he swallowed and looked around and realized where he was. His face changed, and he said, "I have no idea. I don't know what he was doing."

"You think it makes you culpable," said Etta.

Longbaugh shook his head. "No. Selling the dynamite to Prophet that killed his boss makes him culpable."

Horror filled Wisher's eyes. His hands went to his throat, and he began to retch. He turned and fled down the street toward Lexington Avenue. Longbaugh watched him go, and no one followed him and no one stopped him.

Siringo pushed off the building against which he had been leaning and took a step toward Longbaugh.

Etta now saw him up close and realized who he was. "Siringo? Charlie Siringo?" She turned to Longbaugh. "Siringo's here?"

"You didn't see him inside?"

"You were on top of me and there were a thousand people, and he's wearing a *bowler* hat . . . wait, *he* shot Moretti?"

"I have some news."

"No, you don't, no more news, we've had enough news."

"I have to go with him."

She angled her suspicious head. "Why?"

"Under arrest."

"No. Not so, this cannot be." She moved then, right between them and put her arms around Longbaugh as if to hide him, to hug him so tight as to make him disappear, as if she could keep him out of Siringo's hands by the sheer force of her will. Longbaugh felt her arms under his coat, felt her strength and power, and maybe that was all he was going to get, the memory of the fierce way she held on to him.

Then he felt her take his Peacemaker.

His words came as if his shadow were whispering. "Etta, stop—"

She whirled to face Siringo. Holding the gun expertly in both hands, she pointed it at Siringo's chest.

"You may have saved my life, Charlie Siringo, but if you think you're going to take him away, then you shouldn't have bothered."

Longbaugh watched as if the impossible was happening in front of his eyes. "Etta . . ."

"He's mine, Charlie. You can't have him. I've been without him too long. I've got him back and you want to take him away, and I just can't have that."

Longbaugh looked at Siringo's expressionless face, and knew his calm was not good. He looked at Etta holding the gun like that, and knew he had to put a stop to it. Her finger tensed, as if she was about to squeeze, and he stepped in front of the barrel. For a moment he thought he'd made a mistake, that she would be unable to control herself in time. But her trembling hand relaxed and her finger came away from the trigger.

"You can't," he said. "You cannot do this, and you know it. It will make things worse. And anyway, you have your work."

She was enraged. "Someone else can take up the cause, because if it's a decision, then there's no decision, because I won't lose you again."

Longbaugh moved his hand slowly and his palm surrounded the cylinder and he took the gun out of her hand.

She faltered in the rain. "Oh, Harry."

"I gave my word of honor."

"God damn your word of honor."

"I know. But that's why you love me so much."

Longbaugh turned, but before he offered the gun to Siringo, he turned back to her.

"Say good-bye to me."

"No."

"Do it. Say good-bye now. You may not get another chance."

"I refuse."

Longbaugh shook his head, turned, and held the butt end of the gun out to Siringo.

Siringo looked at it a long moment before he took it in his hands. He held it but did not aim it with deliberation. "There's a problem here."

"No, Charlie, there's no problem, the deal was for me, and here I am. I know she pointed a gun at you, but you can't take her in."

"If he's taking you, Harry, he may as well take me."

Longbaugh ignored her. "I understand threatening a lawman is serious business, but that wasn't what happened, that wasn't what you saw."

Siringo showed nothing. "Problem is . . ."

"A little *room* here, Charlie."

"Problem is, I've been looking for Harry Longbaugh, an outlaw of some renown, fellow I knew out West some time ago. I even used to ride with him. Did me a favor once, but I never got the chance to thank him. Heard he might still be alive, despite some international news report of his death. Heard he might have been in prison during that time, and when he got out, some kid came after him. That kid didn't make it."

"A *kid*?" said Etta. "Oh, Harry, why do they always come after you? Why can't they leave you alone?"

Siringo went on. "Thought I'd better check, so I went after him. Followed him out of Wyoming, and on the off chance he'd gone east, I came to New York, spent weeks here convinced he was around."

Etta said, "You know he would never kill a kid unless it was self-defense, you know that."

"Turns out the rumors were true."

"You can't possibly believe he's a killer."

"Son of a bitch died in Argentina."

"You know it wasn't, wait, what?" She looked from Longbaugh's face to Siringo's face. It took a moment, but then a fraction of a smile slipped between her lips. "Bolivia."

Siringo looked down at Longbaugh's Colt Peacemaker. "Probably should have known all along," said Siringo. Longbaugh looked at the gun as well, then looked over at Etta. He heard the words but seemed incapable of understanding them, as they were making no sense. She seemed to understand, and was doing her best to disguise her smile. She was having a difficult time. Siringo said, "No matter how hard you try, no matter how much you want to, certain things are just physically impossible." Longbaugh looked at him, and because he never in his life expected a break from anyone, it sounded like Siringo was speaking a foreign language.

Siringo handed Longbaugh's Colt Peacemaker back to him.

"A man simply cannot arrest a ghost."

THE DAY DAWNED clear and bright with a pale blue sky. The puddles were long and narrow and still as glass. The cobblestones lost their shine as the day baked them dry. The sun was heavy-hot, and thick moisture hung in the air after the scrubbing from the storm. The city waited for a fresh breeze that did not come until late in the evening, and then did not last long. The people did not notice that there were fewer and fewer horses on the streets. Electricity was already being taken for granted, and more people owned telephones. It would be another full year before the continent of Europe went to war.

The heat held on for that week and beyond, and it wasn't long before the leaves turned brittle and browned at the tips.

The man who had once been a legend looked over the rail to the waves creaming along the side of the ship steaming for England. His hand grazed the arm of the woman he loved, and she turned warm eyes to him. Looking past him, she saw that New York was almost gone on the horizon, and she got a look in her eyes, as if thinking of something unexpected. She unpinned her hat, took it in hand, cocked her arm, and let it fly high in the air. The wind caught it and carried it out there to land on a wave, where it fell back and away, and then the hat as well as the city on the horizon were gone.

Together they turned their heads and looked to the ocean ahead, her unpinned hair streaming out and caressing his face.

Acknowledgments

This work of fiction was supported by research, although historians will note that I moved the opening of the Armory Show to later in the year 1913. A significant number of well-known individuals did indeed attend that night, including Lillian Wald and T.R. The remains of the Dutch ship *Tijger* were discovered during the digging of the subway in the same location as in the novel, but in 1916. There are other slights to history, some of them inadvertent, but wherever possible I have attempted to be accurate.

Picasso's sculpture *Bust* is now known as *Head of a Woman*. Barnard's sculpture *Prodigal Son* is now known as *The Prodigal Son and His Father*.

The real Harry spelled his name Longabaugh, although other family members may have spelled it differently. I have chosen to use "Longbaugh" in order to make the character my own. I find it reads more easily on the page, and sounds better in the mind.

Rick Natkin was there at the beginning, and graciously gave his benediction.

Thanks to early readers of the manuscript, Glenn Harcourt and Carter Scholz.

ACKNOWLEDGMENTS

Thanks to Hope Hanafin for wardrobe, ribbons, and petticoats. Thanks to Chelsea Field for her knowledge of horses.

Many books, documentaries, and websites were consulted during the research of the novel. Allow me to single out Luc Sante, Diana Allen Kouris, Kenneth T. Jackson, Eric Homberger, and Anne Meadows.

Thanks to Troy Kennedy-Martin.

William Goldman brought Sundance and Butch into the zeitgeist. If you know of them, it is because of his excellent words.

It has been my particular pleasure to work with the wise, amusing, and wonderfully thorough editor Jake Morrissey. I treasure his support.

A special bow to my agent, Deborah Schneider. You know what you've done. You know how much it means.

And, of course, thanks to my Liz, who goes along for each and every ride.